The Seventh Millennium

Jay Wolfe Friedman

ISBN-13: 978-1507624951
ISBN-10: 1507624956

For my family
my friends
my colleagues
and the strangers
I will never know—
With best wishes and thanks
To all for accompanying me
on this strange journey

The Rubiyat
LXXIII
Omar Khayyam

Ah Love: could thou and I with fate conspire
To grasp the sorry Scheme of things entire,
Would not we shatter it to bits—and then
Re-mould it nearer to the Heart's Desire.

CHAPTER 1

Every morning now, a sense of foreboding. At least the early routine got him going. He was out of bed, showered and dressed by six. Then he'd let the dog and cat out, and make sure Alice was up so she could get off to school on time. Breakfast of a cut-up orange, two slices of buttered toast, a cup of coffee. Sometimes Alice, now fifteen, would join him. More often she would dash into the kitchen, gulp down a glass of milk and run off to school. Mary would still be in bed. He would call good-bye after letting the dog back into the house, grab his bag, get in the car, start the motor—and begin to sweat, little beads of sweat on his forehead, and hands sticky moist on the steering wheel.

A few minutes around the curve, down the main road, and then the mile-long grade from the top of the hill, staring out the windshield, no longer shocked by the apparition. One word— *DIVORCE*—emblazoned on the glass, colorless and cold. It would last only a few seconds, but it remained on his mind throughout the day and into his restless dreams.

Not only divorce but also despair. He had to make a decision that he'd put off far too long, almost from the beginning of his marriage. Early on, the excitement of medical practice was a distraction from nagging marital disappointments. But lately even his enjoyment of work had begun to pale. It was no longer sufficient to protect him from an impending admission of failure.

Divorce meant more than just leaving Mary. It meant the deconstruction of his family and the consequent threat to his daughter's security. Perhaps now that Alice was older, it would not be so bad. But what would Mary, who never did much of anything, do? She would argue otherwise. Wasn't making a home for him and Alice something? Wasn't she always there for him when his colleagues attacked him for being too critical, when he needed her support? Didn't she uproot without protest every time he decided to move to another part of the country just as she was beginning to feel settled? Wasn't cooking and housekeeping and schlepping Alice here and there valued services? And when she was really riled up she would throw in sex to boot. Didn't she deserve credit for anything? Perhaps so, he would concede, knowing that credit was insufficient and beside the point.

Always first in her class, always striving for the perfection her parents expected of her, Mary broke down in the last year of high school and never went back. Rather, she read voraciously, becoming better educated than most college graduates. He married her because she was so bright, because she had—or he thought she had—such great insight that they would resolve all their problems through sound analytic reasoning, and because she was so pretty, and in the beginning they had such formidable sex. And in the beginning all he needed was her companionship. Gradually, whatever more he needed, even though he couldn't say what it was exactly, was not there and he realized it would never be there.

Seventeen years later and she still couldn't take a driver's test without a monumental struggle. It wasn't the actual driving that was the problem. She was a good driver. It was the twenty questions. She had to get them all right. At first he had been sympathetic, supportive, even though her anxiety was hard to understand since he was content with a mere passing grade. Then, when she finally took the test, she had a perfect score. Everything she tried was cursed by this need for perfection. Eventually she did—nearly to perfection—everything that needed to be done, all the necessities. But it was always a struggle.

His sympathy turned to irritation, then to suppressed anger and finally the realization he did not want to spend the rest of his life living with an imperfect perfectionist. Giving her up was acknowledging defeat, admitting a very big mistake, admitting the failure of his own omnipotence. It was symbolic of the diminishing dreams of his declining youth the older he became…the older he became. Last week his fortieth birthday came and went, ignored as best he could, impatiently waiting for it to be over. Alice and Mary bought him a pair of cowboy boots.

Ina cooked him supper the night before. What the hell was he doing having an affair with Ina? She was a medical secretary with little education or experience beyond a high school graduate. But she had the figure of an Aphrodite and the sensuality of every man's fantasies. They fit together like the proverbial hand in glove—on the sofa, the floor, in bed. Every other week he paid the price of small talk, shoptalk, and dull silences for the exalted orgasms she gave him even after two years. If she wasn't so damned accommodating and safe it would not have lasted that long. Another failure. Her intellectual inequality nagged at his pride. If he had to have an affair, why must it be with a woman he felt so beneath him?

Despite his dissatisfaction, deep down he still felt committed to Mary, even though every day he liked her less and less. There was a time when he was proud of her, when they were very young and doing was less important than being. He was proud of the way she looked. More so, he was proud of her knowledge of the arts and literature and history, which made up for his own deficiencies in these spheres. She had superb taste and good common sense, and in the beginning they thought the same way about most things.

Ina had none of that. She was single, in her early thirties and in love with him, or, as she put it, his body. She admired his mind, too, what little he shared with her, knowing that it was the unshared part of him that kept them separate and episodic

Not long after they married, his pride for Mary began to

erode, at first little chunks chipping off, then larger blocks falling away until all that remained was an intangible attachment and caring, which he assumed was love. It was not enough. It did not cover the minor frustrations she developed into major crises. The French laundry ruined her mother-of-pearl buttons. She screamed at the proprietor. The upholstery carefully chosen from one of twenty sample books to match the wallpaper turned out the wrong shade of beige—crash, explosion, rage. Mary's upset was warranted, though totally out of proportion. What was so important to her was no longer of importance to him.

What mattered was that she shared less and less in those activities that were meaningful to him. She would sit upstairs in bed reading when he hosted an occasional political meeting in the living room. "For God's sake," she would say, "don't you get tired of all that bullshit—and tell them to scrape the mud off their shoes before coming into the house." She was right, of course. But he needed to participate, even as his interest was beginning to wane. At least these people were dealing with real issues, or so it seemed until lately.

The steeply descending road turned into a pleasant drive, passing through gently rolling hills crisscrossed by white split-rail fences that formed a decorative latticework separating the mini-estates of what he derisively and accurately called *horse lovers*. Anything connected with horses reminded him of his daughter. How in God's name could he have sired a horse lover? When she was a year old, he brought home a hobbyhorse, and that was it. Barely able to toddle, Alice straddled the plastic horse with its legs stretched across wire springs and started to rock furiously. She had to be dragged off, screaming for more time. She was two years old when they moved from Long Island to Seattle for his residency in Family Practice at a medical cooperative. By then the hobbyhorse was as much a part of the family as the alley cat who wandered into their rented house and adopted Mary and Alice.

When she was four, Alice started riding lessons. By eight, after they moved to Los Angeles, she took jumping lessons and learned how to fall off without breaking her neck. But he resisted buying her a horse. To him, owning a horse smelled of conspicuous consumption. Worse, they were dull and dangerous animals. "Maybe so," Alice would say, "but I like them anyway."

When she was twelve she found a horse to rent for the whole summer. He had hoped that the responsibility of washing and grooming and shoveling up the horseshit would cure her. No way! She loved it. And she taught him something of motivation. When a kid is really interested in something, she'll take all the shit—the nagging parents, the rivalry and snobbery of rich kids with thoroughbred horses over those with common breeds, the favoritism of judges for their own students at the horse shows. All this for the opportunity to care for the dumb beast she loved out of some primordial mystique. Not much different than parents' unremitting love for their kids, their instinctual caring, mostly tender, not infrequently harsh, at times brutal, but unremitting. Not so for their mates, not in California with a divorce rate of fifty percent. Not for Mary.

Damn. He was back to divorce. He'd start the day thinking of it. Then he'd get busy at work and become so absorbed that his own identity vanished. Then there'd be a lull and he would become conscious of himself again, and divorce would intrude like a bad tune stuck in his head.

He parked the car in the area reserved for doctors. Instead of entering the clinic from the rear, as he usually did, he went around to the street entrance. The waiting room was already filled with mothers holding babies and snotty kids scrambling on the floor and old men and women sitting anxiously on plastic molded chairs. He hated the way old people's eyes searched his for recognition as he walked swiftly past, already rigid within the self-protective veneer of his title.

"Doctor Altern," Ina called as he rounded the reception desk.

He had purposely come through the walk-in clinic to avoid her, but there she was, talking with an appointment clerk.

"Doctor, can I speak with you for a second?"

Now she was standing in front of him, her stunning figure masked by the anonymous white jacket that clerks and secretaries wore on the clinic floor.

"John, I have to talk to you."

"Not now, Ina. I'm already late."

"So am I," she shot back.

"You're kidding?"

"No, I'm not."

"I…I can't talk now," he stammered. "I'll call you. We'll get together later."

"Promise," Ina pleaded in a choked whisper.

Jesus Christ, the last thing he needed was a pregnant mare. It was a nasty metaphor to suit his mood. She was on the pill but it wasn't foolproof. He knew he should use a condom, especially now that AIDs was no longer the province of gays and druggies. But Ina was not sleeping around, he was sure of that. So he ignored the safe sex advice he gave his patients. He concealed the probability, however small, that the pill-taker would slip up, all for the unsheathed pleasure that beckoned him like an addiction. With the stupidity of an adolescent, and particularly of a doctor who should know better, he was a victim of the law of happening—if it can, it will.

The morning was unexpectedly quiet. His first patient was a routine physical examination, followed by an obese middle-aged woman with chronic backache, and another with ulcerative colitis who kept falling off her diet. He threatened her with surgery and again she promised to behave. A few more routines and then a cancellation just before lunch.

He telephoned Mary to say a staff meeting was on for the evening. It wasn't exactly a lie since the Family Practice Committee was scheduled from five to six. He called Ina and arranged to meet her at six-thirty at the Border Cafe, a Mexican restaurant some distance away that was so dingy he was sure no one he knew would likely show up there.

Then he decided to check on Stella Manza in the hospital. The attachment of the clinics to the hospital was one of the attractions of this particular medical group. Solo family practitioners tended to lose their most interesting cases when specialists took over. Cases? He had constantly to remind himself that these were people and some, like Stella, were friends.

Being close to the hospital made it convenient to keep in touch with their progress. Except that for Stella there was no progress. Her condition was terminal. In a sense, she had terminated two weeks ago. Yet her body was there, sustained by intravenous feeding and a mechanical respirator because no one had the guts to pull the plug, not the super specialists, not her children, not himself. So she lay there in a senseless coma. He lingered at her bedside for a few moments, thinking how easy it would be to disconnect her, how insensate not to.

Two weeks ago they had talked, or rather he had talked to her, and there was recognition in her eyes between lapses of unconsciousness. He told her she should be proud and satisfied with her life, that her grown kids were okay now, that all was well. As he left, she raised her hand as if a final farewell.

Clarence, her husband, had died a few years before. What John remembered most clearly about Clarence was the size of his heart, not the monstrously enlarged organ of congestive heart failure, but the heart of long distance runner, of an athlete for causes who never gave up. He envied Clarence his courage, his unflappable belief in the future. Clarence would not give up. He would never divorce Stella. How in the world did that pop into his head? Divorce was not in their lexicon. They were born soul mates.

John mused at himself. Here he was, an agnostic and a man of science, at least to the extent medicine could be called a science, thinking of hearts and souls. The heart as the essence of a one's physical and passionate drives, the soul as immortal connection between past, present and future, the undying spirit of this strange species with its unique consciousness, doomed by the unconsciousness of its phylogeny.

Stella and Clarence had lived together for half a century, John barely past seventeen years with Mary. The Manzas were a team, both openly and actively opposed to the Korean and, later, the Vietnam war. Clarence was first censured and then dismissed from the college where he taught creative writing. So he sold real estate to pay the rent and allow them to do what they damned well pleased, which was to support every progressive movement from organizing farm workers to opposing the Cuban boycott, all alleged proof of their communist affiliation, as though one could not arrive at decency by any other means.

John met the Manzas at a conference on national health insurance where Clarence was one of the speakers. Here was this old man, gray, bald and wrinkled, but impressively tall and upright, with the thick body of a lumberjack, and a deep voice reverberating from the depths of his chest like a bull enraged at the injustices done the poor and the helpless. Soon after, they became his patients. Clarence was already in poor health and Stella was not far behind. As disease advanced with the quickening pace of old age, they also became more dependent on him, even as he tried to maintain the barricade separating every doctor and patient so that at least one of them would survive. The cancer the Manzas both shared, as with everything else in their lives, sapped Clarence first. He escaped the miracle of forced feeding and breathing, dying in his sleep at home. Stella was not so fortunate. She was caught by the great caring system that seemed to care for everything but the right to die naturally and in peace. She was caught lingering now between heaven and hell.

Back in his office, he glanced at the headlines of the newspaper that had been dropped on his desk. Always the same corruption, murder and mayhem, only the names and dates changed. He could barely read the paper anymore. He felt more and more detached. But he continued to contribute to organizations fighting the engorged military budget, and government support of repressive dictatorships throughout the world, and subsidies of corporations that were polluting the environment, and regressive tax policies that were making the rich richer and the poor poorer. More and more there seemed less concern for the poor, for civil rights, for protecting the environment, for combating global warming—perhaps the greatest threat, except for the immediate threat of a nuclear holocaust. Not only Russia and the United States but also China and Pakistan and India and France and Israel, even North Korea and maybe Iran, had joined the MAD club, though it had never been satisfactorily explained how anyone could survive mutually assured destruction.

And then 9/11, the shattering of the twin towers in New York by Islamic zealots and 3000 lives lost. You couldn't pick up a paper or turn on TV without being bombarded with stories of international crises, of disasters and near misses, of suicide bombers, of kidnappings and brutal murders, of deteriorating domestic conditions.

It was all so depressing. He felt so helpless. He used to rationalize that at least he was helping his patients. But it was not enough. It just seemed that his whole life was mired in ineffectual and lost causes, not least of which was his marriage.

He joined some doctors for lunch in the hospital's cafeteria. Arthur Sokolsky glanced up at him through thick-lensed glasses.

"John, you don't look well," Arthur observed. He was an older physician, an accomplished musician who also had a degree in theology. Short and pudgy, with a large round head, he was admired by everyone on the staff.

"I'm okay," replied John, somewhat morosely.

"Maybe you need a vacation," Arthur suggested. "You've been working hard."

Yeah, John thought, he needed a vacation—from himself.

One of the other doctors was describing his latest investment in a resort condominium. Two others were comparing the performance of their new sports cars, pausing only long enough to admire the latest voluptuous nurse to join the staff as she carried her lunch tray past their table.

John was offended by their conversation. When he first joined the group practice, he had looked forward to lunch with his colleagues as a source of intellectual and professional stimulation. Oh, occasionally they discussed a new drug or an interesting case. But more often the talk was like today—of cars, investments, tits and ass. Or they would bitch about their low $180,000 income compared to the doctors netting two or three times as much in private practice.

"You're not fair to them," Arthur Sokolsky scolded. "You can't be serious all the time. You've got to relax."

"It's their materialism, their lack of ideology. All they think about is money and sex."

"You know that's not true," insisted Arthur. "You're not the only dedicated doctor."

John protested, "You don't understand. It's happening to me. I'm becoming like them." Decades of disappointments, the fatigue of endless patients, charts, instructions to nurses, angry patients, consultations, treatments, dying patients, and then the rounds again. "I don't see people anymore. I see *cases*, blood and bones. I don't listen to hearts, what's in their hearts. I hear only the squish of defective valves."

"Maybe you should have been a surgeon?" Arthur quipped.

"And bury my mistakes."

"That's sophomoric," Arthur countered.

"No, I heard it when I was a freshman."

They both laughed.

"But I do envy surgeons," John added. "Cut, slice, stitch, pepper with antibiotics, count the money and the glory."

Arthur looked at him seriously. "Have you really become so cynical?"

"I don't know, Arthur. We worship, we idolize the doctor-patient relationship, but when patients come with problems that disturb us as well as them, we prescribe sedatives, tranquilizers, diet pills. Arthur, we're not dealing with their problems. We're perpetuating them."

Arthur shook his head slowly. There was a plaintive tone to his response. "What do you want us to do? Take away their defenses and watch them fall flat on their faces? Tell them to quit their jobs, throw out the kids, leave their husbands and wives? Where can they go? Who can help them? We help a helluva lot. We keep the families together. We get them over crises. We keep them a little sane. What more can we do? We're not gods."

Arthur jostled John's elbow on the table. "Hey, where are you? What's the matter? You seem to be in another world. How about you and me taking a walk?"

"No...I'm okay. See you later."

John picked up his tray and dumped the half-eaten food into the bin. He returned to his office, sat back in his chair and shoved his feet up on the desk. Why should he criticize his colleagues? Deep down, could he say he wasn't envious of their investments, their sports cars, their homes with swimming pools and tennis courts, wanting a new, younger wife, perhaps even another child, maybe a more interesting mistress? *My god*, he implored, *was there nothing more?*

The sun was sinking into the ocean, a rosy afterglow that turned gray as he entered the Border Cafe. For a few moments the dim lighting blinded him. As his eyes grew accustomed to the darkness, he spotted Ina in a booth. He slid onto the bench opposite her. The waitress came over, a cute Latina girl wearing a machine-embroidered blouse and a short, black skirt, skin-tight across well-formed buttocks. He avoided Ina's eyes and ordered a bottle of California Chablis.

"Well, here's to something," Ina said lightly, lifting her glass towards him.

He mumbled, "I don't know what to say."

"You might say you're glad to see me."

"Of course I am. I just don't know what to say about, you know—"

"You could say you're glad," she said in half tones of anger and anticipation and impending disappointment.

He was astonished. "Are you?" His face flushed and burned in the darkness.

There was a long, reflective pause before she replied softly, "Yes, I am…John, I'm thirty-three. I want to have a baby, your baby. I'm not asking you to marry me. I know that won't happen."

"Ina, be realistic." It was the conventional thing to say.

The Latina girl leaned forward as she wrote down their order, her blouse falling away slightly, revealing the cleavage between her breasts.

"Realistic? You or me?" Ina challenged. "If I wait much longer, I'll be too old. Look, I didn't ask for this to happen but it did. I know other single women who have children. They survive. I'm not asking you for anything, except maybe moral support."

"That's what you say now." He also was feeling anger. "You know I care for you, but you've got to be reasonable."

"Care for me? That's a laugh. All you care about is yourself."

"That's not true," he insisted, knowing there was more truth in it than he wanted to admit.

"You care for my body, that's what you said."

"We never lied to each other. We both agreed our relationship was, uh, physical."

"I know," she said, knowing that for her it had always been a lie, that she would always love him.

"Ina, be reasonable. It would never work. An abortion is such a simple thing."

"Damn you," she snapped.

They ate mostly in silence, finishing the bottle of wine. The waitress brought the check. Her skin was smooth and tan and her eyes, darkly mascaraed, met his momentarily. He was annoyed for thinking he might come back to see her again, maybe to…Jesus Christ! Ina's pregnant, Mary's home waiting for him, and he's thinking of fucking a Latina chick a few years older than his daughter.

He followed Ina back to the quadraplex where she lived in three small rooms filled like an arboretum with hanging ferns and broadleaf plants. Her friends, she called them. They had some more wine, smoked a joint, and gazed away from each other. She tuned the stereo he had given her on her last birthday to soft rock. She went to the bathroom, returning a few minutes later completely naked, modeling herself before him.

"Not bad for thirty-three and pregnant," she taunted, slowly moving about the room in an undulating rock dance that beckoned sensually.

Not many women were prettier naked than clothed. Ina's body grabbed at him either way. She could have been a professional dancer—long lovely arms and legs, narrow waist, a firm abdomen, the mound of Venus lightly covered with a triangle of soft brown hair, and a tight full ass he loved to hold as they made love. *Damn her body.*

She gyrated against him and helped as he removed first his shirt, then his trousers. She made love to him on the sofa. Their bodies meshed full length. She wrapped her arms around him, pulling, pressing tightly against his body as if to assure the fertilization of her womb.

It was drizzling lightly as he drove home, tuning in the eleven o'clock news. It was worse than usual. It was calamitous but that hardly startled anyone anymore. A nuclear power plant on the coast south of Los Angeles was overheating. There were rumors of radiation leakage and possible evacuation of Los Angeles. Authorities claimed the danger was small and urged the public to remain calm. *Goddamned liars*, he grumbled to himself.

The international scene was also heating up. That afternoon the United Nations Security Council voted to censure the United States for threatening to invade Iran and North Korea if they did not destroy their weapons of mass destruction. It was a futile gesture, of course, since the United States vetoed the resolution.

China warned the United States that if North Korea was attacked, China would be at liberty to invade Taiwan. *Tit for tat,* John noted. The United States threatened that if China set one sail in the Taiwan Sea, it would risk nuclear war. *Nuclear war over Taiwan! We're nuts*, John muttered. The Pentagon issued a first stage alert, directing all nuclear submarines to ready for attack. The Chinese countered with the astounding revelation that three of its fixed position satellites were poised over the United States, loaded with multiple thermonuclear rockets aimed at strategic communication and population centers. A sudden chill swept through John's body. What if...what if the reactor exploded and was mistaken for a nuclear attack? What if the President panicked and pressed the button? What if some idiot in a rocket silo a hundred miles away saw the flash, recognized the mushroom cloud over Los Angeles, and did it on his own?

He reached home all the more depressed. Everything was wrong. He tried to trivialize his own problems against the world's calamities. He really could not believe nuclear war would happen. It was all posturing, a bluff again like so many times before. He was not going to be distracted from his world, his reality. It was himself he had to come to terms with. He had to face Mary with divorce. He had to stop seeing Ina. He had to regain his interest in his work. He had to rediscover his purpose. His hand trembled as he placed the key in the front door lock. Everything was pressing inside and out. He felt he was going to explode.

"Hello, dear," Mary called to him from the den where she was watching television.

"Hi, be there in a minute." He rushed to the liquor cabinet, poured a bourbon and swished it down, a ritual he performed after drinking too much wine with Ina so the smell of alcohol would appear home-brewed. Only this evening it was also to calm himself, to constrict and numb his fear. He joined Mary before the TV.

Disapproving, she chided, "You've been smoking. I can smell it."

"I had a cigarette after the meeting. What are you watching?"

"A real oldie—*Lost Horizon*."

"Did you hear the news?"

She frowned darkly. "I can't believe it—I'm keeping Alice home tomorrow. I don't want her outside. The radiation—"

"Don't worry. It's not that bad. The rain'll clear the air," he said, knowing that it would not. He turned his attention to *Lost Horizon,* a classic film from the 1930s that occasionally showed on cable TV. He saw it, maybe twenty years ago, while he was still in medical school in New York. It was playing in a cheap movie house on 8th Avenue near 42nd Street. He had never forgotten it—an airplane crash in the Himalayas, a passage through the mountains to a Valley of Eden, *Shangri-La,* and eternal life and peace for the white foreigners. It bothered him that the natives had normal life spans while the Anglos lived on and on. Well, he wouldn't begrudge Ronald Coleman that. He was the perfect lead, sensitive, intelligent, the kind of aristocratic handsomeness that inspired confidence and trust. In the end Ronald had to return. He had to carry the wisdom and the hope and the warning of *Shangri-La* to his own people before it was too late.

"How's Stella?" Mary asked as they got into bed.

"I saw her today—no change."

John reached over to the lamp near his side of the bed and turned out the light. Pellets of rain on the roof pitter-pattered in his ears in a steady calming rhythm.

Mary shuddered. "How awful."

He closed his eyes. She reached over and touched his hand. He didn't respond. Sometimes in the darkness beneath the covers, lying next to her warmth and closeness, it was as if nothing would change and they would remain together always. No matter how dissatisfied and distant he felt towards her, he would inevitably return and cling to her like a security blanket. She had become an inextricable part of him, but someone who could no longer satisfy him.

Tears welled up, pressing, burning, seeping through the corners of closed eyelids. The *wants* and the *can'ts* tore at him. He thought of Alice asleep in her room, the threat of destruction hovering above. Not war, not radiation but him, he was the destroyer. Ina was right, all he cared about was himself. To get what he wanted he would destroy his marriage, his family, his daughter's security. To get what he wanted without knowing what it was.

I t was still raining when he woke up, leaden with fitful, tiring sleep. Mary remained sound asleep. He looked into Alice's room. She was buried beneath the blanket. After letting the dog and cat out, he showered and shaved. He heard Alice shuffling in her room.

"Mornin', Dad," she yawned.

"Hi, sweetheart. Listen, Mom wants you to stay home today. Maybe you should, just in case there's any radiation."

"Aw—mom's always worrying."

"I know, but today she may have a point. Do it for me."

Reluctantly, Alice agreed. "Guess I'll go back to bed."

The dog was at the front door waiting to be let in. He grabbed a bath towel, rubbed her coat dry and wiped the mud off her paws, absorbing affectionate kisses on his cheeks. The cat was roaming his territory and would not be back for hours.

It was raining harder, unusual this time of year. The car started briskly, giving him the pleasure of commanding a marvel of modern mechanization. He backed out of the driveway, slipped into forward drive and slowly picked up speed. Raindrops, still on his forehead from the walk to the car, mingled with the small beads of sweat that wet his brow each morning. The car rounded the curve onto the main road and started down the steep grade. The wipers flapped across the windshield, shaping arcs that appeared and disappeared with each swipe of the blade. Beyond the glass, *DIVORCE* appeared as before.

Suddenly the sky turned black and an avalanche of rain poured down, inundating the road with a rushing wave of water. An enormous bolt of lightning shattered the sky, followed instantly by the deafening roar of monumental thunder. The car bumped, swerved. The sky broke apart, flashing white light—then darkness.

CHAPTER 2

The flash was followed by a loud rumbling thunder and a wind force lashed out viciously. A gigantic white cloud mushroomed slowly upward, silhouetted brilliantly against the clear blue arctic sky. The stalk turned bright orange, capped by a billowy head of vaporized ice that poured back across the polar plains in a torrent of sleet. The roar of wind and sleet gradually diminished, and over the center of the newly formed crater hovered a silvery mist.

The scientists of the Seventh Millennium's Anti-topple Committee viewed the spectacle from within the safety of their globeship miles away. As the sky cleared, a remote drone was sent aloft to survey the area. It skimmed over the surface, returning panoramic images of the ice mantle and measurements of radioactivity. The whole area, covered with mountain valleys and peaks encased in compacted snow and ice before the blast, was now mostly level and glistened in the sunlight. The drone reached the crater, circled the perimeter, and then descended in slow spirals towards the bottom.

Esop, director of the Anti-topple Committee, sat quietly before the large visioscreen that displayed images transmitted from the drone. Assock, the Professor of Pragmatic Rationality assigned to oversee the mission, stood behind him, peering over his shoulder. The drone's scanner swept over the crater's floor. They barely noticed the small black speck.

"What's that?" Assock pointed, just as the speck disappeared.

Esop observed laconically, "Probably rock."

"Go back."

Esop replayed the recorded image.

"Strange," Esop grunted. He magnified the picture. It was fuzzy, shrouded in mist.

"Looks symmetrical," Assock noted, tracing his finger over the surface of the faint image. "We should get a closer look."

"Later," Esop replied, "after the air has cleared."

Assock sucked in his breath. "I have this funny feeling we should go in now."

Esop shook his head negatively. "Radiation's too heavy," he cautioned.

Assock persisted. "We could lose it. It could be swept away by runoff or buried in a backslide. We might not find it again."

Esop was still resistant. "Backslide is more likely now. It might bury us, too."

"I'm going." When Assock's mind was set, he displayed the flexibility of concrete.

Esop studied the screen intently. He hadn't thought much of the object. But Assock had a point. It could be an important discovery. "Okay, let's do it," he relented.

They donned heavy leaded suits and climbed into a large aerobe fitted with grappling hooks. Soon they were over the crater, descending, like the probe before, in slow spirals down towards the unidentified object.

John groaned in pain. His eyes were covered with coagulated blood. He wiped the gelatinous mass away and rubbed the back of his neck. How long had he been unconscious? Groggy, he sat waiting for his mind to clear, vaguely wondering why no one had come to help him. Pounding sleet dwindled to the pitter-patter of rain on the metal roof of the car and then stopped. Darkness turned to gray mist and sunlight began to filter through the windshield. His feet slopped in water. The car was half-submerged and an icy chill raced through his body. He must have been out for hours. Then he looked out the window and blinked rapidly. For a moment he thought himself surrounded by ice. His eyes blurred in a trickle of blood. He rubbed them and looked again, tracing the ice up and up, numbed by the enormity of it. Near the top he saw a silvery object shaped like a teardrop floating down, finally drawing so close that he could make out two helmeted shapes within. Anxiety gripped him in a cold sweat, heart pounding, head throbbing, ears shrieking. And then the cold, the deep penetrating cold permeated every cell in his body and all feeling and sense of self were gone.

A ssock and Esop looked at each other in utter amazement. Minutes before, in the middle of the descent, they realized this was no ordinary object but perhaps an ancient sarcophagus. Now they were abreast of it, and there inside, unmistakably, was a creature, its face tinged ruby-red with blood. For a moment they saw it move and then slump motionless. Esop checked for radiation. Inexplicably, it was nearly zero. The temperature outside was much below. No time for questions or hesitation. He centered the aerobe above the container and extended grappling hooks until it was firmly grasped, and then slowly ascended out of the crater.

They hoped, they prayed the extreme cold would not kill the creature, if it was not already dead. If they could just get it back to the globeship before it froze.

Esop radioed ahead. He spoke to Lank, the Anti-topple Committee's staff physician. "Lank, now listen carefully, we may have a live creature. It's in a...I don't know, like a metal sarcophagus. We hooked it. Inside—I can't describe it—didn't get a good look, but it looked like a head and it moved. The temperature? Minus 40. It'll be hypothermic, if it doesn't freeze again. Get a thawing bath ready. And blank out all home transmission. I don't want any publicity until we know what we have."

In less than half an hour, the aerobe was hovering near the globeship, gradually lowering its load to the ice mantle, and then landing beside it. Assock and Esop, encumbered by their lead suits, climbed out slowly. Shedding the suits, they ran to the container. Lank was already there, scraping away at the ice that covered the window. Esop grasped the handle of what appeared to be a door, but it wouldn't budge. They clawed at the ice frantically, barely able to see the motionless shape inside. Assock pushed Lank and Esop aside and smashed in the window with the butt end of an ice ax, clearing the edges of broken glass. The opening was large enough for him to reach in and grasp the body.

"Careful," Lank yelled. Assock shouted back for help, not caution.

It wasn't until they had the creature fully out that they perceived its shape was like themselves. The body was stiff, the skin an icy blue, the face streaked with frozen blood. They held it by the arms and legs and carried it inside the globeship to the infirmary where it was submerged in ice water.

Lank wiped away the caked blood with a warm sponge, clearing the nose and mouth. He felt for a pulse in the carotid artery. There was none. He forced open the mouth, cleared the mucous clogging the throat and, pinching the nostrils closed, he forced his own breath into the creature's lungs, then watched the chest for movement. There was none.

"We'll have to wait," he said. "We may be too late. It's got to warm slowly. I'll crack the lungs if I exert too much pressure."

He placed an oxygen mask over the face. The temperature of the water was raised incrementally, degree by degree. The clothing was carefully removed as it thawed. They began to massage the skin, kneading it more firmly as it softened. Lank kept his eye on the respirator bag. It remained motionless. They worked on, their hands numb with the cold of the water and of the skin and muscles beneath, but gradually warming as the temperature slowly increased.

"The bag—it quivered." Lank stopped massaging and stared at the rubber bag.

"Are you sure?" Esop said.

"No—keep rubbing," Lank urged them on.

Then they all saw it, a single shallow breath remotely revealed by the quiver of the bag. Another minute—another breath—and then a slow, still shallow steady expansion and contraction. It was breathing on its own. Lank could now feel a weak pulsing of the carotid artery. They lifted the body out of the bath, placed it on a warm waterbed and swaddled it with blankets. The respirator mask was kept on.

Lank found a vein and inserted a needle for intravenous fluids. He attached the electrodes of the electroencephalograph to the scalp. The signal line of the cathode ray tube gyrated very slowly. "There's some brain activity, not much." Lank was encouraged. "We can only wait now." Lank called for attendants, issuing instructions to continue light massage and gentle movement of the limbs and to talk quietly. No sudden sounds, and yes they could, in fact they should have soft music. And to call him if there was any change, any change at all.

They collapsed on deep cushioned chairs in the ship's lounge, exhausted by their physical exertion and emotional tension. Not in their wildest dreams could they have anticipated a live being.

"Can't be sure, yet," Lank cautioned. He was a round man, round shouldered, round bodied, round faced, round lips curved quartermoon upwards in a perpetual half-smile. "It's in a coma. It may never come out."

"We've got to stop saying 'it'. It's not an *it*." Assock was intense. His dark complexion exaggerated a full, heavy face. A broad, flat nose supported thick dark rimmed spectacles that magnified serious, reflective eyes. He lit a cigarette, inhaled deeply and blew the smoke towards the translucent ceiling of the globeship, ignoring Lank and Esop who shook their heads disapprovingly.

"You're right," Esop agreed, "but it's so strange. All the time we were working on it—him—it was an *it*—a thing. When we lifted him out of the bath, only then did it hit me."

"He's not a Species Human," Lank asserted emphatically. "He's not one of us. He's all out of proportion. You noticed how long his limbs are? And his head—the cranium—he's almost microcephalic."

"Oh, I don't think so," Assock contradicted. "The forehead is quite well developed, a good-sized cerebrum even if it is smaller than ours. No, I think—I'm almost afraid to say it—I think we've got a Homo Sapien." He sucked in his breath.

Esop and Lank stared at him incredulously.

Assock continued. "This isn't the first time a frozen creature has been uncovered. Always dead, of course. Remember the mammoths with tropical fruits in their gullets, frozen in the act of swallowing. Compelling evidence of a cataclysmic event. Sapien scientists knew about this cyclic phenomenon. They knew the earth alternately passed from a cold phase to a warm phase and back again, with glaciers expanding and contracting, oceans flowing and ebbing. The polar caps acted then as now as great balance weights to keep the planet on its normal axis. But the earth must have toppled at least once before the Great Cataclysm. Torrid zones became polar, polar zones torrid. At that moment, the mammoths were instantly frozen and preserved for posterity, tropical fruits and all."

The Professor of Pragmatic Rationality paused to light another cigarette, to the frowns of his companions. He lectured on. "Homo Sapiens had the hydrogen bomb, we know that. It's pretty clear that an enormous H-blast occurred, setting off a chain reaction that unbalanced the earth, toppling it much as would happen now if we did not reduce the ice caps. There were survivors—not many—enough to give birth to our mutant Species Human." Assock murmured as an aside, "I've never been sure it was a mutation."

"What do you mean?" asked Esop.

"Oh, never mind," the professor said, and continued his exposition. "What if there was one creature, one Homo Sapien, at the exact center of the blast? What if he was quick-frozen in a virtually complete vacuum as the earth toppled instantly from a temperate to a polar zone. And then we come along and instantly reverse the process with our own H-blast."

Lank broke in. "Yes, yes! It's possible. Zenar—you know Zenar," as if anyone didn't know the biologist at the Universal University in Opalon, "he did just that. He froze mice and years afterwards unfroze them. They came alive as though nothing happened."

Esop laughed. "Do you know how many labs Zenar blew up perfecting that damned vacuum? Three!" He turned to Assock. "Zenar was working on a small mammal, not a man."

"That's beside the point," Assock insisted, clenching his fist. "Zenar's vacuum is not big enough. But the vacuum at the center of a hydrogen explosion is enormous. That's what I think happened. It wasn't a sarcophagus. He wasn't buried there. He got caught in the blast."

"If that's so," exclaimed Lank, "he's over five thousand years old!"

E sop put in a call to Zenar in Opalon, briefly explaining the situation and the need for secrecy.

"Last thing we need," he cautioned, "is a pack of reporters out here. If you have to invent a story, tell 'em we found relics, the usual stuff."

Excitement rose in Zenar's voice. "It's alive, you say. It's really alive?"

Esop continued his instructions. "You should check the medical archives for anything on Homo Sapiens blood types and antibodies. If there are any microscopic slides, bring them. And don't forget your blood kit."

"Really, Esop," Zenar exclaimed, "I know my business."

While Esop was talking to Zenar, Lank monitored his patient. The blood pressure was normal, the pulse strong and steady but the Sapien was having some difficulty breathing. Lank added antibiotics to the intravenous saline solution in addition to nutrients. He checked the encephalogram. The amplitude of the brain waves was increasing, a good sign, but with occasional sharp jerks. All things considered, the creature's condition was progressing satisfactorily.

Esop sent a couple of crewmen out to search the container. They brought back some folded papers that looked like maps, and a small black bag. Then they examined the creature's clothing, which was still damp from thawing.

Assock found a small leather packet with an assortment of cards and papers in the folds that were stuck together in a glutinous mass. He put it aside for drying and separation later on.

Lank rummaged through the black bag. "Look here, look at these tools, some sort of measuring instruments."

Just then an attendant rushed into the lounge. "Doctor, come quick," he cried. "Cardiac—respiratory arrest!"

Lank ran to the infirmary, followed by Assock and Esop. Another attendant had already switched the respirator to positive pressure inhalation. Lank recognized the cardiac muscles quivering frantically like a high frequency vibrator. He grabbed the defibrillator, slammed the electric plates on opposite sides of the chest and discharged three shocks, raising the body in convulsive jerks. The heart resumed a steady beat.

Breathing a sigh of relief, Lank insisted on remaining with his patient. "I'll join you later," he said, sending Esop and Assock back to the lounge.

"That was close," Esop sighed. "What a tragedy, what a waste if he dies."

"He can't...he mustn't," Assock said intensely. "He's got to live. We may never get another chance to..."

Esop looked at him quizzically. "To what?"

"Nothing," replied Assock distantly.

Esop had known the Professor too long to press him further. When Assock was ready, he would tell him what he meant. But he had a nagging feeling, almost of distrust, itching at the back of his brain. They had some major disagreements in the past. Usually they ironed them out. But there were times when Assock's mind was set on a separate course of action. There were times when there was no dissuading him.

Assock interrupted his thoughts. "We've got to speak to him."

Esop shook his head affirmatively. He had been so totally absorbed with the creature's survival that intercommunication had not occurred to him.

"Remember those gadgets in the Language Museum?" Assock reminded Esop. They were used centuries ago for translation between the tribes."

Esop screwed up his forehead. "It was…what was it called, a—yeah—the Electronic Translator."

"And the Psycho-irratica Interpreter," added Assock.

Zenar was located in the Medical Archives. Esop described the translators and told Zenar to bring them along.

"How do you expect me to pick up all this junk without arousing suspicion?" Zenar complained. "How do you know they still work?"

"I don't know," Esop replied to both questions. "Just bring them."

Zenar bristled at Esop's commanding tone. "Yes, sir," he grumbled, terminating the call abruptly.

Esop and Assock checked in with Lank.

"Everything's fine," Lank assured them. "The crisis is over. I'll sleep here anyway." Lank had placed a small cot next to the Sapien's bed. After the last close call, he wanted to be right there in case of another emergency.

Esop and Assock stretched out on the carpeted floor of the lounge. The translucent dome of the globeship was darkening to simulate night in the permaday of the polar region at that time of year. They had been awake for nearly two days. Now their minds settled into the quiet. Only the sound of asynchronous breathing stirred the air as each succumbed to the restless sleep of those anxious for tomorrow to become today.

Hours later they were wakened by the rough sounds of Zenar dragging in the *junk*.

"Sorry I woke you," Zenar greeted Assock and Esop in a deep, resonant voice, not sorry at all. He was tall for the Species Human. Bristling red hair flamed like a torch atop his seven-foot frame. His face was long and tapered, with a long, sharp nose separating narrow blue eyes, and lips thin and pale against a rubicund complexion.

"Did you bring everything?" Esop yawned and stretched.

"Yep—and more." He dropped an armful of books between the still prostrate bodies of his colleagues. "Where's Lank?" His voice, normally loud, boomed and echoed in the lounge.

Startled by how long they had slept, Esop and Assock, now wide awake, jumped up. They were dwarfed by Zenar who followed them through the corridor to the infirmary.

"Are you sure it's a Homo Sapien?" Zenar queried as he bent over the waterbed for a closer look.

"That's what you're here to determine," Esop said curtly.

Assock was unequivocal, stating firmly, "I'm positive."

Lank beamed with confidence not of the creature's identity but of his survival.

"He's doing great," he said to Zenar, but there were lingering doubts masked by his perennial half-smile. The vital signs were good, but the brain waves were something else.

Assock examined the tracings of the encephalogram. "Those jumps, what do you make of them?"

Lank minimized the bursts of jagged peaks that erupted episodically on the graph. "An occasional disturbed dream," he said.

"Terrors," Assock scowled at Lank and repeated, "terrors."

"I know," Lank admitted sheepishly, knowing he should not have minimized his observations but he so much wanted the creature to be all right. "They were even stronger. Look back there."

He showed Assock earlier graphs. "That's when I increased sedation. They've slowed down. He's holding his own now. I'll give him another day on I-V to build his strength. Then we can let him wake up."

"If he wakes up," Assock cautioned. "If the terrors return like before, he may kill himself." He studied the graphs intently. "Look at this series. When did this happen?"

Lank checked the graph against the timeline. "Yesterday, when his heart stopped."

"He was committing suicide," Assock concluded sadly, moving his head from side to side. "We may not be able to prevent it next time."

Lank's face reflected his gloom.

Esop broke the spell. "C'mon, we'd better get something to eat. We've got a lot of work to do."

Zenar dismissed them. "Go on," he said. "I'll take some blood and begin the tests," adding as an afterthought, "if that's all right with you, Lank?" He had almost forgotten that Lank was in charge of the body.

Lank stayed behind to help Zenar draw blood and then joined the others in the lounge that had become their home and study. Food was brought in from the ship's galley. They ate lightly, without appetite, discussing what they knew, what they could remember of Homo Sapiens culture.

The world prior to the Great Cataclysm was part of everyone's education. They knew how difficult it had been for Homo Sapiens to learn from experience. Their history was cluttered with contradictions. How well they remembered the glowing descriptions of the Golden Age of Pericles, a period of astounding art, sculpture and architecture. Less glowing were the Peloponnesian Wars that raged and ravaged up and down the coast of Greece with mercenaries killing, raping, plundering the land and the people. And yet, this same period gave birth to concepts of freedom and democracy so similar in political structure and philosophy to the Seventh Millennium. Their studies carried them through the Dark Ages, into the light of the Renaissance, past the American and French revolutions, to the miracles and enlightenment of 19th, 20th, and 21st century science and technology. And yet wars continued, over 15,000 recorded little wars, big wars, enormous wars. Revolutions renewing hope ended in mass enslavement and genocide. And yet there was literature to stir the spirit, poetry to salve the soul, music to please the gods. The thread of light persisted to the end.

They tried to be objective and unemotional, but they simply could not understand their predecessors. How could any culture be so creative and so destructive simultaneously? It made no sense. There had to be a reason. Was it a genetic defect or was it something about experiencing life within the certitude of death that drove them mad?

Zenar had been standing unnoticed for some time in the doorway, listening to his friends. Esop looked up and saw him. He was more than a little annoyed that Zenar had kept them waiting.

Zenar grinned and boomed, "By Jevh, you're right, Assock. It's a Homo Sapien, no doubt about it. Blood type, antibodies—they match the archival slides almost exactly."

"What do you mean, *almost*?" Assock shot back at Zenar.

"Almost exactly," Zenar yelled back, irritated by what was nothing more than a semantic triviality. "Almost exactly. What more do you want? Nothing is ever exact."

Assock apologized, smoothing Zenar's ruffled feathers. "It's just that I must be sure."

"You can be—almost exactly," Zenar quipped.

"That's great…just great," Lank beamed, pumping his fist affectionately against Zenar's shoulder.

Esop noted Assock's intensity. Reassured by Zenar, Assock still seemed unsure of something, not so much the creature's identification, but of something else. It could wait. Now that they had a live Homo Sapien, a real person, their need to understand his culture was not merely an intellectual pursuit, no study of dead history.

They picked up the materials Zenar had brought from the Library of Antiquity. The librarian had selected a broad range of geographies, histories, books on philosophy, religion and psychology, newspapers—anything that would help them form a frame of reference. The bulk of the materials was more than a normal response to a casual request. Esop suspected Zenar had told the librarian what was going on.

"I had to," Zenar confessed. "Look, old man, the guy's not stupid. He heard I picked up the Translator, God knows how. They must have a pipeline in every archive. He swore he'd keep it secret."

"Fat chance," Esop mumbled. "Well, it's done, and it's a damned good selection."

"Thanks," Zenar replied, as though he was the intended recipient of the compliment.

The four men settled down in the lounge and began reading. Taking an atlas, Zenar studied the Homo Sapiens' geographical world, occasionally whistling in amazement. The mountains, the oceans, the plateaus had all disappeared and been replaced by the geography of the Seventh Millennium. The different colors on the continents, he realized, represented distinctive populations. Nations, they called them. From the bold lines of delineation, he sensed formidable barriers and visualized roadblocks, barbed wire, uniformed police.

Assock picked up a volume on contemporary religions. Regardless of differences in beliefs, values and practices, each sought to calm the anxieties of the unknown. Some religions promised an eternal afterlife for passive acceptance of the deprivations and suffering of earthly existence. Others awarded unconscious reincarnation, which could be good or bad, depending on the quality of the life it succeeded. Assock found reincarnation particularly puzzling since the reincarnated were supposed to have no knowledge of who or what they had been in the past or would be in the future. Then there was the dissolution into the void of insensate nihilism, preceding the inevitability of death.

Religion had its therapeutic value, offering tribal kinship and support, relieving mental anguish, substituting delusions of worth and purpose for the inevitable skepticism and cynicism of a rational mind. But when the fundamentalists of one tribe encountered the fundamentalists of another, all hell broke loose.

Assock remarked to Esop, "Homo Sapiens had only to stand before a mirror to see the most dangerous animal on earth."

Esop barely heard him. He was engrossed in the translations of newspapers, snorting at the motto of one paper—All The News That's Fit To Print—but not all the news. Had he not known otherwise, the papers might have passed for satire. They reflected the times.

The late hours of afternoon glided by silently. The light of the dome followed time like the hemisphere of a planetarium. Shadows emerged from corners and swept over the carpet. They read on, intently bent on understanding. There were the patterns, the boundaries, the blind groping towards unknown goals. The complex social relationships, the families, the institutions. The glories of civilization, and then the final disintegration into social barbarism, economic cannibalism, political infantilism, sadism, masochism, perversion led by deluded prophets, mystics, heretics and hysterics. The guile, the gall, the blazing blunderheadedness. Hopes crimsoned with disappointment. Courage beaten into cynicism. Little men in big shoes. Pus oozing from open sores. Zealots denouncing Zealots, Fundamentalists flaying Secularists, Right-wingers lambasting Left-Wingers, Communists crying Fascist, Fascists decrying Communist, Americans screaming Americanism.

Strained eyes read through dusk. Esop, Assock, Zenar and Lank—Director, Rationalist, Biologist, Physician—thrown back five thousand years, reliving the hopes, the dreams, the failures, the beauty and the ugliness of a destroyed civilization.

CHAPTER 3

The following morning Lank disconnected the life-support systems, allowing the Homo Sapien to function completely on his own. Then he sat back to monitor his patient's return to consciousness. As a precaution, the limbs were restrained with straps just in case the terrors erupted forcibly.

Lank observed the stubbled growth of the Sapien's beard, a good sign. The hair follicles had survived the freezing, the thaw, the near re-freezing, and the final physical restitution. If these superficial cells were in good condition, chances were excellent for the recovery of the deeper tissues and organs. He studied the face. There was noticeable twitching and fluttering of the closed eyelids, and occasionally the lower jaw quivered, accompanied by a shudder of the torso and abrupt jerks of the arms and legs. These reactions were to be expected as the body metabolized the remaining sedative that still coursed through its veins.

"How's he doing?" Assock asked as he entered the room.

"Good," Lank replied. "He's a little slow coming out of it."

"He may not want to," Assock said. "What about the terrors?"

"Subliminal," Lank answered, his forefinger tracing the narrowing amplitude of waves on the encephalogram.

Esop and Zenar carried the translating devices into the room. Esop was skeptical. It was one thing to translate syntax, quite another to transpose context.

Assock was more optimistic. "They should minimize reentry shock, if they work."

"*If they work*," Zenar repeated.

Assock continued. "If we can communicate right off, he should be less disoriented."

The Electronic Translator was programmed for a number of ancient languages. Zenar had been assured by the Universal University's specialist in ancient linguistics that the Translator would work if the creature's language was programmed. As a precaution, it was synchronized with the Psycho-irratica Interpreter, which filtered out transposed idioms and signaled aberrant context.

"And who else did you talk to?" Esop tried to control his annoyance at this further breach of secrecy in Opalon.

Zenar replied defensively, "I had to get the right machines."

"Let's hope so."

They donned headsets, each one containing a receptor, emitter and correlator. Lank gently lifted the Sapien's head, capping it with a similar headset. As he did so, the Sapien groaned. The scientists looked at each other and smiled. No mistaking that translation.

John's eyes fluttered open. Bright light burned through his blurred vision. He lay still for a moment. His head ached. He tried lifting his right arm. It barely raised against the restraining strap. He moved his left arm. It also was tied down. He tried raising one leg, then the other, to no avail. His body rolled gently on the water mattress and he felt nauseous. He waited a moment and then heaved against the straps, grunting, groaning, rolling more violently on the surging waves of the mattress, lifting his head and shoulders, then falling back exhausted.

He blinked, trying to clear his vision. The light was no longer painful, but he was now aware of aches and pains throughout his body. The skin over his face was taut and stiff as parchment, and his chest felt like it was bound in barbed wire that pierced his flesh with each heaving breath. His ears were ringing and buzzing furiously. He strained to see. Slowly the formless blur came into focus. He stared wide-eyed at four heads looming above him.

Sounds, voices, a single voice penetrating the dense ringing in his ears. Speaking sounds, garbled sounds, unintelligible sounds. Wait, he thought he recognized German, then—

"Comment allez-vous?...¿Cómo está?" Esop was switching from one language to another on the Electronic Translator. "How are you?"

John's head perked up. "What happened? Where am I?" His voice emerged thick and granular out of a tight, constricted throat.

"You're all right," one said, the others nodding consensually.

"Who are you?"

"Friends," Esop answered. The Electronic Translator was working perfectly.

"Why am I tied down?" John emphasized the constraints by straining at the straps.

"You had a terrible shock," Lank intervened. "We weren't sure how you'd come out of it."

"Untie me," he insisted.

A bright red light flashed on the Psycho-irratica Interpreter, catching Assock's eye. "Be patient," Assock said softly, adding, "in a little while."

John tugged again at the straps.

"How do you feel?" Lank asked.

"How the hell do you think I feel?!"

The red light flashed again.

"Let me introduce ourselves," Esop interjected calmly. "My name is Esop. I am Director of the Seventh Millennium's Anti-topple Committee."

"The anti what committee?" John stammered.

"Anti-topple. We'll explain in a minute." Esop continued with the introductions.

John's eyes shifted from one to the other, each nodding as Esop identified his colleagues. Then he was asked his name.

"Altern, John Altern."

"We're very glad to meet you Altern John Altern," Esop addressed him warmly.

"No—John Altern. Just John Altern." *Who were these strange people?* There was something odd about them. Their heads were larger than normal, round with swollen foreheads. They looked almost hydrocephalic, but their eyes were bright and intelligent. He noticed how short they were, except for the redheaded one called Zenar. His head was more elongated than globe shaped.

"All right, John Altern—"

"John will do."

"Okay—John. I'll try to explain what we think happened." This time it was the pudgy Professor of Pragmatic Rationality who was speaking. "We discovered you at the bottom of the crater. You were buried...frozen. We can only guess for how long, perhaps five thousand years."

"Are you crazy?" John blurted. The warning light of the Psycho-irratica Interpreter flashed furiously for a few seconds, gradually dimming.

"Our nuclear blast reversed the process. Fortunately, we were able to get you back here in time. If it wasn't for the good Doctor Lank, you would not have survived."

Lank nodded appreciatively.

Assock concluded, "We're really as perplexed as you. I can't find words to express our pleasure in your good condition. And that we can understand each other through the Translator is, well, it's simply remarkable."

"Translator—what translator?" John was indeed perplexed and growing more agitated by the moment.

Esop described the machines, pointing out the headsets they each wore. He explained that if the electronics worked the same on Homo Sapiens as the Species Human, in a few days they will have assimilated each other's language and could dispense with the Translator altogether.

John shook his head. *What kind of nonsense is this? Homo Sapiens...Species Human...what the devil is going on here? The restraining straps could only mean that he was a prisoner of these misanthropes. Maybe they're wearing Halloween masks. But why the charade? Dammit, this isn't funny.* Again he thrashed out against the straps, heaving from side to side, struggling to break free.

Zenar and Esop fell over John's body to hold him still as Lank slipped a hypodermic needle into his arm, injecting a sedative that sent the Homo Sapien back to the physical safety of unconsciousness.

Assock was furious. "Why did you do that?" he demanded.

Lank looked up in surprise. "You saw him. He might have hurt himself. He's still weak. The shock was too much."

Assock turned abruptly and stomped out of the room.

Zenar was bewildered by Assock's outburst. "What the devil's got into him?"

"I wish I knew," Esop answered, shaking his head back and forth. He followed Assock back to the lounge.

"We can't pamper him," Assock admonished Esop, still angry. "How the hell are we going to find out what he's like if he's sedated at the slightest provocation?"

Esop reasoned with him. The Sapien needed time. There would be lots of time now that his survival was assured.

"Perhaps," conceded Assock for the moment, calming down, "but when he wakes up I want the straps off. That was a mistake. We made him a prisoner and he reacted like one."

"What if he becomes violent again?"

"We can handle him," Assock said, dismissing Esop's concerns.

John floated weightlessly in the darkness of sedation, muffled voices penetrating in and out, the ringing in his ears rising to a crescendo until all other sounds were blotted out. His body tingled numbness. Everything was paralyzed except his mind, which raced back and forth like an alternating electrical current. He was in the car, his hands strapped to the steering wheel. The car was speeding up towards the summit of a steep hill. As he approached the top, the engine lost power and the car started sliding backward. He strained to reach the brake pedal but his foot was tied to the dead accelerator. The car gained momentum, hurtling downward, backward, out of control....

He screamed, twisting in the bed, arms bound at his sides, eyes wide open, pupils dilated, the whites of his eyes glazed like a cornered animal. He shouted hysterically, his voice a staccato of fright pleading for help.

"Terrors," Lank observed clinically as Zenar unbuckled the straps and wrapped his long arms around the Homo Sapien, lifting and cuddling him to his chest.

"It's all right...it's all right," he repeated softly, rocking John back and forth.

The terrors ended abruptly. Zenar gently returned him to the bed. John's eyes blinked and the glaze disappeared as he regained consciousness. He raised a hand to his forehead and flung off the headset. Unintelligible voices babbled at him. Zenar replaced the headset and the sounds became words he could understand.

"We released the straps. You're free to move about," Lank assured him.

John moved his hands and legs. "Thank you," he muttered barely above a whisper.

Lank said, "We're very sorry about this morning. You were quite agitated, understandably so. We were afraid you might hurt yourself. We mean you no harm. But you mustn't harm yourself. You must remain calm."

John nodded. Straps or no straps, they were four against one, and no telling how many others to back them up.

"This thing on my head, I don't understand," he said.

"But you do understand," Esop responded enthusiastically. "It's a translating device. Don't you remember?"

John started to say nonsense, then caught himself. No sense antagonizing them. Instead he said, "I understand you quite well. I don't need this." Again he removed the headset. Again their words turned to garbled gibberish. He put the headset back on.

"You see," Esop explained, "we're not trying to confuse you. In a day or two, our speech centers will be programmed to each other. Actually you'll be speaking our language. It's not so different from yours. More a matter of dialect."

John remained skeptical. He supposed it didn't matter what game they were playing so long as they could communicate. He was more concerned with his vision, which was still fuzzy, making it difficult to examine their funny masks more closely. They had to be pretty damned good to look so real. He decided he had better play along until he could get his bearings.

"What you were saying before—about freezing—do you really expect me to believe that?"

Zenar answered, "Seeing is believing. Think you can walk?"

"I'm not sure. I don't feel so good."

"Try."

John sat up with difficulty and moved his legs over the side of the bed, slowly easing himself to the floor. His legs were stiff, wobbly.

Zenar offered an arm.

John declined. "I think I can make it."

He swayed unsteadily but kept his balance. He took one faltering step, then another, and another until he reached the porthole. Outside was an endless expanse of ice, glistening white and bright, causing him to squint.

"How did I get here?" His voice was quiet, subdued by the enormity of the icy plain.

John listened intently, leaning against the wall to steady himself as Assock repeated his theory. Then, still nauseous and rubber-legged, he retreated to the bed, weaving like a drunk, flopping down on his back to relieve the dizziness.

Lank urged him to rest.

"I'll be all right," John said. "I appreciate your untying me."

Esop acknowledged his gratitude, if that's what it was, and urged John to rest awhile. "We'll talk more later, and, oh yes, we'll be going home tomorrow."

"Home? Where's that?"

"Opalon," Esop replied.

John looked up in wonderment as the charade continued. "If you don't mind," he said, "I'd like to be alone. I need to think."

Esop turned to Lank. "Is that okay?"

"Sure, and John, if you need anything, just press this button."

John poured a glass of juice from the pitcher at his bedside and sipped it slowly, his throat soothed by the cool viscous liquid. He was surprised they left him alone. He felt much calmer with them gone, and stronger as he rested. After a while he tried standing again, now on steadier legs, but with joints still stiff and tender. Although his body ached, the pain was considerably less, except for an acute stabbing that pierced his eyes from behind and penetrated to the center of his brain at any abrupt movement. But his sight was considerably improved, now virtually normal except for the bright flash of light accompanying each stabbing pain.

Moving to the door, he opened it cautiously. The corridor was empty. He walked on, through another door, into a narrower passageway. All was quiet, except the persistent ringing in his ears. No one was in sight. At the end of the passageway, near an exit door, were parkas, leggings, boots, snowshoes and ice axes, everything he would need to get out of there. But to where? Absurd as it seemed, sure they would stop him, he had to try.

Donned like an Eskimo, he stepped outside. The subfreezing air shot through his nostrils and mouth, searing his lungs like a blast of heat from a furnace. He pulled the hood of the parka over his head and closed the thermal face mask. Still cold, breathing was now tolerable.

He trudged forward, squinting in the narrow band of light that passed through the slits of the mask. Fifty yards away he spied a dark hulk. As he got closer, he recognized it as a car similar to his own. He moved around to the far side, using it as a blind against detection from the globeship. The driver's side window was broken, but otherwise the car appeared intact. He stuck his head through the opening. The inside was covered with a layer of dry, powder snow. It seemed so familiar. He had this sinking feeling that it could actually be his car. On hands and knees, he crawled to the rear and chipped away at the ice with the broad blade of the ax until the license plate was visible. The blue letters of the personalized plate were more numbing than the frigid air—JAM—John...Alice...Mary.

He fell back in the snow, eyes fixed on the plate, believing, disbelieving, alone, terribly alone. Alice...Mary...where were they? Where was he? He closed his eyes and stared inward. Their faces appeared and disappeared, Alice saying goodbye to him, Mary, her head buried in the pillow, asleep as he last saw her.

He had to pull himself together. Was it possible what they said about his survival was true? No way...absolutely absurd. But there was the car, his JAM.

Joints crackled as he straightened up. He had to see more. He moved away from the car. Snow began to fall, large flakes fluttering earthward, obscuring his vision. The ground cover thickened. He stumbled in drifts that formed mounds over the flat sheet of ice. He stepped into the snowshoes and shuffled towards the horizon that was fast disappearing in the enveloping snow.

They huddled around the visioscreen in the globeship's navigation room, watching the Sapien struggle through the snow, slipping and reeling like a drunken polar bear walking upright.

"We'd better get him," Esop said anxiously.

Assock shook his head negatively. "Let him go on. He must understand there's no place to go."

Esop countered with growing concern, "The snow's pretty heavy. He's barely visible,"

"Don't worry," Assock reassured, "the Locator's got a fix on him. We can't lose him."

"He could fall in a crevasse."

Zenar had enough. Without waiting for comment, much less permission, he rushed out to the ship's storage room where he put on a thermal snowsuit and dragged the motor sled outside. He set the sled's Locator to the signal being transmitted by the tracking device attached to the Sapien's parka. The sled moved full speed over the snow, bucking up and down the drifts. Then it hit an ice pack and capsized. "Damn," Zenar muttered. He punched the starter. It didn't start. The Locator continued to read the signal. He tore it loose and plunged ahead on foot. Visibility was near zero as snow fell in swirling sheets. Following the signal blindly, the beeps of the tracking device became more frequent and louder. He was close.

John sank down in the snow, exhausted, his breathing rapid and shallow. The subzero air cut each breath short, preventing deep inspirations that would forestall hyperventilation. He was becoming dizzy and nauseous. His heart thumped painfully. He was tired, so tired. He would just rest a moment. He was beginning to feel so comfortable, so relaxed. He could just close his eyes—and at that moment he was startled awake by a huge apparition lunging towards him over a snowdrift, its legs sinking knee-deep on the downward slope.

"Here—I'm here," John shouted weakly, adding as Zenar reached him, "Am I glad to see you."

Zenar shouted back at him, unintelligible words lost in the howling storm.

John was too weak to stand. Zenar removed the snowshoes from the Sapien's feet and put them on himself. Extending a hand, he pulled John up, swung him over his shoulder in a fireman's lift, reset the Locator and trudged back to the globeship, following the return signal faithfully through the storm. *It's a damned good thing the Sapien took snowshoes,* Zenar reflected, *Maybe he's not so stupid after all.*

Inside the warmth and security of the ship, they gave John a shot of brandy, a heavy wool robe, thick stockings, and insisted he lie down to rest.

Meanwhile, Zenar, Esop and Assock went down to the cafeteria. Zenar was piqued they had not sent out another sled.

"Thought you needed the exercise," quipped Esop.

"Very funny."

"I'm sorry, old man," Esop said seriously. "We only have one sled."

"You mean to say this whole goddamned expedition brought along just one sled."

Esop shrugged. Zenar had a right to be upset. All this time he had been annoyed with Zenar for leaking the news in Opalon, and here he, who was supposed to be prepared for everything, had nearly lost the prize. But sleds were an anachronism, included as an afterthought, so dependent had they become on aerobes. Fortunately, it was Zenar who went for the Sapien. No one else would have had the strength to carry him back in that storm. He had been wrong to let the Sapien get so far away. He had the authority to countermand Assock. It was Zenar who had the good sense to go after him. Good old Zenar.

After resting a bit, John was escorted to the cafeteria by Lank. The others were sitting around the table and he was directed to the empty chair at its head. He was offered a cup of hot chocolate, its warmth permeating throughout his body. He had not uttered a word since Zenar rescued him. The Translator band was back on his head, so it was not a matter of speaking. They had trusted him and he had tried to escape. Finally, reluctantly, he offered an apology.

"Not at all," they demurred.

"We could have stopped you," Lank further explained. "I was more than a little concerned, but your recovery has been extraordinary. We decided—Assock convinced us—that you had to see for yourself where you are. You were under surveillance all the time, er, most of the time."

John was incredulous. "You mean you let me…you wanted me to escape?"

"Not escape," confided Assock. "Rather, you had to see that we really are at the Pole."

"That's depressing," John admitted sadly. "I saw my car. That was real…my car out there."

Assock nodded, "You needed proof."

"It will take more than my car at the North Pole—"

"South. It used to be North," Esop corrected.

"South—North—what difference does it make?"

"None to you, perhaps," Esop explained. "To us, it's very important. The North Pole's ice cap was also reduced. It was done simultaneously with our blast. The engineers tell us we've been successful. It's a real balancing act. If the timing's not just right, it could cause a major topple, just like what happened to you."

John was exasperated. "We're back to that again. Look, you've convinced me that somehow I got stuck out here, maybe inside my car like you say, but don't give me that deep freeze stuff. It's a bit much."

"Facts are inescapable," Esop declared. "We don't expect you to believe everything at once, not what we tell you or even what you see with your eyes."

"Well, I believe what I saw outside, but I'm not so sure about what I'm seeing in here." He paused, "Would you mind coming closer so I can get a better look at you? My eyes, they're still a bit fuzzy."

Esop leaned towards John who motioned him to come still closer, so close that he could make out the pores of his skin. Slowly raising his hand towards Esop's face, his fingertips barely touched what was unmistakably skin. No mask, no facade. They were as they appeared to be, and that was most disconcerting.

Assock decided it was time to get off this tack. There was little more they could say, and nothing more that would convince the Sapien beyond what his eyes could see. Perhaps it would be better to find out more about him. He began by asking John what he did in his prior life.

"I was," he caught himself and corrected to the present tense. "I am a medical doctor."

"Aha, I thought so," Lank said, pleased with himself. "Those tools, in that black bag, they were yours?"

"They are mine," John corrected him.

"Of course. But what are they for?"

"You're a doctor," John blurted, momentarily forgetting his vulnerability. "Don't kid me, you know a sphygmomanometer when you see one."

"A svig…sfig…what?" Lank tried unsuccessfully to repeat the word.

"To measure blood pressure," John said, further irritated by the developing farce.

"Ah yes, of course. You must show me how it works."

"That's too much." John pushed himself back from the table in complete frustration. "I admit I'm confused, maybe even frightened. I accept the ice, okay, and maybe your…your anti-topple stuff. Maybe that's true, but for Christ sake, why the charade? Species Human or whatever you call yourselves, Seventh Millennium, me five thousand years old. Why can't you just tell me what's going on?"

Esop, Assock and Lank looked at each other, then turned to Zenar who had been unusually quiet. Zenar caught the cue. He ran his fingers self-consciously through his long red hair. His voice curled off his tongue, softly, smoothly.

"Well, my friend, you want the truth, eh? We told you the truth as best we could, and now you want a different truth. Perhaps you don't want the truth at all. You want something to believe. I suppose it would be easier for you to believe that we are aliens in disguise, or maybe not disguised. Is that what you think?"

John shrugged. "I really don't know. I suppose you could be."

"You mean to tell me," Zenar said sarcastically, "that you can't tell the difference between a mutant species and one of your fellow Homo Sapiens? And you a doctor?"

"Damn it, we don't all look alike. Okay, you're not aliens, you're not human beings—no, I don't mean that. I just don't know who or what you are."

"You don't know, but when we tell you, you say we lie."

"I didn't say you lie. I just said I didn't believe you. All I want is to know what happened to me...my family...my country," John pleaded.

"Well, you shall have your truth. The truth is that your world no longer exists. It is gone—your family, your friends, your cities, the oceans, the mountains—your whole goddamned world is gone. There's no use my being pleasant about it."

"I'm not asking for pleasantries." John's throat tightened, his words choked.

Zenar continued, his voice deeper and stronger. "We don't expect you to believe anything outright. In time you will see for yourself. It's hard enough for us to believe you come from a world that's long gone."

John could constrain himself no longer. "That's it! You can't expect me to believe that. You're all mad." He jumped up, thought better of it and slumped back into the chair, arms obstinately crossed against his chest as though bound in a straightjacket.

Zenar's face flushed. Assock tugged at his arm. "Take it easy," he whispered, but was ignored.

Zenar paced around the table, flailing his long arms in wild gesticulations. "Mad are we? By Jevh, we are mad at what happened to your world and to our ancestors who survived. By what standards do you judge our madness? By the standards of a world that mastered the machine only to fall victim to it? The beauty in your world, the good, your accomplishments, your art, your mechanics, your medicine. You were on the threshold of a whole new era, or were you?—you who split the atom. You speak of madness. What do you know of madness? I suspect nothing and everything. You had the bomb. Everyone had the bomb as if that guaranteed your survival. Now you have the truth. With one mighty burst of arrogance, your stupid species blew itself to hell!"

Miserable and indignant, unable to defend himself, whatever the truth they stood as one against him. Without a word, John got up and returned to the infirmary. Lying in bed, alone and lost, he wanted to cry. He closed his eyes and Mary's face formed off in the distance. With all his misgivings, he was still anchored in their home. She was staring at him, puzzled, frightened as though she knew he would not return. Then she vanished and he lay there not caring for this millennium or any millennium, just wanting to melt into the deep blue and cry his heart out and go home. He turned on his side and pressed his head against the pillow.

A ssock and Zenar shuffled through the snow, up a rise to a knoll overlooking the endless arctic expanse. Behind them the illumination of the globeship shone like a lamplight in the afterglow of the storm. They walked the perimeter of the knoll, two figures on a plateau of ice, surrounded by more ice and the infinite universe above.

"Was it too much?" Zenar finally broke the silence.

"No—he needed your bluntness. You are positively the least subtle person I know."

Zenar laughed loudly, echoes of laughter rebounding on polar peaks. "Subtlety? We have so little time. Why waste it on subterfuge?"

Assock contradicted his friend. "Not the same. That's the charm of subtlety. As subterfuge I have as little use for it as you. A strong perfume is obvious, perhaps odious. Dilute it to please the sense, give it that delicate, haunting aroma, distinct but memorable—that is subtlety."

"So what's your point?" Zenar asked with all the interest in poetic license of a biological scientist.

"We were obvious, crude, rough. That's okay for a start. He's got to face up to his situation. We don't want to feed into his defenses. That's what they did. They looked into the mirror and closed their eyes. They were afraid to find out what they were really like, what they really wanted. We've got to give him that chance."

Zenar pressed his lips tight together. He caught Assock's eye, turned aside, avoiding his own thoughts.

"Let's not kid ourselves, Zenar. We've come a long way since the Cataclysm, but we're not out of the woods, not yet. You know the risks as well as I."

The shadow of Jevh loomed ominously over them, adding a deeper chill to the cold wind sweeping the plain. They sat in silence, exhaling white mist, thinking of John lost in this world, needing help, wanting to help, wondering if it was not too late.

The bright morning sun poured into Esop's room, settling warmly on his face. He yawned, stretched, and lay on his back a few moments before getting up to dress. He mused over Zenar's remark that it was sometimes necessary to crack a nut with a sledgehammer. Sometimes the meat is crushed. Then what? He agreed with Assock that they had to get beneath the Sapien's shell. If the meat was rotten, the solution would be simple. But there was more to a man than his outer armor. Beneath the skin was a sentient being, dangerous in fright, yet capable of responding to warmth.

As he shaved, he studied his face in the mirror, comparing his features with the Homo Sapien's. They were different, but not as much as he might have imagined. His head was rounder than John's and his eyes larger, but then John's eyes might still be squinting from fatigue. His nose was sharper, more aquiline but about the same length. His hair was as thick as the Sapien's, with a similar tinge of gray on the sides. He supposed they would have been about the same age. The resemblance was there, even as the difference was so distinctive. He was no longer thinking of the Sapien as an archeological relic. He was a contemporary and that realization was jarring.

He completed dressing and joined Lank in the lounge. Assock and Zenar sauntered in a little while later with a tray of sweet buns and coffee. Lank went to get the Sapien who reluctantly agreed to breakfast with them.

John had little appetite. Although his mind seemed clear and observant, his body was lethargic. His head ached less, but the lump on his forehead throbbed if he moved too quickly. He spoke little, answering their questions politely, cautiously. Their own politeness irritated him.

He sipped coffee, even accepted a cigarette that Assock offered. Coffee and cigarettes, the pacifiers he was addicted to, the latter only an occasional defiance considering the risks. If this was truly a world five thousand years removed from his, how unlikely these similarities would be. That they claimed the differences while indulging in the similarities was disturbing. Were they so certain of themselves that they did not have to destroy the obvious to obscure the past? Even the music floating through the room sounded familiar.

"Bach—Brandenburg Concertos," Assock said. "You see, there is such a thing as immortality." He smiled. "You have touched it yourself."

John snorted and asked, as if to suggest they might yet be on a planet in outer space, "How advanced are you in interplanetary travel?"

"Very little—the usual exploratory treks, mostly with robots."

"You mean this is not a flying saucer, a space ship?"

Esop laughed. "Hardly. We have the usual stuff in outer space—satellites and laboratories—but only unmanned exploratory probes and research vehicles to other planets. Pretty much the same as you were doing. It took us a long time to catch up. Space is really no place for the Species Human."

"Then we're still on Earth?"

Assock threw up his hands in a little helpless gesture. "That's what we've been trying to tell you."

John averted his eyes. What's the use? He would have to find out for himself. But what could he do? He might just as well have been placed on a raft in the middle of the ocean with complete freedom to come and go whenever and wherever he pleased. Hell, you could put anyone in the arctic and frame a pretty convincing case for the destruction of the rest of the world. Circumstantial evidence, provided you remain at the Pole. What if it was true, intruded like a splinter in his big toe. He could carefully step around it, but sooner or later he'd forget and step down and it would send a shooting pain up his spine, like the truth Zenar said he was avoiding.

The nagging loneliness returned. Never again to see his family and friends. Never again to feel their warmth and comfort, to hear their voices, their laughter.

Assock spoke to him quietly, almost whispering, "Every past has a future, a renewal that is as true for you as it is for us. You are not alone. We will help you. We'll soon be on our way to Opalon."

John looked into Assock's eyes and, for a moment, almost trusted him.

He anticipated the flight with mixed emotions, wanting to get away from this godforsaken place, but to where? A city called Opalon, a place on Earth he had never heard of, if indeed it was Earth. A people perhaps as crazy as his captors. There was some small comfort in the cold fact that he could not remain here even if he wanted to. If not here, then there, where there would be answers. Any answer would be better than remaining in limbo. Or would it be? He felt like a defendant at a trial, waiting for the jury to return a verdict. Anxious to end the ordeal, he was panicked by the thought he might be found guilty, that he might be the last survivor, condemned to wander alone for an eternity. He almost wished the jury would never return, that he would never know the truth he feared to face.

Outside the wind moaned hauntingly. The ship was secured, the atomic generators activated and, with the whoosh of its jet propulsion, the giant hemisphere slowly rose in flight. It hovered over the crater as the scientists took one last look at their project. Then the ship steered out across the arctic wasteland towards Opalon.

John's face matched the gloom of his depression. He was on his way to the unknown. Except for the rustling of air against the globeship's hull and the soft murmur of the jets, he heard only the silence that barely suppressed the beat of his heart. He closed his eyes and tried to sleep.

Hours later, the polar cap leagues past, the shadows and creases of his face smoothed with rest, John stretched and looked out into boundless heavens and bright sunshine. Far beneath the ship sprawled a blue-green expanse of water. They were moving rapidly, and patches of billowy cumulus clouds below appeared as cotton balls floating on the surface of the ocean. A thin brown strip of land came into view on the horizon.

Zenar and the others entered the lounge with a tray and glasses filled with a bronze sherry. Raising a glass in the direction of the land, he suggested a toast to Opalon and the future.

John sipped slowly. As they lost altitude details emerged, not unlike the shoreline of his familiar California coast. He asked when they would land.

"About twenty minutes," Esop replied. "We'll fly around a bit. It might help orient you."

John nodded appreciatively with a small smile. It was his first smile and it was refreshing. "And then?"

"I don't know," Esop smiled back. "We'll just take it from there."

"I have a family. I don't suppose I could get in touch—"

Esop shook his head. "I'm sorry."

"I keep forgetting."

"We understand," Esop said. "We're still quite unreal to you as you are to us. But it's not the same for us. We have our reality. You must find yours."

CHAPTER 4

Opalon nestled near the sea, contained in an arc of low mountains, which separated the sprawling city from the seemingly endless plains of the continent that stretched beyond to the horizon. Out of the sea, near the shore, jutted myriad stone spires standing as sentinels to guard the exposed coastline.

"The mountains and sea spikes protected the early settlers," Esop explained to John as the globeship floated over Opalon, affording a panoramic view of the city and its suburbs. "After the Great Cataclysm, bands of marauders—survivors—roamed the continent. One group settled here in Opalon, our ancestors. The sea spikes—they're like a strainer, allowing only small vessels to pass through. The mountains protect our valley from the north winds and winter blizzards."

"And marauders?" John asked impulsively.

Esop laughed. "Heavens no, that was a thousand years ago."

From the sky, the land appeared luxuriously well groomed. Tufts of treetops stippled the surface, coalescing into the dense foliage of parks or thinning out to precise rows of fruit orchards. Rectangular fields, furrowed like thick corduroy, reminded John of California farmland.

"If it wasn't for irrigation, the entire area would be desolate," Esop said, pointing to thin ribbons of water interlacing the fields and orchards.

The dome-shaped roofs of individual dwellings dotted the landscape. Outdoor amphitheaters were located at convenient intervals for symphonies and plays. Swimming pools and large reservoirs mirrored the shifting blue, gray and red of the sky, like so many opals in settings of earth. Narrow paths snaked around trees, in and out of parks, between homes and public buildings. Broad travel ways traversed the length and breadth of the valley, resembling the bands of a patch quilt separating hues of green, yellow, gold, violet and brown, sprinkled with the polka dots of variegated domes.

"What do you think of our city?" Esop asked John, as the ship completed its sweep of Opalon and headed for its home base near the ocean.

"Nice," John replied. He was impressed, not least by the clarity of the air. "No smog?"

"Not since we eliminated the infernal internal combustion machine."

John pointed towards an immense, rough-hewn tower in the center of the city.

"The Tower of Rationality," Assock cut in. "Our monument to the struggle against irrational behavior."

"Looks unfinished," John observed dryly.

The Tower ascended from its mammoth base to the rough edges surrounding the black hole of its summit, which had the ominous appearance of a dormant volcano.

"Never will be," Assock said. "We keep working at it. Every year a little higher, symbolizing endless growth. There's no end," he added, "to the struggle against irrationality."

No sooner had the ship landed than it was besieged by a crowd of news reporters and what seemed the entire city's population. Esop ordered the ship sealed off. Security officers kept the crowd at bay. He huddled with his colleagues while John sat dejectedly in the corner of the lounge, feeling more and more like a freak.

"That shoots our quiet return to hell," Esop exclaimed, surveying the crowd milling beyond the containing ropes encircling the ship.

Zenar lifted both palms upward in response to Esop's accusatory glance. "There's no way to avoid the public."

Esop sensed John's discomfort. He hadn't wanted to expose him so soon to the inevitable circus. He realized it was not entirely Zenar's fault, but surely a little discretion on his part might have lessened the spectacle. "What do you think?" he said, turning towards John, "Are you up to an interview?"

John shrugged indifferently, as if had a choice.

Esop insisted on only a few reporters at first. Contrary to character, they entered the lounge quietly, politely, awed by the presence of the Homo Sapien.

John remained seated off to the side, trying to shield himself from the blatant stares of the reporters, thinking all he lacked was a collar, a leash, and a muzzle to fulfill their expectations.

Meanwhile, Esop described the events at the polar cap culminating in the uncovery of the Sapien. When he finished, the reporters barraged him with questions, virtually ignoring the creature off to the side as though he might have been a stuffed animal.

"How did it survive the radiation?"

"It was zero at the bottom of the crater. The upward draft of the explosion sucked it out," Esop explained.

"Is it stiff from the freezing?"

"Apparently not."

"How do you know for sure it's a Homo Sapien?"

"Positive identification of Sapien blood type, antibodies, DNA, and it's not an *it*, it's a *he*."

"Sorry for that. Any physical problems?"

"None to speak of."

"Is he dangerous?"

Esop smiled and looked towards John. "What do you think?"

"Does he talk?"

"Of course."

"Is he rational?"

"Well, that depends. He's had a great shock."

"What are your plans? What are you going to do with him?"

"Keep him away from you people as much as possible," Esop quipped.

The reporters laughed. "Can we talk to him?"

"Only a few questions." He motioned towards John. "Do you mind coming over here?" He wanted the reporters to see the Sapien walk.

John stood up and walked slowly to center stage, standing at least a head taller than everyone except Zenar, who towered above them all.

The reporters appeared in awe of the Sapien, rephrasing their questions politely. *Are you stiff, sore? How did you feel being the only survivor? What do you think of Opalon? What do you want to do, now that you're here?*

John answered that he was not sore…he felt okay…Opalon seemed nice…he had no idea what he might do.

It was all rather benign until one reporter blurted, "How's your sex drive?"

"That's quite enough," Esop intervened sharply, ending the interview and directing the reporters to leave the ship. Normally argumentative, they filed out quietly, recognizing their colleague's indiscretion, although it was a question that was on everyone's mind.

On Assock's, too. "So," he said to John, "how *is* your sex drive?"

Esop, Zenar and Lank gasped in unison, but John disarmed them all, replying, "Without a woman, how should I know? You do have women?"

"Didn't you notice?" Esop replied. "Half the reporters were women?"

"They all looked alike to me," John confessed, realizing he had been too distracted to notice.

"Interesting," mused Assock.

"By the way," Esop said to John, "you may not have noticed, but the Translator's been off since morning."

John had not noticed. He removed the headset and, to his surprise, realized he no longer noticed the strangeness of their speech. Esop, Assock, Zenar and Lank smiled broadly and each, in turn, grasped John's hand and congratulated him on his rapid acclimation to their dialect.

John still was not sure the whole thing had not been a put-on. Yet, just as they claimed he had acquired their language, he was aware that he had also become more accustomed to their appearance. Now they looked more odd than strange, if that distinction could be made, more like a racial than a species difference. It would be like the first time a Caucasian met an Asian—the Chinese and Japanese must have looked as strange to a European as the European looked to them. In time, each accustomed to the other and the differences between the races became hardly more noticeable than the differences between individuals within each race. It was as individuals that he now recognized his captors.

"What next?" John asked Esop.

"First, we need to have a conference by ourselves—fifteen minutes," Esop answered, adding, "if you don't mind? Then we'll be leaving."

John did mind, not that it mattered. "Where to?"

"That's what we want to talk about," Esop replied. "Why don't you wait in the cafeteria?"

When John had left, Esop turned to his companions. "What do you think?"

Lank spoke first. "I'm absolutely amazed. He's so calm now, so different than at the polar cap, even though he did have a terror last night—calling for his wife. He doesn't remember. He says the headaches are almost gone but he's still got tinnitus. You noticed how well he took the interview—very nonchalant, so calm."

Assock interrupted Lank. "More likely numb, emotionally drained."

"Better than hysterics," Zenar put in. "I agree with Lank. He's shaping up much better than we could have hoped."

"He doesn't trust us," warned Assock.

"Why should he?" Zenar countered. "Do we trust him?"

"I do," Lank declared quickly.

"Enough to leave him on his own?" Esop asked Lank.

Lank paused and his brow wrinkled as he pondered the question.

Assock answered before Lank had a chance to offer his opinion.

"Of course not," he said firmly. "I'm a little surprised at all of you. You talk as if he is one of us, brought back home from a shipwreck, just suffering a little normal shock. You also seem to forget our obligation to learn more about our development through him."

"We have not forgotten," Zenar contradicted the professor, piqued by Assock's presumptuousness. "Perhaps you've lost sight of his human qualities. As a biologist I'm as interested in studying him as you, perhaps more so. He is a unique specimen, but he's also a human being."

"A Homo Sapiens," Assock corrected. "His humanity is the question at issue. Don't misunderstand. I am not immune to his human attributes, but I am concerned that in our enthusiasm we not ignore our responsibilities. We must pursue the question."

Lank, who had been so busy these first days with the medical supervision of the Sapien that he missed many of the early discussions among his colleagues, was startled by *the question*.

Assock explained, "We've assumed that the aggressive, destructive genes of the Homo Sapiens were muted by the Cataclysmic Catastrophe, thus transforming the survivors into a new species—the Species Human—which in turn allowed for the development of a more rational society….Right?"

Lank nodded agreement with Assock's rhetorical question.

"If this is so, then how do you explain our own misfits and miscreants?"

Lank squirmed uncomfortably. "I can't."

"That's right. You can't. Unless the Species Human is not a mutation, but a linear descendent with the same genes and the same innate aggressiveness that led to the destruction of the Homo Sapiens' society, and that could destroy ours."

Shaking his head slowly side to side, Lank responded, "I still don't understand the question. What difference does it make with respect to John?"

"The question is whether the Sapien is capable of evolving into a Human or if his construction is so rigid that he can only destroy himself along with everyone and everything he touches, as he did in the past."

"But that's nonsense," Lank protested. "How can you judge from one individual? You can't generalize to the entire species. He might not be representative. He might be different."

Esop and Zenar nodded in agreement.

Assock persisted. "Maybe so, maybe not. But he's all we've got. We have to make the most of it."

"What are you suggesting?" Esop asked.

"Nothing now. Only that we must not lose sight of the issue, the opportunity for observation and testing."

"*Testing?*" Lank repeated.

Assock was amused by Lank's concern. "Don't look so worried," he assured him. "He won't get hurt. What we've got to decide now is where he's going to live."

"Why not give him a dome," suggested Esop.

"Not just yet. It would be too easy for him to withdraw. Right now he needs people around him. He needs introductions and guidance. He needs to familiarize himself with our culture. Then, if he responds positively, he should have a place of his own."

Assock paused, sucked in his breath, and looked directly into the eyes of his companions. With an air of finality, he said, "He shall stay with me."

He had caught them by surprise. They could think of no reason why John should not stay with Assock, and they might even have suggested it themselves. But they were uneasy with the way Assock maneuvered them into a corner, leaving them no alternative but to agree. They were also reluctant to relinquish some of their own control, as well as to lose contact even if only for a few hours, so accustomed had they become to the Sapien's presence.

John was called back to the lounge. They presented their decision as a recommendation, although he recognized it for what it was. He agreed, anxious to leave the confinement of the globeship, willing to face the crowd that was still milling around outside.

Applause and hurrahs greeted the members of the Anti-topple Committee as they exited the ship. But when the Sapien emerged, the noisy welcome abruptly ended in a hushed, awed silence. John followed up the stairway to a platform that had been hastily erected. Nearing the top, he missed a step and lurched forward. The crowd gasped, then sighed as Zenar caught him by the arm.

Esop took the microphone. "Fellow Opalonians, on behalf of my colleagues and our new friend, I thank you for your patience. Quite frankly, we had hoped to delay his introduction until he had time to acclimate. As you well know, secrets in Opalon invariably make the front page news."

Chuckles rippled through the crowd.

"You already know what happened, so I won't repeat. I do have a request to make of you here and to all Opalonians. Please…please recognize and accept John Altern as a Human. He may look different from us but now he is one of us. Let me now introduce our friend."

The crowd erupted into loud cheers and applause.

Esop tugged at John's arm. "Won't you say a few words?"

John stood firmly, shaking his head. "You told me I wouldn't have to," he said through clenched teeth.

"I know, but it is better that you do. Please, just a few words," Esop coaxed, pushing the microphone into his hand.

John felt like throwing it back at him. *Cool, keep cool*, he reminded himself, but his voice trembled as he addressed the audience. "I don't know what to say. I...I wasn't prepared for this...but…well…thank you…uh...thank you."

He shoved the microphone angrily back to Esop who took it, shaking John's hand as the crowd roared approval. Never a public speaker, John could not have been more embarrassed by his fumbling words. In addition to a presumed relic, now they would surely think he was also illiterate.

They were alone in the large circular living room of Assock's dome, seated on the sofa before the three-dimensional visioscreen. Assock had tuned in the evening news just in time to catch the broadcast of their arrival. John viewed the program glumly, stirring uncomfortably as he watched himself on the platform.

"I sure made an ass of myself," he said, more to himself than to Assock.

"Not at all," Assock reassured him, flicking off the screen at the end of the program. "It's important they got a look at you. Opalonians are a curious lot. We couldn't hide you. Now we can all relax."

"Maybe you can," John said. "I feel so awkward, drained, like every step is a strain."

"Your joints stiff?"

"No—I mean emotionally."

"It can't be easy," Assock commiserated. "I know that. Give it time. Time is such a wonderful balm. It's the only cure for our hurts and disappointments. Give it time....Cigarette?"

Taking a cigarette, John accepted Assock's light, inhaling self-consciously, anticipating and enjoying the slight rush, diminished as it would always be now that cigarettes were on a parity with death.

"I don't understand you," he said. You pretend to be so rational, so mature, so in control, yet you drink and smoke."

"Yes, I do. And I love and hate," Assock responded. "But you have a point. Let me say that I claim only to be more mature, more rational. I am not perfect, you know. And that speaks for all of us." He stirred the logs in the fireplace, added kindling and nurtured the coals into flames.

John stared into the fire, its radiating warmth soothing to his face, which still had the feel of parchment. He was puzzled by Assock who seemed friendly enough, yet always distant, quick to participate in a conversation but often slow to start one, and then he sensed a darkness about him.

Still staring at the fire, he said, "I'd like to know where I stand."

Assock thought a moment. "I really don't know. I suppose you'll still look for escape."

"Wouldn't you?"

"You can't return to the past, not physically anyway, and certainly not to your world—that's long gone. But escape is possible—in your mind. You can deny everything your eyes and ears tell you and live in your private memories. It might work."

John clasped his hands, fingers intertwining and twisting nervously. Yes, he could escape into a dream world. The longer he was here, the more it seemed like a dream. He could spend the remainder of his life reliving past experiences. Would it really matter? Is the past so different from the present when you are absorbed in it? Are dreams to the dreamer different than reality? How is one to know? Was it possible to know? He didn't want dreams. He wanted reality. He could not accept their premises without doubt, without discovering the truth for himself. They were trying to convince him of what they wanted him to believe. Assock was disarming with his apparent frankness, but would he be willing to test their reality against his?

"You say I'm not a prisoner, but what does that mean? Can I get up and go...now?"

Assock rubbed his chin and shook his head slowly. "I don't know. You're not in shackles. There aren't any bars on the door, no guards. You could go now, but I'd have you followed for your own good. Put it this way, you wouldn't let a child who couldn't swim run around a swimming pool alone, unwatched, especially when he is the only child of his kind in the universe."

"I'm not a child," John huffed. "I don't need a chaperon. Am I free to go? Yes or no?"

"Yes and no. Freedom isn't just roaming about at will. True, that's important, but knowing where you're going, why you're going, having some place to go, having real choices, not just wandering around aimlessly. There must be a context. You're in a jungle now. If we turn you loose, you'll get lost. Give us a little time, let us show you around, and then you'll have your freedom."

John flicked the cigarette butt into the fireplace. His first impulse had been to walk out, to test the situation. But Assock had a point. To wander about blindly was worse than useless. Better to be patient and wait for a more promising opportunity. It would come. It had to.

Assock suggested that John come with him to the pool where he was to meet Zenar.

John declined, saying he preferred to be by himself. Then, when he was sure Assock was out of sight, he stepped outside the dome. There were no guards as Assock said, at least none in sight. He looked up at the sky. Never had he seen it so clear. It formed an enormous canopy high over Earth, its blackness sparkling with the brilliance of a trillion shimmering stars. He identified the Big Dipper, the North Star, the rosy glow of Mars. The entire celestial galaxy spread above him, imparting a message he did not want to hear. *This is your Earth. These are the beacons that guided your ships. This is your world.* He would rather have been on Venus from whence he could return to a familiar planet than to be on an earth so strange.

Zenar lay next to Assock in the steam room, sweat pouring through open pores. "I wonder if it's wise leaving him alone."

"He'll be all right," Assock murmured from a lazy semi-consciousness.

John continued to bother him. There was something—he couldn't describe it—a feeling, that was all, a feeling of wrong, of something about to happen. You couldn't disrupt someone, put him in a different culture, much less an alien world, and expect a smooth transition. He wasn't thinking of culture shock, which time usually healed, but of a deeper flaw that sought catastrophe. Perhaps he wanted it to happen to the Sapien as if to prove that what had been true for him was, perhaps, still true and would be true for everyone.

Wasn't his life scarred by disappointment, and by tragedy just when everything was so perfect—only to fall apart. Even as a youth he had learned to anticipate the storm following every calm. He had glimpsed happiness twice, once through Nonam and then with Evol, soaring to ecstatic heights, then sinking not so much into despair but somewhere in between on a barren plateau of work and study. He had come to believe that the Species Human was not constituted for sustained happiness. Perhaps all that could be hoped was comfortable maladjustment.

He had tried so hard to break through the isolation separating him from those he loved and others he wanted to love. He tried to accept the givens—the realities of blemished virtues and frank imperfections in himself and everyone else—believing that in everyone there was some good if only it could be made to surface. He had been taught to believe that love was the medium through which to penetrate resistance. For so many years he had tried to love completely, without censure or judgment. He tried everything—reasoning, companionship, drugs, sex. It made no difference whether one loved a woman, a man, a child. He would talk and touch and hold, giving, always giving of his mind, his body, his sperm and receiving oh so little in return.

What he thought was unconditional love inevitably turned to voracious cannibalism that left him drained and dry. To be loved was to be wanted, possessed, controlled and ultimately consumed. He was fed up with the malarkey of love. To love everyone was to love no one. To be able to love freely without obligation, to give completely without reciprocity was a fraud of self-denial. Always there was a price and that price was *more*. He was tired of giving more than he received, of wanting more than it was reasonable to have. To admit this to himself was dangerous enough. To allow it to be known was blasphemy against the common wisdom. To live with it was consignment to the loneliness of a bared soul. But he had to live with it and to hide his fraud from all the others.

Then he thought perhaps everyone felt the same and, like himself, was afraid to admit it. Maybe that was the difference between the Species Human and Homo Sapiens. Humans had learned to live in fraud, concealing it from the world, controlling their anger, loving safely, loving everyone and no one. Was this the genetic mutation, the rearrangement of a single molecule of DNA to allow tolerance of frustration? Was it really a mutation or could it be learned behavior? Would it have been possible for Homo Sapiens ever to learn to live with *wanting* and not having? How would this missing link now discovered and present in Opalon, how would John Altern respond in the Seventh Millennium to blatant frustration, not the misty-eyed insatiable hunger for the past or the despair of contemporary alienation, but to total disregard of his *wants*?

"Hey, Assock," Zenar called to his friend. He looked over at the professor who lay in a stupor, sweat glistening in globules over his entire body, forming little pools in the rolls of his abundant abdomen.

"The hell with him," Zenar muttered under his breath. He left the steam room wanting no part of Assock's mood. He had learned long ago that the Professor of Pragmatic Rationality had his moments, and these were best left alone.

The elliptical pool outside the steam bath was populated by men and women lounging about, some in groups, others alone reading or meditating. The grounds were large and carpets of clover enclosed in tall hedges yielded privacy for those seeking isolation from the spirited swimmers. A small geyser in the center of the pool circulated a constant flow of oxygenated water. The spiral diving platform rose above the geyser and on the surface of the pool brightly colored floats bobbed and danced with the splashes of aquatic bodies.

Zenar plunged into the clear, cool liquid and glided the length of the pool before surfacing. His head burst through the water, almost colliding with a young girl, her small breasts bobbing up and down in the rippling waves caused by his sudden emergence. She smiled at him and swam away. He grinned and diving underwater spotted her legs cycling slowly above. Grasping an ankle, he pulled her under and tried to embrace her but she darted away like a little minnow. He gave chase and caught her. On the surface they laughed and swallowed water. She wrapped an arm about his neck for support. Her chestnut hair was matted to an oval face and two bright eyes the shape of almonds recognized Zenar.

Hours later Assock roused from his stupor. He found Zenar asleep in an enclosure adjacent to the steam bath, with Vinya at his side. She was not unknown to him, an energetic child half-grown to womanhood. She looked so small and beautiful in the moonlight, breathing softly, evenly. As he watched her, a shadow crept over his eyes and he scowled. For a moment she was a lump of malleable clay and he had an almost irresistible urge to take her in his hands and crush her. Then at once he was protective and had to stifle an urge to cry out to her to run, run before it was too late. Beads of perspiration broke out on his forehead.

Vinya sat up suddenly. She knew the Professor. Everyone in Opalon knew him. "You frightened me."

Zenar stirred beside her.

"I'm sorry, child. I was looking for Zenar." The scowl was gone and Assock's warm, friendly gaze reassured her.

"What time is it?" Zenar looked quizzically at Assock.

"Past midnight. Are you spending the night here?"

Vinya looked at Zenar. "I should be getting back," she said.

"I wonder," Assock said to Zenar, "Vinya reminded me of something. Would you mind if she came with me?"

Zenar was surprised that Assock should ask him and not her. She was not his for the giving. Then again, Assock usually knew what he was doing. He nodded and watched them disappear through the hedge. Still shaking his head, he wandered off muttering to himself about having to spend the rest of the night alone.

The fire had burned down to glowing embers. John was stretched out on the sofa, fast asleep. He looked tired, disheveled but otherwise not as different or as odd as Vinya had expected.

"Shouldn't we let him sleep?" she whispered to Assock.

"I should say not. I want him to meet you."

"Maybe this isn't the right time."

But it was too late. Assock was gently shaking John's shoulder. "Wake up, old man. We have a visitor."

John roused reluctantly, opening his eyes on Assock's fleshy face. It was moments before he was fully awake.

Assock smiled. "I want you to meet someone." He motioned for Vinya to come closer. "You see," Assock said, "we are not all men."

Once John's eyes fixed on Vinya, he could not turn away. There had been instant recognition that, like a fleeting thought, disappears as quickly, yet lingers longingly in one's mind. For just a moment she reminded him of—it wasn't his daughter, nor was it Mary or Ina, but if you merged them into one...

Vinya shifted her weight awkwardly from one foot to the other. She was quite embarrassed and wished she hadn't come. She felt as though Assock was offering her to this...this strange man and she was too inexperienced to know what to do. She sat down on the edge of the sofa opposite John, whose stare was disconcerting.

While Assock went to the kitchen for some coffee, John tried putting her at ease. He, too, was conscious of the awkwardness of the situation. "I hope I don't frighten you," he began.

"Should you?"

"No, I don't think so. It depends on what Assock told you or what you may have heard."

"Not very much. I'm sorry if we've disturbed you."

"Don't be. What else have I got to do?" he said, turning his palms up in a gesture of emptiness. Rather than dwell on himself, he asked, "What about you? What do you do?"

"I'm a student. Just starting at the University."

"Do you have a major, a special interest?"

She thought a moment. "I don't know, I mean, I haven't decided yet."

John smiled at her. He was enjoying her youth and refreshing innocence, which reminded him of Alice. When she smiled back at him with slight dimples and even white teeth and slightly upturned nose, he caught a flash of Ina.

Assock returned with a pot of coffee and three mugs. The hot liquid hit John just right. Assock turned the embers over in the fireplace and threw on some kindling and another log. In a few minutes, flames flared up through the splintered wood and curled around the log, throwing shadows on the opposite wall.

"How about some music?" Assock suggested. "There is something I'd like you to hear. It's called Ode to a Cataclysm. Rather appropriate, don't you think? Lida composed it for the Anti-topple project. She's a friend of Esop. You'll meet her tomorrow—er— later today."

Assock set the disk and then hunched with his back against a corner of the fireplace, opposite John and Vinya who were still separated the length of the sofa. He closed his eyes and listened as the opening strings sketched a delicate pattern of undulating rhythm. Widely spaced bursts of a single horn pricked the background, occasionally stretching to a held note, then sinking beneath the surface. As full orchestration took up the flowing theme, a minor disturbance occurred, the muffled rumble of base drums rippled the calm and atonal disharmonies in minor key mingled sadness and nostalgia. Counterpoints, dichotomies of affirmation and negation, of hope and despair, pitted treble strings against the rhythmic bass fiddles and drums, while the horns carried on an independent abstraction.

The second movement repeated the theme, interchanging major and minor keys, sharps against flats, indefinite nuances strung together by the rise and fall of a single horn. Staccatos jabbed lightly, then plunged into heavy full notes. The tempo quickened, slowly at first, then tumbling on into a finale of whirling frenzy, strings whipping back and forth, drums beating, the horn piping out its ominous warning, the strings spinning on in rising crescendo, loudly, wildly uncontrolled, a mighty spastic clamor, a sharpened horn piercing the cataclysm—a boom, a roar, a clash of cymbals—then deafening silence.

John thought the Ode rather noisy, scattered, melodramatic, but who was he to judge? Besides, he had been preoccupied with Assock who hunched motionless throughout the performance, his thick knees drawn in tight against his chest and his head heavy and downcast. John felt a growing dislike for him, for his dark intensity despite moments of warmth and friendliness. He wished he had stayed with Lank or Esop or, better, by himself.

Vinya didn't like the Ode, either. The horn grated on her ears like chalk drawn sharply against a blackboard, making her wince uncomfortably. To her it was sorrowful, disturbing music and the title was atrocious. It was so negative. It made her sad to think how long the world was in the making. So many people had died without a glimpse of the good life. Sometimes she was jealous of her good fortune. At other times she wished she could have been one of the struggling pioneers of the Seventh Millennium. It was sad that people were not immortal. To have worked so hard and to have died without experiencing the joys of Opalon was an—injustice. To learn so much, to know so much, to love so much, and then to die. There was no escaping sadness in death. They were all sad—she, this strange person, and Assock. Yes, Assock, too, was sad. She was overcome with sympathy and wanted to console him, caress him, kiss him, anything to relieve his sadness. Then Assock looked up, smiled brightly in his familiar warm way, and she was more confused than ever.

It was almost dawn when Assock walked Vinya back to her dorm at the University. They followed along the path to the pool, through the park and around the Tower of Rationality. The air was moist and heavy with fog rolling in from the ocean.

Vinya kept close to the professor, secure in his proximity. She sensed his detachment and was relieved by it. All night she had been dominated by him, as though he had infused her with his own motivations, causing her to act a role she did not recognize in herself. Yet, she was honored that of all the girls—she still did not consider herself a woman—he had chosen her. It didn't matter that it was by accident. If she hadn't come to the pool this evening and met Zenar—she had completely forgotten Zenar— she wondered what he must think of her, if he thought of her at all.

Her pride was hurt that Zenar had passed her on to Assock just like that. They hadn't even thought to ask what she wanted. Her face flushed in anger and she thought they both deserved a sharp reprimand. Then she was apologizing for them. *It's not any girl we'd take into our confidence,* she imagined them saying. But what confidence?

She looked sidewise at Assock. He returned her glance. She felt encouraged. "Why did you ask me to come tonight? Why me?"

Assock reached around her shoulder and pulled her close to him in a fatherly gesture. Their steps slowed to a reflective pace. She was a charming girl, supple and warm. Perhaps one day he would have time for her, but now he was given over to John.

"I need your help," he said simply. "When I saw you with Zenar, I knew you were just the one."

"The one? For what?"

"To love the Sapien."

"*Love the Sapien*?" she sputtered in shocked disbelief. If he had said to go to bed with him, she would have understood. But to love him? To love a Sapien? One doesn't love like that, not because one is told to, not even by someone as important as Assock.

"I don't understand," she barely whispered

"I want to find out—we need to know—if he is capable of love. You know how important that is."

"But if he doesn't love me? Will that prove he can't love?"

He looked at her and smiled again. "With you it may."

She blushed and lowered her eyes. "What if I can't—I mean, it's not real—he's not one of us," she protested.

He patted her gently on the shoulder and said, "We'll see."

She lay in bed staring up at the translucent ceiling, hardly noticing the change from the opacity of the night sky to the increasing brightness of daybreak. She hadn't slept all night. But far from being exhausted, she was keyed with anticipation, and with doubt. How could she love a stranger who was not even a Human, when she had never even loved a friend, not really? Oh, there were times when she thought she was in love. But when you had to think if you were in love, it couldn't be the real thing.

Until a year ago, love had meant nothing more than a sort of warm affection you had for your best friend. It was completely natural, practically unconscious. Then she began to change. Perhaps it was her body changing. She actually began to feel different. Men took note of her. They no longer looked at her as a child, but she had been a child for too long to suddenly respond as a woman.

For many months now, she had been more conscious than ever of her body. She began to measure her maturity by the growth of her breasts. She would pose nude before the mirror, pirouetting on her toes, admiring her lithe form, feeling her breasts and then laughing at herself as she thought how silly she was.

She remembered distinctly asking herself one day, *Where does love fit into all this? Everyone talks about love, everyone says she loves but nobody seems to get excited about it.* She was greatly puzzled because she could no longer think of love as impersonal friendship and caring when her body—when she —was now so different. And, of course, she was not so naïve as to confuse it with sex. No, love had to be something new, something different, something exciting that she had never experienced before. It had to create great desire. It had to give her the strength to do things she had never done before. It had to make her dizzy not so much with anticipation of physical pleasure but with the totality of her being. Yes, she would know when she was in love.

The year passed and nothing happened. Now, just like that, Assock said to love this—this—she didn't know what to call him. She didn't know whether to laugh or cry. It was laughable because he, well, he was a Homo Sapien. He was something out of a book. No, worse than that, he was not out of a book. She could love a character in a novel, for there she could embellish him with all that true love required. But he was not a character. He was an oddity, although not as odd as she had expected. Still, the whole idea was ridiculous and she felt like crying because she wanted to please Assock more than anything in the world, and she was afraid she would fail him. How wonderful to have been chosen by Assock, if only she had not been.

The ceiling was white with sunlight when she finally fell asleep.

CHAPTER 5

John was jarred from sleep by a sharp rap on the sliding panel door. Turning on elbow, he watched as the panel slid aside and Assock's large head thrust through like a mounted trophy.

"Good morning," the professor greeted John sprightly. "I'm sorry to wake you, but we're meeting the others for lunch."

As quickly as it appeared, the trophy withdrew behind the panel.

John sat up, swung his legs over the side of the bed where they dangled loosely, stretched and yawned. He had slept solidly and comfortably. The headache, which plagued him since whatever it was that happened, was gone and he noticed the ringing in his ears only occasionally, although it was omnipresent whenever he listened for it. He diagnosed complete recovery from the concussion. Lucky for him, he thought. He had enough on his mind without headaches.

He stood up, stretched again, and shuffled into the bathroom. It was a clean little room with a shower-tub combination, the ubiquitous toilet and sink. He sat on the toilet and mused that, for all of progress, Man—even Humans—would forever be indebted to Thomas Crapper. The familiar flush and swish of the water in the bowl was a reminder that societal advancement would always be a sanitation department away from complete disaster. After showering, he rummaged through the medicine chest and found an electric shaver that smoothed his face without the slightest tug or irritation and, most remarkably, was barely audible. Definitely an improvement, he acknowledged.

Meanwhile, Assock had brought in some clothing. He sat on the corner of the bed as John tried them on.

"Think they'll do?" he asked, not really considering that they wouldn't.

John slipped into the pants, pulled the frock blouse over his head and buckled the belt about his waist. The sandals fit a bit too snugly and the trousers extended barely to his ankles. Otherwise the outfit was satisfactory, although he was not too pleased looking somewhat like a cross between a South Pacific beachcomber and a Russian peasant. But it was refreshing to have on clean clothes, for which he thanked Assock.

They walked along a lane lined with tall slender palm trees. Sunlight filtered through the fronds. A few men and women waved as they passed by, taking note of John with studied indifference. The kids playing in the park ignored them. Assock motioned John to take a seat on an empty mobench, a small vehicle that hummed quietly and smoothly over the ground at about five miles an hour. It wasn't until they had traveled a short distance that John fully appreciated the absence of cement sidewalks, asphalt streets, and the noise and exhaust fumes of automobiles. Instead there were numerous mobenches, some occupied and in motion, others parked on the side waiting to be used. It was so quiet for a main thoroughfare, as if they were taking a stroll in a beautiful park on a Sunday afternoon.

Assock explained that mobenches were freely accessible to the public, like the aerobes flitting across the sky. "The damned internal combustion engines were suffocating us. We tried eliminating them with public transportation. That didn't work because people were addicted to their own private vehicles. They just wouldn't give them up. The invention of gravity-inverted locomotion made it possible to eliminate the engine, but it's too inefficient for individuals to have their own vehicles, which they would use only a couple of hours a day anyway. So we just made mobenches sufficiently abundant and free. It was that or choking on smog."

Assock turned onto a narrow path. At a distance and above the foliage, the Tower of Rationality gleamed in the sunlight, its tremendous height dominating the view. Circling its base, they were about to go on when a shout from above detained them. Peering upward, from the edge of the summit they spotted Zenar's red hair like a poppy in the sky and his long arms flailing for attention.

A few minutes later Zenar, breathless from the descent, emerged from the base of the Tower. Greeting John, he hopped on the mobench and they continued on to the University to pick up Vinya.

Vinya avoided John's eyes as she sat down beside him. She felt awkward, self-conscious and tense, and hoped he wouldn't notice.

A short while later they came to the inn. The grounds were terraced with stonework and rock formations blending into trees, hedges and bushes. Bypassing the large dining hall, they entered a small enclosure lined by rose trellises.

Esop, Lida and Lank were waiting for them. Assock introduced Lida as the composer of the Ode to a Cataclysm, but it was clear to John she was more than that to Esop. Although he was still conscious of the unique appearance of the Species Human—as they insisted on calling themselves—he had to admit that Lida was an attractive woman. She was as tall as Esop, with high cheekbones tapering into a narrow chin, and teeth as white as chalk that contrasted brightly with her ebony skin. He wondered if they were married.

A glance at the menu was all John needed to spoil what had started out as such a pleasant day. The printing was in Roman characters like English, but otherwise unintelligible. He had doubted they were speaking a different dialect since he had no difficulty communicating with them without that ridiculous headset. But the indecipherable type of the menu was pretty convincing.

Esop sensed his problem. "It completely slipped my mind," he apologized. "You'll get on to it with some lessons. Here, let me help you."

The waiter took their orders, Esop choosing for John.

Conversation was light and casual throughout brunch. John remained silent for the most part, grateful to be left out of their banter. Vinya, too, was quiet. He suspected she was new to this group. She was seated opposite him, next to Zenar. He wondered what she was doing there.

He had hardly recognized her from the night before when her features were dimmed in the low light of the fireplace. Although he had thought then that she was quite pretty, he hardly expected that rare feminine quality which needs no embellishment of dress or cosmetics. Her eyes were green. When she spoke her lips parted just enough to show even teeth. Her skin was smooth with an Asian hue. Her neck was long and slender, her body not yet full. She moved with all the grace of youth.

Esop interrupted his thoughts.

"Uh, what?" John's cheeks burned with embarrassment. He had been staring at Vinya and sensed that they, in turn, had been watching him. More disturbing was his momentarily forgetting where he was. It was as though they were trying to divert him from his principal concern, which was to get out of this place and find his way home.

"We were wondering if there was anything special you would like to do today," Esop said.

John answered slowly, doubting the wisdom of his request. "I'd like to get off by myself, perhaps look around the city. You wouldn't have to worry about me—"

Assock assured him they weren't worried. "You should know a few things about our city," he said. "Don't hesitate to ask anyone for information or directions. If you tire of walking, take a mobench. You know how they work. Our people are very curious about you, but they're friendly and will respect your wishes. If you become hungry, you'll be welcome in any inn or private home."

John was surprised. Just last night Assock had refused to let him go off by himself. He suspected a catch. "I suppose I'll be followed?"

"That won't be necessary. If you return this evening and are not too tired, we'll talk some more."

Assock's permissiveness made John uneasy. It implied too much confidence. He was saying without saying it that he would not find what he was looking for.

When they had finished eating, before they could change their mind, John thanked everyone for their hospitality and asked to be excused. They waved him off as casually as if he was one of their own.

Assock leaned back in his chair. He was amused by the disappointed expressions, particularly those of Vinya and Lida. The original plan had been to take John to the Natoleum or perhaps a Displayer. Zenar had been warming up to the idea of acting guide, especially as it had been some time since he had been to either place. His brow wrinkled disconsolately.

"That frown ill becomes you," Assock observed.

Zenar snorted. "It's contagious. Watching our friend, I must have caught some of his gloom."

"I feel sorry for him," Vinya said.

"My dear, your pity could not be better spent," teased Zenar.

"You're not serious," Vinya protested.

"Not serious? My heart is gushing compassion."

"Oh Zenar!" Vinya's face flushed with angry blood.

Zenar laughed loudly.

"You have no feelings," she asserted hotly.

Rising and taking her by the hand, Zenar bid the others a flourishing farewell. "Vinya and I are going for a long walk. We shall tread the troubled paths of the ancient world. This young lady has much to learn about our Sapien friend. She weeps for poor John. She doesn't know how fortunate he is."

Assock moved next to Lank. "You haven't said a word."

"I was down at the museum yesterday," Lank answered. "Workmen are recreating the crater. The vehicle is already in place. Have you seen it? No—well, it's a masterpiece. Of course, it doesn't have the depth of the original but the illusion is so real. I sat in it for a time, trying to imagine what it must have been like for him. There's blood on the windshield where he banged his head, and I got to thinking of the changes in our evolution. The obvious difference is the size of our skulls, which allows for at least twenty percent more brains. We've always thought that the Sapiens' brain deficiency accounted for their irrationality under stress. John confuses me. He really seems quite reasonable. Maybe we're wrong. Maybe there's not as much difference as we thought."

"Careful," warned Assock, "what seems reasonable may be illusory."

Lank waved his remark aside. "Maybe so, but what if bone growth was inhibited by their poor diet and emotional tension? Is it not within the realm of possibility that, as his diet improves and his tension is relieved, his skull might actually enlarge to allow his brain to grow? Might not John actually develop into a Human?"

Assock pondered this a moment. "Lank, you're too quantitative. Theoretically it might be possible for his skull to enlarge. But judging from the variations in our own species, it does not seem important if one has a little more or a little less brains. What concerns me is the quality of the brain, its ability to function harmoniously with the environment, to respond positively to changes and threats impinging on it every moment of the day and night, to initiate and accept changes.

"Take our friend. What do you think is going to happen to him when he finally wakes up to the fact this is not a dream, that he is forever separated from the past? Oh, he will soon enough accept this consciously. He is already partly convinced, though not enough not to be out there searching for some means of going back. Going back to what? To whom? This Mary—his wife? Momma? Poppa? A sick world on the verge of blowing itself to hell? What will happen when his emotions come to grips with the reality of what has happened? Will a few more ounces of brain make a difference? I think not.

"Take a long hard look at the world he came from, Lank. What sort of people were they? I'll tell you. They were lonely, isolated, frustrated. Their families were breaking up. They had no security. Their work had no meaning except to buy and buy and pay the bills. There was no enthusiasm, no belief in a future for themselves or their children. They substituted and confused instant pleasure for love. They lived in constant fear whether of a nuclear holocaust or a stranger next to them. When their parents died a part of them died, sometimes all of them. They clung to their children in incestuous strangleholds, just as they had been strangled from birth on, and at the mere mention of incest they retched in agonizing guilt. At twelve they might have still been alive, by twenty they must have been a curious mixture of youth and old age, hopeful yet fearful. By the time they reached middle age—what were they when they reached middle age, Lank?"

It was a rhetorical question, of course, and Lank did not attempt an answer. His perennial smile had long vanished and he looked tired.

Esop stared at Assock curiously, almost detached, but Lida was entranced.

"They were walking apothecaries and mental cesspools," Assock answered himself, "Their physical senses were numbed with aspirins, barbiturates, synthesized hormones, vitamins, alcohol, marihuana, cocaine. Their bowels were gorged with the decaying rot of emasculated foods, their minds gutted with religious garbage and illusions of their own infantile irrationalities."

Assock sucked in his breath. "Well, what do you think is going to happen to our friend now? Do you think it is only a question of a little more brains? Will his twisted, distorted brain untangle itself just like that?" He snapped his fingers sharply. "No, Lank, you'd stand a better chance throwing a ball of knotted yarn in the ocean and having the waves unravel it. What do you think is going to happen inside his brain when he fully realizes he can't go home?"

Lank was stunned. He shook his head and looked to Esop for support. He wanted to contradict Assock, to defend John. But Assock had shaken not only his enthusiasm but his confidence.

In a quiet, dispassionate voice, Esop countered, "What makes you certain John is typical?"

Assock scowled darkly at Esop. "Don't be a fool," he uttered harshly. Then immediately his face softened into a quiet smile, as though he had been caught off guard and was now retreating behind a mask of kindness. His voice sank to a whisper. "He needs help. We'll help him. But we'd better not fool ourselves. His mind is like a balloon buoyant on air. Let him settle on thorns and—pop!"

John walked for a good half hour, as rapidly as he could without drawing attention to himself. He wanted to get as far away as possible, in any direction, almost as though he was fleeing instead of searching. He paused along the side of a wide lane, reluctant to yield even a moment towards passive planning, yet realizing he could not just run on blindly. He stared blankly at the ground…waiting…hoping for some idea to fill the void. He didn't know where to begin, what direction to take. To the west lay the ocean and for a moment he thought of commandeering a boat. The unsettling recollection of the sea spikes, the tremendous expanse of water traversed in the globeship, and the possibility, if not probability, that he would end up adrift and lost at sea was an even worse nightmare.

He had no choice but to wander on. Perhaps he might come across something that would be helpful. He was totally without a frame of reference. Like a newborn baby, he would have to discover his bearings through the painstakingly slow process of observation and experience. He walked on, more calmly now, only to feel his little toe pinching in the sandal. He cursed and stretched the strap to ease the chafing. He noticed an empty mobench parked beneath a tree. It was a postman's prayer come true. But no sooner had he sat down on the mobench than he was startled by a woman's voice.

"Hey, where'ya going with my mobie?" She was of average height, slightly overweight, and speeding towards him. When she came within a dozen steps of the mobench, she stopped short and uttered, "Oh, I'm sorry. I didn't recognize you."

"You know me?"

"Why yes, you're the...the—"

"The ice man?"

"Yes," she said, flushed with embarrassment.

They stared at each other like two animals of opposite species confronting each other in a forest, tense yet curious. John got off the mobench, apologizing that he did not know it was hers.

"That's okay, you keep it," she offered quickly. "I don't need it." Her voice was coarse and she remained firmly planted on heavy legs, conveying the impression that once having made up her mind, she would not budge.

"No, it's yours," John insisted politely.

She stood there shaking her head. And then they caught each other's eye and burst out laughing at the impasse.

"I'm Nola." She stuck out a firm hand that grasped John's like a man. "Tell you what, I don't live far from here. Drive me back and then you take it."

John welcomed the opportunity to talk with her, although he was not pleased that she had recognized him on sight. Recalling Assock's remark that the entire population knew of his presence, if he was to pass unnoticed he would have to be unseen. Perhaps it was not merely to inform the public but to keep him under surveillance that they had broadcast his picture. They were clever, no doubt about that. Perhaps even now they were watching him. No matter, he could not help it.

Nola guided the mobench while they talked.

"I guess I kind of stand out like a sore thumb," John said.

Nola nodded affirmatively.

"Do you know where I'm from?"

"The United States, I heard."

"Could you tell me where that is?"

"Not exactly—I suppose it was around the crater where they found you."

"Was? You mean it isn't there now?"

She turned and faced him. "You were there. You should know."

John pressed his lips tightly together and shook his head. "This may sound strange to you, but seeing isn't always believing. How do I know I wasn't taken there, say from another planet? How do I know this is really Earth?"

Nola frowned. "Guess you have to take our word for it."

"How do I know you're not lying?"

"Why should I lie? What have I got to lie about?" Nola objected.

"I don't know. That's what I'm trying to find out."

"Well, let me tell you something," she stated, annoyance entering her voice, "from what I've heard, your world was full of liars. Lot of good it did telling the truth. Who'd believe you? Well, let me tell you, we don't lie. You don't believe me? That's your problem."

"Yes, I suppose it is," John agreed, not only to mollify her but because she was right. Would he ever find sufficient facts to satisfy himself? He was beginning to doubt it.

He decided on a different tack with this woman. "You seem to have a rather dismal view of my world," he said. "What do you think of this Seventh Millennium?"

"It's all right," she conceded simply.

"You don't sound very enthusiastic."

"Never been anyplace else." She thought to herself, *What stupid questions these Homo Sapiens ask.*

John continued. "Are you happy?"

"I suppose."

"Surely this isn't perfection?"

"Who said it was?"

"Well then, maybe some things aren't so good."

She looked at him suspiciously. "Why are you asking all these questions?"

"I'm confused, that's all. I need to know, I want to understand what it's like here."

She answered, her voice barely audible as though debating whether or not to terminate the conversation, "Look, I'm a nobody. What I think, who cares?"

"I care. I want to know what you think," John pleaded. He had touched a sensitive nerve. This most perfect of all perfect worlds had its defects, too. He would not learn of them from Assock or Esop or Zenar. "Please, what is it, what are you afraid to tell me?"

She pulled the mobench off to the side beneath some trees that shaded them from the midafternoon sun and looked directly into his eyes. "I'm not afraid," she said, "just not sure it's right talking to you like this." She fidgeted uncomfortably on the seat of the mobench,

"Take a chance," John coaxed.

Shrugging her shoulders, she said, "Maybe it doesn't matter. I have a good life. I have fun. But suppose I love someone who doesn't love me?"

"Is that what's wrong?"

"Yeah," she murmured. "Shouldn't surprise no one. I'm not pretty. He says I'm not feminine enough."

"No—you exaggerate," John said truthfully,

"That's nice of you, but it's so. Men don't like me."

"You'll find someone."

"That's what they say. I'm supposed to get over it. But what if I don't? Then I get the treatment."

"The what?"

She laughed hollowly. "The treatment. You know. No, guess you don't. If that don't work, then it's up to Jevh."

"*Jevh?*"

Nola looked up at him, startled, as though she had been speaking to herself all this time only to discover that someone was listening. "Sorry…never mind…sorry…have to go."

She jumped out of the mobench, and before John could ask her to stay, her stocky legs carried her into the thicket, out of sight.

He sat there puzzled and disturbed. Had he pushed too hard? There was nothing so wrong in what he had asked or what she had said, certainly nothing all that unusual. Weren't her problems the problems of all people of all time? Yet, at his repetition of *Jevh* she stiffened, and a moment later was gone. Had she revealed something forbidden to him?

He rode on into the country, looking not at the landscape but for clues. He spoke to a number of people, all of whom recognized him at once and were friendly. But they couldn't or wouldn't tell him anything more than he had already been told. There was no United States, no Europe, no Asia. Yes, they had once existed, thousands of years ago, but now there was only the Seventh Millennium spreading over the many continents of the Earth. One world, one government. No, there was no interplanetary travel. They had enough to do here without flying off into space.

Whenever he asked about Jevh, they froze him out. Yes, they heard of him. No, they never met him. No, they couldn't tell him more, thank you, and good day.

As night approached, John's hopes faded with the light. He knew no more now than when he had set out, except for the disquieting awareness of someone or something called *Jevh*, a silent force intervening between himself and those he met.

Damn Jevh, he mumbled and slumped to the ground beside the mobench. He was at the end of his rope. There was nothing to do but turn back. He was so tired and alone. If only he had been left alone, unconscious and entombed in ice, for all intents and purposes dead. Better to be dead than to return to nothing.

He felt like a hollow shell mindlessly walking and breathing. No, it was worse than that, for he could not forget. *Damn memory. What good was a wife who no longer lived, a child who no longer laughed, a lover who no longer loved?* It would be better to be truly dead than to know all one knew was gone.

Hours later, the cool dew of morning wakened John. He had slept in the mobench through the night, dreamless sleep of drained emotions. Open palms rubbed sleep from his face and smarted against the coarse stubble of his beard. He felt unclean. Pangs of hunger rumbled in his stomach. His mouth was dry and his tongue chafed against the furry film of dried saliva coating his teeth. His clothes clung to his skin in sticky discomfort and his legs cramped when he stretched.

He scanned the open field about him. Removing the sandals, he stepped off the mobench and slid his feet over cool moss. The rippling flow of an irrigation channel beckoned to him. He undressed and eased into the water, submerging chin deep as the cold water rinsed away the fuzziness of his body and mind. He pulled his head beneath the surface, rubbing stiff fingers against his scalp, then climbed out of the channel and stood in the sunlight to dry. The sweet smell of clover filled his nostrils and his depression mellowed.

As he rode back towards Opalon, John pushed aside thoughts of himself to observe the land. It was not easy. His mind did not want to see what his eyes beheld. It wanted familiarity and even though the earth felt like earth and the sky looked like sky, it was not his earth, not his sky. Nonetheless, here he was and he had to make the best of it.

He passed fruit orchards and vineyards and helped himself freely of their offerings. The soil shifted from deep black to reddish brown to plush carpeted green, alternating crops of lettuce and squash and other common vegetables. The country dwellings were mostly single story, many with the same round, translucent roofs as in central Opalon.

He stopped a few times to talk with field workers who pointed out barns, storehouses, and country amphitheaters. He gazed back at the cattle grazing in pastures who paused to gaze at him. He came upon factories, which fanned outward from central hubs, the spokes of production interspersed with parks and recreation fields and large patches of cultivated flowers.

The transition from country to city was so gradual that John was well within Opalon before he realized it. The Tower of Rationality, visible far beyond Opalon's boundaries, had set his bearings. He was struck afresh by the poise and the power of the Tower. The city was dimming in the late afternoon, yet the Tower still glistened in the slanting rays of the setting sun, shifting colors as though its surface was composed of millions of prisms that transformed the descending light into myriad rainbows. The Tower was both inspiring and awesome. Its massive mass seemed to generate a gravitational force that drew John towards its bosom. Long moments passed before he shook himself loose and continued on to Assock's dome.

CHAPTER 6

Assock slouched in an overstuffed armchair beside the fireplace, an open book on his lap. He nodded to John without rising, scrutinizing him through his thick black-rimmed glasses. "Well, are you satisfied?" he asked after a long silence, as John eased onto the sofa opposite him.

"With what?"

"With whatever you were doing."

"As if you didn't know," John replied curtly, disappointed by Assock's coldness. He had resolved to be more open on his return, to make a fresh start with him. But the man was so quixotic, one moment warm, intimate, friendly, and then almost menacing.

"If I knew, I wouldn't be asking." Assock said, his thick lips curving into a forced smile.

"Oh, come off it," John uttered in exasperation, making no effort to conceal his annoyance. "What do you want to know? Did I find a way to escape? You know I didn't. Am I happy to be back? Hardly. For all I know, you were watching me all the time."

"Oh, that wasn't necessary."

"You mean you know what everyone does anyway?"

Assock shrugged, grinned enigmatically and, as if there was no antagonism between them, offered to get him a snack.

"I'll help myself," John declined, then decided he wasn't hungry and went to his room to wash. He lay down on the bed, closed his eyes and must have dozed off for an hour or so. When he returned to the living room, Assock was gone and the fire had reduced to glowing embers. He picked up the book Assock had been reading, only to be reminded once again that he could not decipher the print. He slammed it on the floor and kicked it with his bare foot, inflicting more pain on himself than damage to the book. *Damn it, I've got to get out of here.* He rushed out the door and stubbed his sore toe on a rock. Limping back into the dome, he put on his sandals and, as he passed back through the living room, he gave the book another swift kick across the room.

Just then Vinya stepped through the doorway, the book landing at her feet. She looked up startled and stepped back, and then entered cautiously. "I was looking for Assock. I didn't know you were back."

"That surprises me," John said tersely.

She remained just inside the door, anticipating a hasty exit.

"Please, come in," he said.

Vinya smiled.

"I'm really quite harmless."

"I know that." She still felt awkward, uncomfortable in his presence. "I was looking for Assock. He said to meet him here."

"He was here. I don't know where he went."

"The pool, I guess." She picked up the book, straightened out the creased pages and placed it on the end table. "That's where people go at night." Her face brightened. "Perhaps you'd like to?"

"I don't think so, not tonight."

"Oh...then I'll go."

"Wait," he said hurriedly. "Please...stay. I've spent the last two days looking for something that everyone says doesn't exist, asking questions that don't get answered. I don't know if I want to walk or talk or sleep or just get drunk. Right now I don't want to be alone, so please keep me company...for a little while anyway."

"I'm not sure I'll be good company."

"Let me be the judge. Can I get you something, a drink perhaps?" She followed him into the kitchen. He sniffed some open bottles. "Ah, this smells medicinal. Want some?"

"A little," she said. "I don't drink much."

John poured himself a full glass after measuring out a smaller amount for Vinya. The amber wine slid smoothly down his throat, soothing his general irritability.

They sat back on the sofa. She kept turning the glass in her hand, trying to conceal her discomfort.

He tried to put her at ease. "Tell me some more about yourself."

"Not much to tell," she said.

"How old are you?" he asked for starters.

She answered slowly, as if counting on fingers. "I'm sixteen. I think I told you I'm at the University. We study a lot and, of course, there's swimming and dancing and listening to music, and things like that.

"Any brothers, sisters?" John asked.

"Yes, but I don't think in the way you mean. It's different here."

John raised his hand. "No sociology tonight. I want to know about you." He was relaxing as the alcohol infused into his blood, warming and numbing, spreading out into his arms and legs, seeping into his brain.

"Do you have a boyfriend?" he asked, as though that was what an adolescent girl would expect to be asked, not sensing any personal interest.

"No one special. I have some good friends, like Zenar and—"

"Zenar," John echoed in surprise. "That's not what I meant. I mean a real boyfriend."

Vinya smiled at him. "Zenar is a friend. He's very nice when you get to know him."

"But he's too old for you."

Vinya laughed. *Are you?* she almost blurted, shocked by the thought. Then she remembered the professor's remark the other night and realized it was no accident he was not at home. Avoiding John's eyes, she sipped her drink.

"It's just that I have…I had a daughter almost your age and…," the words caught in John's throat and his eyes burned with tears. He wiped them away with the sleeve of his tunic and shrugged helplessly. "It's very difficult, all this—"

"I really am sorry," she said, reflexively reaching across to touch his hand.

He looked at her through prisms of tears and placed his hand over hers, needing to touch and be touched. "Thank you," he sighed deeply. "You're the first person to treat me like a human being."

"I'm sure they mean to,"

"Perhaps. Maybe I'm just angry. I walk through the door and Assock greets me like an iceberg. Before I left he said he wanted to talk. I come back and it's like he's challenging me. I don't understand him."

Vinya shook her head slowly from side to side. "Nor do I."

"I wanted to talk to him. It may sound odd but I almost felt relieved. All this time looking for an escape, for a clue, something to show me a way out, some crack in this…this charade. Not a thing. I found nothing. I'm here. That's all there is to it. I'm here and I don't know where here is."

The wine was affecting Vinya a little. "I guess here is here," she giggled and immediately felt foolish because it was not a joke to him. Then, hoping to lift his mood, she suggested they walk down to the beach.

Afraid she would leave if he declined, he reluctantly agreed. He had been walking all day and his legs were stiff, but he was still restless and distracted and didn't want to be left alone.

A cool breeze wafted in from the ocean as they ambled slowly towards the shore. He wanted to hold her hand as he would his daughter's, but she was not his daughter and the difference laid bare his need, his yearning to hold a woman, even someone so young. He was embarrassed by the thought.

He, five thousand and forty years old, give or take a few hundred. She—sweet sixteen.

"What are you thinking?" Vinya asked.

"While I was wandering out there I got to thinking—I know this sounds foolish—but what if I was dead and this was an afterlife, possibly heaven, perhaps hell. People really believed that nonsense, but what if...? I can see this being a heavenly place if you're not a misfit. But if you don't belong, if you feel like a misanthrope, it could be hell."

She pondered that for a moment and then said very seriously, "In our study of old world religions, I seem to remember there was a place in between heaven and hell—"

"It was called purgatory."

That' right, *purgatory*. It seems to me that if you didn't know where you were, then you'd be there."

Her response surprised him. "You're a wise old lady," he joshed.

"I wish I was," she demurred, still serious.

They reached the beach. It was deserted. Sitting on the sand with hands clasped over knees, they watched the whitecaps rolling in on ocean waves. Behind them the glowing domes of Opalon were darkened one by one as the population went to sleep.

Inhaling the fresh salt air cleared his head of the lingering effect of the wine, and for the first time in so long he felt not unhappy and relatively free, though not completely, of that lurking anxiety which had been constant since coming here.

"Thank you," he whispered, putting his arm around Vinya's shoulder and giving her a fatherly hug.

She looked up at him. "For what?"

"For being here with me now." The warmth of her body suffused into his and a tingling adrenaline rush swept over him like a surging wave. Her face turned towards him. Her eyes, large and translucent as a porcelain doll, locked onto his momentarily and drew him towards her. As if in a trance, he leaned forward and kissed her lips. Momentarily she responded, then pulled away.

"I'm so sorry," he said in a voice flustered by his unexpected behavior. "I shouldn't have...."

She let him hold her hand as they walked back in the silence of the night. Before the door of her dormitory she kissed him back, a moment's touch of lips, and disappeared inside.

He glided back towards Assock's dome on a cushion of exhilaration, not so much with the lingering, tingling impression of Vinya's lips on his, as with the sense of suddenly coming alive. After days on end of pain and depression, of bereavement at the loss of his family and his former life, of loneliness in a crowd of strangers, he could see a future just as this day he came to accept the present.

Late as it was, he didn't want to sleep. He wanted to talk, to continue the contact with people here and now, to get to know all of them better. And he could hardly wait to see Vinya again.

The light was on in Assock's bedroom. John looked through the doorway and Assock motioned for him to come in.

"I was waiting for you."

John sat down in a chair opposite Assock's bed, "Vinya was here looking for you," he said awkwardly, trying to dismiss his past antagonism.

Assock nodded. He also wanted to meet John on new terms, recognizing that his own emotions had been a barrier to a constructive relationship. "I was beginning to worry about you," he said, referring to the lateness of the hour.

"We walked down to the beach."

"A lovely girl," Assock noted. "We hoped you would like her."

John bristled at the implication of a setup, but tried to stay calm. "Assock, no matter what we say to each other, somehow it doesn't come out right. Just now, for instance, you make it sound like prescribed therapy. I take a walk with Vinya who just happens to come by looking for you who just happens not to be here. Isn't that a little obvious?"

"I can understand you're thinking that," Assock replied. "Anything I do for you will look that way. If you were one of us you wouldn't give it a second thought. But you're right. I arranged for her to come by this evening and then conveniently wasn't here. Call it therapy if you like. I felt you needed some companionship—what better than with a woman who wasn't threatening, someone with whom you could just be yourself."

John was disarmed by Assock's candor. "Maybe I have been too sensitive," he said, meeting him halfway.

"Not at all. You've been very open about your feelings. That's good—healthy."

"Maybe too open," John reflected.

Assock reassured him that was not so. "We've been pretty hard on you. You can blame me. I felt it better not to coddle you. Sure, we're all glad to have you here. But not until you come to terms with yourself will you be able to live and work with us. I think you understand that."

John nodded. He wondered if he could come to like this odd Human. "I appreciate your concern," he said, "and you're right about Vinya. I felt comfortable with her, but she's so young."

Assock smiled. "So are you, if you want to be."

"You don't understand. I have...," again he choked on the present tense, which was past. He continued hoarsely, "I had a daughter her age. I'm old enough to be her father."

"That's not an issue here in Opalon," Assock assured him. "When you get to know us better, you'll see how free we are at any age."

John wondered if Vinya was really free, or if—child or not—she was playing an assigned role.

Assock continued, as if reading his mind. "Vinya may be young but she is no longer a child. Relax, enjoy yourself. She has a mind of her own."

"There's something else bothering me," John said hesitantly, far from relaxed as he recalled the anxiety of some of the people he met earlier in the day. "Who is *Jevh*?"

Assock's mood changed instantly and he demanded abruptly through tightly pursed lips, "What? Who? *Jevh*? Who said that?"

"I don't remember," John lied in defense of the woman he met on the mobench. "Everyone I asked shut up like a clam."

Assock's grimace softened into a smile as he contradicted himself, "Oh, yes, it's one of those fishwives' tales. God knows where it came from. Anthropologists have been trying to track it down for years. Some say he was the leader of an ancient band of marauders who was thought to be immortal. Legend has it that he haunts the hills, an omnipresent specter of retribution for the destruction of his tribe. It's pure nonsense, of course."

"They didn't seem to think so," John challenged. "Quite the contrary, he seemed very real to them."

"Did anyone ever see this *Jevh*?" Assock challenged back.

John shook his head.

"Then, you see," Assock concluded with satisfaction, "it's just superstition. Don't take it seriously. We don't."

John was far from convinced. Why did Assock deny *Jevh* at first and then concoct such a cockamamie explanation? But it was clear there was no point in pursuing the subject further.

Assock terminated their talk, saying, "We should get some sleep. Then I'd like you to see our Natoleum. You'll find it quite interesting, I'm sure."

As John got up to go to his room, he reached a hand out to Assock who grasped it firmly. "I hope we'll be friends," he said.

"We are..." Assock responded, "we are."

CHAPTER 7

Esop rolled over and stretched full length against Lida who lay facing away from him, still asleep. He put an arm across her shoulder and his palm came to rest upon a velvet textured breast. She stirred as he entered that warm, sweet harbor with its flowing and ebbing tide, rising and falling, absorbing the offering of his insatiable need.

"You're lovely," he whispered against her ear.

"You're impossible," she laughed contentedly.

Esop rolled out of bed, put on some old clothes and went outside to his neglected garden. The sun poured over his shoulders as he pruned the fruit trees and scratched away at weeds in the lettuce furrows. The smell of fresh turned earth and young plants refreshed his lungs, and the rich black soil between his fingers and toes was moist and lush. Reaching above his head, he pulled an orange from its stem, peeled it, tossed the skin onto the compost pile and sank his teeth into the juicy pulp.

His work on the Anti-topple Committee's final report was nearing completion, and he looked forward to spending more time with Lida.

There was also his obligation to the Homo Sapien to consider. He was more than a little concerned with Assock's assumption of individual responsibility when it was the Committee that should be in charge. He couldn't figure Assock out. Ever since the discovery he had been unusually moody and irritable. When he tried to talk to him, Assock dismissed him as though he was a fool. *Trust me*, Assock said, *I know what I am doing.* He might just as well have said, *I outrank you in these matters. Do not question me.* That sort of thinking went out with the Inquisition. Still, it was hard not to trust the Professor of Pragmatic Rationality, for it was he, more than anyone else, who embodied the *raison d'être* of the Seventh Millennium.

Lida argued with him on that point. "Really, Esop," she chided, "he's just as crazy as you—maybe more so. You men act as though emotions are a thing of the past, as though anything you think and say is immutable rationality."

"Darling, that's the difference between men and women," Esop joshed. "You know it's pretense. We pretend it isn't. Just think what it would be like if we let our emotions rule the roost."

"Like women?" Lida laughed and knuckled him in the ribs.

He loved her for her laughter, for the way she penetrated his defenses, for her iconoclastic good humor, albeit a bit more emotional than his.

A fter breakfast, Esop and Lida sauntered over to Assock's dome, anticipating an enjoyable visit to the Natoleum.

Assock and John were waiting outside. It was another bright, cheerful day and fluffy clouds roamed lazily in the pale, robin egg blue sky. They acquired a mobench for the short trip to the Natoleum.

The Natoleum was structured like a wheel with the administration centered in the hub and wide lanes separating the spokes that formed the five divisions. Every metropolis had its own Natoleum modeled on this basic plan.

They walked up the lane separating the first two divisions. It was lined with a variety of bright yellow, white, and bronze tracts of blooming chrysanthemums. Knee high close clipped hedges separated the flagstone walk from the grass. Through the open windows of Division I drifted the squeals and wails of babies, sounds to which Esop's ears were not sympathetically attuned. They reached the hub and entered the large reception room through automatic sliding doors.

Lank rushed up to meet them, greeting John warmly, beaming proudly. This Natoleum was his baby. He had planned its growth from the original blueprints to the final construction. Except for occasional diversions such as the anti-topple project, Lank spent most of his time here.

He led the group to the center of the room so that John could view the fresco covering the upper half of the circular walls and the dome-shaped ceiling. It portrayed in rich pastels the cycle of creation from the fertilized ovum to the young woman and man cuddling a newborn infant. Home life, schools, and work scenes completed the panorama. There was a raw vitality in the mural that appealed to John.

"The Natoleum covers the first twelve years of childhood," Lank began, directing his words to John.

He described the admitting procedures and the detailed records that were kept of the developing child. He brought them around the reception area to a large room where clerks sat before small visioscreens on which clinical records were updated. To make an entry, the clerk spoke into a microphone and the material was electronically transcribed in the computer bank. Hard copies were printed on demand.

John was impressed, especially by the voice transcription. "We had a similar system," he commented, "but it wasn't in widespread use." He asked to see a printout.

"Certainly," Lank said, pleased with John's interest. He spoke to a clerk and a few minutes later a neat file issued from the printer. Lank handed it to John who leafed through the pages, which contained not only the medical history but also photographs of a young girl at different ages.

"Recognize her?" Lank asked.

John smiled as he spotted a picture of Vinya when she was no more than twelve. "How do you assure confidentiality of records?"

Lank looked up quizzically.

"Our records are…," John caught himself, "were kept confidential to protect the patient's privacy. That was very important."

Assock answered, "We don't have that concern. here. We've nothing to hide."

"It's not a matter of hiding. There's the principle of privacy. Why should Vinya's records be open to the public?"

Assock dismissed the question. "No one would ask unless there was a reason."

John persisted. "It just seems to me that personal details about one's life should be protected."

"Protected from what?"

"I don't know—people prying—getting information that's none of their business, which might be embarrassing."

"You'll just have to take our word for it. It's not a problem," Assock said, ending the discussion.

Sensing Assock's annoyance, Lank suggested they go over to the Prenatal Division.

"This is where pregnant women stay and work as assistants," Lank began as they entered the Division.

"Are they required to stay here?" John queried.

"Not required. They want to, most of them anyway. A few odd ones don't come, but we get the children. Their husbands, as you call them, live here with them. Want to see their living quarters?"

They rode the stair ramp to the second floor and entered an apartment occupied by a young couple who seemed indifferent to their intrusion.

"You see," Lank said, pointing about the room, "they have their privacy and, of course, an ideal environment for fetal development."

John shook his head skeptically. *How is it so private if they can walk in just like that?* he questioned to himself. Assock had made it clear privacy was not up for discussion, at least in this place. Instead he asked, "Why do you want them all here? Isn't it a tremendous burden, everyone living in the hospital?"

"Natoleum," Lank corrected. "They want to be here. It's not a burden. This is our custom, our way of life. It's what we want. All these people here, they don't just sit around doing nothing. They make the Natoleum work. Women don't come just to give birth. They come to raise children. So do fathers."

The young couple nodded affirmatively, then abandoned the apartment to the uninvited guests who had settled into their living room.

"Look at it this way," Assock intervened, "each Natoleum is a communal society. Parents participate in the development of their children but bear in mind that children belong to society. They are not private property. Living in the Natoleum is voluntary for the parent, but for the child it is compulsory. After all, not every woman makes a good mother, or every man a good father. If they stay here with their child, they can't help being guided by the example of others."

Esop interjected, "Except for breast feeding, there isn't that much difference between a mother and a father."

"Oh, I don't believe that for a moment," John blurted. "Men and women are not identical, not when it comes to bonding with infants. A man can never have the same attachment as a woman to her child nurtured in her womb and at her breast."

"Maybe so, maybe not," Lank picked up before Esop could reply. "We recognize the unique character of maternal bonding, and that fathers also bond. But that misses the point. Excessive possessive bonding is what we avoid because it is stifling and reinforces the isolation and separateness that stunts full development."

Esop added that the Natoleum instills a sense of community that is manifested in shared responsibilities.

John was not convinced. "You know, the idea is not new. You didn't invent it. We had communal societies. Some were based on religion, some on socialist ideology like the kibbutzim in Israel. Yet, when the kids grew up they wanted their own apartments. They wanted independence."

"You're right," Esop concurred. "That's why we also have our own place when we grow up, if that's what we want. Lida and I live together in what you would probably call a villa. Assock has his own dome, while Lank chooses to live here in the Natoleum. What we do later in life is not the issue. It's how we are raised, how we are socialized to be good citizens. That's why we are all raised in a Natoleum—to have instilled in us shared concerns, obligations, and responsibilities, and to learn how to live and work together."

Esop was tempted to add, *Isn't that so, Assock?* but thought better of goading the professor.

"Sounds like indoctrination, not education," John suggested, more as a question than a criticism.

Assock agreed. "Of course, it's indoctrination, no different than what you did with your kids—only we do it rationally."

What John heard was control with a capital C, no matter how benignly described.

Lank again picked up the description of the Natoleum that was, after all, his pride and joy. "Yes," he declared, "it's shared responsibilities. That's the crux of it. Mothers and fathers, they both work here so it's a matter of sharing, day and night. A mother may come alone. Not all men want to participate, and maybe the mother doesn't actually know who the father is. Even if she comes alone, she's not alone because once here, she becomes part of the extended family of the Natoleum. The child always has a father—many fathers and mothers."

John thought how such an arrangement might have solved Ina's problem. Poor Ina, she was gone, too. But he was here—he had to concentrate on the present. He had to shake the past to remain in the present.

"I'm a bit confused," John confessed, referring as much to his internal state of mind as to the immediacy of the cultural lesson they were offering him. "Do people marry?"

"In a sense," Assock explained, "but not in bondage. We live together as long as we want to, so long as we get along—in a manner of speaking, *symbiosis*. When we tire of each other or become incompatible, then we separate. Couples aren't stuck together permanently because they sleep together for a while, not even if they share the birth of a child. Many do, of course, so long as the relationship remains symbiotic."

"It wasn't bondage," John retorted, "at least not in civilized countries. Really, we weren't that much different, except where children were involved." He decided not to mention that marriages were breaking up all over the place, half ending in divorce within five years.

Remembering the attachment that had sustained his own marriage, he insisted that parents have a greater responsibility to remain together when children are involved. "They should at least try."

Assock nodded affirmatively. "Of course—if they can. But forced cohabitation doesn't guarantee they'll be good fathers and mothers. Take your world. Many of your families were very unhappy. There was constant friction, and whether it resulted in separation, divorce or continued but dishonest relationships, everyone suffered—husbands, wives, children—all of them."

"It wasn't all that bad," John maintained, resenting Assock's constant criticism of *his* world, even when he agreed.

Assock wasn't through. "Having a child is not sufficient reason for two unhappy people to stay together. Unhappy parents breed unhappy children. Preserving the union is pragmatically irrational."

John thought if only it was that simple, but life was not the blacks and whites of the professor's generalizations and exaggerations. Where children are involved, you just can't walk away from a marriage.

Then Assock surprised him. "I'm describing not only your world but ours. We had the same problems. We also had your example to learn by. We tried an experiment. It was small in the beginning but it caught on fast. The child weaned from the mother became part of a group instead of remaining attached only to the biological mother and father. We gave to all parents every child. Birth parents were allowed to follow the growth of their own child with specific interest but not with special favor. Parents gradually assumed the role of general guardians. Out of this experience emerged individuals who were part of an integrated group."

By now Assock was in full swing, pacing back and forth, gesticulating with arms and hands as he spoke. Esop and Lida shared the sofa of the small apartment. Lank squatted on the ottoman while John leaned back in the easy chair.

"We are all fused into a homogeneous community, probably like some of those Utopian societies you referred to. Only here we are very conscious of what we're doing. That is the difference—being conscious and rational. No hokey pokey religious nonsense. No romantic idealism. No egotistical gene doting. Just a general sharing. Parents develop interests and attachments for children outside their bloodlines. Children come to regard them all the same.

"I'm not saying there are never conflicts. It's bound to happen. Parents sometimes split and form new relationships. Sometimes there is jealousy, even hatred. But the group gradually resolves these conflicts by offering understanding and sympathy, and helping them talk out their problems and, most of all, providing the elixir of love. I've oversimplified, of course. The Seventh Millennium wasn't born whole overnight."

John started to object that *understanding, sympathy* and the *elixir of love* were platitudes, but the professor was not to be interrupted.

"The principle of communal guardianship is now fully accepted. Even if a woman has a baby outside a Natoleum, as when she is living and working on a special project in some remote area, the baby must be raised here. No exceptions. The system generates universal love, not the highly charged possessiveness of Homo Sapiens. Child abuse and cruelty are a thing of the past, not like in your—"

'Wait a minute," John finally interrupted Assock. "It sounds wonderful—ideal—but that doesn't make everything we did all bad. You don't miss a chance to say how terrible everything was, how cruel, how stupid. To say the least, it's tiresome. I agree we had much wrong just as I know there is much wrong here."

"What do you mean?" Assock shot back.

"You seem to have taken the worst of my past and assumed it was ordinary. I am only suggesting that you are showing me the best in your world and ignoring the bad. That's all. I mean, it's a bit much to expect everyone to go around loving everyone else." John was thinking of the woman he had met outside Opalon.

"Why is that?" Assock challenged.

"Because, dammit, not everyone is lovable! For Christ's sake, some people are just damned unlovable."

Assock laughed, but it was not a good-natured laugh. "Is that so? Isn't it a matter of degree?"

John answered with exasperation, "By that measure you can make anything fit."

Esop felt the discussion was leading nowhere. "John," he intervened, "We'd like you to see the rest of the Natoleum. That's what we're here for."

Lank led them out of the apartment to a small conference room where he began a detailed description of the Natoleum. Taking into consideration John's medical background, he went into further explanations concerning basic physiology. He might have done so anyway, for he loved to talk about his work.

"John, you asked why it is necessary to bring the prenatal mother to the Natoleum. It isn't necessary so much as it is desirable. You are familiar with the development of the brain."

Lank turned on a large visioscreen and dialed a time-motion image of the brain.

He continued, "We want women here by the fourth month of pregnancy. The fetal brain is still unruffled, no convolutions.

Note the smooth cerebrum." He pointed to the screen. "By the sixth month the brain has changed radically. See, it begins to look like an adult brain. During the fifth and sixth months, the surface of the brain becomes convoluted, increasing the total surface area many fold."

Lank turned away from the screen to face the small group. "It is during this period of tremendous brain growth—the Critical Phase—that prenatal asylum is particularly important. We maintain ideal conditions from before the Critical Phase, through it, and afterwards when the brain is increasingly sensitive to both physiologic and emotional influences.

"As far as the early fetus is concerned, the major influences are physiological—the acidity of the blood and suspending fluids, nervous stimulation, hormonal balance, blood pressure. These are all affected by the emotions of the mother. If she is upset, her pulse and respiration increase, body fluids become more acidic, glands secrete excessively. The changes are transmitted to the developing fetus. Sometimes the cellular growth of the brain is retarded, at other times accelerated. Tissues may lose some blood supply and microscopic nerve endings in the initial stage of development may wither never to complete their growth or properly attach at their assigned destination."

Then, addressing John directly, Lank concluded, "All this was known in your time—the importance of sound synapses, perhaps the difference between genius and insanity, the trauma of perinatal memories, the limitations of a life founded on an insecure birth. It was all known, but perhaps knowledge is not always sufficient."

Lank was pleased with the flourish of his last sentences. It always came as a surprise to hear himself shift from the assurance of concrete facts to the grandeur of generalities.

Esop and Lida were content to remain passive, she leaning against his shoulder. Assock, hunched in an armchair, appeared distracted or disinterested. Lank's lecture was academic and they enjoyed his presentation, except perhaps Assock.

They snacked on the cake and coffee that had been brought to the room.

John sipped his coffee, then said, "This isn't exactly new to me. We recognized the importance of the prenatal environment. But some of your assumptions are highly speculative. I have serious doubts about uterine and perinatal birth trauma memories."

Assock stirred from his apathy. "Why should there not be perinatal, even pre-birth memories, though I doubt spearing the ovum is one of them? Perhaps memory is not the right word since they're completely unconscious. You know how children, even adults, often curl up in the fetal position in sleep. This is an obvious tactile memory so why should there not be others?

"Not everything has to be remembered to be a memory. Some individuals may claim that their conscious memories date back to their birth, albeit vaguely. They are probably just projecting from documentaries of intrauterine development without realizing it. Anyway, it's not memory that's the key, but the environment that counts, especially the conditioning of the first years."

Lank brought the discussion back to the Natoleum. "Infants and mothers are separated but not immediately."

He walked over to the visioscreen, adjusted a few dials and an image appeared of Division I.

"Here is where mothers and newborn infants live. Unbroken contact is maintained between each mother and child. It was a rude enough shock for the child to have been expelled from the womb in the first place. They shouldn't be separated afterwards.

"Here mother sets up house in much the same manner as she lived in the Prenatal Division. The only difference is that the facilities are specialized for her needs and she gets more help. Also, she can associate with other mothers. They discuss their problems together, fondle each other's babies, and begin to feel emotionally that in a broad sense each has given birth to all the children. Later on, if you like, we can walk over there."

"When are they separated?" John asked.

"That depends on the infant's development. Division I is the *Stage of Diminishing Utopia —Early Infancy*. I think you will agree that Utopia is an impossibility."

"I'm glad to hear you say that," replied John. It was an admission that modified their projection of a super-superior society.

"Not that we don't approach it," Lank corrected himself quickly. "We have developed a society that is nearly free of conflict. But there are always unpleasant tasks that have to be done. Sharing these tasks minimizes their unpleasantness. The mature mind will not completely resent them. Though we might conceivably create an ideal physical world, it is impossible emotionally. Why is this?"

Lank paused as though he were the only one to know the answer. He was allowed to indulge himself.

"It's because for the infant Utopia once existed. During uterine development every unconscious need, every demand is satisfied—effortlessly. It's all free, no price to pay. Then the rude shock of birth. Utopia is shattered. Still, it's not all that bad. For a short time after birth, all or almost all desires of the infant are fulfilled, more or less on demand. The newborn is still virtually omnipotent.

"From age zero to perhaps a year after birth, the infant has everything she wants and needs. she has her mother's breasts. She can urinate and defecate and fart and burp without inhibition. Mother is always there with eyes so loving, breasts so full and lips so soft and tender. The infant in its helplessness is more powerful than it will ever be again.

"As she grows in size and coordination, as she discovers things about herself and then her world, she senses the change. She is not quite so helpless, therefore she is helped not quite so much. The world lets her cry a few minutes longer. She will stop as soon as someone picks her up or tickles her ribs. She must eventually forego mother's breast. She is still a pretty powerful baby, although she is already nostalgic for those days of omnipotent helplessness. If she receives sufficient attention and affection during this crisis, the repercussions are not serious."

Lank paused to focus the screen on Division II, showing living quarters, recreation rooms, play areas, nurseries. He pointed to mothers in the division caring for infants, performing the unceasing routine and personal functions.

"Division II is usually entered at the end of the year and is known as the *First Stage of Frustration*. It begins the gradual separation of infant from singular mother. The child begins to identify with other children and mothers. And the mother cares for other children to whom she also becomes attached. Thus, mother and child reduce their mutual possessive dependency and spread their interests over the entire group."

John interrupted Lank. "What about the fathers? You seem to have left them out of the equation."

"They also care for children," Lank answered. "It was tactless of me to dwell solely on the mother's role. Fathers share in those activities that are not specific to mothers. They cuddle and play and change diapers. As you can see in the visioscreen, there are many men in the nursery.

"Depending on how well the infant develops new ties and identifications, she passes into Division III, which encompasses the *Second Stage of Frustration—Late Infancy*. Age ranges from two to three years. Here the child begins group living. Mother may enter this division if she likes, but as a participant in the group, not as a parent. She may still show specific interest in her own child but not special care. If she is not capable of cutting the umbilicus, so to speak, separating herself from her birth identification, she is barred from this particular division so as not to hinder the development of the child. She will be transferred to another Natoleum to work in its Division III without the temptation of blood ties. Or, she may leave the Natoleum and return to her former life. Actually, it is much harder for the mother to make the break. The child has no difficulty identifying with the group, having many mothers and fathers and many playmates, so one less mother, even if the genetic source, makes little difference.

"Next we come to Division IV, which is the *First Stage of Independence—Early Childhood.* It covers ages three or four to five. By now children have overcome much of the frustration at losing Utopia. They are acquiring more self-assurance. They are beginning to reason and to make some decisions themselves. They have learned to cooperate with each other and to work with adults. Each lives in his or her own room with a friend the same age. They are closely supervised but they no longer have to be watched continuously. They go to the toilet alone. They feed themselves and play their own games. They are now prepared for the beginning of formal education.

"Around age six, they enter Division V, the *Second Stage of Independence—Late Childhood.* This is a difficult period, for their intellect is beginning to conflict with their emotions. Although they can do much of what they want, they cannot do everything. There are group responsibilities that place some limitations on individual activities. They learn to accept them. They also try to imitate adults but are not pleased they no longer have their complete attention. It is most important they enjoy their own age."

John raised his hand as would a student in a classroom. "Let me get this straight. What you've described is an attempt—"

"Not an *attempt*, an achievement," Lank submitted.

John persisted, "an attempt to wean the child away from the family, to destroy familial love."

"No—no," Lank asserted, "We don't destroy familial love. We enlarge the family to include everyone. It's possessive love we modify, the clinging, suffocating love of a single parent for a single child. The Natoleum *is* the family, don't you see?"

"I see what you say but I'm bothered by the neat package," John admitted. "If you scratched the surface of those Utopian societies, you found something quite different. More often than not, a strong leader and a lot of rivalry and jealousy. Few survived a generation. Some primitive societies looked utopian to outsiders, where everyone was supposed to be happy. When they were studied closely, they were far from perfect. They hardly had choices. There was enforced conformity. You know, a place for everyone and everyone in his place. And god help you if you were out of place."

Lank beamed. "Then you can appreciate what we have accomplished. We don't have strong leaders. We have strong people who move together. After all, if it takes a strong leader to build a monument, another can tear it down. This can't happen when leadership is shared by all."

John repressed his reservations. He wondered if there was any leadership if leadership was shared by all.

Lank picked up where he had left off. "Division V children exhibit overt social sexuality. They had experienced infantile sexuality but were not conscious of its implications. It is a trying period for they are not yet emotionally prepared for sexual intercourse."

"Not yet!" John exclaimed. "And when might that be?"

"In a few years, when they are ready emotionally," Lank answered matter-of-factly.

John was incredulous.

"This surprises you?"

"It amazes me."

"You agree that six year olds are conscious of sex, that they're curious about their bodies, that they have erotic feelings, that they masturbate?"

"Yes, of course, but not all of them, not overtly anyway," John answered in partial agreement. "We didn't encourage it. You yourself said they're not yet ready, not emotionally. Yet you allow them to do it anyway."

"We don't allow it. They *do* it. It's not harmful."

John was adamant. "How can you say it's not harmful? Six year old girls have gotten pregnant."

"Oh, that's such a rarity, and not by six year old boys," Lank countered. "Besides, we can handle that."

"The emotional damage," John argued, "you can't dissolve that with a chemical."

"Suppressing natural behavior is more damaging and leads to preoccupation with what is suppressed," Lank reminded him.

John could appreciate that. Perhaps if he had real sex earlier, not just adolescent masturbation, sex might not have been such an obsession all of his adult life. Often, even when he wasn't thinking about it, he would be thinking that he wasn't thinking about it.

Assock pushed into the conversation. "You're right, John. In your world such an experience might be harmful. *Might*, I said, for it is a question which is worse, the morbid suppression of sex or its too early enactment. We think suppression is worse. Uninhibited children will accept sex as a pleasurable physical function and a release of tensions. But just suppress it, tell them it's bad and wrong and sinful and you have laid the groundwork for future neurosis."

Assock looked directly at John, through him. "Our attitude towards sex upsets you. Let's not argue that now. We have lots of time to go into it later."

"Anyway," Lank continued, "they live in Division V until puberty. And to put it into proper perspective, their overt sexual activity is largely curiosity. Two children are usually assigned to a room but they can interchange roommates if they wish. Sex play is uncomplicated, mostly narcissistic—feeling their own body. Intercourse is a late development, the natural consequence of adolescence, around twelve or thirteen.

"I don't want to overemphasize sexual activity. The children are just as concerned with learning to read and write, studying history, mathematics, rationality. When they have developed sufficient maturity and understanding of themselves and their world, they move on to the Elementary University.

"There they live in dormitories for the first year, attending courses, honing their study habits, and participating in a variety of extracurricular activities. The second year is a major shift from communal to quasi-independent living, for those who want it. These student, often two or three together, can live with a citizen, a man or a woman, usually both, who accepts them. When the mentors, as we call the chosen citizens, feel their students are ready, they matriculate full time to the Universal University, usually around age fifteen or sixteen. There they are pretty much on their own. However, the mentors who passed them on continue to mentor them, both as friends and advisors.

"You may wonder why we have mentors when we suppress this type of relationship between parent and child. Well, we don't have to worry about infantile possessiveness between a mentor and an older child. More important, adolescents gain a great deal from living with adults apart from school. It affords an opportunity to develop on their own a mature relationship with a mature person. Equally important, it gives the mentor a chance to view the world through the fresh eyes of a young person."

Lank's round mouth opened before he realized he had run out of things to say. He stammered and chuckled. "Well, that's it, that's how it works."

John thought the Natoleum might be good for orphans or children from broken homes. But he remained skeptical of forcing everyone into the same mold, and he could not accept the lack of privacy permeating the institution. There seemed little opportunity for individuality, despite what they said. So much appeared controlled, regimented. He doubted that all the mentors were as good and trustworthy as Lank portrayed them. He couldn't help thinking there might be—there most probably were—child molesters who would gladly volunteer their services. As for early sex, he remained highly skeptical.

As they toured the divisions, some of his misgivings were tempered by observation of so many cheerful and enthusiastic children and adults. He was aware that his ingrained biases—what he had been conditioned to think—might be a barrier to perceiving the benefits of this life. He was trying to maintain an open mind. He could accept almost everything, but sex among very young children still bothered him. Nonetheless, he envied their freedom and wished he had experienced more of it when he was a child. And he sure could have used a mentor when he was struggling thought adolescence.

Then he thought of Vinya. He tried not to, but he could not help feeling she was besmirched. He wanted her pure and innocent, yes, a virgin as she seemed to him even now as he knew it wasn't so.

CHAPTER 8

"How about a swim," Esop suggested to John as they left the Natoleum. "You might as well take advantage of your leisure."

John glanced sidelong at Esop, whose features, once so strange, were now familiar, taking special note of the creased crow's-feet at the corners of his eyes and the close-clipped mustache that accentuated his serious and calm demeanor. "I'm not exactly on vacation," he said.

"You're right. When you don't have a job, you can't be on vacation. I don't care much for vacations anyway, especially long ones. Not working enough is as much a problem as too much work. We have a saying here that *work is the salvation of humankind.* You have to work to feel useful, to be happy, or at least not unhappy."

"I wonder if happiness is all that important," John mused aloud.

"Perhaps not. Whatever it is, it's not something you can control. It's quite ephemeral. One moment you're up in the clouds, the next your down in the dumps. One thing for sure, it doesn't come by doing nothing. You can't just lie around and wait to be happy."

"Sounds like the good old Protestant ethic," John said. "Our problem, well, my problem anyway, was trying to avoid the dulling effect when work becomes so routine it's only work, when you have lost your enthusiasm for it."

"That's the dilemma," Esop agreed, "except for people like Lank. He eats and breathes the Natoleum. He is so involved, I doubt he has a sex life. Maybe that's the answer. He's too busy to worry about whether or not he's happy."

"You're one to talk," Lida chided Esop.

"At least I have a sex life," he countered, squeezing her hand.

"What about Assock?" John asked.

"Ha!" Lida snapped. "That's a good question. I doubt—"

Esop cut her short. "Assock changed a lot after—"

"You'd think he was the only one to suffer," Lida said caustically. "He takes himself so damned seriously."

John had not expected Lida's quite obvious dislike of Assock. She gave no inkling of it when they were all together. Rather, everyone appeared to revere him. And they all deferred to him whenever he asserted himself.

As they neared the pool, John asked Esop if he could borrow a swimsuit.

"What the devil for?" popped out of Esop's mouth.

They passed through the hedge that served as a windscreen and stepped onto the thick carpet of grass surrounding the pool. As a physician, John had seen enough naked bodies not to suffer puritanical scruples over nudity. It was more a matter of esthetics. Children and adolescents he found comely enough, but adults—most adults—he thought more attractive clothed. Then again, he had to acknowledge that nudity was not to satisfy his esthetic eye, but to allow people to relax and enjoy the freedom of their unfettered bodies.

They entered the locker room. To John's discomfort, the room was shared alike by men and women. Despite his generally liberal disposition, he had always been a bit of a prude outside the clinical setting. His eyes averted as Lida and Esop undressed, even as he followed suit. He felt awkward and self-conscious but averted eyes could not resist observing Lida's lissome shape.

"You'll get used to it," Esop said, trying to put him at ease. "You never swam nude?"

"Of course, but not since I was a boy at camp. We had nudist colonies, some nude beaches. It was a fad."

"Some fads survive to convention. First thing you know, everyone's doing it," Esop noted.

John wrapped a beach towel around his waist, commenting that he felt like he was entering a dream where he was the only one naked in a crowd, except for everyone else.

They went outside to the pool. Esop and Lida launched in headfirst. John dropped the towel and quickly followed after them, gliding beneath the surface in short breaststrokes. He surfaced, pleased at the distance traversed, enjoying the clean silken smooth water gently coursing over his body.

Slender birch trees leaned over the edge of the pool in clusters, throwing shadows along the sides. He sidestroked along the rim, treaded water and watched children playing tag.

At the far end of the pool a young woman poised on the high board. She recognized him and waved. He watched as she tested the board's spring. Then, high-stepping to the edge, the board rebounded her upward and she soared out into a graceful swan dive. Her form knifed through the water, throwing up the small splash of a good diver. She glided along the bottom and surfaced next to John, taking rapid, shallow breaths. Her eyes blinked off droplets of water and her face broke into a smile. She treaded close to him. The water was so clear he could see her legs cycling slowly for buoyancy, rising from narrow ankles to dimpled knees to the suppleness of shapely thighs. He had this urge to reach out and touch her, to see if she was real. Just then Esop floated up to them.

"I might have known you'd be here," Esop teased Vinya.

Vinya laughed. "I see you here often enough. Where is Lida?"

Esop scanned the pool and spotted her on the other side, her skin glistening like bronze in the sunlight. "See you," he said and swam off to join her.

"C'mon," Vinya motioned to John as she kicked into a slow crawl. They swam side by side, taking air facing each other. They had nearly circled the pool when John, his chest heaving heavily, pulled up for a full breath and accidentally gulped water. He coughed violently and managed to utter that he was calling it quits.

"You're not leaving?" She sounded disappointed.

He hesitated. "No—think I'll get a little sun."

"I know just the place."

"Thought you wanted to swim."

"I can swim anytime. You don't want me to come?"

His face flushed. "I don't mind," he shrugged, trying to sound nonchalant, as if it mattered little either way.

Vinya climbed out first. He avoided looking at her, though his eyes strained to take in her naked form. He followed, certain everyone was staring at him between his navel and his knees as if to verify that male Homo Sapiens were shaped the same as Humans.

They wrapped themselves in large beach towels. Vinya led the way through the hedge to a small clearing carpeted with clover. Spreading her towel on the ground, she exposed her body to the warmth of the sun, motioning for him to do the same. They lay side by side, eyes closed, breathing deeply and quietly.

Vinya broke the silence hesitantly. "Last night...I was afraid you might think...I don't know what I'm saying... I just...you seemed so...alone."

Her voice tingled in his ears. "You mustn't feel sorry for me," he said.

"I don't." She responded with more assurance. "You lived in such a crazy stupid world. I think you're much better off here." She raised her hand to chase off a bug, lightly brushing John's thigh as her hand came back to rest, and she closed her eyes.

Every sense in his body stirred at her touch. It was casual, unintended, accidental, and meaningless. Yet, he was consumed as though it was an inviting caress. His mind reminded him she was just a child and that it would be impermissible to...but his mind was losing control. He listened to her breathe and her body fragrance merged with the sweetness of the clover. He longed to taste her lips and his lips tensed in anticipation, and his fingers ached to reach out to her.

He hunched up on elbow and looked down at her. Her eyes half-opened. She seemed almost in a dream. He tried to hold himself off but was drawn to her as if they were the opposite poles of two magnets with invisible forces pulling, encircling, enclosing...his head swirled dizzily, his heart pounded, his skin burned with yearning. He lowered himself, enfolded her in his arms and matched his lips to hers. She responded to him with such delicate sweetness as only an adolescent could dream was possible.

"You have totally captured me," he said later, as they walked along a stream running through the park.

Vinya turned her head sidewise and looked up at him with a small smile of sincere reciprocity.

John's heart skipped, and suddenly he felt very depressed. "I know for you making love isn't, well, all that special."

She turned away from him.

He flinched inwardly at his callousness. "That was a stupid thing to say," he apologized.

"Yes, it was," she pouted.

She turned back towards him. "With you," she whispered, "it was like...well, like nothing before."

He pulled her close and kissed the corner of her mouth. "Like nothing before," he repeated.

"Nothing before," she breathed between her lips, wrapping her arms around his neck and kissing him deeply.

He pushed her away at arm's length and looked intently into her eyes. "If I'm not careful, I'm going to fall in love with you."

"I don't like it," Assock said to Esop. "You shouldn't have left them alone."

"Why not? We anticipated it," countered Esop, perplexed by Assock's turn of mind.

The professor pursed his lips. "Yes, I know, but it's too sudden. We have our responsibility to Vinya."

"It'll be good for her. He's a nice enough fellow."

"You surprise me, Esop. This isn't any ordinary affair. It's loaded with dynamite."

"Oh, I dunno," Esop drawled calmly. "If it doesn't work out, we can stop it."

"You should have seen her face when she told me. I've never seen a child less aware of what she has gotten into."

"She's no longer a child."

"She can't see him as we do."

"I'm not so sure we see him clearly."

"We know what he is."

"He's not a stereotype."

"Maybe, maybe not. But we mustn't forget that he's still a Homo Sapiens."

"More like a semi-Human," Esop mused.

"You see…you see," Assock said, jumping up and waving his hands in exasperation. "All of you—Lank, Zenar, and you too—you don't want to face reality. *Semi-Human*," he parodied, "what the hell!"

Esop was finding it increasingly difficult to talk to Assock. They had all discussed the pros and cons of involving Vinya and it had been agreed that this would help uncover much of the Sapien's behavior patterns. Now that it happened, Assock was reacting like a Sapien father. Would it not have been worse if John had not responded to her? That Vinya responded also was all the better. It spoke well of John. Why all the fuss?

"You'll see…you'll see," Assock repeated ominously.

Esop left in obvious irritation.

They had been friends for so long that Assock was tempted to confide his plans to him. But there was enough doubt in his own mind not to risk Esop's censure. He wanted Esop to support John, to reinforce the Sapien's actions while he chipped away, giving a little, taking a little, appearing at once supportive, then disruptive. They were all being seduced by John's apparent reasonableness and adaptability, just as they were seducing the

Sapien by showing him how the Seventh Millennium was so much better than his old world.

Better? Wasn't that really the question that nagged at him? Everything was planned so well. Didn't they have an answer for everything, except the ultimate question—WHY? *Why are we here? Why does it matter? Why do we care?* They perambulated like a herd of contented cows. But beneath their contentment was fear—fear of contradiction, fear of conflict, fear of ambiguity—their unspoken fears concealed in peasant myths. Security was their obsession and instant gratification their drug. They avoided frustration like a plague, or tried to.

There was no free lunch. Everything had its price. To do as one pleases, to have what one wants on demand was paid in full by conditioned conformity disguised as free choice. Where were the peaks and valleys of pleasure and despair that in contrast to each other gave depth and breadth to the soul? How dull is this broad, unbroken plain of everlasting satiation....

The Sapien was closer than he realized to the sapping of the vital syrup cut short by aborted frustration. His disturbance over uninhibited sex in the Natoleum struck at the heart of the problem. Can the ultimate society be accomplished by instant gratification? Where will the energy and the drive to exceed the present come from if none is left over to combat the dulling contentment of unrestrained orgasm? Champagne and caviar every day for lunch becomes nothing more than alcoholic soda pop and raw eggs.

Then again, the search for new tastes, new experiences, new understanding may derive from the vulgarization of the exotic. There he was caught in his own dilemma. If instant gratification ultimately becomes boring, can it any longer be gratifying? Would not sooner or later frustration and dullness give rise to the need to overcome it, and thus provide the impetus for society to improve on itself?

He was too impatient to wait a lifetime for an answer to that or any question. But was it fair to risk the Sapien to satisfy his own thirst to know? Was one test the proof of anything? Perhaps not, but there was no alternative when only one test was to be had.

John eyed Assock curiously from the doorway of his dome. He had returned wondering what he would say to Assock, whether he should mention anything about Vinya. But in the moment of greeting, he knew that Assock knew.

"So you had a nice swim," the professor said.

"Yes, it was pleasant."

"I'm glad you enjoyed it. Sit down. I want to talk to you." He waited for John to take a chair, poured him a cup of coffee and offered him a cigarette, which John declined.

"Today at the Natoleum, you seemed to think that we were picking on you."

"I wouldn't say that," John answered suspiciously,

"Perhaps there's been too much talk about our differences and not enough about what we have in common."

"Yes, I think that is so."

"I'm glad you feel that way. If we're to get along, we've got to know each other."

"What are you driving at, Assock?"

The professor smiled. "You seem to have taken a fancy to Vinya?"

"So?"

"She's a young girl, and I think we're both mature enough to know how easy it is to be hurt at that age."

"I take it you don't like my seeing her."

"On the contrary," Assock replied benignly, "I'm glad you like her. It's good for you."

"Then what the hell are we talking about?"

"She's only a child," Assock said quietly.

Assock was making it sound like he was a child molester, John thought. From what he had learned at the Natoleum, there was no justification for this Victorian pretense. Still, they knew so little about him that he was not unappreciative of their concern. He would probably have reacted the same if Alice had come home with a man old enough to be her father.

"It's not the sex," Assock continued, "it's how a young girl romanticizes an experience, no matter how inconsequential and episodic it is. We do not object to experimentation as long as it doesn't get serious, if you know what I mean."

"I wouldn't worry about it," John parried, knowing full well what Assock meant. "I take it you don't mind my continuing to see her." That was foolish, he thought. Did he need Assock's permission? What if he said No?

"Not at all. Enjoy yourself. Have fun. But remember, we have a responsibility towards her, the same as we do towards you."

He would remember. The warning was clear enough. He was free only as long as they wanted. But it was a little late to scare him off. He had nibbled at the bait and was hooked.

The maître d' seated John and Vinya at a small wrought iron table on the terrace. A warm breeze laden with salt spray from the ocean drifted inland, rustling gently through the leaves of laurel surrounding the dining area. Vinya leaned forward with her arms folded on the glass tabletop, her eyes momentarily meeting John's, then turning shyly towards the candle between them. The flickering light sparkled in her eyes and cast warm moving shadows across her evenly tanned skin.

"I didn't think it was possible," John said in a whisper.

She looked at him quizzically.

"You're even more beautiful tonight."

She reached across the table, placing her hand on his. "You're making me very self-conscious."

"I take it all back," he said, holding her hand.

"No, not all of it."

"I couldn't anyway."

She withdrew her hand and rested her chin on the upturned palm. "If you don't stop staring at me, I'm going to laugh."

"Then laugh," he said lightly. "You're even prettier then."

She looked at him very seriously. "There are lots of pretty girls. I want to be special."

"You are," he said softly. He wanted to lean forward, to inhale her fragrance, to kiss her but he knew others in the restaurant were watching them. He hated being out in the open, sensing their stares, certain of their censure for transgressing the boundaries of youth and age. As he glanced about, he realized no one was paying any attention to them. The transgression was of his own mind.

She sensed his discomfort and tried to put him at ease by saying that she had dinner in the same restaurant with Zenar a few nights before. So, there was nothing unusual with a young woman being here with an older man. That was the last thing John wanted to hear. He couldn't help asking, "And after dinner, you and Zenar?"

She shook her head from side to side, but was she saying No or simply marveling that he could ask such a question? She held his hand across the table, offering visual commitment for everyone to see, if anyone cared. It was worth more than words to quell his unease.

After dinner they sauntered down to the beach. The ocean glistened in the moonlight. They took off their sandals and strolled barefoot on the warm wet sand. Shallow waves rolled shoreward, transporting long horizontal whitecaps that stretched out like curls of cotton.

They slept on the sand that night beneath a large beach umbrella made into a lean-to. Early in the morning they woke to the cries of gulls skimming the sea's surface for breakfast. Hand in hand, they walked down to the water and into it until their bodies became weightless and John's toes barely touched the sandy bottom, and Vinya wrapped herself about him as they bobbed up and down in harmony with the rhythm of the sea.

CHAPTER 9

It was midmorning when they returned to Vinya's room. After showering to wash off the salt and the sand and the stickiness of the beach, they stretched out on the bed. Vinya suggested they might go to the arboretum later on, but John wanted to spend the day there in the room making love, and sleeping, and dreaming. They were still lounging about when a voice sounded through the intercom.

"Anyone home?"

"That you, Esop?" Vinya called back.

Esop waited outside while Vinya slipped into a robe and John hurriedly dressed. He greeted Vinya as he entered the room, then turned to John and asked how he was getting along.

"Fine, thanks," John mumbled self-consciously.

"You two look as if you could use a good night's sleep," Esop teased, trying to put them at ease.

Vinya smiled. "We had a wonderful time. We spent the night at the beach and went swimming this morning." She sat down on the bed beside John.

Esop became serious. "I want to talk to both of you. I don't like what I'm going to say."

"Then why say it?" John rejoined.

"For your own good. Mind you, I'm not trying to tell you what to do. But John, I think you should know that we're a little uneasy."

"You or Assock?"

"Let's say all of us. We're glad you like each other."

"I'm beginning to wonder," John said.

"I don't blame you. I suppose we seem a little contradictory. We say that sex is fine and at the same time we're not sure if it's right for the two of you."

"You've been watching us?"

"Of course not. We don't have to watch to know what people do. We just don't want you to do anything rash."

John stared straight at Esop. "What are you saying—are you warning us?"

Esop returned his stare, barely nodding affirmatively. "If you want to put it that way. It would be better for you not to see each other for a while."

"But why...why?" implored Vinya, who had been listening quietly. Her eyes filled with tears. "Must it be all or nothing?" she barely whispered.

"Perhaps not," Esop replied sympathetically. "I guess there's no reason why you can't meet during the day. But any idea you might have of living together is out of the question. If you feel the same in a few months, maybe it can be arranged."

John gritted his teeth in exasperation. "This is the damnedest place. I guess we don't have a choice."

"There's a right choice and a wrong one. I think you can make the right decision."

"Thanks for the confidence," John said sarcastically.

Esop shrugged. "What plans did I spoil for today?"

"I have to go to school," Vinya replied quickly, only too glad this stupid conversation had come to an end. Besides, she sensed Esop preferred she leave.

"Well, then," Esop said to John, "perhaps you'd like to visit a Displayer? How about it?" He added with quiet sincerity, "John, I've never done anything like this before. I hope I never will again."

But John's mind was already at work planning on ways to be with Vinya. It was not only a matter of his need for her, but also of his self-respect. He did not doubt Esop's concern for his well-being. But if they insisted on treating him like an adolescent, he would return the favor. His adolescence had not been without resource.

The Displayer was a large rectangular building that towered above the domes of Opalon. By daylight, clouds reflected on the glass facade. Sunset gave the building a fairy tale glow of bright orange and pink hues, while at night the walls formed a dark mirror of the universe.

Inside, elevators and escalators carried shoppers from floor to floor, the elevators traversing transparent tubes in the center of the building. Esop worked their elevator slowly from the ground level so they could observe the succeeding floors. On the first level were heavy items such as mobenches, aerobes, farm equipment and shop tools.

Esop explained that personal mobenches and aerobes were not necessary for individuals within the metropolis as they were public property and widely accessible. People in remote areas might need their own vehicles.

The second level displayed household goods such as fine sterling and stainless steel utensils, translucent porcelain china and more sturdy stoneware, along with electronic kitchen ranges and refrigerators. The next level exhibited clothing, sporting goods, hobby equipment. Other levels were devoted to furniture and interior decorations, and such a multitude of articles that John was reminded of a combination Macy's, Sears, and Home Depot all wrapped into one building embellished with the interior decor of a more exclusive designer store like Neiman Marcus.

Esop explained that articles not on display could be ordered through catalogs. Out of stock items were filled in turn as they became available. The delay was seldom more than a few weeks when styles were changed or improved models developed.

Innovations were the responsibility of the central Research Commission, which was made up of specialty committees. Each committee handled a group of commodities with the assistance of engineers, artisans, and technicians. Consumers contributed ideas and inventions. They also participated in experimental studies and surveys to judge their utility value and durability before mass production was authorized.

The decision to produce something—whether an object or an educational program—was not made on the basis of popularity ratings so much as the absolute number of people served. To illustrate, Esop chose visiobroadcasts.

"Some programs are not universally popular as measured by the majority or even a large minority of viewers. The Advanced Program broadcasts technical lectures on scientific matters, courses in art appreciation, poetry recitals and chamber music concerts. Assume only one percent of the audience likes any of these programs, which is certainly a very small percentage. But if the total audience for all the programs is, say, nine million, this one percent represents 90,000 individuals, the equivalent of thirty large theaters. The principle is not to make each program appeal to the maximum number of people, but to make it the best of its kind regardless of popularity.

"If you seek maximum popularity all of the time, you end up with minorities that are dissatisfied all of the time. By aiming at many levels of taste and education, both minority and majority are served."

"I suppose you can do that," John surmised, "because you don't have to worry about bottom line profits. For us it wasn't even the bottom line. It was more like an insatiable appetite. You had to feed it constantly. If you didn't grow, if you didn't make more and more money every year, even though you were profitable as you were, it was as if you were on the verge of failure."

"We're more concerned with consumer satisfaction," Esop countered, "although I must admit there are times when what satisfies the consumer leaves much to be wanted."

John chuckled to himself, *The more it changes, the more it remains the same. Even they are elitists.* He wondered aloud what it would be like to order anything he wanted and not have to pay for it. It was even difficult for him to accept a simple gift without an urge to repay it in kind, as if everything had a price that had to be satisfied.

Esop assured him that if he felt the need to pay, he could always work once settled in Opalon, perhaps at a hospital or a Natoleum.

"That's the problem—I am not settled," John jumped at the thought. "If I had my own place—don't misunderstand—I'm not ungrateful staying with Assock, but I really need my own place, where I don't have to apologize for what I am or what I do...I need my own place."

Esop pondered John's appeal. It was not unexpected. Put in his position, he would want the same. That, after all, had been their intention until Assock commandeered John to his dome. Staying at Assock's was all right for a few days, but he could see that the sooner John was on his own, the better it would be for everyone including, he truly believed, Assock. He would make the decision himself and argue it out with Assock later.

"Agreed," he said, "let's go dome hunting."

They left the Displayer and went over to the Domiciliary Registry. In the center of the room was a large circular contour map, which delineated the different sections of the city complete with miniature models of all the domiciles and other buildings. Esop pointed to Vinya's dormitory, the Natoleum, Assock's dome and where he and Lida lived. John surveyed the map, calculating that if he got a place on the ocean side of the university Vinya would be closer, with Assock on the far side. He suggested to Esop that a dome by the ocean would give him the privacy he sought.

They checked through the file of vacancies and located one with an ocean front. Each file contained interior and exterior photographs of the dome, not that the furnishings or views mattered much to John so long as it was his own.

"Here, look at this one. Just what you ordered. It's yours," Esop granted, without waiting for John's concurrence.

They took a mobench, passing Vinya's dormitory on the way. John estimated it was twenty minutes further by foot to his new residence on the coast, only five by mobench. He could not have asked for a better location.

Esop checked out the dome to make certain all the facilities worked. He showed John how to have food delivered and how to operate the appliances. He gave him a list of numbers where they could all be reached by visiophone. He assured John that he would have complete privacy. There were no *bugs,* as John put it, no hidden cameras or microphones.

"I'm surprised you should think that," Esop said, genuinely hurt.

John apologized, recalling that at the Natoleum they were able to tune into the private domiciles of the residents.

"Those were only showrooms for visitors," Esop explained. "Believe me, we're as protective of our privacy as you seem to be of yours."

As Esop was leaving, John asked if he would explain to Assock why he had changed location.

"Of course," Esop replied. "I'll see you in the morning. You're sure you'll be all right?"

"Very sure, thanks."

John kicked off his sandals and stretched out on the divan before the floor to ceiling window fronting the ocean. The sun was settling like a gigantic fireball on the thin line of the horizon, shimmering in the atmospheric dust. Alone at last, he luxuriated in his newfound privacy. It had happened so quickly, so easily, so unexpectedly. Assock had been like a presence he could not shake, as if under his constant surveillance. Now he felt free of him, free to be himself, to think about himself, to be alone with himself.

He had lost count of the days—or was it weeks?—that had passed since coming to Opalon. He was caught between two lives—one a memory strong in the beginning, now receding further and further away—the other a future of promise, exciting in its uncertainty. The present was still so unreal. It seemed as much a dream as the past was a memory, as though time and the sequence of his life had been suspended. The ambivalence and indecision that had plunged him into the worst depression of his life had been destroyed by the Cataclysm. Now he could barely recall the alienation of his marriage and of his work. His thoughts of Mary were no longer of divorce, but of sorrow and sadness that she was dead. There were moments when he longed for the comfort and security they had once given each other, followed by guilt for having wanted to abandon her.

It did not escape him that if Mary were still alive, he would not have met Vinya who was responsible in no small measure for his anticipation of the days to come. But when he thought of Vinya on the threshold of her life, he had to struggle against memories of Alice who would never know the joys and fulfillment of growing up, whose future was threatened by him when she was alive, and whom he could no longer help no matter how much he still cared for her deep in his heart.

As he lay in the stillness and the darkness, drifting from one thought to another in complete absorption, he became conscious of the pulsing of his body and the chill of the night air. Suddenly, he felt numb all over. The sound of feet pummeling the carpet pummeled his ears and body shadows raced swiftly around the room, about to pounce on him. He cried for help but the words choked in his throat. He stared helplessly in the dark, paralyzed from head to toe, frozen in the terror of fear, desperately denying whatever it was in the hope it would disappear.

The room was quiet now and in the darkness he saw his old friend Arthur Sokolsky standing above him, shaking his head from side to side, and Mary beside him, and beside her, Alice silently crying. He tried to call out to them, to beg forgiveness, to plead for help. Mary bent over him. Her face was so near he could feel her breath, and he cried out *No...no...no,* and his voice echoed in concentric rings of anesthetized sound.

The night was interminably wretched. Somewhere in the middle of it, he dragged himself to the water bed and spent hours rolling from side to side in every conceivable position, slipping in and out of sleep, in and out of dreams, some placid, others disquieting and others raging nightmares he could not recall on wakening. At daybreak, he finally made it to a deep dreamless slumber. When he woke sometime later, the room had warmed by the morning sun and Esop was sitting in the corner reading a book.

"How long have you been here?"

"An hour or so," Esop answered. "I hope you don't mind my coming in. I knocked. You were sound asleep."

"I'm glad to see you."

"Ready for breakfast?"

John showered and shaved while Esop put the remaining groceries in the cupboard and then made a pot of coffee, toast, and fried eggs and bacon.

"Good, huh?" he said as they sat down to eat. "How was it last night?"

"Why do you ask?" John replied suspiciously.

"No special reason, well, yes—I know you haven't been sleeping well."

"I slept all right. How about you?"

"Not too well. I was worried about you."

"I don't see why."

Esop decided to mention their concerns from the first days on the globeship when they feared he might not survive, that he might even attempt suicide.

John assured Esop he was not the type to kill himself.

Yet, there were the night terrors, Esop reminded John, and asked if he recalled them.

"Not really. I had so much pain and confusion—the whole thing was a nightmare. Besides, if they were truly night terrors, I wouldn't remember them. Terrors are quashed by amnesia."

"Yes, if you remembered them, they'd be bad dreams, not terrors."

John acknowledged he had some pretty bad dreams.

"Good," Esop said, not unkindly.

John laughed. "My misery makes you happy?"

Esop laughed in turn. "Your memory of your misery does. That's progress."

"Speaking of progress, you know what I might be eating if I was home? Bacon and eggs...so much is different here, so much the same."

"We have common roots."

"What puzzles me, what I don't understand is if you're as free as you say you are, or if you're the most controlled people on earth."

"Maybe the essence of our freedom is our self-control."

"That's too glib, Esop. Anyway, I'd like to get away from me...I was thinking about the Displayer and how everything is for the asking. I don't see how you get along without money. How do you keep people from making gluttons of themselves? Where are the incentives? How do you get anything done?"

"It's not easy," Esop acquiesced. "We have to work at it. We do have a work ethic, but it is not motivated by accumulation of individual wealth. We look at work two ways. First, to solve problems, to do what needs to be done to keep the society running. Second, to consume our excess energy, to occupy time that is, in a sense, outside ourselves, or should be kept outside, so we don't dwell inside all the time. Nothing more depressing than too much of oneself."

"Tell me," John murmured.

As for money, Esop explained that it was necessary only in an economy of scarcity. If demand exceeds supply there has to be some way of regulating distribution. But if there is such an abundant supply of goods that no one is left wanting, money has no value.

"Supply is regulated to meet demand," he said, "so everyone can have just about everything he or she wants. As for gluttony, even that has its limits. And as for getting things done, if work is pleasant and not too difficult physically, it becomes almost recreational as well as social, because it brings people together. Most of us don't like to work in isolation. It's more fun to work with others, to share some common goals, and to achieve them. It's really quite necessary. The human animal does not adapt well to isolation and idleness."

"What if someone flat out refuses to work?" John persisted.

"That can be a problem but there's a lot of peer pressure to conform and perform. People are expected to work up to their capacity. Not everyone works the same. But if someone refuses to work at all—well, we look at it as a sickness that requires therapy."

"And if therapy fails?"

"It rarely does. There is always something someone can do. Work doesn't have to be measured by units of production, like counting beans in a cannery. It must be viable for the individual. It can be as simple as visiting with patients in a hospital or keeping an eye on children at a playground or helping the elderly with their chores."

"We had volunteers in our hospitals and nursing homes," John recalled. "They weren't paid. I don't know what we would have done without them."

Esop disagreed. "They were paid. They had a function. They were useful. They were appreciated. Their pay was what *they* got out of it. Money had nothing to do with the value of the work they performed. That is an illusion of a money economy.

"Here, volunteers are on equal footing with workers in a factory. There is no discrimination. They all have free access to the Displayer and everything else they need."

"You make it sound so simple. Surely there must be some limits, some regulation, some control, some coordination," John challenged.

"Of course. That's where government comes in. Production and manpower are allocated and coordinated by the Central Survey Board with representatives from all geographic areas.

Each region has its local Survey Board and subcommittees, which conduct studies on what is needed, from diapers to heavy machinery. If needs can be satisfied locally, that's where decisions are made. If it's necessary to get goods or materials from another area, the request is reviewed and resolved by the Central Survey Board, which establishes priorities. When there are major demand and supply problems, the Board commissions a study that concludes with recommendations to the Assembly.

"The Assembly is comprised of members chosen by lottery, similar to your jury selection system. Their five year terms overlap. The Assembly is the consumer-controlled supreme legislative body. It oversees the various expert committees on manufacturing, farming, communications, education, and so on. Assembly members are guided by special interest experts, not special interest politicians. The experts first present plans and projects—proposals—for consideration by the local population. The people vote on proposals that represent their needs, not on personalities. The approved plans are then forwarded to the Assembly for final determination."

"But some people are always more persuasive than others," John insisted, resisting the temptation to add, "Look at the way Assock gets *his* way."

"That's true," Esop agreed. He continued to describe the legislative process. "There must be merit in the proposal. There is usually more than one way to get something done, in which case the plan is carried forward by opposing advocates. The advocates argue their position before the full Assembly, which makes the final decision.

"The advocate whose position is adopted—this is most important—becomes the administrator of the plan along with his defeated colleague. Together they select an independent third member, the three of them making up the implementation team. The plan is activated with decisions determined by at least a two-thirds vote. The advocate whose approach succeeded supplies the enthusiasm for its success, while his opposite will exercise critical restraint, and the independent member prevents a paralyzing stand-off."

A triumvirate made sense for implementation, John thought, but that was only part of governance. "What about laws? Who makes the laws?" he asked.

"We don't have many laws. Our constitution is nothing more than common sense accumulated over the centuries. What laws we have are codified in a single volume. More like rules of conduct. Anyone can read the law for himself."

"Reading is one thing," John countered, "but how laws—or rules as you call them—how they're interpreted is another. We believed that justice requires rule by law, not by men. If all you have is an etiquette book, how can you assure just resolution of disputes?"

"By arbitration," Esop replied. "Disputes are submitted to an arbitration board, again of three people, each disputant choosing one member, these two choosing a third."

"We did that," John said, "but it was less than perfect. Let's say you and I have a disagreement and it goes to arbitration. What if I refuse to accept the decision? What do you do then?"

Esop looked puzzled. "You have to accept the decision. You agreed to. What would be the point of rejecting it?"

"It was a lousy decision, so I changed my mind and refused to go along. What happens then?"

The question was almost beyond Esop's comprehension. "In that event—I'm not sure—I think we'd treat it as a psychiatric problem. I suppose you'd have to undergo treatment."

John exhaled. He started to say he had heard of *treatment* from Nola, then caught himself, saying instead, "We called that brainwashing."

"In a manner of speaking, you might call it that," Esop acceded, "but what's wrong with cleansing the brain?"

"I suppose it depends on whose brain and who is doing the cleansing."

Esop seemed to think that brainwashing was merely mental hygiene, like tooth brushing. John thought better of arguing the point. Shifting gears, he asked, "What about serious crime? You can't arbitrate that."

"Crime as you knew it is long gone," Esop assured him.

"Oh, come off it, Esop," inadvertently slipped out of John's mouth.

Esop rejoined matter-of-factly, "Humans are quite different, you know. Oh, there may be an occasional assault or murder by a deranged soul. That's petty stuff compared to what went on in your world."

Esop paused for a moment, debating whether to continue. He rubbed his mustache and then proceeded with no outward sign of emotion.

"If you will permit me, the crimes and the criminals you tolerated are beyond our comprehension. It was a crime to kill someone, unless sanctioned by the state, whereupon you might be elected governor by promoting capital punishment. It was not a crime to poison the air or the food of millions of people for profit. It was a crime to steal an apple but not to exploit the public by deceptive advertising and selling shoddy goods. It was a crime for a woman to sell her body but the biggest prostitutes were politicians indebted to corporations and banks and organized crime, to the extent there was a difference. For loyal service, they were rewarded with honorary degrees and private fortunes instead of the jail sentences they deserved."

John started to interrupt but Esop carried on.

"A secretary of state could endorse massive bombing and napalming of peasant populations in a disgraceful war—killing tens of thousands—and receive a Nobel peace prize. Your CIA could murder the presidents of other countries. A homophobic homosexual could head your FBI and destroy the lives of your best intellectuals and have a crime-fighting building named in his honor. To say the least, your attitude towards crime and criminals was very perplexing."

"I wish you wouldn't say *your attitude*. It wasn't mine," John protested.

Esop apologized, "I don't mean you personally. I've been reading so much, trying to understand what your world was like. There was all that talk about freedom, but as soon as some threat came up those famous freedoms dissolved in obeisance to patriotism. Dissent became disloyalty. Agreeing with the government doesn't require a constitutional guarantee. The right to disagree, to dissent in times of crisis, does."

John concurred. "In my country, the public was pretty docile. Things had to get really bad before discontent spilled over into open opposition, like during the Vietnam war. It didn't seem much at first, but as *our* casualties increased from hundreds to thousands, akin to an open sore spreading into a fulminating infection, when the students began to rebel, when they refused to be drafted, when they burned their draft cards, when American soldiers were dying by the tens of thousands and there was no end in sight, public opposition swelled across the country and the government was finally forced to end the war. The war was a crime. It was disgusting. But it was a lesson unlearned. The public turned back into sheep. We were soon back at it in Iraq and Afghanistan and..."

He paused as if trying to wipe away a bad memory.

"War had become perpetual. It was good for business. There was no end to it."

He mopped his brow. "That was then—this is now? Maybe you don't have wars and massive crime, but people still kill each other, don't they? What do you do when someone commits a murder?"

Esop dismissed murder with a wave of a hand. "It's such a rarity," he said. "Sure, it happens, though not for property or power, but out of uncontrolled rage, more likely a frustrated love. It's strange," he said, as if musing to himself, "that the tenderest of passions sometimes leads to the most violent crime."

"And when it does—" John prodded.

"A murderer, like anyone exhibiting antisocial behavior, would be committed to the Institute of Rehabilitation. If he couldn't be rehabilitated—I don't know of any such case in recent times—he would be restricted to institutional life. It might interest you to know that in the past half-century only one murderer ever repeated and I can't recall a killing here in ten or twenty years."

John remained skeptical. "You seem to have an answer for everything."

Esop shrugged. "Almost. We are only Human."

John was tempted to remind Esop he was also human, but it seemed pointless. Instead he said, "One other thing puzzles me, this *pragmatic rationality*—what the hell does that mean?"

"You should rather ask Assock," Esop said, then realized that John might rather not, although it was the professor's realm of expertise. He would have to explain.

"It's pretty much as it sounds. *Reason that works* might be the simplest way of putting it. You can construct a theoretical model but if it doesn't serve any useful purpose, what good is it? Besides, things change, nothing remains the same. We might have general guidelines but it's their application that counts. Does that make sense?"

"Sounds pretty vague to me."

"Do you believe in a god?" Esop asked abruptly.

"That's an odd question from a pragmatist," John responded. "Do you?"

"There's no way to prove god exists, or does not. It's a nonsensical question, isn't it?"

John agreed.

"Yet, the philosophy, the concepts, the moral and ethical principles that are attached to god have meaning. They are real whether one believes in their deification or not. It isn't laws embedded in stone against murder or adultery or incest that makes them effective, but their connection between belief and practice. God is just a symbol for belief. Since the belief has not been shown to prevent murder, adultery and incest, it cannot be considered pragmatically rational. As to god being an actual being, that is totally irrational."

"How can you say it is *totally irrational* when you admit there is no proof one way or another? How can you say there really isn't an eternal man with a flowing white beard—a god? I wouldn't argue it, of course, but I can't deny it absolutely, even though to me it is utterly absurd."

"To me also," Esop said. "There's so much we cannot explain, but that doesn't mean there might not be an explanation someday. We simply refuse to accept mystical explanations for what we do not know. You can theorize all you want but until it has been found applicable, perhaps I should say perceptible to our senses, it's only a theory.

"We reject mysticism as another form of reality. We don't say that hallucinations and delusions are unreal. I mean, people have them. They may even share them as in formal religions, but mass addiction to a delusion does not make it less a delusion. Mysticism by definition is irrational because it cannot be studied, controlled, reproduced and understood by rational means."

Perhaps so, John thought, but not everything was subject to test by the scientific method. Hell, he doubted that he could prove to anyone that Opalon or the Seventh Millennium were real even though their reality was recorded by all his functioning senses. Sometimes he wondered if there was any difference between reality and belief.

He posed a hypothetical question to Esop. "What if an event happens just once and never again? It won't, it can't repeat, and it cannot be reproduced experimentally. By your definition, it would have to be classified as a mystical experience."

"Not at all," Esop responded. "If it happened—if only once—it happened. The Big Bang was a one-time event, for which we have astronomical evidence. The Great Cataclysm happened once. We have proof in archaeology. Indeed, you are proof. Simply because an event cannot be reproduced doesn't make it mystical, not if there is proof that it did in fact happen, if only once.

"Isolated physical events are not what we're talking about. Pragmatic Rationality has nothing to do with isolated events. It is the system by which we derive our moral values and our code of conduct and assess their effectiveness. You have to find out what people really do, as well as what they want to do, and what they can do, and what they should do before you can moralize.

"We look at our own culture the way anthropologists observe primitive societies. They observe, they don't moralize."

"That's hardly the way you react to my world. Seems to me you do a lot of moralizing there," John asserted, not without a little rancor.

"You can thank yourself for being here to remind us," Esop chided. "but I don't think we're far off the mark. We go beyond anthropological observation and description to consider effects. If mores benefit survival and well-being, they are pragmatically rational, which is good. If they do not, and many of your mores did not, they are pragmatically irrational, which is not so good. At least a lot of good rubbed off on you."

"You mean I'm not all bad," John quipped.

Esop stretched his arms, poured out the last of the coffee and leaned back in his chair. "Far from it," he said earnestly, then apologetically, "I hope I haven't bored you with this discourse."

"On the contrary," John said appreciatively, "if I am to live here, I must know what you're all about."

He looked at his watch. It was nearly noon. The morning had passed so quickly. "I suppose I should tell you—you'll find out anyway—I'm meeting Vinya at the pool."

"I'll walk you over."

"As a chaperone?"

Esop chuckled and shook his head.

How could one day change a lifetime? Since yesterday she was a totally different person. Everything about her was different. Shapes and colors that she had taken for granted came into sharper focus as though she was now wearing corrective lenses. Overnight, her friends seemed callow, immature, unaware of the deeper meanings in personal relationships and especially insensitive to the new person before them. Could they not see the aura of womanliness that only yesterday was the mere prettiness of adolescence? Could they not sense the incredible voluptuousness his touch had made of her sensuality?

Assock said she was only infatuated and that she must not confuse it with love. He said that infatuation was generated by physical frustration. Once frustration was eliminated by sexual indulgence, that heightened feeling would dissipate and then she would know if she was really in love, or if it was only a physical attraction.

What did Assock know about love? Nothing, she concluded. He was a man unaware and incapable of knowing a woman's feelings. He belittled the excitement and referred mystically to the calm of true love. For her part, she would rather love with the passion of infatuation then succumb to the placidity of Assock's sterile assumptions.

Esop left John at the hedge. He was uneasy, eager to see Vinya but anxious that her feelings for him might have faded in the night. He walked along the side of the pool to the far end, through the bushes to the small clearing padded with clover. She was there. He knelt down beside her.

"I thought you'd never come," she whispered.

"I was afraid you wouldn't be here."

"I said I would."

"I know, but when you leave me I'm afraid Assock will talk you out of seeing me."

She reassured him no one could.

Isolated as they were in their small enclosure, the sounds of bathers at the pool were reminders of the limits set by Assock and acceded to by Esop.

Vinya wanted to meet him at his dome. No one would know. She wouldn't be watched. They didn't do things like that, she insisted. Despite Assock's objections, there wasn't anything he could do about it.

"I don't know," John said. "It's not as if I'm just anyone. They may tolerate our meeting here, so long as nothing more comes of it." He added, without conviction, "We should wait."

That night she was there. He had been lying in bed staring at the stars through the transparent dome, consumed by her absence. The hours passed. At each sound, he started, hoping it was she, disappointed it was not, and embarrassed at behaving like a moonstruck adolescent. Then she was standing by the bed and he thought he must be dreaming until the warmth of her body and her breasts pressing softly on his chest dispelled the fantasy.

She was gone almost as suddenly as she had come, before the first light of dawn. She came and went all that week and the next, materializing out of the darkness and vanishing before daybreak. The few hours in bed were enough to sustain but not to satiate their hunger. When their bodies separated there was left the impression on each of the other still there. It would last until the next night.

John would visit with Esop some mornings while Vinya was at school, but he steered clear of Assock. Then he would see her for an hour or so after class, often at the pool. They pretended to be casual friends, which was not easy as their bodies craved contact. The daytime abstinence only served to heighten their anticipation of coming together late at night.

Occasionally, Lank or Zenar dropped in but he was wary of too much intimacy with them. He suspected they were reporting to Assock.

Much of the time he watched educational and current events programs on the visioscreen. It was a therapeutic distraction from thinking too much about himself, and a relief from the anxiety and depression that plagued him since coming to this new world. And, if Assock knew of Vinya's visits, apparently he was not going to interfere. Yes, everything was beginning to settle down.

CHAPTER 10

When it came time for young Assock to leave the Natoleum and enter the Elementary University, he had to choose a mentor. The boy admired one man above all others, although he knew him only by reputation—Nonam, Professor of Pragmatic Rationality, the most revered man throughout the Seventh Millennium. Assock trembled with anticipation as the time approached for his interview, even though he was assured he would be kindly received.

That first meeting made an indelible impression. Long after Nonam was gone, Assock would often recall the easy manner of the old man who treated him as an equal. He remembered Nonam's small piercing eyes, the folds of skin about his jowls, the thin wrinkled lips, ears that appeared excessively large aside the wizened head. He remembered the skinny legs, the small frame with ribs outstanding on a sun browned chest. And the large hands of the craftsman, the knurled knuckles and hard callused palms. How he liked to feel the strength in those hands.

Assock sat opposite him. "How old are you, son?" Nonam asked in a quiet, reassuring voice untouched by age.

"Twelve." He was annoyed by the high pitch of his voice. He wanted to sound older.

"Why did you choose me?"

"I...well...my advisors said maybe you could help me."

Nonam smiled. He had heard of Assock's persistence. The boy was always searching beyond the conventional wisdom. "Perhaps," he clucked. "I'm told you are more interested in life than living, that you're very serious, that you don't like to play."

Assock said that wasn't true. He liked to play. He played as hard as anyone, but he also wanted to know more, and for that he had to ask questions. It was not his fault he was dissatisfied with pat answers.

"Are you good at games?" Nonam asked.

"Not very…I think I think better." He looked long and hard at Nonam.

"Tell me, young man, what are some of these thoughts?"

A small smile lighted the boy's face. He perceived Nonam was now playing a game with him, a game that he liked. "When I ask why are we, nobody seems to know. All they ever say is because we are."

Nonam took the child's hand in his. "Perhaps that is so. There may not be answers to all questions. Shall we explore together?"

"Oh yes."

Assock's early childhood had not been the happiest. Some combination of genes, infant impressions and innate sensitivity set him apart from most children. His movements were a little slower and more deliberate, his physical development a little behind his age group. He seemed to have been born more introspective, more serious than most others. Nonetheless, he was part of a group that demanded group participation. He had plenty of time to dwell on himself but he was also conditioned to accept the activities of others. If he was pulled into a game, he played hard, forgetting himself, exhausting his young body in the excitement of exertion. All in all, he was content at the Natoleum. But he was not sorry when he had to leave. There was so much to learn that he could hardly wait.

What loneliness he experienced vanished with Nonam. He never quite understood the strong empathy between them. When he was by himself he felt terribly inadequate compared with his mentor. In Nonam's presence his sense of inferiority vanished. Then he was simply a boy with his teacher and friend.

Every day for three years Assock walked to Nonam's retreat. It was located on the outskirts of the University among some uncleared hills and fields. A narrow rock-strewn path led to the small adobe hut perched beside a vegetable patch, which Nonam tended himself. Often as they talked, he and Assock would prune the plants and bushes and fill baskets with ripe fruits and vegetables. He was happy with Nonam. He dreamed of spending the rest of his life with him, doing everything Nonam did, thinking his thoughts, being him.

Nonam did not encourage him. "I am an old man," he would say. "My strength is leaving me. Even now I must sometimes lean on your shoulder as you have leaned on mine. We are men in different stages of life. Your life is yet to be, while I am gathering loose ends and tidying up a bit before I part. You must live your way as I have lived mine. Don't look so sad, my son. There are many years left for both of us."

Assock wished he could die with Nonam. He didn't want to be left alone. Only Nonam understood him and he alone understood Nonam.

About this time he discovered a friend his own age. Zenar was tall, thin, completely extroverted and full of the devil. They so contrasted that they were drawn together on sight. Nonam encouraged their friendship and became Zenar's mentor also.

The two boys were a comical sight. Zenar towered head, shoulders and chest above Assock, and insisted on being his protector. Assock protested. "I don't need protecting."

Zenar insisted he did.

"From what?"

"From yourself."

And that was all there was to it. Assock needed protection, it was true, from growing up too soon. But as Zenar drew Assock out of his shell of shy self-consciousness, he suffered the consequences of becoming friends with an intellectual. Their discussions were not always placid. Zenar would out-holler if he could not out-argue, but as with others who dealt with Zenar, Assock learned to raise his voice.

One day they hit upon a subject that stymied them. Zenar had casually asked, "What is the greatest wisdom?" They consulted their mentor. Nonam's reply was the story of the king who commanded his wise men to compile the wisdom of the world and bring it to him so that he could understand the meaning of life.

It was a monumental task and took many years. Meanwhile the king was busy with affairs of state and when his wise men presented him with a dozen thick volumes, he insisted they shorten their report, as he was much too busy to read all those books. The wise men condensed, distilled, evaporated and finally reduced the wisdom of the world to one volume. By then the king was on his deathbed. He pleaded he had not enough life left for even one volume. If the wise men were truly wise, surely they could answer him in one sentence.

The wise men, who were now not only old themselves but even more wise than before, said to the king, "O Noble lord, you commissioned us to explain the meaning of life. Would that it were otherwise, but it is this and no more: We are born—We live—We die."

They often remained with Nonam late into the evening. There was something special about evening time, sitting on the rock wall watching darkness envelop the earth and sky, naming stars as they appeared, listening to their voices drifting out into endless space as fireflies glowed their secret light to the steady chirp of crickets.

Then Nonam died, quietly, in his sleep. The boys were just fifteen. Zenar heard of it first. Assock was devastated. He called Zenar a liar, insisting it wasn't true, tearing himself away from Zenar's grief-stricken embrace. He ran towards the Tower of Rationality, climbed the thousand steps and was tottering on the topmost ledge when Zenar reached him, pulled him back from the ledge, and told him simply to stop feeling sorry for himself and grow up.

Assock always remembered those words and never quite forgave Zenar. Nor did he forgive the world that hardly paused to mourn Nonam. Slowly he returned to his studies, slowly he regained his philosophic interests and accepted that another's death was not one's own, that life renewed through continuity, that Nonam lived on in himself. And when he died, he, too, would live on in others. So it went, one life compounded of another, our ashes scattered in the sea, corporal complexity reduced to harmony in elements. Assock no longer walking the path to the adobe hut. He had found himself in Opalon.

Assock developed into a highly civilized product of the Seventh Millennium. He moved to the Universal University, studying history, philosophy, mathematics and the physical sciences. He was interested in these courses but always felt detached from studies that were removed from the daily personal relationships between people. He wanted to be with people, to know them and feel what they were, to really understand them.

Nonam's seminars at the University were carried on by other faculty until a permanent successor could be appointed. Assock had attended the seminars since he first met Nonam. As a boy he had secret fantasies of taking over where Nonam had left off, but as he matured he realized it would be many years and much more experience before he would be ready, if ever. Nevertheless, he was an active participant, seldom missing a session although the demands of his general studies were great.

Some of the faculty suggested that Assock groom himself to succeed Nonam sometime in the future, but the young man's doubts about himself persisted. Besides, he did not want to narrow his perspectives to a niche already prepared for him. He decided to study medicine.

As he passed from such basic courses as physiology, pharmacology and anatomy to clinical treatment, his interest intensified. Now he was working with Humans, not tissue specimens and cadavers. Theory became practice. Still it was not enough. Diagnosing physical ills, prescribing drugs, instituting mechanical therapy, performing surgery—all had their rewards in success, disappointments in failure—none answered the basic questions. What caused the disease? What upset the balance of natural resistance? What initiated the stimulation that produced the excess or deficiency of hormonal secretions and nerve excitation? What caused premature degeneration, headaches, ulcers, atrophy, paralysis, senility? Why did one individual succumb and another resist? The answers did not lie solely in the scourge of pathogenic microorganisms, of physiological imbalance, of malicious genetic permutations. There was more to disease than biological mechanics.

Assock's probing led inexorably to psychiatry. Here at last was a field that struck at the core of life and its relation to disease and, ultimately, to death. The pathology of emotional stress and distress might be as significant as that of physical illness but its definition was elusive and speculative.

The sheer number of patients demanding his attention numbed his sensitivity. Just as he had become bored with general medicine and gave it up, he abandoned the practice of psychiatry to concentrate on the generic causes of disease. He was convinced that limiting treatment to individuals without attacking the root source of their illnesses would only perpetuate the general miasma.

The only way to wipe disease off the face of the earth was to create a society that nurtured health instead of feeding into the destructive forces that put an end to all previous civilizations. Far more progress had been made by improving nutrition and vaccination to strengthen the population's resistance to disease, and by sanitation to destroy lethal organisms. Otherwise the world would be little changed despite the miraculous cures of modern medical science applied to individuals one by one.

As the common diseases that once caused major epidemics were conquered, others took their place and it became inescapable that some diseases derived from within the biological and psychological organism. Heredity down to the core elements of genes became a focal point of his attention. He wondered how much the variations in sensory structures and, indeed, in the emotions were influenced by heredity. By altering genes and producing mutations, it might be possible to breed Humans as resistant to emotional diseases as they had become to some bacterial, viral and parasitic diseases.

Had not the Great Cataclysm done just that, producing the mutant Species Human? The effect had been less than perfect. Genetic experiments with Humans, promising in theory, had resulted in so many grotesqueries that they were now forbidden. Instead, the emphasis was on environmental controls to reduce stress. From infancy onward, individuals were bred like a plant in the monitored atmosphere of a terrarium, sheltered from conflicts and the paralysis of possessiveness. Yet, there were some whose aberrant behavior required treatment to cure, if indeed they could be cured at all.

Assock wondered if the controls of the Natoleum might not be too extreme. He was appalled by the emphasis on conformity, the ease with which most of its graduates were directed and controlled, and their lack of spontaneity and creativity. Though they lived longer and seemed more content, he was far from certain that better fed cows was the answer.

Might it not be better to compromise with nature? Were parents by definition bad? Did not other species raise their young successfully in monogamous harmony? Were not parents entitled to share in the responsibilities and the rewards of child bearing? Could not mature parents avoid the stunting and crippling of possessiveness? He would have to find out.

An experiment of this kind would require the approval of the Assembly's Research Committee. Attitudes toward private rearing of children were clearly defined and prohibitive. A child was not a guinea pig. Centuries of experience had taught that children belonged to society, not to parents. For their own happiness, they must mature unfettered by restrictive familial dependencies.

Assock agreed, but he reasoned convincingly that it need not be *all or none*, that variation was not without merit, and that if the experiment failed, it would be further proof of the wisdom of traditional policy. He was thus permitted to proceed with the proviso that his emotional responses be closely monitored. He was well thought of, but his judgment, like anyone's judgment, was not totally immune to emotions. The first sign of a deleterious possessiveness towards the child would terminate the experiment.

The next step was to find a suitable mate. Few women would be either willing or capable of going completely against the established convention that children belonged in a Natoleum. Assock decided he must choose a maternal figure, some woman who represented the classic concept of what a mother should be like. She must be full-breasted, with firm bones and wide hips. She must be gentle in demeanor, desirous of giving her milk. She must be willing to sacrifice her personal *wants* in favor of the well-being of her offspring. Above all, she must be capable of selfless love.

As for himself, Assock felt he was quite capable of providing all the qualities of a father without harming the child. He could not imagine himself becoming possessive. He would of course like his child, but no more so than other children. Together he and the woman would provide warmth, security and love just as at the Natoleum, but with the additional intimacy of a private family stimulated by the uniqueness of their own individuality.

While visiting the Natoleum he met a young woman, one of the daily attendants in the nursery. He was immediately struck by her resemblance to his idealized image. She was his height. Her eyes were a gentle gray, but clear and perceiving. She had long, auburn hair. Her lips were thin, her forehead untrammeled, her breasts wholesomely large. Her name was Evol. Assock introduced himself.

"Ah, the monogamous researcher. I've heard of you."

Assock grinned, then said straightforwardly, "Will you mate with me?"

Evol took his bluntness as a jest.

"I mean it. I want you to be the mother of the experiment."

"Why that's positively the most romantic proposal I've had." She barely restrained laughing in his face. "Why me?"

"You look like a mother." *What the hell is so funny*, he thought,

"And you look like the perfect father," she teased, then turned serious as she realized he was serious. "What makes you think we'd be compatible?"

"I'm easy to get along with," Assock assured Evol in magnificent self-deception.

She compressed her lips and shrugged. "No, it isn't right. For two people to have a child outside the Natoleum, there must be love between them. Have you ever been in love?"

"What do you mean?" He loved Nonam. He loved humanity.

"Look, it's one thing to ask me to nurture your seed, quite another to have me live with you. What if we don't like each other? The experiment would flop. Would that prove anything?"

Assock considered for a moment. "That's true. I just assumed we'd like each other. I guess we'll have to find out. Incidentally, I do like you—I think."

Evol grinned. "It will have to be more than incidental. Do you sail?"

The abrupt change of subject confused the prospective lover.

"I'm going sailing this afternoon. Want to come along?"

"Uh—fine, yes, I'd like to."

Assock did not care one way or another for sailing but he dutifully sat in the bow of the small craft and adjusted the jib to Evol's command. The waves were high and slapped against the hull, throwing spray over the railing, soaking him clear through to chilled bones. He did not agree it was "Fun, eh?" She laughed and he enjoyed her laughter and laughed, too.

They docked shortly after dark and Assock invited her home for dinner. She accepted on condition that she prepare the meal.

It had been some time since the smell of home cooked food permeated his dome. He liked it and suggested they cook often.

"If we're to be a family, you'll have to help," she said.

"Okay, but one thing—I abhor dishwashing."

"When did you ever wash a dish?" The image of Assock sloshing in a sink amused her.

"Just the thought. From what I've learned of families in the past, that was the epitome of male domestication. My refusal shall be a torch of independence."

"Before you refuse, you should know what it is you are refusing." Her smile was sweet as she handed him a dirty dish.

Assock accepted the assignment, which amounted to little more than scraping the dishes and placing them into the dishwasher, protesting all the while but enjoying it all the same.

Afterwards they lounged around and talked about their plans. The decision to live together infused them with a warmth and interest that was lacking in more casual affairs. But before Evol would have his child, she would have his love.

"I do love you," he declared, hungering for her. "I feel you pulling me, and there's this sense of anticipation that if you touch me I'll dissolve, and if you don't I'll cry. All my life I've thought of love but never loving, not like this. I'm like the flame on those logs. If you don't kindle me, I'll die,"

She moved close to him. Flame shadows reflected unevenly on their faces, their eyes bright with their own warmth.

Most of Assock's life had been an indulgence in solitary thought and study even though he conceptualized himself as a highly social person. He had friends that he enjoyed. He assumed he loved them although it was more or less intellectual and without emotion. There was Zenar for whom he felt the deepest affection. His feelings for Nonam had been even more intense, the strongest sense of attachment and an overwhelming sense of loss, of abandonment when he died. What he felt now with Evol was different, but he did not know how to describe it, except that it was a total preoccupation. He could not get her out of his mind.

Evol insisted on being courted. She had denied her body during the first days until she was certain Assock really wanted her, not as some maternal symbol but as herself, a woman of feeling and passion.

His hunger was real, his desire for the ultimate intimacy exaggerated by her denial. There were sensations he had not experienced since his first adolescent affair, like the hot flash and tingling of his skin when he thought of her, and the anxiety bordering on faintness if she was late coming home. What was more, he was genuinely fond of her.

Their first month together was full of discovery. Each had established some picture of what the other would be like. It was a rough sketch, which only the experience of living together could fill in. They revealed unexpected quirks.

Evol was less fond of people and tired easily of the repetition of daily conversation. She scoffed at his assertion that one might always learn something new. She would rather listen to music, or attend a play at the amphitheater, or sail by herself, although she did not object to Assock accompanying her.

Assock could not comprehend why anyone would want to do anything alone, even as that was the pattern of his life. At times he felt excluded by her independence, and was annoyed if she was not at home waiting for him when he finished work at the University.

They grew accustomed to each other. Sitting in a room, each in his own thoughts, was sharing just as much as lying side by side asleep, each in touch with the other. Walking in the park, sunbathing on the dunes, toasting marshmallows in the fireplace. Weren't these things as important as talk and study and games? That was exactly it. They had no need to play *games* to impress the other. Now when they talked it was to exchange ideas and discuss plans for the day, the weekend, the future. They toasted marshmallows because they liked the taste. They were already intimate.

Assock was much puzzled by all this. He had lived with other women for short periods. Why did she satisfy him more, in all respects? He had liked the way others looked but the familiarity with Evol's features pleased him more. He enjoyed sex with others but she gave him more pleasure. Why should this closeness have developed with her?

Their relationship stretched to months. Although the purpose was to produce a child, Assock was unexpectedly annoyed by her pregnancy. At first anxious for it to happen, it muddled his analysis of why he loved Evol more than anyone else. He could no longer think of her solely in juxtaposition to himself. There was a part of him growing in her that united their bodies even when they were apart. For the first time in his life, he was jealous because the child would be more of her than of him. After all, he had only planted the seed. Evol insisted they harvest together. Nonetheless, he remained envious of maternal creation. His jealousy and envy were short-lived. Evol was still herself and it was she he loved, not an unborn, unknown child.

They were happy. Evol grew bigger. From a slight bulge in her abdomen the fetus pushed out, remolding the mother's contour to its own curled shape. Her breasts became more dense and the nipples firmed invitingly. Evol was exhilarated by the fulfillment of her gender. She wondered more and more what it would be like to raise her own child in her own home.

"Our child—and Opalon's," Assock cautioned. "A tree belongs to the field but the field belongs to Earth."

Term approached and they talked of how they would behave with the child. Infancy held few problems, but as childhood approached there would be need for playmates. They would bring him to the Nursery at the Natoleum during the day and take him home at night. How would the child feel when all other children lived in one place and he in another? Would he resent them for it?

"Perhaps," Assock said, "but we've lots of time before we come to that. Right now we have a problem of our own. It will be more a test of ourselves than the infant. We were brought up not to be possessive in love, yet isn't a love such as ours possessive? A child can grow up without parents but can parents allow their child to grow up? That's the problem."

The problem finally arrived—a hungry-mouthed, lusty-voiced girl. How their lives changed. The first month was regulated by the tyranny of the irregular newborn timepiece. Assock left work so that he could devote all his energies to helping Evol, and observing the infant's reactions and their own. It was a merry-go-round of changing diapers and sheets, of back patting and burping, of gurgling, suckling, cooing and cuddling. They only went out to sun the baby on the verandah or to take short strolls with the carriage. Assock was so attentive that, except for lack of protruding breasts, he might easily have been mistaken for the mother. As he explained, he was merely asserting his right to share in creation. Now he understood why some men were so active in the Natoleum's nursery.

Birth took strength from the mother. The strains of new life, the constant attention, waking at odd hours, short periods of sleep, left little time for recuperation. If a woman created a child with relative ease in nine short months, the following months and years of hard work were more than enough to make a man think twice before envying the task.

One afternoon Evol went down to the dock. She hadn't been sailing for so long. She found her boat, dropped the keel and rigged the mainsail and jib. The wind puffed out the canvas and pushed the small craft at a swift clip. The water was slightly rough but Evol was an experienced sailor. She stretched out, her head just protruding from the small cockpit, the rudder's handle nestled between her arm and side. The salt spray brushed her face, the sun beat down and she was so comfortable, so relaxed. She closed her eyes and dreamed. The boat became a dot and the sail a speck from the shore, and then there was only the horizon stretching to infinity.

The search for Evol failed to uncover a single clue to her fate. There had been no sudden storm, no sudden violence in the elements, no possible explanation for her disappearance. It was as though the ocean had opened up and swallowed her.

Assock continued to look long after the search parties had given up. He flew back and forth over the ocean, traversing areas far beyond the land. More than once, in his despair, he was tempted to plunge into the waters after her.

He was held back by thoughts of their baby—now his baby. He would raise her himself. She was part of Evol, the remnant of their love. He would not give up any more. He was in a daze. Friends offered sympathy and tried to help but there was no helping. Their words and gestures passed unnoticed. He was tired, so tired. He was tired of thinking and feeling, tired of searching for answers. Evol was lost. There was no sense to this life? There were no answers, no meanings, just bits of wax, a little flame, and darkness.

He guarded his daughter jealously. At least their child would come to no more harm. More harm? What more harm was possible? She had lost her mother. He would make up for the loss. He would live only for his child. She would not let him forget Evol, even as the pain of Evol's loss intensified with each passing day. He would not give up their child.

They came to him. The child must go to the Natoleum, they said. Assock would not have it. They explained patiently that he was being extremely possessive, that he would stifle the child, that it was impermissible for her to grow up in such an unhealthy environment.

"The hell you say. What about me? Don't I count? She's all I've got."

They pointed out his irrationality.

"I don't want to be rational. All my life I've been rational."

Assock wearily watched them bundle up the baby. She was placed in a Natoleum far away.

Twice before Assock had suffered the shattering loss of dearly loved ones. First Nonam, then Evol. He had clung to the child as though possessing her would delay the complete loss of

Evol, just he had clung to Zenar for months after his mentor's death. But they would not permit him even that small solace. He could not raise a child alone. Damn them and their smug certainty. How could they be so sure he could not raise his own child without insufferable possessiveness?

He was numbed by the separation. In the midst of the general contentment, how much suffering could one person endure? Gradually he succumbed to the inexorable perspective of Time, with its dulling suppression of passion and distancing of memory. He opened his eyes to the world about him.

Years passed and he was grateful for having lived at least a while with Evol and to have shared their child for as long as it lasted. He remembered their happiness and in that memory lingered the pain of his grief.

Assock and Zenar walked along the path to Nonam's old retreat. It was more than a decade since Nonam's death. The hills were vibrant with the brilliant hues of autumn. Splashes of orange and gold ran up and down the hillsides in bright relief against the softer hues of brown bark and evergreens. Then the breeze broke the leaves last hold and they fluttered earthward, forming a soft carpet on the ground.

They reached the retreat and wandered aimlessly about the overgrown fields. Dead twigs crackled beneath their weight. They sat on the rock wall behind the adobe hut. Zenar picked up a slender stick and carved figures in a small patch of dirt between his feet. He had completed his formal studies in biology and was working on his own research. He described his experiments to Assock. When he finished, he turned to his friend, "And you, what are you up to?"

Assock doodled in his patch of earth. "Not much—reading, some writing—still obsessed with the inexactitude of the mind."

He paused, kicked at the dirt and slammed his stick like an arrow between his feet. "Why must we be tyrannized by the brain? How is it that the ideas of science can appear so clear and precise but our deepest thoughts are in such a muddle? If our mind could only be reduced to the clarity of physical laws."

"Spoken like a true Professor of Pragmatic Rationality," Zenar responded grandiloquently.

Assock scowled at him. "We've been through this before. You know I wanted to succeed Nonam. But you have to more than just want something. You have to be capable of it and I am quite incapable."

"You amaze me," Zenar raised his voice to a holler. "You're like a child afraid of the dark. You still haven't gotten over your idolatry. Nonam is still a god who would castrate you if you dared challenge his authority. He was only Human." He stuck the point of his stick into the ground in emphasis.

"It's not that simple, Zenar."

"The hell it isn't," Zenar bellowed, and then lowered his voice to a reasonable shout. "Look, old man, there's been a dozen leaders of the seminars since Nonam died. They're not right. They'd all be glad to hand the job over to you. They're just waiting for you to grow up and take over."

"I'm not ready."

"You're exasperating. You're so damned scared of Nonam. I give up…go on back to your isolation." He stood up, broke the stick in disgust and stomped down the path, yelling back, "I hope you're miserable."

Assock's laugh was hollow. He could not shake Zenar's challenge. He argued back and forth with himself, changing his mind with each breath, recalling the faith Nonam had placed in him, wanting and not wanting to succeed him.

A week later, he became the second Professor of Pragmatic Rationality at the Universal University in Opalon.

CHAPTER 11

Zenar's laboratory was no longer located in the biology section of the University. Once he began using explosives to create the vacuums required for his quick-freeze experiments, he was moved to the isolation and safety of an underground concrete bunker. This suited him fine, as he preferred to work outside the traditional surveillance of colleagues, especially, administrators. Few people came to his lab and then only by invitation, except once each year when all scientific facilities were open to the general public for a day of acknowledgment.

Zenar was particularly grateful to Esop for encouragement and assistance in cutting through the red tape surrounding scientific experimentation. Perhaps if he was using animals, instead of tissues and microorganisms, it would not have been so easy. The regulations for experimenting with live animals became increasingly restrictive as they climbed up the evolutionary ladder. It was practically impossible to sacrifice anything larger than a frog or a rat without first obtaining permission from the SubHuman Society. The rules had become so complex that one needed the informed consent of, if not the animals, their Human proxies.

Zenar explained all this to John, whom he had invited to visit the laboratory along with Lank, who was surprised that he had been included.

"I thought John might need your protection," Zenar kidded. "After all, he's proved my theory of organic freeze reversal. It would be tempting to try again."

"That's not funny," Lank said seriously, "and not a very polite thing to say in front of our friend."

John laughed. "Your SubHuman Society wouldn't approve. Thank god for that. We could have used more restraint. The slaughter of animals in the name of science was horrendous. One experiment really got to me. Dogs' legs were broken to study fractures, as if they couldn't find enough broken arms, legs and heads in any orthopedic clinic. But no, they had to use dogs. Millions of cows, pigs, and chickens were slaughtered to satisfy our excessive craving for meat, at the same time polluting the environment. We were so out of control."

"I am in favor of controls—for others," Zenar quipped with a chuckle.

"Be serious," remonstrated Lank.

"I am serious."

"You can't be."

"Why do you think I accepted this dungeon? It gives me complete isolation. Not even a visioscanner can penetrate these walls."

Lank's rotund face exhibited genuine surprise.

Zenar looked at him directly. "Can I trust you?"

"What do you mean?"

"You know damned well what I mean. Why do you think I asked you here? To talk about animals?"

Lank stammered, "Well…what?"

"Our friend here, and Assock," he turned to John, "he hasn't been himself since you came along—has he, Lank?"

Lank's eyes reflected puzzlement.

"Didn't it strike you as odd that Assock barely recognized me at the crater? He acted as though we hardly knew each other, except that time when we were together out on the ice, away from everyone. We were brothers. Now, I can't get through to him."

Lank frowned. "No one can."

"I don't know what's come over Assock," Zenar said. "He seems to have lost interest in his work. He dropped out of the seminars and has yet to complete his part of the Committee's report. It's as though he's severed his connections with the past and has even withdrawn from the present. He's made strangers of us all. Frankly, I think it's deliberate. I think he's setting us up for his own experiment, with John the guinea pig."

"I can't believe that," Lank protested weakly. "He doesn't have that right."

"You're so damned naïve, Lank," exploded Zenar. "You know who he is."

Lank started to respond, then fell silent. He stared at the floor and shook his head slowly from side to side, saying in a faltering voice, "I...I don't think I should get involved. This...it's none of my business. Have you talked to Esop?"

"I was hoping you would help me."

"What about Esop?" Lank repeated.

"I wanted to talk to you first."

"You should ask him." Lank squirmed, his discomfort pouring through the pores of his forehead in glistening beads of perspiration.

"I'm sorry I troubled you," Zenar said derisively, with barely concealed contempt.

Lank, ever the conciliator, ignored the barb. "That's all right, really it is." Glancing at his watch, he sighed in relief. "I've got to go," he said, "I'm due back at the Natoleum."

"Can I trust you?" Zenar repeated. Now there was urgency in his voice, urgency and demand, which failed to conceal his doubt.

"I won't say anything," Lank promised quickly and left, not once having looked at John who had been staring at them both in shocked silence.

"Goddamned coward," Zenar mumbled to himself.

"I don't get it," John finally uttered, shuddering in the chill of the laboratory, which had come on him as he listened to Zenar and Lank. "What experiment? What were you talking about?"

"I wish I knew," Zenar answered. "I thought maybe Lank would help. I was wrong." Zenar's eyes clouded as if he was engaged in an internal debate. He motioned for John to follow him. "Here, let me show you something."

Zenar removed a key from his pocket and unlocked a thick thermal insulated door that opened into a smaller room. A blast of icy air frosted their faces as they entered. The walls were lined with refrigerator pipes coated with ice like a meat freezer. Lying on an oblong table in the center of the room was the tiny body of a newborn infant, its skin blue with cold and covered with frost. Zenar extended the long finger of his right hand across the infant's palm. John gasped as the tiny hand slowly curled around Zenar's finger. There were no other signs of life. Zenar placed a sensor on the infant's chest. It amplified the tiny heartbeat, which thumped at ten second intervals.

John looked up at Zenar. "Can you revive it?"

Zenar shrugged and led John back to his office, which was furnished as a one-room apartment, complete with an oversized bed to accommodate Zenar's length. Bulging bookcases rimmed the room. The large oak desk was littered with papers and small laboratory tools. It supported a microcomputer and an electron microscope.

"You live here?" John asked as he sipped hot coffee. The chill of his body was unrelieved, and he shivered at the thought of the near-frozen infant.

"Most of the time...can't be gone for long." Then, with the same urgency and plea he had addressed to Lank, he warned, "Nobody knows what you just saw. Do you understand?"

How could he understand? What Zenar had shown him contradicted everything that had been said of the prohibition on experimentation with live animals, much less human beings. What did it have to do with him? Why should Zenar share secrets with him? Why was Lank so afraid? Had he just witnessed the prelude to his own demise? He wished he could stop shivering. Even his teeth were chattering.

"I could be hanged for this," Zenar said, "not literally, of course."

"H-how did you get the baby?"

"It's a Horde child."

"A what?"

"A Horde child. We told you about the Hordes?"

"Oh yes, but you said that was long ago, that they were extinct. I distinctly remember—"

"Ah, but they're not, thank Jevh."

"Jevh?"

Zenar waved his hand dismissively. Jevh was not up for discussion. As for the infant, Zenar again cautioned John that it must be kept a secret. He explained that a live Horde had never been captured before. The occasional report of a sighting was passed off as a high altitude hallucination.

He also believed them to be extinct until a few weeks ago, when he was climbing alone high up in the mountains. He had been caught in a storm and bivouacked in a cave at over 20,000 feet. When he woke in the morning, there was a body lying at the mouth of the cave. At first he thought it was an animal, a mountain goat. He moved towards it slowly, expecting at any moment it might spring up. Then, to his amazement, he saw it resembled—it was—a Horde, a Horde woman wrapped in a bearskin. Her face was blue as the sky and glazed with ice. He pulled the frozen coat apart and felt for her heart. His palm came to rest instead on a little form, so small he recognized it as a newborn.

He surmised that the Horde woman had fallen behind her band and was trying to get inside the cave when she collapsed at its mouth and there gave birth. With her strength fast ebbing, she had placed her baby inside the fur against her chest, shielding it from the cold, draining her body warmth to keep it warm as she froze to death.

Instinctively, he picked up the baby and pressed his ear to its tiny chest and felt, or thought he felt, the slightest shimmer of a breath. It was faintly alive.

He feared her band would come back looking for her. If they found him, he'd be a dead duck. So he threw the woman's body over the side of the ledge, and then withdrew to the deepest recess of the cave, the half-frozen baby nestled inside his parka against the warmth of his body.

The Hordes returned not long afterwards. They spotted the woman's body on the snow far below the ledge, too far and too inaccessible to retrieve. There was deep sorrow in their guttural grunts, and one Horde fell to his knees and wept and wailed his grief. He was gently lifted to his feet by his companions, and pulled along as they continued on their way.

Zenar left the cave as soon as he was sure the Hordes were out of sight. The baby inside his layered thermal insulated undershirt pressed against his chest like a ball of ice. He doubted it would survive, if indeed it was still alive. He backtracked down the mountain, hurrying, but not so much as to risk the fate he had visited on the baby's dead mother.

Not until he was back inside his laboratory, and had lain the infant on the table and pressed the stethoscope against its chest and elicited a very slow but steady heartbeat, was he sure it was still alive, barely. The heartbeat and respiration were so weak, Zenar was sure it would not survive for long. Perhaps if he lowered its temperature to just above freezing, perhaps he could sustain the thin thread of life within, and slowly bring it back, degree by degree.

It was the baby's only chance. It would have to be done secretively. If it became known, if the Horde infant died, he would be accused of gross negligence for not turning it over to the neonatal specialists. His failure to report to the authorities immediately would likely destroy his career.

There was more to his concern than the infant's survival or what might happen to him if and when all this came out. He had made a discovery that would rock the foundations of the Seventh Millennium. His analysis of a drop of the infant's blood revealed that the Hordes were not a post-cataclysmic mutation, a variant of the Species Human as everyone believed. He had performed the same tests on John's blood. There was no doubt— they both lacked the Human Factor. The infant was a Homo Sapien!

"That's wonderful," John exclaimed. He was not alone.

"You don't understand," Zenar went on. "In the millennia following the Cataclysm, they failed to Humanize. They were monsters, cannibals, killers. They tried to destroy us. They fought among themselves. They did more to destroy themselves than our ancestors who tried to exterminate them. We thought they were all gone, but some must have survived. They are totally incapable of changing and adapting to our advanced ways. Don't you see, they're barbarians, a malignancy—"

"Nonsense," objected John. "Didn't they come back for the woman? What about the man's grief? You witnessed that. You felt it. Maybe it's *your* behavior that's barbaric to them. For Christ's sake, you tried to exterminate them."

"Let me finish," Zenar said. "All this time we believed the Hordes were a mutation like the rest of us. Perhaps their extreme aggressiveness was a reaction to fear and persecution, but it was beyond restraint, it had to be in their genes. Since they were survivors of the Cataclysm, the same as us, we assumed the radiation destroyed whatever human qualities Homo Sapiens possessed. But we had no proof. They disappeared. We assumed they were extinct. We should have known the sightings were true. But the Hordes have all the cunning and deception of...of—"

"Homo Sapiens," John finished his sentence.

Zenar's story reminded him of the reports of Big Foot and the Abominable Snowman who haunted the folklore of his time. If one had been captured, the whole world would have known. He failed to see why Zenar had to keep it secret. Surely the authorities would understand.

"If this gets out," Zenar tried to explain further, "it will prove Assock's theory. He believed the Hordes were Homo Sapiens and that was why they could not assimilate in the Seventh Millennium. Don't you understand? That's what he believes about you, that you are genetically incapable of co-existing with Humans."

"And you?" The chill had penetrated to the marrow of John's bones.

"If I agreed with him, you wouldn't be here," Zenar replied, even as he still harbored some doubts.

"Doesn't he credit environmental influences, I mean, there's more to character than genes."

"Certainly for Humans there's no doubt. Some of us believe that was also true for Homo Sapiens. Assock won't accept belief. He insists on proof."

"Is that what you meant by his *experiment*?"

"Yes, but I don't know what he intends to do."

John swayed unsteadily. He had been standing all this time as Zenar paced about. He slowly eased into a chair, feeling the stiffness of his joints, folding his arms across his chest to diminish the chill and stop his shaking. He asked weakly, "Can't you find out?"

"I was hoping Lank would help. I also wanted his help with the Horde infant. I'm not a physician, you know. You saw for yourself. He can't be trusted."

"Aren't you taking a chance with me?"

"I had to warn you. You'd gain nothing by reporting me. And I think maybe you can help me."

John shook his head. "I have no experience with neonatals. I wouldn't know where to begin."

"It probably wouldn't work anyway," Zenar said wistfully. "I don't know what the authorities will do if they find out."

"To you or me? What'll they do, put me in a cage for the rest of my life?" John said, disgusted by the absurdity of it all.

"You *are* in a cage."

"Well, you don't seem so damned free yourself," retorted John angrily.

Zenar started to laugh, softly at first, then rising to loud raucous laughter that brought tears to his eyes.

He spread his arms wide and shouted, "You're right. This cage, this concrete dungeon is my freedom. You don't know how funny that is."

When he had calmed down, he said very seriously, "Take my advice, stop seeing Vinya. I don't know why, but whatever Assock has in mind, it has to do with her. Stop seeing her and you'll be all right."

John's chill turned feverish. He was angry, but not at Zenar, who he believed was sincerely trying to protect him. "Is she in danger?"

Zenar responded slowly, "No, I don't think so."

"You don't think so," John repeated, "but you're not sure."

"Can one be sure of anything?" Zenar cringed inwardly at the inanity of his reply. John Altern might be a Homo Sapien but he was not stupid. Surely he would have sense to leave well enough alone, unless—unless Assock was right. And if so, he also was in jeopardy.

When Lank got back to his office at the Natoleum, he immediately phoned Esop and asked him to come right over. He started to make notes of his conversation with Zenar, then thought better of it. He knew, of course, that Assock and Zenar were childhood friends. Everyone knew that, just as they mused over how different they were. Still, it surprised him that they were no longer close. It was strange, as Zenar said, that Assock chose to ignore their friendship. The Sapien's presence was affecting them all oddly.

Zenar's precaution was so unexpected it had put Lank on guard. Ordinarily he would have been flattered to be taken into his confidence. But he sensed that Zenar was testing him, pretending concern for John when it was something else he was after. He figured it had to do with Zenar's experiments, and the flap about Assock was a ruse.

When Esop arrived, Lank ushered him to a chair, thanking him for coming over so quickly. "Nothing urgent," he said, mopping his brow, fumbling for words to begin, not sure he should. Cautiously, he recounted the conversation with Zenar, watching Esop's face closely for reactions, noting none, and ending with the disclaimer that he was probably exaggerating its importance.

Esop listened patiently, observing Lank's discomfort. "Was there anything unusual in the laboratory?" he asked.

Lank shook his head.

"How did the Sapien react?"

"More like a bystander…he didn't say much."

"What were you afraid of?"

"I don't know…it was what Zenar said about Assock. No, it was more than that—his secretiveness and his resentment over restrictions."

Esop reassured him, "You mustn't take Zenar too literally. He keeps me informed." Esop was not about to admit that the biologist had not spoken to him about his work for weeks, even though he was obligated to report to him. It would not stand him well to have it known that Zenar disregarded his surveillance.

"There's something else," Lank recalled. "Zenar's been browsing around the neonatal intensive care unit. He borrowed a cryogenic tank?"

"Hmmm—did he say for what?"

"No. I assumed for freezing tissues. Didn't he mention it to you?"

"He's kept pretty much to himself. We talked over lunch the other day—nothing about cryogenics. I'll ask him about it."

Lank fidgeted, clasping and unclasping his hands. "I'd rather you don't," he said. "He talked to me in confidence. I…I had to tell you."

"You did right. Now leave it to me."

Lank's shoulders sagged in relief. He could rely on Esop. He regretted breaching Zenar's confidence. However, rules had to be followed and he had to protect himself. He didn't want to get Zenar in trouble, but if everyone went about on his own, how could order be maintained?

"What about Assock, shouldn't he be told?" Lank suggested hesitantly.

"What do you think?" Esop extended the leash and watched Lank squirm some more. Lank was such a ninny, almost always a fatuous smile on his immature face, the faith of a child, never really acting on his own. Making such a fuss over something clearly beyond his responsibility. Violating a confidence that hardly warranted a second thought...or did it? Why Zenar should have gone behind his back was a nagging question he must have answered.

A buzzer sounded on Lank's desk, rescuing him from a reply. He pushed the button and a voice announced that Dr. Altern was at the reception desk asking to see him.

Lank looked at Esop.

"Send him up," Esop answered for him.

"I didn't expect to see you here," John said to Esop as he entered the office, nor was it a pleasant surprise. He wanted to talk to Lank alone. Esop's presence could only mean that Lank had already broken Zenar's confidence.

"What can we do for you?" Lank said stiffly, with a forced smile.

"It's time I got to work," John replied, trying to sound matter of fact. Zenar had convinced him that he should help with the Horde infant, and Lank had been encouraging when he had mentioned some time ago that he wanted to get back to work. Perhaps Lank would let him start in neonatal care, where he might be able to pick up the knowledge and experience that Zenar so desperately needed to keep the infant alive.

Lank beamed, now genuinely. "I would be delighted to have you." He looked to Esop for confirmation.

Esop concurred, though not without suspicion. Surmising that John had come straight from Zenar's lab, he sensed a connection. He knew John's main interests were in adult medicine, not babies. Why would he ask to start with newborns? They had talked before about his working at one of the medical centers but never at the Natoleum. It had to do with Zenar.

He said to John, "I understand you visited Zenar at his lab this morning."

"Yeah," John affirmed nonchalantly. "He showed me around —very interesting. Made me itch to get back to work."

Esop marveled at his reserve, and liked him even more for keeping Zenar's trust. "I understand Zenar talked to you about Assock's experiment. You don't seem much concerned."

John stared at Lank, contempt in his eyes even as he was relieved that Esop now knew of Zenar's apprehension. His throat was tight as he tried to reply casually.

"Of course, I am concerned. It would help if you could tell me more."

"We're as much in the dark as you," Esop answered, "but I assure you whatever Assock has in mind, it can't be as bad as Zenar made out. We are civilized, you know."

Are you really, all of you? raced through John's mind. The smell of paranoia permeating Zenar's laboratory still clung to him and he found it in the eyes of Lank and Esop, in their quick glances at each other.

"I have to rely on you," he said mainly to Esop. "I understand Assock's position. He thinks I am genetically disadvantaged, incapable of adapting to your ways. He can believe what he wants, but he's wrong. I hope he'll change. Regardless, I'm here. I don't want to be a parasite. I want to work. Maybe when he sees that I'm not a monster, he'll change his mind."

"I'm sure he will," Esop reassured him, then shifted back to John's choice of work, probing, "Why do you want to begin in Division I? I didn't think you were interested in pediatrics."

"I'm a family practitioner, and that includes children," he explained, although he was actually an internist specializing in adult diseases.

"Wouldn't it be better to start at a medical center, where there'd be patients of all ages?" Esop knew the difference between a family practitioner and an internist.

"Perhaps," John conceded, not wanting to appear overly eager. "It just seemed knowing Lank, it would be easier for me here."

"Very well," Esop agreed, still suspicious of his choice. "Lank will arrange it." He got up and shook John's hand. "If you'll excuse me, I have to get back to my office."

Lank expressed his pleasure at John's decision and asked him when he wanted to begin.

"What did you say to Esop?" was John's curt reply.

Lank was taken aback. "I don't see that's your concern."

"Not my concern?" John exclaimed. "Zenar scares the hell out of me with talk of Assock's experiment. He asks you to keep the conversation confidential and you blabbermouth it all to Esop."

"I...I'm sorry," Lank stammered. "You don't understand. Zenar, he's wrong. He should have spoken to Esop."

John apologized for his outburst. He realized Lank was, as he put it, just a doctor. He had known these kinds of doctors all his life. Gutless sycophants, medical dictionaries for minds. It wasn't Lank's fault if that was all he was. He suggested he start to work next day.

"Good. I'll be here." Lank was outwardly gracious, inwardly bristling at John's reprimand. Who did this Homo Sapien think he was? He wiped the moisture from his palms on the sides of his pants and walked with John to the reception area where they parted.

Vinya was at the pool. John was eager to tell her about his decision to begin work but he decided against mentioning his meeting with Zenar or the reason he chose the Natoleum. They went for a brief swim and snacked in their special enclosure from a picnic basket Vinya had brought along.

John talked a great deal about himself now. Vinya was an eager listener. He told her of his life at home, his boyhood, what he did and how he felt when he was her age. What surprised him as he grew older was that his emotions—especially how he felt about himself—seemed to have reached a plateau, so that he always thought of himself as an overgrown adolescent.

"I guess that's why you seem so young," Vinya offered as a compliment.

If only it was so, John thought, but he was not about to contradict her. She might think less well of him if he revealed all his thoughts and feelings. He had learned long ago that total honesty, total revelation about oneself, could be not only self-defeating but also be very painful and cruel to others.

His mind wandered back to his wife and how he repressed his dissatisfactions for fear of hurting her. It wasn't her fault that marriage circumscribed his life and curtailed his freedom to experiment, even to be irresponsible. He wondered if the occasional lapse, like his affair with Ina, was not only self-indulgence but also his protest against the conventional harness, or perhaps also a denial of aging by proving he was still attractive to a younger woman. He preferred to think of it as the simple pleasure of recreational sex.

Even then it could never be as it was before he was married. The affair was marred by the anxiety of exposure. It lacked the spontaneity and the excitement of a boy in the blush of discovery. It had to be secretive, and always in the back of his mind was disloyalty to Mary. It didn't matter that she had not known and now would never know. He carried the violation of her trust within him, including the fault of survival. He was like all survivors harboring guilt while irrepressibly grateful for their good fortune.

More to the point, Ina and Mary were gone and he was now with Vinya. He was angered that they had to hide behind bushes during the day. He was growing increasingly impatient with their furtive visits at night. He wanted them to be together openly, honestly. He wanted her to move in with him.

Vinya was equally impatient but begged John not to push too hard. "I can't stay all night, not just yet. You know that." Then she suggested half-heartedly, "Maybe I shouldn't come at all?"

"Is that what you want?"

"You know it isn't."

"Then why don't we just tell Assock it's none of his damned business."

"It's not that simple."

"It is simple. He introduced us. How can he then say we can't see each other? He doesn't control us. I mean, really—"

"He only said we can't live together, that's all."

"It shouldn't matter what he says. My lord, he's not God." John paused and then confessed, "What worries me is that you'll meet someone your own age, one of your own people. Maybe I'm selfish. Perhaps I'm asking too much, but when you say you love me, you have no idea what that means to me. When they first found me, all I could think of was going back. I couldn't accept that I had lost my family—everything. It wasn't until I met you that I began to think maybe I can pick up the pieces and go on. I don't want to, I can't forget my past, but being with you is my dream, my hope that I can have a life again."

"Oh, I can't mean that much to you."

"You do, really you do. You speak of being frightened. You don't know what it's like being completely alone, so totally apart from everyone and everything. It's worse than being dead. You have that overwhelming sense of wrong, of everything gone wrong, of something dreadful hanging over your head about to fall, and then you wish it would fall and be done with.

"It's not just the loneliness but the feeling that somehow you're to blame, that you might have done something different even though you know there was nothing you could have done to prevent it. And then to find someone to give you hope, to push back that loneliness, to give meaning back to your life." He exhaled audibly, "I don't expect—you couldn't possibly feel the same."

She leaned against him and ran her fingers through his hair. "Whether it's the same or not, I'm happy with you. I don't want it to end—never."

"Nor do I." He looked longingly at her, as if they were already forced apart. She was so beautiful, so vulnerable. Then he said, as if to challenge her, "You'll forget me."

Tears welled in her protesting eyes.

He wrapped his arms around her. "The hell with Assock," he said. "Stay with me tonight… all night…every night."

"I will," she whispered and kissed him and promised to come to him after dark.

His gaze lingered after her as she disappeared through the trees, calling back to him, "I will...I will."

When he left Lank at the Natoleum, Esop decided to call on Zenar without delay.

"It didn't take Lank long," Zenar grumbled as he led Esop down the passageway to the underground laboratory. *Just passing by, hah.*

He observed Esop's casual perusal of the lab and described a new mechanism he was developing to intensify the heat exchange in the thaw chamber. Esop noted the external dimension of the chamber was nearly twice the size of the old one.

"Didn't I tell you?" Zenar said innocently.

"No." Esop was in no mood for games.

Zenar chuckled and draped an arm around Esop's shoulder.

Esop pulled away, plainly annoyed. "There's a lot you haven't told me," he said.

Zenar turned serious. "Look, old man, I'm worried about Assock. I've been meaning to talk to you."

He followed Esop around the room. They stopped before the thermal door.

"What's in here?" Esop tried the handle. It held fast.

"Cold storage."

"Why is it locked?"

"To keep the cold in," Zenar answered flippantly, then seriously, "and to keep my assistants out. It takes too damned long to get the temperature back down again when the door's been opened." He fumbled for his keys. "Want to go in?"

"Maybe later. What about Assock?"

"That's what I want to ask you. Assock doesn't talk to me." Zenar sighed inwardly, wondering what he would have done if Esop had called his bluff.

"To me neither," Esop confided. "Maybe we should talk to him instead of whispering behind his back and conjuring up hideous experiments. It might put a stop to all this nonsense."

Esop was finding it hard to concentrate. What the devil was behind that door? It was locked to keep him out, not assistants whom he knew Zenar had dismissed weeks ago. As curious as he was, he sensed Zenar's anxiety and decided not to challenge him, not just yet. He wanted to give Zenar a chance to be forthright. He would get to see inside the chamber soon enough.

Taking Zenar by the arm, he said, "Let's go now. We'll pick up Lank on the way."

Esop guided the mobench to Assock's dome. Lank had at first refused to join them, protesting that he was too busy and, besides, he didn't want to be involved. Esop pointed out that whether he liked it or not, he was involved. Lank acquiesced, hiding his anxiety and guilt behind a smiling facade, unable to look directly at Zenar whose expression roundly condemned him for breaching his confidence.

Assock welcomed his colleagues, effusing self-assurance and taking pleasure in their unease. To relieve the tension he offered snacks—crackers, cheese, raw vegetables and a decanter of apricot nectar—and small talk about how busy they all were, and how little they had seen of each other recently, and wasn't it a grand spring, and—

"The weather's fine," Esop cut in curtly. "It's you we've come to talk about." He sipped the nectar, peering over the rim of the glass directly into Assock's eyes. "We want to know what you're up to."

"Sit down, relax." Assock motioned to the chairs and sofa in the living room. Esop and Lank sat on the sofa, Zenar on the floor, cross-legged with his back against the wall. Assock chose a side chair facing the three of them.

"Well?" Esop said.

Zenar gave words to the question. "What are you planning with the Sapien?"

"Ah, that's what this is all about," Assock mocked. "What makes you think—"

"It's what you think...what you're planning." Accusation was in Zenar's voice.

"What makes you think I'm planning anything?" Assock would like to have added, "Zenar, my friend, soon...soon you will know."

"That's why we're here—your experiment."

"What experiment?" Assock parlayed back.

Esop reached for the decanter but Assock, acting the good host, intercepted him and refilled all the glasses.

"Please, Assock," Esop said, "enough of this parrying."

"Well then, get to the point," Assock countered sharply.

Esop began, "Ever since we discovered the Sapien you've been contradictory, obscure, at times hostile, and you virtually ignore us. You've been very unsettling to John and Vinya, as well as to us. We agreed—"

"We agreed," Assock abruptly interrupted, "that we had an unprecedented opportunity, as well as an obligation, to study the difference between us and Homo Sapiens. We also agreed to allow the Sapien the freedom to move about, although I questioned if it was safe to let him roam without constraint. At your insistence, I set aside my skepticism. I introduced him to Vinya so he could have sexual companionship. I didn't object when you found him a dome at the beach." He paused, his head moving side to side, then threw up his hands and said with displeasure, "I gave in too easily."

"He's getting along fine," Lank cut in. "I admit I haven't been around much. I've been so busy. But I've stopped in now and then to see him, and he seems fine, just fine."

"Yes, Lank, you have been too busy," Assock said blandly, and added not so blandly, "You're always too damned busy."

Lank reddened but words failed him.

Assock accused them all of superficiality. That was his stock in trade when others differed with him.

"What are you getting at," Zenar growled, as he sprawled lengthwise on the carpet, propped up on an elbow.

Assock drew a deep breath. "We're supposed to look beneath the surface for deeper insight and understanding" he said, "not just at what takes place before our eyes. We're supposed to be objective, yet I must say that you have allowed your subjectivity to blur your vision. Instead of remembering what he is and how he came here, you project your own vision on him, seeing in him what you would like to see, closing your eyes to what you don't want to see."

"It seems to me you're doing a little projecting yourself," Zenar prodded.

"That is exactly what I mean," scoffed Assock. "I haven't forgotten his origins. I haven't projected my own sexuality onto him, vicariously enjoying his relationship with Vinya as though it was an innocent Human affair? I warned you—we're not dealing with an emotionally stable Human."

"I beg to differ," Esop said, shaking his head. "I've spent more time with him lately. You're exaggerating his responses. He's really quite reasonable."

"Ah, yes," Assock breathed deeply.

"He's an individual. He warrants respect," Zenar asserted, clearly annoyed with Assock's haughtiness

"Aye, I respect his individuality." Assock continued slowly, "Indeed, I fear it. It is his individuality, his uniqueness—his Sapienism—that I fear. You should fear him also.

"Let me remind you, if we were in his time, before the Cataclysm, observing the way people lived and worked and loved, would we not say what you are saying now about this Sapien? On the surface they seemed like reasonably intelligent people. They loved their children, took care of their families, acted decently towards one another. They were against evil, for good. Yet all about them was disease and poverty and war and they just stood by and let it happen…and happen…and happen… until it all blew up. You or I, would not we have run out in the streets screaming *Stop! Enough! No More!*"

"Would it have made any difference?" Esop reasoned, wondering if he would have had the courage to dissent openly, blatantly. "Would anyone have listened? As individuals, they could do nothing."

"They called themselves individuals, but you could scarcely tell them apart," Assock said, "In fact, they were just part of the herd. Assume our Sapien was not insensitive to this debacle—what good was his sensitivity? Perhaps it made him feel a bit superior. 'Yes,' he says to himself, 'it's inane, they're all insane, but what can I do? I'm only one person without power, without influence.' So our friend absolves himself and goes on about his business with all its perks and privileges and his obscene indulgences as though in a dream world. And if the less privileged, if the have-nots tried to take away the smallest part of what he had, there was the power of the State—the police, the judiciary, the military—to put them down, if need be to kill them."

Assock's complexion turned beet red, reflecting his anger. He challenged them in deep guttural tones. "This relic, this Sapien, this beast—you would him let roam free?" He wiped the sweat from his brow. "You see him as a reasonable person trying to adjust to a new environment and ignore the innate biocidal misanthrope lurking beneath the surface."

Zenar disagreed vehemently. "We're not idiots. You speak as though we know nothing. We're not assuming the Sapien is suddenly Human. But if we've learned one thing, it's that a healthy environment can modify destructive tendencies. This is what we have been putting to test." Esop and Lank nodded in agreement.

Assock's demeanor changed. Now he seemed more himself, calm and professorial. He contradicted Zenar calmly. "You have not put it to test. That is where you are mistaken."

"I remember when I wanted to test him," Zenar lamented at his missed opportunity.

Assock scoffed, "I remember, too. You wanted to freeze him again. Really, Zenar, he may be a Homo Sapien but he's not a guinea pig."

"What's your point?" Esop interjected, trying to bring the conversation back to a rational level.

Assock removed his glasses and pinched the bridge of his nose. "Let him have a little more rope. His possessiveness towards Vinya is developing very nicely. It's infecting her, too."

"We didn't think it would go this far," Zenar said.

"You mean *you* didn't. I had no illusions. It has been exactly as I thought it would be."

"Despite your interference?"

"No—because of it." Assock shook his head from side to side. "I don't understand how you all can be so naïve. Do you think this is a game?"

"I'm not sure." There was an accusatory note in Zenar's reply. "However we intended it, we've got to think of Vinya."

"Yes," Lank chimed in. "We've got to think of her. She must not be hurt."

Assock dismissed their concern. "She understands…she will survive."

Then, as suddenly as before, Assock's demeanor hardened, as though he had become another person. "It'll take its course. The Sapien will be true to character. This great love," he sneered, "will wither."

"And you'll help it." Esop said pointedly.

Assock's false laugh grated on their ears. He gazed at the floor and his words came out slowly. "The Sapien needs no help from me. He'll follow the dictates of his genes."

"That's all you're going to do—just watch what happens? No testing, no interference?" Esop pressed.

Assock deflected the question. "Let nature take its course. Maybe I'll be proved wrong."

They hoped he would.

As they rode back on the mobench, Zenar spoke bitterly and skeptically. "I don't believe a word he said. He stonewalled us. He's hiding from us. Historical objectivity—historical bullshit! Damn it, Esop. You let him off too easily."

Esop shrugged. What could he do? That's a cop out, he admitted to himself. Assock intimidated them all. He was afraid to challenge him just as he had been afraid to challenge Zenar in his lab. *What the devil does Zenar have in that room?* What more could he have said to Assock? Call him a liar? Insist on the truth? About what? Weren't they all playing a waiting game? What Assock said seemed reasonable enough. He had no grounds to doubt him, even as he did.

They separated at the Natoleum, agreeing to keep closely in touch and to report anything unusual.

It had been an altogether frustrating afternoon.

CHAPTER 12

Vinya entered Assock's dome warily. As Assock ushered her in, she saw they were alone. She had expected others would be there, perhaps Zenar and Esop. She wished it was daytime instead of night, and that they were meeting in some public place like a restaurant. The dimly lit room did nothing to lessen her apprehension.

"Thanks for coming," Assock welcomed her.

"You asked me to," she answered stiffly.

"Do you do everything I ask?"

"I try to," she replied, repressing the anxiety she felt welling within.

"You look very pretty tonight," Assock said, squeezing her hand.

She pulled away from him.

"Can I get you something—a little wine?" He poured from a bottle that had already been uncorked and placed in a ceramic cooler on the coffee table. Burning logs crackled in the fireplace. Assock motioned for Vinya to sit on the sofa.

"It's so dark," she said.

"You have to forgive me. I'm photophobic. Besides, I look better in this light."

Was he kidding? Why should he care how he looked to her? She wished this night, which had just begun, was over. She sipped her wine and half-emptied the glass before she realized it.

Assock refilled her glass and sat down beside her, sighing like an old man relieved of the burden on his feet. "How's your friend?" he asked blandly.

"Which one?"

He laughed. "C'mon."

"He's okay. We see each other during the day."

"And at night?"

"You told me not to," she answered evasively. He could think what he wanted. He probably knew, but she was not going to admit more than she had to. She felt his stare and avoided looking at him. She had hoped they could have a good talk, but the moment she entered the dark room and saw the fire and the wine and that they were alone, her whole body tensed, as she perceived beyond disbelief what was happening.

"How have you been feeling?" Assock jostled her thigh as if to direct the question between her legs.

Her skin recoiled at his touch. "Why did you ask me here?" Talking was always a good defense.

"Isn't that rather obvious?"

He couldn't mean it, not with her, especially now when she was in love. She must have misunderstood. But his hand returned to her thigh. She stirred to move away but it tightened ever so slightly, holding her still. She pretended to ignore it, even as the sight of his pudgy hand on her leg made her feel slightly nauseous.

"Assock, please...aren't we going to talk?"

"We've talked enough." He released his hold and leaned forward for the wine.

"I don't want any more," she said, but took it nonetheless, thinking that if she sipped slowly, Assock would drink a lot more, and get drunk, and leave her alone. Why was he doing this to her? Assock had never once touched her, not this way. Why should he? He was her teacher, her friend. Surely he didn't want her that way? She could hardly think the word. His hand returned to her leg and she stared disbelieving as the fingers wandered upward like a crab's legs, making her flesh crawl.

"Assock, please…," she repeated, sipping nervously, not wanting to drink, not knowing what to do. It was her third glass, more than she was accustomed to, but it was not the alcohol that numbed her.

"Please don't," she protested as the fingers crawled to the buttons on her blouse and one by one picked them open. "I don't want to—"

He reached inside and cupped her small breast in the palm of his hand. Her head began to swirl and a dull paralysis crept over her body, as though she was being bound by threads in a spider's web.

He slid his other arm around her waist, pulling her towards him, feeling no sensuality, only a cold determination.

"Let go…don't hold back…." His voice was thick, coarse. He felt the tautness of her body as he removed her blouse, then knelt before her and slipped off her pants. Her legs reflexively clamped together but he forced them apart and buried his head between her thighs.

She came out of her torpor abruptly. "No—don't—I won't," she screamed at him, pushing at his head with both hands. It was too late. His arms were wrapped around her and his tongue plunged to its length. She writhed and tried to pull away but he held her firmly, moving his tongue in and out until her juices flowed into his mouth and she fell back in submission, hips involuntarily gyrating to his rhythm as her body succumbed to its own sensuality.

He let go of her and then undressed himself. Shifting her lengthwise on the sofa, he lay down beside her, taking her hand and curling it around his still limp shaft. "Rub it," he commanded and she obeyed as if in a trance. Slowly it took form and when it was fully shaped he commanded her to kiss it.

Her head shook and her eyes and lips closed tightly.

"Do it," he commanded once more, pulling her around and forcing her down on him, holding her head in both hands, pushing between her lips, into her mouth, gradually releasing his hold as she succumbed.

Her mouth was empty of sensation, as numb as her mind. She felt no will of her own, enslaved by his. *I hate you*, screamed in her brain, *...come...please come and let me go.* She had no desire but to earn her release.

His eyes clamped closed as he sought sensuous thoughts to overcome the passionless mechanics. He reached out and rubbed her back and let his hands slide down to her narrow waist and up to her breasts, circling the small mounds, squeezing them gently. *Oh Evol...Evol*, he murmured beneath his breath and he thought only of her and he remembered them together and he felt her skin and her mouth and he came in convulsive jerks and a surging flood of semen. "Enough, Atir, enough."

Her throat constricted tight and burned against the backflow of sour acid and rejected scum as her stomach convulsed to purge itself. She wiped her mouth with the back of her hand and fell back on the sofa. A trickle of semen rolled down between her breasts and her palm recoiled as she smeared it off. Her eyes began to focus but could not bear to look at Assock. Her hand trembled as she reached for the wine glass and brought it to her lips, drinking to wash away the salty film and tinge of vomit that covered her tongue and throat.

Assock stirred, raised up, and looked down upon her. The light from the fire fluttered on her body and her face reflected the anguish in her heart. She was so young, so beautiful, so distraught. He smoothed the creases on her forehead with both thumbs. Her eyes closed and she lay motionless. He caressed her body gently, feeling the shape of her legs and knees, her smooth, flat abdomen, the curve of her hips. He kissed her breasts, her chin, her mouth. His fingers traced around her mound, spreading lips and delving in-between for the special spot that moistened to his touch and made her move against her wishes. He rolled on top and entered her, sliding in and out, each thrust driving deeper, stronger, forcing her hips to meet his, her arms thrashing helplessly from side to side, grunting in her ear, "You disobeyed me." He dug his fingers into her buttocks as she convulsed against his orgasm.

She began to cry, at first in her heart, then in her chest and eyes. Sobbing softly, she got up slowly, dazed and trembling.

He helped her dress and smoothed her hair and sent her home.

The moment she was gone he started to shake all over. His hands tore at his hair and he sank to his knees before the fire. His arms crossed his chest and held tightly to his shoulders, swaying like a mourner as a low moan shuddered through his chest and broke into uncontrollable sobs of grief. *Oh god, what have I done?* He grasped his hands and pressed them to his forehead, rocking back and forth in the agony of his torment.

She was so deeply ashamed. Her resistance against his determination had been so weak. She had succumbed to him like a puppet on a string, even as she despised his fat ugly body. He commanded her and she obeyed like a slave. She was powerless, overwhelmed by his power, humiliated by perceived punishment. What right did he have to punish her? She loathed him. She hated him. If he touched her again, she would kill him—she swore she would. Her knees buckled in the shower and she nearly fainted as she recalled his orgasm surging through her loins. She caught herself and, standing with legs apart, tried to scrub away the memory of his wretched touch.

The shame was unrelenting, burning through her cheeks, intensifying the lingering numbness of the wine. She stumbled out of the shower, dried herself carelessly and wrapped a towel around her wet hair, grateful that the mirror was clouded with steam. She crawled into bed, wishing she was drunk, that she had the excuse of intoxication. But her mind told her that the force that gripped her was not intoxication, but rather the incomprehensible power of Assock.

From the first moment she had met him, she knew that he dominated her, that his will was hers. Always he had made it seem voluntary, explaining what he wanted in such a gentle way that his wish became her choice freely chosen. He made her feel secure and she luxuriated in that special tenderness, which she alone seemed to draw from him. Then he began to change. His wishes became orders. He told her to see John, not to see him, when to see him, how long to see him.

She began to resent Assock, to be reserved, even devious in her recounting of John's responses, which he demanded she describe in clinical detail. But she never dreamed he would force himself on her. Never in her wildest thoughts. It was so...terrible.

Maybe it was all a dream this night, a nightmare. Oh how she wished it was. How could she love John and not have fought harder? Could she really blame it all on Assock? Could she not have broken free, walked out, run away? No, she told herself. Assock had forced her. He had held her. She was powerless in his hold. It was as if there was a special history between them that made her bend to his will. But John was real and she loved him. In violating her, Assock had violated him, too.

The thought forced itself on her that she loved John because Assock told her to. That could not be true. John was so sweet and gentle. He would never be cruel to her. He would have protected her. She wanted to cry out to him, *I love you, John, truly I do. Oh John, I need you so.* She closed her eyes and tried to see him. But Assock's image intruded and his face was dark and clouded. Then she felt his hands on her head, and his penis in her mouth, and his sperm squirting down her throat, and her stomach convulsed again and again, and she gasped at the recall of his words, *Enough, Atir, enough.*

She woke up with a terrible headache. When she tried to stand, a sharp pain shot through her temple behind her eyes, which smarted in the light. Her forehead was moist and clammy. She felt weak all over and sick to her stomach. She fell back on the bed, thankful for having a hangover. She had been drunk after all. Then it hadn't been all her fault. She could blame the wine and she resolved never to drink again. She pulled the blanket up to her chin and snuggled in the warmth of the bed.

No school for her today. She just wanted to lie quietly. What had she done that was so terribly wrong? Absolutely nothing. It was no crime to have stayed with John at night, all night. Oh, how she loathed Assock. She would never forgive him. She would never stop hating him.

It was not Human to bear such hatred. It went against everything she had been taught. He had no right to make her feel guilty, and to force upon her the vilest punishment. Never in her life had she heard of such a thing. Why should she be punished for going to bed with John when that was what he told her to do? It was crazy. She cringed at Assock's lingering presence, not wanting to remember—*Atir*—a shiver crept up her spine as the name rebounded in her brain. It was a mistake, a slip of the tongue. Surely, but she could not dismiss it. *Atir, I know you, but who are you?* She tried to think where she had heard it before. She knew no one of that name—no one.

It was nearly noon before she could stand. The headache was mostly gone unless she moved too quickly, when her brain felt like peas in a pod rattling inside her skull. John would be waiting for her at the pool. She was hesitant to meet him, more fearful of any change he might note in her than of Assock's intimidation. In some way, what Assock did moved her closer to John, as though she was more on his side than ever before. On his side? Against whom? Assock? Her own people? Well, if she had to make a choice, she now knew what it would be.

She saw him from a distance as she approached the pool. He waved and started to walk towards her. Her heart raced as she ran to meet him, flinging herself in his arms, hugging him, burying her face against his chest. *My darling, my love*, she cried silently as tears filled her eyes and flowed down her cheeks.

"What is it? What's wrong?" John implored.

"I'm so glad to see you," she said, wiping at the tears with her hand.

"I was worried. I expected you last night."

"I couldn't come. I should have called."

"That's all right. You're here now." John looked at her more closely. Her eyes were bloodshot and darkly ringed, and there was little color in her face.

"Are you sure you're all right—nothing happened?"

"I'm okay. I was sick, but I'm okay now, really I am. I just want to be with you." More tears rolled down her cheeks. "I don't know why I'm crying...I'm so happy now."

But she wasn't happy. She was miserable in her shame, and in the fear that if John found out, he would no longer want her.

John knew something was amiss last night when he tried to call her and there was no answer. He had walked over to the dormitory and waited for her outside until the pain of her absence became unbearable. Then he returned to his dome, angry and jealous of whomever it was she was with. He tossed and turned throughout the night, fearing she would not be there today. He had come early, waiting for over an hour, checking and re-checking the time, barely responding to the greetings of others who also frequented the pool and now recognized him as a daily visitor. It would have been unbearable had she not come.

He took her by the hand and started towards their special place where they could be alone. She pulled him in the opposite direction, towards the Natoleum. He barely concealed his disappointment. He had no wish to go to the Natoleum, or to see or be with anyone else. He wanted to take her to the enclosure where they could lie on clover and be as they were before. He wanted her to talk to him, to tell him what had disturbed her so.

"Not now," she said. "I have this feeling...there's something I have to find out. I know it's there. Please, I need you to be with me. I have to go there."

He picked up the tremor in her voice. The cold of her hand chilled him.

At the Natoleum, she went directly to the record room and asked to see her personal file, not a copy but the original. The file clerk looked up, surprised at this unusual request. He called over his supervisor and had Vinya repeat her request.

The supervisor eyed Vinya and John curiously. "Originals are kept in storage. The copy is identical," he said. He was an older man, one of the permanent staff.

Vinya persisted. "I want to see the original just the same."

The supervisor started to say, "I am not permitted—"

Vinya cut him short. "Who is?" she hissed.

"I don't know—this is most unusual."

"Then find out!" she ordered with a flash of anger, the tremor in her voice gone.

The supervisor was startled. Who did this girl think she was? "Wait here," he said curtly and retreated to his office. A few minutes later Lank appeared, smiling broadly at both John and Vinya. The supervisor rejoined them.

"Now, what's this all about, child?" Lank asked.

"I want to see my records—the originals," she answered firmly.

Lank pointed out that there were certain difficulties.

She addressed him formally, "Doctor Lank, it is my right."

"Of course it is, but this is not a good time. We're very busy. Perhaps tomorrow—come back tomorrow."

"No—now," insisted Vinya with a determination that wiped the smile off the good doctor's face. "Now!" she demanded.

Lank shrugged. There really was no reason to deny her, except that it was such an unusual request. No one had ever requested an original file before. Why would Vinya want to see hers? The copy was just as good and instantly available. Clearly she was implying some discrepancy, but that was impossible.

He wondered if perhaps Zenar had spoken to her. Since his conversation with Zenar yesterday, he had been brooding over his refusal to help him. Now he felt he was being drawn into exactly the situation he had been hoping to avoid. He was afraid of—of what? Of helping Vinya? Poor child, what could be so important in her file? He would let her see—and himself.

"Come with me," he motioned to Vinya.

John started to follow. The supervisor blocked his path and ushered him to the waiting room.

Lank led Vinya through a door at the back of the record room, down a long, narrow spiral stairwell into the cavernous labyrinth below. It was filled with ceiling-high steel racks that contained the records of all the children that had been born in the Natoleum. They walked a distance through the narrow corridors of the racks until Lank found the one indexed to Vinya's file number. Thumbing through the folders, he located hers and handed it to her.

She took it gingerly, her heart thumping almost audibly. Her hands began to shake and she had difficulty opening the folder. She turned to the first page. There was the usual birth information, as she recalled on the visit to the Natoleum when John had been shown copies of her record. She remembered her embarrassment and resentment that her permission had not been requested. John also had been ill at ease at—what did he call it—the lack of confidentiality. Since there was nothing to hide, however, it mattered little.

She glanced down the page, beginning to relax. She turned to the second page. It was stuck to the first. She tried to thumb the pages apart. Her heart skipped a beat. The two pages were as one overlaid on the other with an adhesive. Picking at a corner with her fingernail, she gained a hold and slowly peeled back the top page so as not to tear the paper. An artery throbbed in her neck. Her eyes fastened on the first line of the true original. Her face blanched and she shrieked and dropped the folder and ran headlong back towards the stairs, screaming, "No—No!"

Lank stared after her and then at Vinya's folder on the floor, as if a choice was to be made. He reached for the folder and turned to the page that had been concealed. A cold sweat swept over him as the entry pierced his eyes, *Atir, daughter of Evol and Assock....*

She raced up the stairwell, stumbling midway, gashing her shin on the edge of the iron step, feeling no pain but the pain in her heart. She reached the top landing, chest heaving frantically, head spinning dizzily. She almost blacked out and fell backwards but was able to grasp the rail and hold on. Her stomach churned acid. Retching vomitus spewed up her throat and out her mouth and nose, abdominal muscles contorting and doubling her over in agonizing cramps. The heaving passed, enabling her to straighten up. She spit out the remnant foul film clinging to her tongue, but the bitter sour taste lingered. Unsteadily, she dragged herself to the reception area.

John, engrossed in a magazine, did not see her enter until she was standing before him. He raised his eyes and started to smile, his expression turning to dismay as Vinya's distress poured out to him. Her face was streaked with tears, her hair twisted in straggled strands. He dropped the magazine, jumped up and reached out to support her as she wavered on the brink of fainting.

"No—don't touch me," she whispered hoarsely, and then fell forward into the strength and security of his arms. She couldn't, she wouldn't tell him what had happened, not now. Just being with him was enough, she said, pleading for his patience.

He took her back to his dome, washed her face, cleansed the wound on her shin and combed her hair. She was completely passive, accepting his caring, his tenderness, slowly reviving from the shock and the disgust that masked her beauty with inner-felt ugliness.

They walked along the beach in the warmth and brightness of the midday sun. She limped a little from the cut on her leg and accepted his arm around her waist, smiling wanly when he kissed her on the cheek. Later he made a fire in the living room and they snacked on cheese and crackers. She watched in silence as the sun set, shifting her stare to the fireplace when it became dark, avoiding his eyes, which searched hers for explanation. When it was time, he helped her undress and they showered together. She cuddled close to him in bed and let him caress her until she fell asleep.

He lay quietly beside her, staring into space, knowing the most he could give her at the moment was his presence, confident that sooner or later she would tell him, wondering what it was that was so terrible she could not speak of it, grateful she had come with him when she needed him as much as he needed her. She stirred and cried out in her sleep. "It's okay, I am here," he whispered. She was quiet again, except for the sound of deep, disturbed breathing.

His mind spun crazily as it retraced this day, and the past days and weeks, recalling the ice, their strange appearance in what he thought at first was a lunatic asylum, the pain and the terrors of the night, the cold, the interminable cold. He shivered and pressed closer to Vinya's body, careful not to waken her, absorbing her warmth, fearing he was the cause of her distress.

CHAPTER 13

It was not unusual for children of the Seventh Millennium to grow up without knowing the identity of their blood parents, or to find out later when such knowledge was little more than historical curiosity. A child might be disappointed, Esop supposed, as Lank described Vinya's reaction, but it was hardly cause for hysterics—unless something extraordinary happened. He knew she and Assock had become very close and that Assock had been guiding her relationship with John. That had been their agreement, though he had come to doubt its wisdom. Assock's unpredictable behavior was disturbing, but surely he would not intentionally harm an innocent child, surely not his own.

Zenar was equally nonplussed. He had known of the infant and remembered well Assock's attempt to keep her after Evol disappeared. But it was decided that she would best be placed in a Natoleum outside Opalon. Assock had been warned that his extreme possessiveness could not be tolerated. Somehow he must have arranged to have the child returned to Opalon, covering up his parentage with a falsified birth record. To have been so close to her all these years, so close and yet so distant, must have caused him great pain. Zenar's sympathy rekindled the warmth and love for his old friend that had been suppressed during these months of antagonism. No doubt, Assock was under a terrible strain.

Esop was not so charitable. Assock deliberately set up Vinya with the Sapien, using her as a guinea pig. But why her, his daughter? He could have chosen any one of a dozen other young women. And now that she had developed a deep dependency on John, he seemed about to destroy it. It made no sense.

Turning to Lank, Esop said, "John's the best tonic for her now. We have to get to Assock before he does more harm," not knowing what harm had already been done.

They went to Assock's dome, to his office at the University, to the pools he frequented, but he was nowhere to be found. They left word to be contacted when he showed up. If he didn't appear in a day or two, they would put out a public warrant for his location.

Zenar returned to his laboratory. He was really worried about Assock. He had gotten used to the professor's moods, his irritation and hostility alternating with solicitous concern. Sure, he'd get pissed at his friend, but never enough to diminish the depth of his love for him. Something had gone terribly wrong, and he was at a loss to understand if Assock's strangeness, as he preferred to think of it, was cause or effect. Perhaps if he could get to him before the others, perhaps he could help. He tried to put himself in Assock's position. Where would he go if he wanted to be alone?—probably to Nonam's old retreat.

First he had to check on the infant in his lab. He unlocked the iron door and quickly slid inside the refrigerated room. The ice-blue baby lay stiff on the table. He slipped a dropper filled with a viscous nutrient between the thin lips and slowly emptied the contents into its mouth. He checked the heart, which maintained a steady ten-second beat, then brushed off the accumulated frost and massaged the baby's skin from head to toes. It felt like cold parchment. He let himself back out of the room, closing the door behind him.

The sun was dipping beneath the mountain ridge as he strode up the path to Nonam's retreat, stopping before the closed wood plank door. The adobe hut had been kept in good repair by farmers who worked the surrounding fields. He called out to Assock, receiving no answer. He rapped on the door, then slowly pushed it open. The light was failing fast, but there was enough for him to make out Assock sitting cross-legged in the far corner of the hut. He bent over, lowering his head beneath the mantle, and entered. Assock remained immobile. Zenar squatted opposite him on the dirt floor.

After a few moments, a sigh passed through Assock's lips. He straightened his back, raising his eyes to Zenar. They were darkly ringed and liquid. "Welcome back, my friend," he whispered hoarsely.

"I wasn't gone," Zenar replied in a voice lowered to the surrounding dusk. "Are you okay? You look terrible."

Assock cleared his throat and stretched his legs, rubbing at the stiffness in his thighs with the heels of his palms. "It's been a long time since we were here."

Zenar felt Assock reaching out to him, yet he remained distant. He seemed so lost. "We found out about Vinya," he said softly.

"Oh?" was Assock's hesitant response.

"Why did you do it?"

"Do what?"

"Deny her all these years."

"Does she know?"

"That's how we found out." He recounted what Lank had told him.

Assock's face remained impassive, concealing the emotions surging within. So she heard the slip of his tongue. It was unintended, or so he tried to convince himself, knowing that such slips were seldom innocent.

"What went wrong?" Zenar was pleading for Assock's confidence.

"Perhaps you should ask her."

Confused by his friend's aloofness, Zenar tried hard to be sympathetic but Assock was not making it easy. "It must have been difficult—not acknowledging her."

"You will never know," Assock sighed. "I appreciate your concern and I thank you for coming alone." Now he wanted

Zenar to leave. Time was running out. He had to finish. "Did you tell anyone I might be here?"

"Everyone's looking for you. I'll tell them you're not here."

"Zenar, I need one more day—one day, a day and a half. Then we'll talk. I'll explain everything. Make up some excuse. Tell Esop I contacted you, that I'll be back. And stay away from Vinya, please. Will you do this for me?"

Reluctantly, Zenar agreed. He would help his friend although he was not comfortable with Assock's delay.

A ssock resumed the lotus position in the darkness of the adobe hut. He had fasted all day, sipping just enough water to quiet the rumbling of an empty stomach and ease the hunger pains. Long hours passed before he could free his mind of the tormenting guilt. For so long, he had suppressed all feelings for their child—his and Evol's. After he secretively arranged her return to the Natoleum in Opalon, he intended to follow her progress through the succeeding Divisions, knowing he would have to avoid even a hint of a personal connection. But it was too painful. The sight of his child evoked memories of Evol and the loss of the family he had wanted them to be. He discontinued his visits to the Natoleum, and for more than a decade he managed to bury the past and deny the presence of his daughter.

Then one day she appeared at the pool. He had been lounging on the side, soaking up the sun, oblivious to others around him, when someone called out her name. There were other Vinya's, but instinctively he knew it was she. Adrenaline shot into his heart, which jumped and thumped, although outwardly there was no sign of recognition. At the opposite end of the pool. a half-dozen adolescent girls lined up at the diving board. Vinya was one of them. He waited impatiently, guessing wrongly as each took her turn on the board. Then "Vinya" was called out again and his daughter climbed up the ladder to the high board. He watched her all afternoon.

Her visits to the pool were infrequent at first. But as she grew older, she became an avid swimmer. Now he would see her almost every day, occasionally speaking to her, mostly just watching with seeming indifference. Then the disruptive discovery of the Sapien with its unique opportunity to study the past, and his decision to involve her, as though in some odd way it made her once more a part of himself.

His relationship with Vinya developed easily enough. It was natural for her to accept him as her mentor. He encouraged her feelings towards John. At first, he was pleased with her response to the Sapien, but as the days passed and she reported back to him, he became more and more irritable. Her affair with John was turning into his obsession. It had to continue even as he wanted to break it off. By limiting them to afternoons at the pool, he hoped to abort the extreme possessiveness for each other that it had been his intention to develop.

In the beginning he was envious of their affair, which brought to mind his own barren love life. He soon recognized that his envy was transforming to anger, as he sensed Vinya's diminishing dependence on him. He was no longer objectively testing the reactions of the Sapien. He had become emotionally involved, as though this was also a test of himself.

He tried convincing himself the experiment was working exactly as intended, and that his involvement was essential to its success. But the more attached Vinya became to the Sapien, the less she confided in him. She had shifted her allegiance to John, defying his order to stay away from him at night. His anger drove her further away, which is what he had anticipated, though not at the expense of his own rationality.

Beyond anticipation, was it not identification with John that he also wanted? He had allowed himself free reign to experience the emotions of Home Sapiens as though he was one himself. To know anger, to sense the power of manipulation, to feel the urge to punish and, if need be, destroy. That was the Sapiens way, but he was still hesitant. To feel was one thing, to act out on those feelings quite another. He was not sure he could do it.

The visit by his colleagues forced his hand. Esop and Zenar were getting too close. If he waited much longer, they might intervene and take Vinya under their protective wing.

That night—the moment she entered the room—he had begun to panic. He kept telling himself over and over that she was just another young woman, that there was nothing meaningful in their blood tie, that what he was doing was in the interest of science and should not be confused with sentiment. He anticipated her resistance, even her submission, but was totally unprepared for the intensity of his own response. It was as though all the censors of the mind had been lifted and the soul laid bare to satiate its archaic drives. And then the shock—the sudden grief—that gripped and wrenched his soul. He felt such shame and guilt and fear that if she knew, it would scar her for life, even as he felt the scars of Sapienism tearing at his own flesh.

He sought the solace of Nonam's retreat, which retained the aura of the old man's comforting presence. He sensed it in contemplation throughout the day of fasting, but not all he contemplated was reassuring. Though Human, he was flabbergasted by how easily he had succumbed to the emotions of Homo Sapiens. He should not have been surprised. Wasn't that what happened to him long ago when he became obsessed with the possession of his infant child? He should have known then that there was more to Human evolution than a genetic mutation. Still, there was the lingering doubt—no—the hope that he was wrong, that John would prove to them all that Sapienism was not a hopelessly self-destructive contagious disease. The others had been content to let it rest, not to put it to test.

In the quiet of the day and the night that followed, his resolve returned. Pragmatic rationality was not the empty rhetoric of seminarians contemplating their navels. Proof of the pudding was in the eating. Bitter or sweet, he would have his way.

Vinya slept fitfully through the night, tossing and turning, her face buried in the pillow, which muffled an occasional sob that penetrated John's restless sleep. Each time she turned, the mattress rocked gently and their bodies rolled close into the center, only to have her move away to the edge. In the morning he cuddled up against her, but she was rigid and non-responsive, moving away when he became aroused.

He got up and made a pot of coffee, feeling as tired and depressed as when he had gone to sleep. He poured two cups and carried them into the bedroom. Vinya was sitting up, her back cushioned by a pillow against the wall, the cover drawn tightly across her shoulders. He sat on the edge of the bed sipping coffee, waiting for her to say something, anything that would acknowledge his presence.

He waved his hand before her eyes and said lightly, "Hey, remember me?" The water mattress rippled and slurped along with the coffee in their cups. He leaned forward and touched her hand.

She withdrew and awkwardly moved off the mattress into the bathroom, with a limp favoring the injured shin. She emerged a little while later—face washed, hair brushed, fully dressed, looking refreshed.

The hours of the morning dragged on interminably. John made breakfast. They drank more coffee. He suggested they walk along the beach, but she declined because her leg hurt. When he asked her again what happened, tears welled in her eyes, and she did not answer. He tried to be patient, to suppress the gnawing sense of wrong, recalling how it was with Mary when they had fought and could not speak to each other, but remained together anyway out of the mutual dependency of their marriage, each craving the presence of the other, even as it prolonged their pain.

He could stand it no longer. "Damn it," he cried, banging his fist on the table. She cringed at the shock and started to cry. He put an arm around her, then dropped it to his side in frustration at the way she shuddered to his touch.

"I...I can't stay...I better go," she stammered despondently, but made no move to leave.

John pleaded, "You've got to talk to me."

"I can't."

"Is it Assock?"

She barely nodded.

"What happened?"

She managed to whisper through a throat choked with despair, "He's...he's my father."

Her words, distorted and faint, roared to him like a thunderous outburst. He leaned back in the chair, emitting a long sigh, shaking his head in stupefaction. That was what she discovered at the Natoleum. But there had to be more to it. "It's not like he was a real father to you."

"I know," she acknowledged, feeling a little relief in having revealed the smallest part of her burden.

"Parentage means nothing here," he scoffed. "That's what they say.... You didn't know he was your father?"

"Not until yesterday."

"What made you think—"

"Something he said, my name—Atir—I didn't know it then. Later I seemed to remember..."

Even worse was the suspicion she might have known, deep down, all along. She obeyed Assock as though he had a special hold on her. In the beginning, she met John at the pool, had dinner with him, went to bed with him, all at Assock's direction, all in submission to him. Yet, she laughed when Assock suggested she might fall in love with John, but she did— with an intensity as unexpected as it was fulfilling. It was too late when Assock commanded her to slow down, to stop seeing him at night and soon to end the affair. Her submission had turned to defiance.

John knew he should not be angry, but he could not help himself. "So he's your father. What the hell does it matter?"

All of yesterday and all of today she wanted to tell him everything, but each time she tried, her throat tightened until she thought she'd choke. She was so afraid if John knew what Assock had done, if he knew how she had yielded, he would leave her in disgust. She just wanted to be with him, but she could not let him touch her, such was the revulsion for herself. She would not let him be sullied by her shame.

"If you don't talk to me, I can't help," John pleaded.

"It may be worse if I do."

"You have to trust me."

"I want to…I do." She knew she could not hide from him forever. She did not have to tell him everything. But it was so difficult to find the right words and, even more, to force them out. "He…he told me to come to his dome. He said it was an important meeting," her voice trailed away. She bit her upper lip, looking away from him. "When I got there, he was alone." Her fists clenched tightly, baring white knuckles.

John encouraged her to go on.

"He…he…" she turned her face to him, her eyes spread wide like a terrified animal, uttering barely above a whisper, "forced me…to—"

John gasped both question and answer. "He raped you?!"

She wanted to say, "Yes, yes, it was all his doing," but her tongue refused to cede the lie as her head shook sidewise, and she tried to explain in faltering words what she did not herself understand—the shock of Assock's advance, her loss of will, her disbelief that it was happening, the paralysis that prevented her from fleeing. She did not tell him how she succumbed, how her mind snapped in received punishment through the satiation of his body.

John was seething. "I could kill him," he hissed through tight lips.

She reached out to him, placing her hand on his fist, which was clenched like hers before. "You mustn't say that, not even think it."

He pulled away, covering his eyes with both palms, pushing back at his rage. She moved behind him and put her arms around his shoulders. Now it was her turn to plead against withdrawal.

"I didn't want to tell you. I was afraid you would blame me," she said, as if it had not been out and out rape.

John offered that Assock drugged her—he made her drink too much. She could not be blamed. She must not blame herself. If anything, John felt he was to blame. He thought he could defy Assock and have his own way. He had been warned. But instead of protecting Vinya, had he not put her in jeopardy as he indulged himself? His anger turned inward, at himself for not having protected her more, as if he could have done otherwise. She needed him now, as he needed her. He pulled her towards him, cradled her in his arms and carried her to bed, lying down beside her.

Drained of emotions, beyond words and tears, the hours of the afternoon passed slowly as the room darkened into evening.

John roused from a twilight sleep that was filled with floating, unsettling dreams he could not remember. He slipped on sandals and went into the bathroom to wash the remnant film of sleep from his face. He thought a walk to a nearby restaurant for a late dinner would do them good. He passed back through the bedroom, kneeled on the bed, and kissed Vinya on the forehead. She opened her eyes and smiled weakly, saying she felt better and would be ready in a few minutes.

He went into the living room, fumbling in the darkness for the light switch, blinking in the sudden brightness—and then at the apparition of a figure standing before the door. It wore a full-length saffron robe, its hair tied in a topknot pointing skyward like the spire of a temple. John shook his head and blinked again to dispel the image that remained immobile. Before the creature's eyes were Assock's thick-lensed, black-rimmed glasses.

"You!" John uttered, freezing in recognition.

"I have come for Vinya." Assock's voice wavered but was nonetheless commanding.

A chill rippled up John's spine, raising the hairs on the nape of his neck. "Wh…what did you say?"

"I've come for Vinya," Assock repeated in monotone.

"How dare you! How dare you come here?"

Assock shrugged, "It's not your concern."

"I should think it is! Who the hell do you think you are?"

Just then Vinya came into the room. She caught her breath at the sight of Assock, her hand coming up to her mouth to stifle a cry.

John moved beside her. "Get out," he spat at Assock.

The professor raised his right hand in a gesture of peace. He said stiffly, "It's better she come with me."

"The hell you say." John would not be intimidated by Assock, ludicrous in his absurd imitation of a Buddhist priest.

Assock stepped towards them, stopping an arm's length away, a full head shorter than John who tightened his hold on Vinya. "Come with me, child," he said firmly to Vinya, who pressed closer to John.

"No," John answered for her. Assock was no match for him. "After what you've done, do you think I'd let her go with you? What kind of animal are you?"

It was more than a rhetorical retort. How could this man who had seemed so wise and decent, how could he have done such an abominable thing?—and to his own daughter!

Assock was perspiring so heavily that his glasses fogged. He took them off and dried the lenses on the sleeves of the robe that symbolized the rising and the setting of the sun, the time of wakening and of rest. He again ordered Vinya to come with him.

This time she answered, refusing as John had before.

Assock flashed angrily, "He can't have you."

John's cheeks burned. "Can't have her? I've got her!"

Assock laughed in his face. "That's what you think." He shook a finger at John, asserting forcefully, "I will not let you destroy her."

John was astonished. It was as though their roles had been reversed and it was he who had abused Vinya.

He tried to reason with the professor. "What's got into you? After all you've said about—"

"The hell with what I said," Assock snapped. "It's what you do that counts."

"Not what you do?" John flashed back.

"Assock!" Vinya called out to him.

"Keep out of this," Assock warned bluntly.

"But I have a right—"

"Child, you have no rights."

"For god's sake!" John yelled.

"For god's sake—for god's sake," Assock mimicked, then thunderously declared, "This isn't a theocracy! There's no goddamned God here!"

"You're making a good try," John shouted back.

"Don't get smart with me," Assock snarled.

John shook his head back and forth and tried once more to be conciliatory. "Assock, please, I'm not trying to be smart. I'm sorry if it sounded that way. But you make out as if we have no right to—"

"That's right—you have no rights, none at all."

John could not restrain himself. "The hell you say—you don't make the laws here."

Assock looked right through him, his dark face twisting into a malevolent grin. "Don't I?"

"Dammit, you don't. Where's Esop? Zenar?"

Assock brushed them aside and said grimly, "I don't have to argue with you. She must come with me. Do you understand?"

"Yes, I'm beginning to understand," John sneered. "You don't give a damn so long as you have her—you will never touch her again."

Assock's face flushed crimson. He turned angrily towards Vinya. "What did you tell him?"

"Everything!" John spit out.

Assock grinned. "As if you are innocent. You are finished with her?"

"Don't you care what she wants?"

"Not one whit. She wants what I want."

"That's not true," Vinya cried.

"Shut up! You don't have a say in this." Assock might as well have slapped her.

"I won't shut up. I'm staying with John," she said defiantly. Then she added, almost as an afterthought, in a pleading tone, "You can't stop me."

Assock turned on her slowly, his eyes squinting as he growled, "Vinya, if you know what's good for you, you'll keep out of this."

"She stays with me," John stated with finality.

"You'd better let well enough alone," Assock threatened.

"Get out of here," John hissed.

"I'm warning you." Assock was firmly planted in front of them.

Vinya's resistance crumbled in the face of Assock's compelling demand. "It's no use," she said, "I'll go."

It was all she could do to move, but John pulled her back, encircling his arm about her waist.

Assock grabbed at John's elbow.

John turned white. "Take your hand off me."

Assock's grip tightened.

John jerked his arm down, breaking Assock's grasp. As Assock reached for him again, John swung his fist up into his belly.

Assock's mouth dropped open as he gasped for breath. Vinya screamed.

John followed with a right uppercut that sent Assock sprawling back across the room.

Assock struggled to keep his balance.

John pursued him in a rage, unconscious of Vinya clinging to his back, trying to hold him back. He smashed his fists against

Assock's fleshy face until blood spurted from his flattened nose and his eyes rolled in pain.

Vinya tried to get in-between them. She fell aside as Assock clutched at John, closing his arms around his assailant's chest, but there was no strength left.

John shoved hard, throwing Assock back over the divan where he landed with a dull thud, battered and unconscious. John stood over him like a madman, eyes dilated wildly, fists clenched hard, knuckles bruised and bloody. He stared at the broken body lying motionless like a heap of refuse stuffed in an orange sack.

Vinya crouched on the floor where she had fallen, terrified not only by the fight but also the sight of pure hatred and rage distorting John's features. Slowly his fists unclenched, as did the muscles of his arms and body. His shoulders sagged but there was still a glaze to his eyes.

Hesitantly, Vinya stood up, still afraid, caught in the dilemma of Assock's command and her love for John, moving warily towards Assock who lay injured, needing help. She leaned over him and gasped, not so much at the blood pouring from his face as at the contorted expression, as though he was grinning at her. She looked into eyes that were vacant and dull, and her grief turned to anguish.

The fear of John in his crazed rage turned to fear for him. She tugged at his arm and whispered, "Come, quickly."

Her words barely registered as she led the way. Walking in a daze, his mind protested it didn't really happen. It was all a dream.

Vinya guided him to a cluster of dense trees where they could not be seen. He slumped to the ground and closed his eyes. Vinya knelt beside him.

"Are you all right?" she asked softly.

"We shouldn't have left him," he said.

"There wasn't time."

"He needed help. I...I—"

"It wasn't your fault."

"I don't know what happened to me. I couldn't stop."

"I should have gone with him," she said, utterly dejected.

He pressed her hand. "No."

She started to cry.

"We'll go back and explain."

She caught her breath. "We can't go back."

"Why not?"

"You attacked him. He wanted you to attack him, don't you see? Even if he isn't dead, it doesn't matter. If they find us..." her voice broke into a sob, "he'll find us."

"Who?...Who will find us?"

"Jevh."

In hiding there was no refuge. John felt completely lost and trapped. In another place at another time, he might have known where to go, where to hide, where to seek help. Vinya wanted to help. He was thankful for that, but all she offered was the certainty of capture and punishment for a crime he was not guilty of, but had no way of disproving except for her witness. And it was probably true, as Assock said, that she did not count. Now the specter of *Jevh* who haunted him since coming to Opalon.

Vinya could not or would not tell him more, pleading in a tone of foreboding that she had only heard of Jevh. She huddled against him. "You won't be blamed. I'll tell them everything."

"Assock was after me. He baited me."

Vinya shook her head. "It was my fault. I let him use me."

"What do you mean?"

Nothing mattered now. So she told John how Assock had chosen her for him, arranging for them to be together, even suggesting she love him. She followed his instructions at first because she thought it would help, and then because she wanted to.

John turned away, knowing that if he looked at her he would cry.

"I didn't know what love was," she went on, "or if I could love you. After a while I only wanted to be with you. I was in a dream—"

"You can stop dreaming now," John said cruelly.

"John, look at me. I love you."

"Yes, it fits. Assock sets you on me. You get me to trust you, tell you everything so you can report back and round out the *experiment*. Well, I hope he's dead. That would be one satisfaction."

"It wasn't that way. Maybe it started out like that but…but it changed. I fell in love with you." She started to cry again, leaning, clinging to him.

He was so confused, his mind a jumble. He didn't want to doubt her. Impulsively, his fingers stroked her hair, pressing her head gently in the crook of his neck and shoulder, at first renewing her sobbing, then gradually calming and reassuring her. He wanted to protect her, but he knew he could no more protect her than himself. "Maybe it would be better if you go back alone," he said.

"I can't leave you," she protested. "What would you do?"

"I don't know. What can I do? I have no place here."

"We can help each other," she pleaded. "I don't want to leave you."

"You better go."

She shook her head resolutely. "I won't. Even if you make me, I won't go back—I can't. You don't understand."

He did not understand. After all that had been shown him of this great and civilized land, with its touted rational behavior, why should she fear it so? Wouldn't Esop and Zenar help her? Surely they would protect her against Assock, if he was still alive. Moreover, he doubted that Assock would violate him again. *Him*? He meant to say her. But it was him. What Assock had done all along was directed against him. He could see that now. Assock was maliciously bent on destroying him through his rotten experiment. Surely Esop and Zenar would understand.

He recalled Zenar's antagonism towards Assock, his concern over the "experiment," the Horde baby hidden in the secrecy of the laboratory. He remembered Zenar saying that not even the visioscanner could penetrate the walls of the underground structure. If the child could be hidden there, why not him? He might be safe there, at least for a while. And, however remote, it was possible that Zenar might help him.

He tried again to dissuade Vinya from staying with him, convinced she stood a better chance on her own. She insisted he needed her. He really didn't want her to go. Perhaps she was right…if they were after her, too.

Together they made their way through the darkness, skirting the few pedestrians who were still about. They reached the entrance of the laboratory and descended the stone stairs, not knowing if it would be better or worse if Zenar was there. The main lab was empty and cold. Glancing sidewise at the closed iron door, John led Vinya into the warmth of Zenar's interior apartment.

He wondered if he should tell Vinya what lay beyond the iron door. Perhaps later, he thought, although it might be better if she didn't know at all. He went to the sink to wash his hands and was startled by the blood smeared over his fists. His or Assock's, he wondered, surmising it was both as the water cleared the skin, exposing a deep cut over the right middle knuckle. It began to bleed again. He found a roll of tape and wrapped a strip around the injured hand. Then he rummaged through the cabinets and found fresh vegetables, fruits and cheese.

Vinya sat quietly in the swivel chair by Zenar's desk. Her eyes followed John's movements in silent connection to him. She took the plate of snacks he handed her and placed it on the desk. She wasn't hungry but he urged her to eat anyway. She nibbled at the food, her mind unable to focus clearly on where they might eventually go. They could not stay in the lab for long.

John found an open bottle of brandy and insisted she take some. The bronze liquid burned her throat and had the intended effect of sharpening her senses.

John sipped his brandy slowly. "Feeling better?"

She nodded.

He asked if she had been here before and if Zenar had ever mentioned his work.

She shook her head. "Why?"

"Just wondering."

He tried to dismiss the refrigerated room from his mind, but the harder he tried, the more compelling became his need to see it again. He told her he was going to have a look around, closing the apartment door behind him as he reentered the main laboratory, going directly to the oval iron door. He tried the handle, anticipating it would be locked. But it was not. He was so surprised that he dropped the ice-cold handle as though he had grasped a hot poker. For a moment he wished it was locked. He turned the handle again, carefully pushed in the door and stepped over the arc of its opening into the cold ultraviolet light that covered the table on which lay the Horde child, infusing it with an eerie blue aura that shimmered through the coating of frost.

The infant was much as he recalled. Fragile, almost transparent—except that there was no umbilical knot! Brushing away the frost, his hand passed over the smooth belly, palpating for the depression of the navel, feeling for the remnant of the lifeline. There should be some indication, perhaps a scar. He examined the area closely. The skin where the navel should have been was completely smooth. His fingers were stiff with the cold and perhaps too insensitive to feel any irregularities, but his eyesight was sharp. Without an umbilicus, the baby could not have developed naturally. The thought was as chilling as the frost in the room.

He stared at the infant and began to doubt Zenar's story. With all their sophisticated scanning devices it was implausible to believe Hordes could exist without detection. But why should

Zenar have concocted such a cock-and-bull story unless it was to deceive him. If not a Horde, then what?

The question held the answer as he suddenly recalled Zenar's talk of cloning experiments. No, he would not, he could not believe it was a clone of himself. He had not been here long enough. There wasn't that much time, even if they had the technology. Why should he even think of it? Why not? Was anything inconceivable anymore?

The cold was becoming unbearable. He turned to leave. Vinya was standing there in the doorway. He motioned for her to come all the way in. "You may as well get a good look."

She leaned against the table, breathing mist and shivering. "Is it dead?"

"No, but it's barely alive," he replied, staring at the frozen form, fascinated by the thought it might be him, appalled by the grotesque implication, at once wanting it to live, and repressing the impulse to assure it did not.

Back in the warmth of the apartment, he asked Vinya what she knew about cloning. She said she had heard of it but had never been much interested in science. As they were talking, he heard a noise outside the room. Quickly, he turned off the light and opened the door a crack. He saw Esop and Zenar standing in front of the iron door.

"You still insist," Zenar said. He shrugged and slipped the key in the slot. "I'll be damned. I left it unlocked."

A few minutes later they emerged from the refrigerated room. Esop was furious. "How the hell did you expect to get away with it?"

"I thought—"

"You thought—" Esop interrupted, "You didn't think. And you showed it to the Sapien!"

"I told him it was a Horde child."

"That's very funny. He believed you?"

"I made up a pretty good story. Fact is, I needed help. Lank refused. Of course, I didn't tell him what for. I had a hunch I could trust the Sapien and—"

Esop interrupted him again. "How did you grow it so fast?" Flapping his arms, he suggested they get into the warmth of Zenar's office.

John pulled Vinya away from the door, scurrying with her beneath the desk supporting the microcomputer, getting out of sight just as Esop and Zenar entered.

"That's better," Esop sighed, rubbing his cold hands to warm up.

Zenar described how he had cultured the sperm taken from John at the polar cap. During earlier experimentation, he had discovered that the electron microscope occasionally stimulated rapid growth of some single-celled organisms. So he placed the culture containing the Sapien's spermatozoa under the scope and one by one exposed them. One sperm became unusually active. He infused it with estrogen and then implanted the fertilized sperm in the uterus of a fecund rabbit. It grew at triple the expected rate. At the end of a month he removed the embryo from the rabbit and placed it in a container of synthetic amniotic fluid heated to a temperature twice that of the body. Using a micropipette, he was able to feed the fetus orally and to oxygenate the lungs.

The growth was phenomenal. By the end of the second month it appeared nearly full term. That was when the trouble started. It turned blue, cyanotic, as though it was drowning even though he had rigged up artificial respiration through the nostrils. He delivered the baby from the fluid but was unable to stimulate normal breathing. It seemed to be dying. He had no choice but to slow down its vital functions by near freezing and to slowly nurse it along until it could sustain independent life. He thought John, being a doctor, would be able to help, since Lank would not.

"How about a drink?" As Zenar started towards the cabinet, he noticed the bottle of brandy on the table. "That's odd, I don't remember—"

"What?" Esop queried.

"Oh, nothing." He slipped the two glasses beside the bottle into the sink. He noticed the roll of tape on the counter and what appeared to be a drop of blood. Taking two clean glasses, he poured them each a stiff shot.

"Ah, good…thanks," Esop said. "Brilliant, really brilliant but you should have told me."

"How could I?"

"I guess you couldn't. All the same, you know Human cloning is absolutely forbidden."

"But the Sapien is not Human. What if he died? We'd have nothing."

Esop replied irritably, "What do we have now? Let me remind you, Zenar, monozygotic clones are totally without moral capacity. That was well established. Homo Sapien hordes were nothing compared to the band of monozygotes that escaped the island and nearly destroyed our civilization. And they came from us. They were Human clones, but without a mix of male and female genes their destructive instincts were totally uninhibited. You know that. How much worse would a monozygotic Homo Sapien clone be, especially a male? I can't even guess."

"Damn it, Esop," exclaimed Zenar, "why do we have to guess? Why can't we find out? We're scientists, not moralists."

Esop glared at Zenar. "I did not hear that, and I hope I never will again, not from you or any other Human. If you really believe that, you're no better than that clone in there, no better than the Sapien, no better than—" He stopped at the ring of the telephone.

Zenar activated the speaker. The voice was Lank's. "That you, Zenar? Is Esop there? Yes, you'd better both come quickly. The Sapien's dome—something terrible happened." The voice broke off. They looked at each other, gulped the remaining brandy, and left hurriedly.

John and Vinya crawled out from beneath the desk. John's knees crackled as he stood up.

"They found Assock," Vinya said dejectedly, "They'll soon find us."

"What difference does it make?" He matched her gloom.

"Maybe we could get away. The island Esop mentioned, I know where it is. It's deserted." Her voice held a hint of hope.

John shook his head. "They'd find us, even if we got there."

Ignoring his pessimism, she was determined to commandeer an aerobe. It was worth a chance. Anything was better than remaining here. She was taking control. She seemed to have grown older, more mature in just a few hours. Promising to return shortly, she hurried away.

When she was gone, he went back into the refrigerated room. Was this—this thing—really him? Was it, as Esop said, the incarnation of all that is evil in his species, in his genes? Could this small, helpless, innocent creature really develop into a monster with destruction its only pleasure? Would it not also love and love to be loved?

Perhaps not, if it was only the half of him that gave in to Assock's provocation? But there were two parts to him, and more—his father's sperm received by the ovum of his mother, nourished in her womb and at her breasts and in the warmth and tenderness of their home. Could this thing, if it was him, be totally devoid of the good that was them, given to him? He was not a monster, no more so than this ill-begotten progeny. He would not kill. He started to shake, his knees buckled and he cried out, "Oh god, I don't want to hurt anyone."

CHAPTER 14

The hour passed…then two…then three…until he was no longer waiting for her but for them. They would come. And come they did—suddenly—with searing searchlights and the Immobilizer. Paralyzing forces pressed his arms inward, holding him in an invisible vise. He was powerless to speak, with open eyes blinded by the light, and his ears burning hot and ringing, ringing him into unconsciousness.

The cell was damp and dark, except for a thin sliver of light slanting through the small oblong opening near the ceiling. Fetid odors reeked age and decay. He lay on a thin, lumpy mattress crumpled on a slat-wood bed in the corner opposite the window. He could move now, but his muscles ached with tension and the narrow light burned at his pupils. He scanned the room. It was perhaps eight feet by twelve, with a small table and stool in the center and a backless bench on the far side. He raised himself unsteadily, leaning against the wall. His hand passed over the coarse stubble of beard. Two or three day's growth, he reckoned.

At full length, his head was short of the slot window by two feet. He slid the bench over, its legs grating unpleasantly on the concrete floor. With difficulty, he raised himself onto the bench. Now he could see out and down. He was not long in recognizing Opalon stretching towards the mountains and the sea, and the grounds of the University immediately below. His abdomen knotted and his chest constricted painfully. Only one structure was this tall in all of Opalon—the Tower of Rationality!

He let himself down and slumped on the bench, waiting, watching the light beam slide across the room as the hours crept interminably slow. Muffled voices outside broke the silence as the heavy oak door creaked open and then closed behind a short, fat man. He had difficulty recognizing Lank without his perennial smile. The doctor stood in the dim stillness of the cell for a few moments. Then he came forward and placed a gentle hand on John's shoulder. "Are you all right?" There was neither friendship nor hostility in his voice.

"I think so," John mumbled.

Lank took his wrist and felt his pulse. "Stand in the light."

John rose stiffly and stood unsteadily as Lank squinted in his eyes. "What's going on?" he managed to get out.

Lank shook his head. "I can't tell you anything. Strong enough to walk?" John nodded and Lank turned and called to the guard. The door swung open. He motioned for John to follow.

They stepped into the rectangular square of the uppermost floor. A steel ladder led above to the summit of the Tower. A narrow ledge rimmed the edge, surrounded by the open sky.

The guard followed Lank and John down the winding center stairwell. The Tower broadened towards its base, with narrow passageways tunneling from each landing into other cells. Near mid-level they stepped into a narrow hall. Lank ushered John past two doors and stopped before a third. Turning, he stepped around the guard and disappeared down the stairs.

John grasped the handle and slowly pushed the door open. The room had little more light than his cell. Inside was a desk with a chair behind it supporting a small, moldy man.

"Come in—come in," the man motioned testily. "That's right, over here—no, here, not there, here—that's right, that's right."

John felt sick to his stomach. He was nauseous and hungry. His throat was painfully tight and dry. Only with effort and concentration could he keep his knees straight. Even so, he swayed unsteadily as he stood before the little man who impatiently drummed his fingers on the bare desk, scrutinizing John through narrow birdlike eyes.

"You know why you're here," he said, then contradicted himself. "No, I don't suppose you do." His tone was thin, nasal, irritating. He identified himself as the Recording Clerk of the Court.

"Would you mind if I sat down? I don't feel very well." John glanced about for a chair.

The clerk pointed towards a small three-legged stool in the corner. John dragged it before the desk and sat down, lowering himself a head's length beneath the clerk who peered disdainfully down at the Sapien.

The clerk continued, "You've been accused. How do you plead?"

"Accused of what?"

"Of what?" the clerk repeated in surprise. "Surely you know."

"No, I don't know."

"No matter, no matter—I only arrange the papers. Well, come now, your plea, how do you plead?"

At John's silence, the clerk—musing aloud to himself—continued in the manner of the professional bored by his work but mechanically competent. "Guilty—yes, or you wouldn't be here." He scribbled with a thin scratchy pen across the paper on the desk. "Now, what form of guilt?"

Addressing the question to himself, he ignored the Sapien. "Guilt by reason of insanity? No, not very good. If he's crazy, he couldn't tell right from wrong, so I don't suppose he'd be guilty. On the other hand, if he's sane and can tell right from wrong, then he would have to be insane to do wrong. Perhaps he doesn't know what he did. Hmmm, then it would be by reason of ignorance."

He mechanically drummed the desktop in a little area worn to the shape of his fingertips. "Ignorance, with innocence an extenuating circumstance. Hmmm, before and after the fact. Yes, that will do nicely."

The clerk scribbled and repeated aloud to himself, "*Guilty by reason of ignorance and innocence before and after the fact.*" Pleased with himself, the clerk pointed to the Sapien and directed him to sign.

"I don't think I should sign anything," John mumbled numbly.

"Come, come, it's not important, but you must sign. It's procedure. Everyone signs. You do know how to write?" He handed him the pen.

Fatigued beyond resistance, John dragged the pen slowly across the designated line like a drugged convict. The clerk terminated the interview by calling the guard who took the prisoner back up the narrow spiral stairway to his cell.

The sun was down. A slight mist filtered through the open slot. He was given a candle for light, a tray of cold food, and solitude.

The next day—he could not be sure—he was roused early and led by the guard down the stairwell, past mid-level to a large hallway ending in a broad Gothic archway blocked full length by imposing judicial double doors. As he approached, the doors swung apart and he entered a large, austere chamber. The walls of the chamber were bare. Small, narrow, evenly spaced windows high above eye level cast thin shafts of light. Heavy wood ribs arched to the center of the Gothic ceiling. The air was gray and sullen and damp.

He was led to an open box surrounded three-fourths by a waist-level railing. Before the box was a raised judicial bench. Behind the bench loomed a large figure cloaked in a black velvet robe, with a blank white mask blocking its face.

John leaned against the railing…waiting. He felt eyes staring at him through slits in the mask. After a few moments, a muffled voice curled around its edges towards the prisoner. The voice was even, toneless, yet fully commanding.

"By the powers invested in me, I—Jevh—hereby open these proceedings against the Homo Sapien known as John Altern."

There was more condemnation condensed in that toneless voice than in a jury of twelve men rendering a verdict of guilty.

John felt himself sinking further into despair, but the realization that at last he was face to face with the mysterious Jevh stiffened his resolve. His voice quivered but did not break. "Who are you?" he asked, trying to appear calm.

The mask replied, "I just told you."

"I can't see your face."

"Of what importance is that?" the mask queried benignly.

"I have a right to know my accuser and—"

"I am not your accuser," the mask interrupted. "My role is to determine the nature of your guilt. That is all. The size of my nose or the shape of my mouth are of no importance."

"Then why the mask?"

"That is something you must answer for yourself."

"What does it have to do with me?"

"If you do not know, I cannot tell you," the mask replied, not without a little derision.

"Then you won't reveal yourself?"

"Ah, that is another matter. What I am, who I am shall most certainly come out. In a sense, that is the point of this trial. Let me say only this—and let it end the discussion—the essence of a person lies not in his appearance but in what he is. I have an identity, yes, and perhaps you will soon come to recognize it. But we are concerned with your trial, not my appearance. Whether my face is a blank mask or a classic profile is of no consequence."

John listened carefully to the voice as it crept around the mask. There was a familiar ring to it, but it was too muffled to place. He knew this person, knew him well—he was sure of that. But what could he mean by his identity being the point of the trial?

Jevh continued, "Now, let's get on with the business at hand. You are accused—let me see"—he shuffled through some papers—"ah, here it is. Let's see…you are accused of *Adultery, Perversion, Murderous Assault* and *Inconsistency*. Having before me a signed confession, I hereby acknowledge and accept your guilt."

"What? I signed no such thing," John said vehemently. He had found his voice.

Ignoring John's denial, Jevh continued, "In accordance with the laws of the Seventh Millennium, the accused shall have a fair trial, with full opportunity to defend himself, after which he shall receive his just reward."

"Fair trial!" John raised his voice. "You have me guilty already."

"Lower your voice," Jevh remonstrated. "There will be no bellowing in this court. Now, did you not sign this?" Jevh waved the clerk's paper before him. "Was it not a confession of guilt?"

"No, I did not. I mean, I didn't mean to. I was exhausted." He pointed at the clerk who was recording the proceedings. "He said I had to sign, that it wasn't important, that it didn't mean anything."

"We shall see whether it is meaningless or not," Jevh replied. He turned to the clerk, asking if the prisoner had not indeed signed the paper. Without losing a scribble, the clerk nodded affirmatively.

Jevh redirected himself to the forlorn figure in the dock. "We have before us certain facts, to wit, on or about a certain date you engaged in certain activities with a certain Vinya and that these activities were by your own admission adulterous and perverse. And furthermore, that as a result of the aforesaid activities coming to the knowledge of a certain Assock, Professor of Pragmatic Rationality, you thereupon murderously assaulted him. How plead you now, John Altern?"

John swayed in dismay, answering, "I need a lawyer."

The muffled voice laughed and replied that there was no need for a lawyer since they were not here to argue fine points of law, but to determine truth and the appropriate response to it. If the prisoner wished to change his plea to insanity, Jevh offered, there would be no need for a trial. But if he declared himself at the minimum not insane, or perhaps even sane, then he would be assumed competent to stand trial on his own two feet.

John protested he did not know the rules—the law—what he must answer, and what he had best not reply to on grounds of possible self-incrimination.

"Ridiculous," Jevh said. "To refuse a question because the answer would incriminate you would make every refusal an admission of guilt. It would make a mockery of this inquiry. It would make every No a Yes. Hardly the way to ascertain the truth."

"You misunderstood, your—your honor. I didn't say it *would*, I said it *might* incriminate me. If I knew what was behind the question, if it was a legitimate question, you might be right. But it is not fair to make a man convict himself. I must be assumed innocent until proven guilty. I must have the right to remain silent if the way a question is posed and answered would misrepresent me. And I have a right to face my accuser."

"Well said," Jevh said, "just like a lawyer—all those *musts* and *mights* and *rights*—poppycock," he scoffed. "The determination of guilt, not its equivocation, is what concerns us."

"Then I plead innocent."

"That is just the point, my dear sir, You have already pleaded innocence. That is part of your confession." Jevh turned to the clerk. "Let it be so acknowledged that John Altern extends his plea to innocence."

"If you'll excuse me, sir, I said *innocent*, not *innocence*."

Jevh waved the distinction aside for the moment, raising his voice to punctuate the attack. "Did you or did you not sign this confession of guilt by reasons of ignorance and innocence?"

"Yes, but—"

"And did you not in fact have an adulterous relationship with Vinya?"

"No—of course not!" John answered vehemently.

"You mean you did not have an affair with her?" If the mask had an eyebrow, Jevh's tone would have raised it.

"No—I mean—yes, but it was not adultery. How in the world could it be adultery when I am no longer married. My wife—she died in the Cataclysm."

"In your heart, can you really say that in your heart there was not adultery?"

John dropped his gaze from the judge's mask, wondering what in hell was going on here. What sort of justice examined one's heart rather than what happened? Sure, there were times when he felt it was wrong with Vinya, much as if Mary were still alive, absurd as that seemed. It was no different with Ina when Mary was a real presence and his lying and cheating on her had become habitual. Yet, here—now—in the present, did he not still feel a twinge that he had violated their marriage, if only the memory of it?

"The chamber acknowledges adultery," the monotone droned.

John shrugged. "Surely this is not a crime in a society as openly promiscuous as Opalon."

"Would you rather change your plea from innocent to innocence? By admitting adultery you are guilty of the charge and thus cannot be guilty and innocent simultaneously. By the same token, guilt of an action does not by itself constitute a crime. The clerk very properly advised that you plead guilty by reasons of ignorance and innocence, which at least gives you a chance, though I doubt it will withstand close scrutiny."

Jevh glanced appreciatively at the clerk who responded with a smug smirk. He continued, "The chamber will take note that the accused, by acknowledging adultery and confessing thereto, effectively denies his innocence and ignorance both before and after the fact."

The mask nodded in agreement with itself. The voice continued, "To be guilty of something, one need not necessarily have knowledge of it. After all, who among us has never committed an innocent crime?" He surveyed the spectators in the chamber. "I see no raised hands." He turned back to the accused. "Lacking the knowledge would assure your ignorance as well as innocence which are, perforce, one and the same. However, in this case you were very much aware of the nature of adultery and your participation in it. In your heart, you knew it was wrong."

"That's too much!" John objected. "It's not wrong here. It can't be. By your own standards, if you don't have marriage, you can't have adultery."

Jevh pointed a long finger at the figure in the dock and said with obviously glee, "Ha—it is by *your* standards that you shall be judged."

"It's not fair—"

"There is a law in your heart that says, 'Thou shalt not commit Adultery.'"

"Oh my god, this is ridiculous," John exclaimed, completely frustrated.

"Is it now?" Jevh retorted and then intoned, "It is *you* who committed adultery, *you* who are not innocent, *you* whose innocence is denied by your guilt-ridden conscience."

With each *you* he pointed palm up, two fingers outstretched and the voice became deep and resonant and final so that John knew he had been convicted of the first charge, and had to admit that there was some measure of truth to it.

Jevh called to the clerk, "Let us have the first witness."

The clerk jumped up and waved to the guard standing before the doors of the chamber, who then pushed them apart to allow the witness entry.

Lank acknowledged John grimly as he took his place before the judge. His face was drawn, worried. He did not relish his appearance before the court.

"Doctor Lank, tell us what you know of this Sapien," Jevh said.

Lank spoke quietly, without his usual exuberance. "I am a doctor, you know. I can only tell you what I observed as physical fact."

"Yes, yes—" Jevh seemed impatient.

"I was at the crater when he was discovered. I did the initial medical work-up." He clucked his tongue. "I had no idea he would turn out like this."

"Like what?"

"Well, so aggressive—so unHuman." He twisted around and looked at John as though anticipating an attack from the rear. "You see, he gave all appearances, at least to me, of being a rational, considerate creature, and really quite capable of living peacefully among our people. Nothing in his constitution—"

"His what?"

"His body— his internal organs, glands, bones, reflexes—he is physically healthy."

"Okay," Jevh said, trying to speed Lank on, "but what of him as a person?"

Lank shrugged. "I thought he was nice. I was beginning to like him. You know, he had been a doctor…"

Yes, he *had* been a doctor, John repeated to himself—past tense, imperfect. If asked what sort of patient he was treating, how often must he have answered that he was only a doctor, how should he know? Of course, he could classify neurotic, passive, aggressive, manic depressive. He knew the labels. But where was the person who was none of this and all of it, the human being with a heart and a soul? Here was Lank describing him down to the revealing frequency and consistency of his bowel movements.

"A mesomorph, with strong passive masochistic tendencies, anxiety derived nervous stomach, night terrors—"

"Yes, doctor," Jevh said curtly, "I appreciate your clinical details, but did the defendant at any time express interest in your body?"

Lank squirmed, his face flushed. "What do you mean?"

Jevh suppressed a laugh. "Was he curious about the Species Human and the advances in medical science since his time?"

"Oh, why yes. He often said he wanted to talk about it."

"Wanted to, but did he?"

"Well, just last week he asked about working in the Natoleum, but there wasn't time—"

"I'm asking you for facts, not excuses," Jevh reminded Lank.

"He told me a lot about his own medical experiences."

"In other words, he didn't seem too interested in your medical knowledge but was essentially preoccupied with himself?"

"You could say that," Lank acquiesced.

"Thank you. Is that a general characteristic?"

"Of Homo Sapiens or John?"

"How many Homo Sapiens do you know?"

His sarcasm was lost on Lank who replied, "One, just him."

"Then would you say this was characteristic of him?"

"I don't like to generalize on so little experience."

"On the basis of your limited experience?" Jevh persisted,

"I suppose you could say that."

John waved has hand as if seeking the attention of a teacher. The mask looked up. "Yes, Doctor Altern?"

"Your honor, I appreciate that I am not allowed to cross-examine the witness. You have made it quite clear that all cross-examination shall be between us."

Jevh corrected, "Not cross-examination, your examination."

"It's unfair not to let me raise questions as they develop. I can't be expected to remember everything. You won't let me take notes."

"Only what you remember is important."

"Well, I object to your leading the witness—I believe it is called."

"What is called?"

"Leading the witness—questioning him in such a way that he will give the answer you want"

"Are you suggesting that I misled the good doctor?"

"I didn't say you misled him."

"Then what's your point?" Jevh demanded.

John shrugged, "You make it very difficult to have a point by the time you twist everything I say."

The judged agreed. "Semantics is a problem. We could use the Psycho-irratica Interpreter, but it lacks the fine distinctions we must sometimes make. Now, what were you saying?"

"You led Lank into assuming that a general characteristic of mine is preoccupation with myself."

"Is it not?"

"That's beside the point. I object to you leading him."

"My dear fellow," the judge opined, "how many times must we go over this? We all learn by repetition. But when we have reached our age we should learn a little faster. You still insist this is a replica of your courts, in which you had a verdict of innocent or guilty determined by a jury of untrained citizens chosen at random, who were led by clever attorneys and judges through hoops of allegations, and innuendoes, and associations, until there was enough confusion and creative or circumstantial evidence, or lack thereof, to satisfy or dissatisfy, beyond a reasonable doubt, what no reasonable person could possibly decide.

"Your courts required concealing or revealing what was harmful or helpful to the accused or the accuser, truth or untruth quite irrelevant to either or. So once more I say to you, this is not an Anglo-Saxon court of justice, not even a Judeo-Christian court. It is, if you will, a chamber of truth. We are here to determine not only the crime, but the nature of the criminal. If you object to truth, then say so. But, please, do not lead us into irrelevancies."

John gritted his teeth. There was no defense. Apparently his so-called crimes were only a pretext for attacking the essence of his being and making him admit that truths, even if only half-truths, were total.

Jevh dismissed Lank who turned and barely nodded to John as he left the chamber. He called for the next witness.

Zenar bounded into the chamber in full stride. "How are you, old man," he said to John, as though it was a social occasion.

"You will confine your greetings to the court," Jevh ordered.

Zenar smiled boyishly. "I was only being civil. Well, what do you want to know?"

"I understand," Jevh said, "that you are a polar biologist."

"That's right. My specialty is frozen organic tissue. I don't see how that matters."

"Wasn't the defendant frozen?"

"Yes, but I wasn't permitted to pursue the effects on him," he said with more than a tinge of disappointment.

"You were able to observe him, were you not?"

"As a man, not a specimen."

"Would you like to disqualify yourself?"

"Not at all. I came to testify."

"Then what have you to say of him as a man?"

"He qualifies in every respect as a Homo Sapien."

"But not as a Human?"

Zenar smiled. "What do you expect? After all, he was only frozen, not metamorphosed."

"How does he differ from a Human?"

Zenar answered with surprise. "Isn't it obvious? I assume—"

"You will assume nothing," Jevh interjected peremptorily, "not even your reliability as a witness."

"I am a scientist," Zenar asserted haughtily. "I am not accustomed to having my reliability questioned."

"Oh, really," Jevh jeered, equally haughtily. "Shall we assume that scientists are always reliable even in those areas that normally fall outside their particular field? Because you are a biologist, shall I assume you are also an authority on everything else? Shall I further assume that even as a biologist you are never in error?"

Zenar hedged a little. "That isn't exactly what I meant."

"What exactly did you mean, Mr. Scientist?"

"Only that you and I, even though we never met before, that we are on a level of understanding because of our similar background, which makes it unnecessary to verbalize certain basic assumptions."

"Quite the contrary," Jevh said. "You take too much for granted. We do not look alike. What makes you think we think alike? I can assure you we do not. Now tell me in your own words, how do you distinguish a Homo from a Human?"

Zenar was relieved to get back to his testimony. "Well, at first I thought the difference was physical, determined by evolution. You know, survival of the fittest following the Cataclysm. I would have been satisfied with analyzing his genome, but Assock insisted we also test his social adaptability. I had to agree, although if I had known what would happen, well, that is something else. Assock insisted that *frustration* would strike at the core of his character. We would facilitate a possessive social relationship that was typical of Homo Sapiens, and then frustrate it to see what would happen."

"Let me get this straight," Jevh said. "As you implying that Humans are not possessive?"

"We're possessive all right, but not exclusive."

"You mean you are promiscuous."

Zenar scratched his chin. "Yeah...sort of, but not exactly. It doesn't mean we don't feel more strongly for some than for others, and that we don't settle down with a mate, but it's not like total and eternal ownership. That's why I couldn't see anything wrong with the Sapien's early reactions. As a matter of fact, I sympathized with him."

"A scientific observation," Jevh commented sarcastically.

"When his relationship with Vinya grew into such an obsession, when his whole security was tied up in possessing her—"

John had been listening to the proceedings with growing impatience. He was compelled to conform to the rules of the court, but if it meant such a gross distortion of everything he did and believed, he would have to protest.

"If the court pleases," he summoned his most respectful tone, "I would like to explain—"

"The court does not please, not now," Jevh said curtly.

John persisted. "You said you were concerned with the truth."

"You shall have your turn."

"I'd like it now."

Zenar intervened. "Why not, Jevh? I'd like to hear what he has to say."

The mask turned sharply on Zenar. "You will refrain from interfering. You are here to testify, not observe."

John threw up his hands in a helpless gesture and lapsed into silence.

"Now, Zenar, you may continue," Jevh directed.

Chastised, Zenar picked up in a lowered voice, "As I was saying, I don't blame John for fighting to protect his interests."

"That was Human?" Jevh queried.

"No—Sapien, the way he did it. When everything was okay, he seemed to act rationally, but when Assock interfered, that's when the real difference came out."

"How would you have behaved?"

"If I were John?"

"If you were you," the judge answered with mounting exasperation.

"I've given that a lot of thought, Jevh. As much as I loved Assock, I might have gone against him."

The judge sat upright. "You would have assaulted him?"

"No, no!" Zenar said quickly. "I mean, I might have taken Vinya anyway. What did John have to live for if he believed that anytime he got attached to someone, Assock could break it up? It must have been his insecurity and, of course, the obsession that she belonged to him, that he would kill for her—that was so typically Sapien. He should never have attacked Assock. After all, that is perhaps the most important distinction between Sapiens and Humans."

"Yes, well, thank you, Zenar. You have been most helpful."

Zenar shrugged. There was more he wanted to say in the Sapien's defense. He stepped towards John and said, "Don't worry, old man, Jevh's not so bad—"

Jevh cut him short. "The exit's that way."

Zenar shrugged again and started out.

"Wait," Jevh shouted, stopping Zenar in his tracks. "I almost forgot. There's one small matter. I understand you've been carrying on your own experiment."

"Oh that," Zenar waved aside, as if it was of no importance.

"Yes—*that*!"

"It's all over, Jevh, finished."

"Would you mind explaining for the Sapien's benefit, if not mine?"

Zenar looked accusingly at John standing in the dock. "He left the door open. The clone thawed—it died before I got back. After I reported that he was in my laboratory—"

"Son-of-a-bitch!" John blurted. So it was Zenar who turned him in. He should have known better than to have trusted any of them.

"Be quiet," Jevh ordered, turning back to Zenar. "You are guilty of a major crime—the crime of cloning, albeit brilliantly executed."

"Thank you," Zenar said appreciatively.

"It is fortunate for all concerned that the experiment failed, but that does not relieve you of responsibility for your intent."

Zenar fidgeted nervously. "Surely," he offered in his defense, "the preservation of an extinct species merits some consideration. What better means than a clone? Oh, we had some bad experiences before, but that doesn't mean we shouldn't try again."

"Bad experiences!" snorted Jevh. "It was a calamity of the first magnitude and, I might add, thoroughly deserved for indulging in the worst form of narcissism."

"Narcissism?" Zenar questioned.

"What could be more narcissistic than to seek immortality through replication of oneself?"

Zenar shook his head violently. "It was John, not I. It was his sperm, not mine."

Jevh raised his hand to silence Zenar. "The child is his father's son. I must compliment you on your cleverness, but it just won't do." The mask turned towards John. "Please have a seat over there. Would you like some tea?"

He motioned to a guard who led John to the seat, poured him a cup of tea, and sat down beside him.

"Now, Zenar, would you please step into the dock."

Zenar protested, "I am not on trial."

"Do as you are told!"

Zenar's ruddy complexion blanched. For a moment he thought of refusing, then shrugged and moved to the dock.

The judge continued sternly, "As I explained to our Sapien friend before you came in, this is not a contest of wits but a chamber of truth. You say you are a scientist— I have no doubt you are—but it puzzles me that the rigors of the scientific mind so often fail to influence the moral mind, though both are housed in the same shell.

"Surely it is not unreasonable to expect the truth to match your speech. But you have lied to your colleagues, you have lied to the Sapien, and now you have lied to this court. Perhaps you deceived them, though I suspect there was as much self-deception on their part as deceit on yours. However, there shall be no deception and no deceit here."

Zenar pulled back his sagging shoulders. He wondered how much Jevh knew. Leaning against the railing of the dock, he mopped the sweat off his forehead with the sleeve of his shirt. Which was worse, the small lies or the breeding of the clone that had turned him from witness to felon?

"Jevh, your honor, sir..." he began.

"One will do."

Zenar straightened up full length and looked directly into the mask. "I have no wish to deceive the court. I freely admit I was not exactly candid, but there are times when a scientist must protect his work."

The mask nodded and commented, "Call it what you will."

"I tried the Sapien's spermatozoa but the radiation from the Cataclysm, or maybe our blast, rendered them impotent. So…I—"

"Say it," Jevh said, knowing what he would say.

"I…I," he choked, "used my mine. I didn't intend to deceive anyone, but under the circumstances I had to keep it secret."

"I'll make a note," Jevh noted. "Secrecy is not deception. Go on."

"I had to. You see, the fetus was taking the shape of Homo Sapiens. How could my sperm generate a Homo Sapien…unless I was a…," he could not say it. "Naturally, I was confused."

"Naturally," Jevh assented.

"I went to the archives for the records of the Human clone colony. I'm sure you know the history of our clones."

"I do."

"There were no biological records, just anecdotes of the wars and their final extermination."

"And the prohibition of all future cloning," Jevh added.

"Yes, but the records, they should have been there. I was afraid if I asked too many questions someone might suspect what I was doing. I took a chance and mentioned it to Assock. He said he wasn't surprised."

"Oh?" Jevh uttered, surprised. "Did you tell him about your clone?"

Zenar hesitated. What did it matter? It could do Assock no harm now. "Not exactly. I told him I was experimenting with mammalian sperm replication. He said he doubted if genetic mutations accounted for the whole difference between Humans and Homo Sapiens."

"And you—what do you think?" Jevh asked.

"I don't think—I know!" Zenar exclaimed with a note of triumph in his voice. "We are essentially the same, genetically speaking. That's why the clone records were destroyed, to maintain the myth of genetic mutation."

"Then how do you account for our differences?"

"Nutrition and elimination of environmental toxins."

"Is that all?"

"What else could it be?"

Jevh answered, "Have you considered social toxins? Isn't there more to Human development than food and refuse? Would you ignore the difference in the way Human children are reared and Humans relate to each other?"

"Of course not. That was Assock's point. That's what he was aiming at with the Sapien. Unfortunately..." Zenar wavered and fell silent.

"Very interesting," Jevh remarked. "Now what shall we do with you?"

"What do you mean?" Zenar would rather not have asked.

"For all your brilliance, you know so little," Jevh declared, shaking the mask from side to side. "Don't you understand? A clone is neither a Species Human nor a Homo Sapiens, no matter how much it resembles one or the other. It is a sterile replication both in conception and conceptuality. A clone has a present but no future. Incapable of procreation, it is consigned to self-extinction, the ultimate nihilism of an organism that cannot pass its life on to progeny.

"A normal soul is sustained by its sense of immortality, that its life gives life. Deprived of bisexual fertilization, a clone's mind is as sterile as its gonads. Denied the nourishment of both maternal and paternal inheritance, it is devoid of Human feelings and responds like a starved animal surrounded by the fruits of a love it cannot consume. It turns on its creator in unrepentant rage, its only satisfaction retribution for the crime that has been committed on itself."

Jevh looked fiercely at Zenar and intoned, "*You* have committed that crime."

Zenar gripped the railing of the dock, shaken by Jevh's condemnation. He had come to the Tower of Rationality prepared to testify not in defense of John, so much as sympathetically. He should have known better than to think he could escape the wrath of Jevh.

The judge continued, "The more serious crime…"

Zenar swayed unsteadily against the rail—*the more serious crime*—what crime was more serious than cloning? He knew that cloning was forbidden but his curiosity had gotten the better of him. He expected that sooner or later he would be caught but it was worth it just to see himself develop. The shock of his clone's resemblance to Homo Sapiens—the realization that his discovery destroyed the cherished myth of Human distinctiveness—convinced him the clone must not survive. Murder, even of a clone, would be a more serious crime than cloning. Fortunately its death had been an accident. He could not be accused of murder.

"How can a society protect itself from those privileged to be its leaders if lying is tolerated?" Jevh hammered home. "If one strikes a blow it leaves a mark for all to see. But if one lies, the truth is hidden behind a facade of false honor that is as much a blow to the mind as if struck by a clenched fist. One might excuse an error of judgment, a lapse of responsibility, even a violation of the law. But there can be no excuse for the dishonor of a friend's faith or the desecration of Human honesty."

Zenar's face reflected his bewilderment. Jevh spoke as though he was an inveterate liar when he could not recall having told a serious lie until the Sapien arrived, and then only to protect his cloning project. Damn the Sapien. None of this would have happened but for him. He said as much to Jevh.

The judge's staccato laughter shook the mask askance. He carefully straightened it and pointed a finger at Zenar. "You excuse yourself by blaming him as though he infected you with his own deceit?"

"In a manner of speaking," Zenar admitted uncomfortably. He was not pleased with himself for shifting blame onto John, but had not Assock warned that Sapienism was like an infectious disease.

Jevh shook his head slowly. "It will not do. You had an obligation to the Committee, and to Esop who befriended you in a special way, permitting you to work without the usual supervision. Small lies, you say. Perhaps, but small lies compound to big ones. The big lie was not to the Committee, or to Esop, or even to me, though that is most inexcusable. It was to yourself."

"I did not lie to myself!" Zenar exploded, raising his voice, which had been subdued all this time to its normal timbre.

"Poor Zenar," Jevh sighed. "Even now you cannot face the truth."

Zenar scowled derisively. "Mine or yours?"

Jevh ignored the barb. "When you observed your clone resembled a Homo Sapien, what was your first reaction?"

Zenar ran his fingers nervously through his hair, which was damp with perspiration. "I...er—"

"Come, come—your first thought."

"To destroy it," he blurted, relieving the pressure of another lie that had been building up, "but I couldn't."

"Nor could you admit it was a replica of yourself."

"I don't know what I thought." But he did know. He would deny it was him. If he was discovered, he would say it was John's clone. He forced himself to speak on. "I was afraid—look at me—I'm seven feet tall. My face is long and narrow, not like...like a normal Human. In John's world I could have passed for—"

"A Homo Sapien," Jevh assisted.

"You see, even you thought it. But I'm not—I am Human!"

"But you are not sure," Jevh taunted. "So you lied."

"I had no way of knowing if other Human clones would be the same. Don't you see," Zenar begged, "something may have gone wrong with me. I might be a direct descendant—I might be a Homo Sapien—if Assock is right, there is no hope for me. I did not lie to myself. It was to protect myself that I lied."

"No, Zenar," Jevh contradicted, "the lie is your insistence that if you face the truth alone and conceal it from others, you will be what they think you are, and if that is so, then that is what you are—the embodiment of the lie."

Zenar's mind reeled in the confusion of uncertainty. Always so sure of himself, Jevh had forced his face to the mirror, and what he saw was as featureless as the mask concealing Jevh. He turned towards John who sat silently beside the guard, returning his stare with an expression of bewilderment that matched his own.

Jevh recalled his attention, speaking to him so softly that Zenar had to strain to hear his words.

"I cannot avoid my responsibility to this chamber, no matter how heavy the burden of my command. You know what I must do."

Zenar nodded submissively.

"You may step down."

Zenar moved slowly from the dock, pausing in front of John who started to rise but was constrained by the guard's hand on his shoulder.

"Good-bye, my brother," Zenar managed to whisper in a voice choked with emotion.

John looked up into Zenar's drawn face, his eyes blurring with the mist of commiseration. Then Zenar was led away and John knew he would not see him again.

CHAPTER 15

The trial had begun early in the morning and it was late afternoon when the masked judge sent John back to his cell. Dusk was settling over Opalon. He lit a candle to dispel the gloom. His sense of time was in a shambles. How many days had he been here? He stretched out on the cotton mattress, propping his head against the wall with the thin pillow curled into a roll. The medieval character of the interior of the Tower of Rationality continued to puzzle him, its austerity all the more startling in contrast to the opulence of Opalon's buildings and domes below. It was like a caricature of a prison, or perhaps a child's fantasy of an ancient castle drawn down to the ultimate absurdity of light by a candle in the midst of a world illuminated by electricity. He could only guess that it was intended to break down his resistance. He would not have been surprised if a guard clad in medieval armor should suddenly clank into his cell with a barbed truncheon for a lesson in obedience.

What he could not fathom was the extreme view of honesty put forth by Jevh who hid behind a ridiculous mask that seemed itself the ultimate deception. There was something so familiar about the judge. It tantalized him to the point of exasperation. It was ludicrous to demand honesty without reservation and restraint, and then hide behind a mask. Unless the revelation would be too hideous to behold.

Like Dorian Gray, there is a soul-revealing portrait in everyone's attic? Dorian's masculine beauty was no less a facade than Jevh's mask. To look into a mirror without drawing an opaque veil over the flaws and weaknesses, the scars and misery—the death mask—staring back beneath the glass would destroy the hardiest soul. One cannot survive without deception and protection lest the horrors all about and in ourselves would drive us mad.

At what point does an essentially honest person's little lies and deceits become a misdemeanor? At what point does the compounding of our faults become a felony? In Opalon the line seems drawn thin. To the judge there was no line, not for an Opalonian, not for him.

He was still piqued at the judge's censure. He would not again give in so easily and he kicked himself for a defense so poor that at Jevh's declaration he actually felt guilty of adultery. He was outmaneuvered by Jevh's twisted logic, which ignored the separation of time and space between his past life and the passage to Opalon. Yet, he could not deny that he had been an adulterer and that in his memory there was the guilt of his affair with Ina, and of others in fantasies almost as real to touch and memory. But was not adultery more the perversion of the mind than the violation of a universal law? It did Mary no harm and himself much good so long as Mary did not know. There were times when he wondered if she did know.

He remembered once returning home late after an evening with Ina and getting into bed with Mary who exclaimed, "Whew, you smell of perfume." His response was quick, if doubtful. "Must have been the soap in the men's room." He was supposed to have been at a dinner meeting. He was not sure if she believed him or chose to let it pass. He remembered thinking that if she challenged him, he would have to tell the truth—not that he wanted Ina but that he was tired, tired of their marriage and the little lies that sustained it.

Little lies compound to big ones, Jevh said, and on that count Zenar was guilty, too. The big lie for him had been his insistence that the only reason he and Mary remained together was for the sake of their child, when it was also a shield for his own indecisiveness. He could blame Mary for not doing this or that or whatever would make their life together better. But he could not blame her for preventing him from doing what he was afraid to do, because he did not know what it was he wanted, except that the undefined *wants* were driving him up the wall.

Continuation of the marriage had not been an entire lie. They still cared for each other. They still took care of each other. *Still*? Would he never come to terms with the past? Even though Mary was gone, she was still part of him. With all his misgivings, all his dissatisfactions, he still cared for her.

Why should caring not be enough? It simply wasn't. If not for Alice, if not for his indecisiveness, he would have divorced her long ago. But whenever he reached the breaking point, or thought he had, he would recall an argument with Mary in front of Alice who began to cry. She said, between sobs, "I'm afraid you and mom are going to get divorced."

So he put off the divorce but not the thought of it. His marriage continued as before. He would wait for Alice to finish high school. Had it not been for the Cataclysm, he wondered if he would still be waiting. That was the measure of his determination. Nonetheless, it was over, the topple happened. Memories of Mary and Alice were blurred and less frequent.

He was in the present, and he loved Vinya for what she was, not as a replacement—he was sure of that—even though he was as preoccupied with her in the present as he had been with his wife and child in the past. Now Vinya was gone. The loneliness she had displaced covered him like the frost on the clone.

His thoughts were disrupted by the opening of the cell door. He got up quickly, hoping it might be someone else, but it was only the guard bringing him supper. He took the tray from the extended arm, which quickly withdrew as the door clanged shut. He placed the tray on the table and glared at its contents—a slab of cold meat, boiled potatoes, a slice of bread, and a pot of tasteless tea. Also two candles. "Thanks for nothing!" he shouted towards the door. Pouring a cup of tea, he slumped against the wall, dreading the hours before he could fall asleep, wishing he could think of something else besides himself.

"**G**ood morning, doctor," the judge greeted John cheerily as he approached the dock. "Did you sleep well?"

"Hardly."

"Oh, that's too bad. You'll get used to it. Now, let's see, where were we? Hmmm. Adultery? We finished with that."

John addressed the judge. "Your honor—"

The mask looked up from the sheaf of papers it was perusing.

"I've given a lot of thought to yesterday's session. It was very unfair, very one-sided. I'm not a lawyer but I have certain inalienable rights—the right to a fair trial."

"Inalienable rights?" The mask once again would have raised an eyebrow if it had one.

"Yes—inalienable," John persisted. "If this...this...I don't know what it is. I can't continue unless my rights are respected."

"My dear fellow," Jevh exclaimed, "You may not be a lawyer but you do sound like one. You have no choice—"

"I could remain silent," John threatened. "I refuse to be put in the position of convicting myself without a proper defense."

The mask stirred from side to side on the axis of its neck. "*Inalienable rights—proper defense*. Interesting, but I fail to grasp your point. Rights are not inalienable. They stem from struggle. You have to fight for rights. If you win, you have rights. If you lose, you have no rights. Every school child knows that. There is no such thing as an inalienable right, except, perhaps, the right to fight. Is that what you intend?"

"I do," John replied, encouraged by the judge's response.

"Very well, what shall we fight about?"

"For one thing, the mask—why you are hiding."

"Oh, still on that. Why do you keep insisting on seeing my face?"

"It's my right to know who you are."

"Without a struggle?" Jevh's tone reflected disappointment. "I thought we had settled that yesterday, or was it the day before? It is for you to see beyond the mask, not for me to reveal the color of my eyes. We shall not confuse the issue with physiognomic irrelevancies."

"What is the issue? It's all so vague," John whined.

"What is vague about adultery?" Jevh answered. "You're guilty. That's as specific as you can get. You still want to argue about what you have admitted to yourself as well as to this court. We talked about your lies and deceptions, your guilt. Don't you remember? Certainly you would not expect me to countenance an improper defense of half-truths or not truths or flat out lies."

"That's my point," John countered, "You convicted me on half-truths and lies."

"You were convicted on your own confession and testimony. Are you now telling me that you lied?

"No, damn it! What I am saying is that truth is not so simple. There is no absolute truth. What one believes to be true is not the same for everyone, not even always for yourself."

"Quite true," Jevh said amiably. "That is why we are concerned with your present truth, no one else's. Don't you see?"

What choice did he have? It sounded so simple but it was not simple. Jevh had a way of turning everything back on him until he agreed because he could not disagree, no matter how strongly he resented his involuntary concession.

"I suppose I should be grateful for you forcing me to see my own truth." His sarcasm was not lost on Jevh, who commented that he could do without John's gratitude.

You will have to, John muttered beneath his breath, then aloud, "Let's get one thing straight. I am going to appeal the charge of adultery. I did not commit adultery here."

"In your heart—in your heart," Jevh repeated.

"The hell with my heart," John retorted hotly. "My wife is dead. I'm free to do what I like."

"Not in your heart. She is not dead in your heart."

"My heart is none of your damned business. I'm fed up with this *in your heart* bullshit. Yes, I committed adultery but that was long before I came to Opalon."

"Oh? Then the past is not present?"

"What do you mean?"

"Time *is* peculiar," Jevh answered like a schoolmaster addressing his pupil. "Can you always be sure an event that you remember as clearly as if it happened yesterday took place yesterday or the day before or years before? What of events of today? Have you never had an experience today that you seem to have had in the past? Is not old age senility the past becoming present? Is the old man living in a dream of the past? Or, has his past become as present to him as your present is to you? You know, there are those who believe reality is only what one's mind perceives—"

"Solipsistic rubbish," John retorted. "More of your half-truths. You may be senile! I am not."

Jevh responded tolerantly, "I must admit that nothing is more aging than trying to prove the unprovable. Whether it is half the truth or the whole of it, you have confessed adultery. If it pleases you more to be half an adulterer than a whole one, so be it. In your mind there may be a difference, not in mine."

John's face burned with anger. "Damn you and your differences."

Jevh slammed his fist on the bench. "Enough of your bad manners. If you can not speak civilly, you can return to your cell."

John refused to apologize, though he tempered his tone. "It's the constant reiteration of these..." he started to say damn but checked himself, "differences between me and everyone else. The more I see of you people, the less different I seem to myself. Look what Assock did to Vinya, his own daughter. Would you call that civilized?"

"Incest was not uncommon in your society. Since you claim to be civilized, then perhaps it was civilized," Jevh reasoned.

John grimaced in disgust. "Certainly not," He shifted on his feet and leaned heavily against the railing. "Could I have a chair?" he asked. "My legs are still a little weak."

The mask shook negatively. "I would like to accommodate you but the rules do not permit it. You must stand on your own two feet."

John was not amused by the cliché. He recognized it as an extension of the medieval cell, as if the discomfort would weaken his resolve. Yet, he had hoped for some relief. The judge alternated between considerateness and callousness, sometimes speaking to him in a kindly manner, sometimes not so kindly. He supposed it might be worse. He could be chained.

The trial had so concentrated himself on his own plight that his concern for Vinya had remained locked in the cell whenever he was brought to the chamber. He knew she could not have escaped. When he asked the guard if she was also imprisoned in the Tower, the guard laughed and said nothing. Not knowing where she was, how she was, was never far from his thoughts.

"Would it be too much to ask if Vinya is all right?"

"Yes, it would," Jevh answered dismissively.

"Why, what harm would there be in just a word of reassurance?"

"The harm is in what you did to her."

"What I did! I did nothing. I love her. I'm concerned for her," John countered with rising emotion.

"That is what you say, which brings us to the fact of incest."

John nodded. "What Assock did was—"

Jevh cut him short. "It's what you did that concerns us here."

"What do you mean, what I did?" John exclaimed heatedly. "It was Assock. You're twisting everything again."

A forced staccato laugh spilled from the mask, echoing in John's memory the sound of Assock at their last confrontation. He swayed against the railing, flinging his right arm forward, pointing his forefinger straight at the mask. "You...," he growled, "you—yes, you—I wasn't sure—it's you!"

"Oh," Jevh feigned surprise.

"You can take off the mask, Assock."

More staccato laughter from the mask, now unforced, ricocheting throughout the chamber like bursts of a machine gun.

John triumphantly folded his arms across his chest, confident the charade was over.

Jevh pulled himself together and said, "Come now, you will have to do better than that. You cannot avoid guilt by mistaken identity. Listen closely. Is mine the voice of Assock?"

John stumbled in auditory confusion. "You sound like..." throwing up his hands in exasperation, he realized the mask masked the voice. He could not be certain it was Assock? Yet, who else could it be? Finally, he had to admit, "I'm not sure, not absolutely...the mask—"

"And so it is intended," Jevh acknowledged.

"It makes no sense."

"We shall see. What does make sense is your confession of perversion." Jevh picked up the signed confession and waved it tauntingly at John.

"Pure crap!" shot out of John's mouth before he could block it, but Jevh seemed not to notice. "I told you I was forced to sign. It means nothing."

"Is that so? You said the same about adultery. Why should your confession of incest be less true?"

"Because my daughter...Alice is..." John's throat tightened and his voice quavered as he tried to speak above the sadness of his child's death. "I loved her. I could never do such a thing. I never thought it." He fought back tears, unwilling to grant the judge the satisfaction of his upset.

"Wasn't Alice Vinya's age?"

"No, she was younger by a year. There was no resemblance. My god, I didn't go looking for Vinya. Assock introduced us."

"The difference in your age and her youth didn't bother you?" Jevh probed further.

"No...well, a little in the beginning."

"She didn't remind you of your daughter? Can you say it never occurred to you?"

The question jolted John's memory unpleasantly. It was as though Jevh was reading through the protective screens of his mind, peeling back memories, forcing him to remember what he had suppressed to save himself the embarrassment of their admission.

Yes, it had occurred to him when he first met Vinya. She reminded him of Alice, but it was only the closeness of their age. What he felt afterwards had nothing to do with his daughter. True, Vinya's youth bothered him at first as it always bothered him when he saw an older man with a much younger woman. It bothered him not so much as reflected lechery as with envy, and the frustration of his own lost youth and missed opportunities.

When he met Vinya, it was as if his sweetest fantasy had been fulfilled. She was the embodiment of his adolescent dreams, of the girl that would love him as he loved her. At first he was very conscious of being older, and he was uncomfortable in the presence of others who might not approve. But he also enjoyed their envy. That was only in the beginning and had nothing to do with incest.

"*Nothing?*" Jevh repeated.

John was tempted not to answer, but he knew Jevh would interpret silence as a further admission of guilt. He had nothing to be guilty of, not with Vinya. So what if he admitted that the resemblance, at least in age, had crossed his mind, and that he had also wished Alice was still alive here with him.

"I wanted her to live a full life," he said, tears flooding his eyes, eyes burning and blinking in the grief of his child's lost life. "I wanted her to have a future, to grow up...," his voice broke and his chest heaved in deep sobs. "I...I wanted her to have a life like Vinya's. Please—please leave her alone, leave her out of this. Vinya had nothing to do with her." He wiped at the tears and struggled to regain his composure.

"I have no doubt," Jevh said sympathetically, "that you loved Vinya much as you loved your daughter."

"She is *not* my daughter. I love her for who she is and what she means to me."

"Quite so," Jevh agreed, "what she means to you. That is the essence of incest—the ultimate indulgence of the self. Let me be blunt." The distaste of what he was about to say preceded his choice of words. "You indulged yourself worse than an animal. With rare exceptions, Homo Sapiens among them, animals do not mate their offspring. The relationship between a child and a parent—don't forget, adults are proxy parents to all children—is one of trust and protection. When you indulged yourself with Vinya, no matter how willing the child, you violated that sacred trust. In your mind's eye, blind as it is to reality, Vinya is as much a child as was Alice. I do not say that you violated *your* child. I say that you violated the sacred trust a child has for her parent."

Jevh's statement shocked John beyond restraint. "You are contemptible," he spat out.

"Yes, thank you. But these are your thoughts, not mine," Jevh contended. "I did not make them up."

"You're out of your mind," John shouted at the mask.

"If so, then so are you."

As Jevh peered down at John, a ray of sunlight streamed through the slit window high above, reflecting off the mask like a mirror concentrating its brightness on John's face. John squinted and raised a hand to shield his eyes. "Is the truth so painful?" Jevh asked.

John moved his head out of the light, ruminating on Jevh's direction, finally catching its drift. He tried a more conciliatory tact. "I know I've been indulgent and I admit that what I did, my relationship with Vinya, could be seen as very self-indulgent, even hedonistic."

"That's a kinder way of putting it," Jevh said kindly, "but it's not that simple. Remember what Lank said, about how little interest you had in this new world, how you seemed preoccupied with yourself."

"That's only partly true. I admit I was self-centered. Under the circumstances, can you blame me?"

"*Partly true*," Jevh bounced back. "Another half-truth. Your life here in Opalon has been a model of self-indulgence. I dare say, you are the most narcissistic person I have yet to encounter. I am told that was characteristic of Homo Sapiens. It was no accident that Assock challenged you with Vinya. He had to see how far you would go. His incest was your incest. His indulgence your indulgence, and your refusal to give it up drove you to attack him."

"I can't believe you believe that. I suppose Assock didn't provoke me," John said derisively.

"You provoked yourself."

"You don't know that. You weren't there. How can I make you understand?"

"How can *I* make *you* understand," Jevh thrust back, "if you will not recognize yourself?"

"You keep throwing everything back at me as though I was the cause of it all. Children do have incestuous fantasies towards their parents. There's nothing new in that. I suppose parents could have the same fantasy towards their children, but there's a difference between a fleeting fantasy and reality. What Assock did to Vinya was real. What I did was—"

"A fantasy?" Jevh interjected.

"No! You're doing it again, twisting everything."

"If not a fantasy, then it was real and you are guilty of incest. You just admitted it," Jevh intoned.

"Oh, what's the use," John sighed, relinquishing the argument. Jevh's mind was made up. To the judge it all came out black and white no matter how he tried to explain the subtlety and complexity of his feelings. Let him just admit the smallest element of truth in the accusation and it became the whole of it. He was too fatigued physically and mentally to argue further.

Jevh was not yet through with him. "The court acknowledges that perversion of the mind is not the same as its abusive enactment upon a child, what you refer to as fantasy and reality. But your violence—what you did to Professor Assock—is consistent with what we know of Homo Sapiens, not how a Human would react."

What next, John thought. First adultery, then incest, and now violence. He protested that he was not characteristically violent. There might be innate differences between him and them, but it was not a crime to be different.

"Not in the Seventh Millennium," Jevh agreed.

"Why was it necessary to provoke me and make a capital offense of it?"

"No matter how great the disagreements among Humans, under no circumstances is physical assault tolerated."

"Assock grabbed me. What did you expect me to do? Not defend myself?" He had hoped to argue his actions were understandable under the circumstances, if not excusable. Yet it seemed he was on trial not for what he did but for what he was.

"Was it really to defend or to possess? Did it justify killing?" Jevh challenged.

"Sometimes I think it did. My lord, we were only human."

"Human or Sapiens?" Jevh tilted his head sideways. "How do you justify the murderous assault of another person, no matter how provocative that person is?"

"He wouldn't listen. I...I lost control. It was a madhouse!"

"Are you pleading insanity?"

Perhaps it was temporary insanity, John conceded to himself, and then challenged the judge. "It's not insane to protect the one you love. You say, just don't give a damn and everything will be okay. Well, I don't see it that way."

"Oh my," Jevh said with rising inflection, "a truly noble sentiment. You were selfless, not protecting your possession, only defending this poor helpless little girl. It just won't do. You cannot hide behind her. You must face the obvious."

John's eyes dropped and he leaned back wearily. It seemed as though they were going round and round and the trial was beginning all over again.

Jevh continued, "You have this insatiable need for love, as if you cannot survive alone. Only that perfect mate could recreate the perfect unconditional love you once experienced—the mother for the child, the child for the mother. It is an affliction of tunnel vision with no light at the end, doomed to dissipate. When you finally find that one perfect mate, your whole being demands its total, exclusive possession. Heaven help anyone else who dares to enter."

John shook his head slowly, more in wonderment than disagreement. "First you say I loved her as my child, now as a child would love his mother. I wonder who's more confused, you or me?"

Jevh was gracious. "It is not either or but all of it. Why the obvious should be confusing is indeed confusing." Abruptly, he ended the session. "I'm hungry. We'll recess."

John flopped down on the mattress in his cell. He closed his eyes and tried to rest, but his mind would not shut down. Arguments, retorts, protests swirled within. It was so easy to think what he might have said, so difficult to find the words. If only they allowed him pen and paper, he could prepare his remarks for the next session, but the judge denied his request, asserting it would inhibit spontaneous interaction, as though spontaneity was foolproof. He had known many people, patients especially, whose capacity to lie matched the rapidity of their speech. *Doctor, I have never been unfaithful. I must have got the clap from a public toilet seat.* Poetic justice, he would think as he injected penicillin and prescribed a condom for the next trip to the toilet.

As bad as the trial had gone, it might have been worse. He supposed it would get worse. Jevh was toying with him, playing little word games until he tired of the charade and pronounced with chilling condemnation, *Guilty of Adultery—Guilty of Incest—Guilty of god knows what else.* No one was immune to Jevh's judgment, as witness his contempt for Zenar.

If only he could remove the mask. It had to have meaning beyond anonymity. On that point, he agreed with Jevh. Yet, absurd as it seemed, he had grown accustomed to the faceless visage, visualizing features much as a blind person *sees* people through the sound of their voices. Small wonder that the voice irritated him more. At times it sounded exactly like Assock and the mask would appear almost pudgy, colored like putty. Then the voice would turn deep and toneless, as though rising from the recesses of a hollow chamber, and the mask would darken to a void. He wouldn't put it beyond Assock to be mocking him. Everything about him could be made to fit Jevh—his changing moods, one moment warm and reassuring, the next cold and cruel, impervious to the rules Esop and the others were bound by, forcing them to comply with his damned experiment. It was not inconceivable to John that the trial was an extension of Assock's experiment.

What a laugh, locking him up in a prison they call the Tower of Rationality. Only he wasn't laughing. If they were trying to frighten him, they could have saved themselves a whole lot of trouble. He had been frightened from the moment they stumbled upon him at the crater. Even as his hopes for a new life had risen with Vinya, Assock was there plotting against him. He had hoped Esop and Zenar would help him, but he should have known better. They were no match for the professor.

He did not have to be told that beyond the trial lay the *treatment,* the undefined punishment for transgressing laws that he did not know existed or that he was violating. He wondered how he would hold up to the *treatment*. He was not a coward, but his bravery had never really been tested. He had never been in battle, never had to face an enemy intent on killing him, never had to dodge bayonets, bullets or bombs.

He had escaped all that, only now to be drenched in the sweat of a fear unknown. He tried to visualize his worst fear. Would it be a debilitating illness, or a stroke that left him paralyzed, speechless, and imprisoned in the grasp of his skin? Might it be pain? He had never experienced great pain, but even pain has its limits.

As bad as torture would be, intuitively he sensed that physical pain was not his worst fear. He recalled the recurring debates over capital punishment and the do-gooders who insisted life imprisonment without hope of parole was better. Better for whom? For the convicted killer who might prefer death by lethal injection to confinement like a rat in a cage for an eternity? For his advocate who would not for a moment exchange places, much less insert the needle and push in the plunger? What would be his choice if sentenced to this cell for an eternity, let out only to amuse Jevh in his Chamber of Truth—in and out, on and on and on? Would he not beg for a syringe to end it all?

The thought of Assock smirking behind the mask strengthened his resolve not to give him that satisfaction. As long as the trial continued, he would defend himself as best he could, even if part of his defense was against accusations of the heart. It was almost as though he was accusing himself, against which there was no defense. It was not a trial but a persecution that forced one's heart to testify against oneself. It was medieval—and they called it a rational society.

Then his resolve would give way to unbearable fatigue and he would crawl into his bed, knees drawn tight to his chest, shivering beneath the threadbare blanket, hopelessly unable to fall asleep and escape his depression. Why should he go on living? What did he have to live for anyway? His past was buried under the polar ice cap, and the present promised, if not a cell in the Tower of Rationality, imprisonment in some other equally macabre institution.

Then, without reason his mood would lift. Faced with extinction, prudence reminded him that once gone there were no second thoughts, that deep down he was fighting for a second chance. If there was any sincerity in this trial, surely Jevh would see the good in him, that he was not just a miscreant Homo Sapien, that he had human feelings, and, even if he had guilts and had done wrong, it was not too late to make amends and live the rest of his life as a decent human being.

Jevh rapped the bench with his gavel, opening the afternoon session. Addressing John he said, "We must now resolve the matter of murderous assault. That this charge was not given priority should not lead the defendant to assume it is of lesser importance."

"Your honor, if I may interrupt?"

"You've been doing it all along."

"You speak of murderous assault, but not murder. Am I to assume that Assock is alive?"

The mask again voiced incredulity. "What does it matter?"

John was equally incredulous. "*What does it matter?*" he shouted back. "It does matter! If Assock is alive, then I can't have murdered him."

"Tautological irrelevancy," Jevh sighed. "I am trying my best to be patient with you. Will your assault be more murderous if I bring in the victim's corpse and let you look at it? Is this the measure of your crime? Again I say to you, we are concerned with what is in your heart, if there was in fact intent to murder. It is immaterial whether or not we have a corpse. Did you or did you not wish Assock's death? Did you or did you not act on that wish?"

John protested, "I did not wish anything. I was reacting—"

Jevh scoffed, "Is a person nothing more than a mass of conditioned reflexes? Push one button and he laughs, another he cries, a third he murders. Really, what sort of nonsense is that?"

John threw up his hands in despair.

"Please, no histrionics," Jevh admonished.

"What I mean is that if you tried everyone for murderous impulses the court would be filled from sunup to sundown."

"Are you suggesting it is not?"

John hesitated at the implication. "I don't know. If it is, then I have made my point."

"Not at all, dear boy. The only point you have made is what I have been trying to make clear. Murderous assault is a heinous crime. If you wish to distinguish between intent and action, that is something else."

"That is what I'm trying to say," John said, relieved at the clarification.

Jevh sighed again. "You make so much of so little. You committed an action, an assault. Are you claiming that an action has no intent, that it is merely a random release of energy?"

"Perhaps there was intent, but it was not to kill Assock," John hedged. "All I wanted was for him to leave us alone. Vinya wanted to stay with me. I did not force her. When Assock took hold of me—I struck back."

"Are you equating the placing of a hand on an arm with a fist on the jaw?"

"Since you put it that way, yes."

"Whew," Jevh exhaled, "Now *I* am confused. I think what you mean is that the intent may be the same even as the actions differ. Is that correct?"

John felt as though he was stepping into a trap, but he could not disagree.

"That is the chamber's position also. You argue that you had no intention of killing Assock. All you wanted was to be rid of him. That was why you struck him again and again. That is why you did not stop beating him until he lay helpless and unconscious. You did not want to kill him. You were merely pushing him out the door."

"I grant you that I was angry," John responded in classic understatement.

"Yes, and I suppose that should excuse you. So we are back to conditioned reflexes. Why cage the psychopathic killer who kills only when provoked?

"You and your ridiculous analogies," John said. "Sure, if I went around assaulting anyone who angered me, I should be caged. But I don't."

"Ah, I see your point," Jevh said. "Since you only assault people who interfere with you, you should be set free."

"Oh, what's the use," John murmured half aloud, grasping the railing, wishing he could tear it off and throw it at the judge.

"If we take your remarks as the closing of this portion of your testimony, perhaps I can summarize our position. Under no circumstances is assault condoned or allowed to go unpunished. We are not a tribe of barbarians. If a member of society cannot restrain murderous impulses, then he must be recognized as a threat to society. It is that simple. Physical assault contains intent to murder."

John tried once more. "I did not intend to kill Assock."

"Are you now pleading irresponsibility, perhaps temporary insanity?"

"I suppose so," John said wearily.

"Then we're back to where we started. Is not every assault an irrational act? Shall we excuse it simply because it is insane? How long can society survive if every time a person is frustrated he assaults someone? It doesn't matter if you killed Assock, does it now? You assaulted him. That is enough."

"It is not enough," John countered. "Can't a man defend himself?"

Jevh replied, "That is an entirely different matter. Assock tried to defend himself. He tried to restrain you. That he failed was his misfortune. The difference is that he did not assault you in return."

"He would have, if he got the chance," John flung back at Jevh.

The judge wagged a finger at the Sapien. "That is your perverse assumption. You are still trying to excuse yourself. It simply won't do. You are plainly guilty of murderous assault."

"I guess there's nothing more to say."

"I guess not," Jevh replied with finality.

He stalked back and forth in the cell, his brain smarting at the penetration of Jevh's thrusts, which once gone in stuck like barbed darts tipped in a drug that was exasperatingly irritating. There was constant pressure in his forehead as though the frontal lobes of his cerebellum were pushing to expand and reshape the outer plate of bone. He wondered if the survivors of the Cataclysm might not have experienced similar agony as they wrestled with the shock of their world's destruction, and if somehow these mental pressures might have pressured the brain to expand and transform the skull in succeeding generations to the shape of the Species Human.

Far from expanding, his brain felt humiliated and diminished before Jevh's onslaught. Everything was turned on its head. His defense of Vinya became on assault on Assock. In his day, in a court of his time, he would have been exonerated. He should not be judged by what was in his heart. Jevh was not a cardiologist.

He stopped pacing before the clouded mirror above the sink next to the toilet. He had avoided the increasing despondency evident in the reflection since the first days of imprisonment. It had been so long since he looked at himself. He was shocked by the image that faced him. The beard was neither full nor thin and yielded no sense of time. It could have been a few days growth, a few weeks, or longer. The eyes were withdrawn and encircled by rings as black as coal. The cheeks were hollowed out beneath their arches and his lips, once full, were thin and wrinkled. It was a portrait not of aging, but of injury and pain, of a wounded animal staring out at him.

And then, as the cloud that dimmed the sun and darkened the cell passed by, the mirror brightened and the shadows lifted from his face. It was as if he had witnessed the regeneration of new tissue and the covering over of raw nerves and the reintegration of the scattered parts of his soul.

He had to go on, to get out of this cell, away from the Tower. He moved the bench over to the window and stepped up on it. Leaning over, he scanned the park below. The grass was greener than he remembered. Tantalizing specks of colored flowers reached up to him. Children were playing in the park and he watched them run and jump and tumble. There, far beneath him, was life, not up here in the quiet of a cell pierced only by the occasional grating of the oak door opening for the guard to pass him stale food, or lead him back down to the chamber.

He had to stop feeling sorry for himself. He had to stop wallowing in self-recrimination. He might have lived a better life, he knew that now. So might everyone. If anything had to be destroyed it was this isolation, this separation from the world about him, from himself. He was tired of cynicism and hopelessness and despair.

It was not only the good people who became discouraged, giving the world over by default to the mean and the selfish. It was also the masses, the poor and the downtrodden, who lived and died in passive submission. Yet, not all had not given up. Civilization did not come easily—not without the fighting and scratching and biting of those with the sense and the guts to care. Even if it was not utopia, it was better than the jungle.

At the last session, Jevh spoke of contradictions existing side by side, of right and wrong, of good and bad, of progress and reaction. *The world does not advance through fixed gradations, through steady unretracing progress, but rather ebbs and flows in everlasting overlapping patterns.* There was reassurance in the repetition as though bad as things were, and worse they might be, sooner or later the tide would reverse. People would be kinder to each other. Life on earth would improve for everyone.

Perhaps he had jumped forward too fast and been exposed to attitudes and circumstances beyond his comprehension. If only he could go back and try again. Of course, he could not. But he could go forward. Given another chance, he would be different.

Jevh was unconvinced. He had been given a second chance in Opalon, and failed miserably. His weakness was ingrained in his soul.

John accepted the criticism, but not the judgment. True, he had been too self-centered, too indulgent, but not intentionally at the expense of others. He was not beyond redemption. He had not given up all hope. To give up would be to deny not only himself, but all those before him who had not given up, to whom everyone was indebted for whatever decency there was.

He marveled that this glimmer of hope could surface and survive in prison. Perhaps that is what kept lifers alive—the grand illusion of eventual redemption. His ray of hope was like that thin band of daylight streaming through the window in his cell, a narrow slanted transparent path with the strength of mylar that would carry him to freedom. He would follow that hope no matter how small it seemed. Somehow he would squeeze through that little window into the world below.

"We come now to this matter of your inconsistency," Jevh began the session.

John was jarred by the shift to a subject that was so far removed from his thoughts that he resented the intrusion. Only a moment ago, it seemed he was pacing back and forth in his cell and now, with no recollection of transition from cell to chamber, he was standing in the dock. With effort, he forced his mind back to Jevh's attention and asked the judge to repeat the question.

"How do you manage on the one hand to reject the major features of your society and on the other to pledge allegiance to it? How do you rationalize your claim to humanism without objection to the capitalist system that defiles it?"

John stared at the judge as if he was unreal. "I can't believe this—*capitalism* an issue in this court? What does it have to do with me—the crimes I've been accused of?"

"It's a matter of your inconsistency," Jevh repeated. "How can you be a humanist and a capitalist simultaneously? If that is not an inconsistency, what is?"

"But it can't be a crime? Besides," he added petulantly, "I'm a doctor, not a capitalist."

"Perhaps—let us see."

John recalled a similar conversation with Assock when they were still on speaking terms. Now, as then, he tried to explain that living in a capitalist society was an accident of birth, not an ideological choice. If he had been born into a communist society, no doubt he would have been a communist. even if he did not believe in communism. Investing in stocks, earning unearned income was something everyone did, or hoped for. That did not make him an apostle of capitalism. He did not believe in making money off other people's labor, but investing was not exploitation. It created jobs even though he had to admit that, when he bought stocks, he wasn't thinking of jobs for the unemployed but of capitalizing on his investment. In that sense, he supposed there was some truth to the accusation.

The judge rocked back in his chair. "*Some truth?* Will we never get to a whole truth?"

John started to laugh, settling instead for a smile of commiseration. "Would you recognize one?"

"Speak for yourself," Jevh retorted, unamused.

John played along. What harm could it do? It was a welcome relief to talk about something that had nothing to do with his inner turmoil. It was like his conversations with Esop, when they were explaining to each other how their worlds differed and how they seemed in so many ways so much the same. It was like the pleasant talks he had with Assock before everything turned upside down.

"We avoided clichés like 'capitalist'," John explained, "except when someone with progressive ideas was called a *red*—a socialist or, even worse, a communist. But it's true, most people in my country claimed allegiance to the God of Capitalism with a capital *C*, even if they weren't capitalists and didn't know what it meant.

"But if you looked at the history of modern governments, it wasn't the capitalists who pushed for basic services like sanitation, police and fire protection, public schools, public health, public transportation, so much as those they called *socialists*, and many of them were. Some of my colleagues called me a socialist because I, like the majority of the public, was in favor of national health insurance. In a sense, anyone who supported government was a socialist—otherwise, we'd all be anarchists.

"But I also believed there was a place for free enterprise and the market—you know, private initiative and all that. But when you really looked at it, government was subsidizing big business in a big way. It was like socialism for the rich. It was a mixed bag, and there was so much emotion. It was a lot like religion. What you said in church on Sunday had little to do with what you did on Monday. We couldn't help ourselves. No matter what our beliefs, we had to go on living. Assock said I supported the system. Well, I guess I did to the extent I was part of it. But it was different for me—"

"We know you're different," Jevh affirmed.

"Jesus! Let me finish."

"Please do."

"Most doctors believed in the fee-for-service system. You know, when a patient got sick, you charged a fee for everything you did, even for things you didn't do. I hated to charge a person who was sick and maybe had no money. What could he do, not pay me and die? Believe me, it happened—not to my patients, of course. That's why I chose to work as a salaried physician in an HMO. No, I guess you don't know. But that made me different. It was my choice, not something that was forced on me. I got paid whether people were sick or not. I didn't profit directly from their illness."

"But you did profit."

"Well, I earned more than most people, but that didn't make me a capitalist."

Jevh was skeptical. "You said you got a bonus at the end of the year if there was a surplus. Isn't that like a dividend? You didn't give the money back to your patients. You kept it, right?

No matter how you slice it, you profited off the backs of your patients."

"That's unfair. A lot of doctors in private practice made a lot more. I wasn't overpaid for what I did."

"A rather self-serving assessment," Jevh observed.

"I worked hard for my money."

"So did the ditch digger, and he sweated a lot more."

"A doctor has a lot more responsibility. A ditch digger doesn't take his work—his worries about his patients—home to bed with him at night."

"So you think you should be paid for going to bed?"

The relief John felt in having a straightforward discussion was squashed by Jevh's constant needling. Instead of an objective discussion, the judge kept forcing him back to a defensive posture.

"You don't have to be sarcastic," John chided. "You asked me and I tried to explain how it worked. As long as I lived in that society, I could not avoid being part of it. It was not as bad or as one-sided as you make out."

"So, you supported the system?" Jevh asked again, reducing the question to its basic element.

John issued a long sigh, "I suppose so—mostly."

"Even though it was essentially immoral—you do agree it was immoral?"

John shook his head back and forth. "I'm trying to explain. It's not that simple. It isn't black and white. If you lived in a country, you supported it even if you tried to change it. I mean, you paid taxes. That still didn't make me a capitalist." A surge of anger swept over him. "For Christ's sake, it wasn't only capitalists who were immoral and killed anyone who got in their way. Catholics, Protestants, Irish, Jews, Muslims, Communists, Socialists—every goddamn one of them—they were all killing each other."

The mask tilted down towards John, giving him time to calm down. "You miss the point, good doctor. We are concerned not with your politics or their politics, but rather with your inconsistency. If you believe in exploiting your fellow man, if you condone irresponsible social behavior, if, for you, the ends justify the means, then your allegiance to capitalism would be logical and consistent. But when you say you are opposed to all of that and at the same time thrive on that system, then it would seem not unreasonable to find you inconsistent, if not totally irrational. That is the point."

"You make too much of it," John said firmly. "You take everything to its extreme. It is not all or none. There's nothing wrong with supporting a system while you criticize it."

"Is that the way you practiced medicine, doctor?"

"What do you mean?"

"If a patient had a heart attack, perhaps you prescribed emotional distress?"

"C'mon."

Jevh continued, "You had a world sick at heart, longing for peace, and you prescribed bullets and bombs and profits to kill the disease created by bullets and bombs and profits. You killed the patient. Too bad."

"I wish you wouldn't keep saying *you,* " John hollered.

"But it was *you—you* supported it," Jevh hollered back, thumping his fist on the bench. "You just don't make sense."

"Who the hell does?" he responded angrily. "Is it a crime?"

"Certainly not if you are stupid or ignorant. Then you would be innocent. But you are not stupid and ignorant. You are not innocent. What you plainly are—is guilty."

Even though John's face burned at the finality of the verdict, Jevh's condemnation had lost its edge. "Where does it end?" he murmured wearily.

CHAPTER 16

The hours passed as the sun slowly disappeared. He had just finished the cold meat and potatoes, which had been his daily dinner since imprisonment, and there still remained half a candle to light the room for another hour.

Unexpectedly, the door to the cell creaked open. Except for that one time with Lank, only the guard had so much as come to the door. Squinting in the dimness, he could barely make out a form, but there in the doorway was someone cloaked in shadows. He blinked hard and in disbelief as his vision fixed on Vinya closing the door behind her, seeming so small and fragile. She took a step towards him, hesitating in the flickering candlelight. She smiled slightly and said softly, "I had to come."

He was so choked, he could barely speak. "I…I thought I'd never see you again."

She lowered her eyes as if ashamed. "I tried before…they wouldn't let me."

He moved to the end of the mattress. Leaning against the wall, he motioned for Vinya to sit beside him. "What about you? Are you all right?" He felt strangely cold, not indifferent towards her so much as distant, uncertain, as if in a dream.

"I guess so," she said without conviction. "I've been in the Tower, too."

"You know about the trial?"

"It's on the visioscreen. It's terrible—watching and not being able to say anything. There were so many times I wanted to say it wasn't so, not that way, not the way they made it sound. It's horrible. I felt so helpless."

"Do you believe what they say about me?" he said, hoping for her denial.

She looked up at him, sadness in her eyes. "I don't know...I don't know what to believe."

"We're even there," he said, hiding his disappointment. "What are they going to do to you?"

"Nothing—I think. Esop visits me. He says after the trial I'll go back to school. He's very kind. He says I don't have to worry, but I am worried. I'm worried about you." She stared at the wavering flame atop the candle on the table before them, avoiding his eyes,

An uneasy feeling came over him that she was hiding something. He wondered why they would imprison her if, after the trial was over, she was to be released. Her story was unconvincing. Was it possible she had been sent by Jevh? He studied her closely. Her clothes were clean, her hair neatly combed, her skin still deeply tanned. He doubted she was telling him the truth. "You haven't been here at all," he said.

Her head jerked around and faced him, eyes wide and welling with tears.

She seemed so forlorn that he couldn't help but feel sorry for her.

With effort she controlled the tremor in her voice. "He wanted me to find out if...if I still love you. I know it sounds silly but—"

"After all this, can you feel anything?" The question was a statement of his own inner anesthesia.

"You don't care for me anymore," she said sadly.

"That's not what I meant. I've been through a meat grinder and it's not over. It will be a long time before I know how I think or feel about anything.

She shook her head slowly. "I guess maybe I was afraid to see you. I was afraid I might still be in love with you."

"I suppose I should laugh," John said, then wished he hadn't.

"Don't be cruel, John."

"I'm sorry...."

"When they put me here and tried to make me testify, I couldn't…I wouldn't…" her voice quivered, "You must believe me." Her eyes brimmed again with tears and pleaded with him.

"They let you refuse?"

He struggled to remain impassive, untouched, unbelieving but his resolve dissolved in her tears and the pleading in her voice. Impulsively, he moved towards her and she towards him, their arms reaching hands out to touch and hold and press each other close together.

The candle burned down to a small, lightless nubbin, replaced by moonlight straying stingily through the narrow cell window. They lay stretched out on the mattress, barely perceiving each other's features in the dark, whispering softly, almost apologetically, when all they wanted was to hold on and never let go.

"We won't see each other again, will we? I suppose they'll know…"

"It doesn't matter," she whispered through a kiss with arms around his neck.

She was smiling now, as she used to after they made love, a warm, quiet, satisfied smile. The tenderness he felt for her was so exquisitely pure and filled with gratitude. He whispered back, lips pressed against her ear, "I love you so much."

Her voice failed and her breath became short and shallow as she tried hard not to cry. "I love you. I will always love you. I will never forget you."

He repeated over and over, *my dearest, my sweetest, I love you…I love you…I love you,* but there was no sound to his voice, only heaving sobs and tears flooding shamelessly down his face, as he clung tightly to her in one last embrace.

A sharp rap on the door jarred them apart. He had to let her go and she left as quietly as she had come, slipping out of the cell and his life as gently as a warm summer's breeze, with no good-bye, no more promises, no more words, knowing that in his heart she would always be there, not as he saw her for the first time, or the last, but as she had come to him those many evenings, as she lay close to him in the moonlight, her eyes reflecting the brightness of her first love—and theirs.

He was ready now for what would come. No matter how Jevh characterized his relationship with Vinya, no matter how he broke it down into this insecurity or that frustration, she would remain secure in his heart. Jevh could call it narcissism or incest. He could name the elementary substances like a chemist describing water. But two parts hydrogen and one part oxygen was not water until combined to make it so. Separating the subterranean elements of his mind might provide analytic insights but the raw symbols did not make up the whole. And the whole of it was that they loved each other, and a part of them would always retain that love for as long as they each lived and could remember.

His calm did not last long. He was returned to the trial without any reference to Vinya's visit. Jevh kept picking and pecking until he was again a mass of raw, exposed tissues and nerves. He sealed Vinya off in a little corner of his mind, preserving her for the quiet of the cell where he could treasure their victory over Assock—and Jevh.

The dissection continued, forcing him to shed the last fragments of the tough protective skin he had been a lifetime building. All the little defenses—the clichés of conditioned thinking—were shredded and scattered like discarded husks. Those he thought sympathetic had systematically turned against him. First Lank, then Zenar, and finally Esop testified to his weaknesses and inconsistencies and the differences between him and them, *ad nauseam*. Jevh led them like puppets on a string, and they picked up his cues and barbs and thrust them at him, striking deep, but the pain was no longer sharp. It was more a dull ache relieved only in sleep, except he was no longer sure he slept. He had lost all sense of time. The dialog of the trial and the monologue of his thoughts merged in a continuum of blurred consciousness. Yet, he was no longer as fatigued. He sensed an increasing alertness. As resurgent attitudes broke to the surface, sometimes singly, often in clusters of unexpected responses, he understood at once that they were part of him even though he disliked much of what they imparted.

At times, as he stood in the dock before Jevh, he seemed also to view the scene from afar. He heard his voice and listened to his arguments as though it was someone else speaking. He no longer wanted to argue. He wanted to reflect on what was being said. He wanted to engage in intellectual introspection calmly, as in meditation.

But Jevh was relentless, rejecting his rationalizations, which to a reasonable judge would have been reasonable. Jevh kept saying over and over that it was not what he did so much as why he did it, and how he thought about it, that was wrong.

He could not understand why this should be of such concern to a judge hiding behind a mask. He was still convinced that Jevh was someone he knew before the trial, and he could not get Assock out of his mind even though Jevh deflected the association. Assock was the only one who filled the bill, the only one with the intellectual breadth and the psychological jargon to match Jevh's persona. He was the only one who had not appeared at the trial, assuming, of course, that he was still alive. It was the only explanation for the mask, the carefully guarded voice and what he had come to recognize as the similarity of their views. Only the voice and the face were masked.

Jevh had to be Assock! Small wonder Jevh was so certain of his guilt. The signed confession, the arguments, the repetitious rhetoric were purely and simply a continuation of Assock's sadistic attacks on him. Well, he would make short shrift of that. No more of this farce. Assock had had his fun but he was finished with it.

"So you think this is a farce?" Jevh answered without humor.

"You can take that damned mask off, Assock," John shouted at him defiantly.

Jevh sighed. "Not again. How tedious. Well, what if I am Assock? How does that change anything?"

John glared at the mask, wanting to reach out and smash it to bits.

Jevh was silent for a long moment. At length he raised his hand and the doors to the chamber swung open, and in came Assock.

John was stunned. His eyes fixed on Assock shuffling towards him, limping noticeably. His face was bruised and puffy, his left eye half-closed, black and blue. He passed John with a nod and stood before the bench.

The mask turned towards John. "Well, we're waiting."

"I...I don't know what to say."

"Aren't you at least glad he's alive?"

John fumbled for words. "Yes...yes, of course I am."

"Would it help to know that the good professor has defended you?"

John turned towards Assock who nodded and said, "What is done is done. You have suffered for it."

"I don't want your charity," John blurted, his suppressed anger at Assock rising to the surface, still beyond his control. Of course he was glad Assock was alive, but that was as far as it went. He wasn't forgetting, he wasn't forgiving, and he wasn't seeking forgiveness. Assock had gotten what he deserved. He turned to Assock and uttered between clenched teeth, "You got me into this."

Assock shrugged. "If you had listened to me, we could have worked it out. And let me tell you, forgiveness is not in my lexicon. Perhaps I'll feel differently when I can see out of my left eye again."

"I'm sorry for that," John offered without conviction. "I tried to be reasonable."

Assock countered pointedly, "I hate to think what might have happened if you'd been unreasonable. And what if I did provoke you. Don't you think you provoked me?"

"All right, children, that's enough," Jevh intervened. "Professor, what is it you wish to state before this court?"

"Your honor," Assock said, "I had hoped to avoid a direct confrontation with the Sapien. It is true I offended him to the extent he was unable to control himself. I admit I pushed him to the limits. We had to find out how far he would go to have his way. The evidence is there, or rather perhaps I should say here in my injuries. It is done now. The skeleton is laid bare."

John snapped, "Yours or mine?!"

Jevh rapped the bench with his knuckles. "Enough!"

But John would not be silenced. "I don't see why this sanctimonious bastard should be allowed—"

Before he could finish his sentence, Jevh bellowed, "Silence!" Then he motioned for Assock to proceed.

John muffled his mouth and tried to listen, but it was difficult to contain his rage. If it wasn't for Assock, none of this would have happened.

Assock picked up, "When we realized we had a surviving Homo Sapien, I was struck by the different reactions among us. Lank was concerned mainly with his bodily functions, whether he had been impaired by the long entombment in ice. Zenar went to the opposite extreme of wanting to test his theories on the freezing and unfreezing of live tissues. Esop was willing to identify with the Sapien by attributing our own rational processes to him without adequately taking into account the differences that were manifest from the start.

"Initially, I tended towards Esop. I looked to a relatively brief period of recuperation, after which I expected he would be fully integrated into our society, the differences between us seemingly not so great. But as I reviewed the history of his culture, I realized this creature was a potential threat far out of proportion to his singularity. Now we had a unique opportunity, beyond testing biological theories as Zenar would have done, but to test our own rationality—our reactions and resistance to Sapienism.

"I needed a frame of reference. John and I had conversations on many subjects—art, politics, economics, love. He seemed reasonable enough on the surface, but when the surface was scratched, he became—how can I put it—irrational. I'll give you an example—"

The mask interrupted, "Professor, please be brief on this point. It is beginning to wear thin."

"I'll try," Assock acquiesced. "Love was for him exclusive possession. It was almost as though Homo Sapiens had never learned to count beyond one. One mother, one father, one wife, one husband, one lover on the side. It's a wonder any of them ever had more than one child. They lived in such isolation, venturing out only to work or to shop, then retreating back within their own little enclaves, not unlike the ostrich with its head in the sand while all that craziness raged about them. In the face of impending catastrophe, they went on about their lives like there was no tomorrow, no responsibility, no day of reckoning."

"We have more than ample evidence of Sapien irrationality," Jevh sympathized.

"The issue is not that Sapiens were irrational, but why? Jevh, you made much of John's inconsistency but that also misses the point."

Jevh stirred uncomfortably but decided against censuring the Professor's impertinence. "Your point?" he prodded.

"It comes down to a species defect—the inability of the Sapien mind to control its emotions. The defect was not totally dominant. Far from it. What they had accomplished by way of art and science and social welfare was quite remarkable, but in the end the bestiality of the species won out. It was not just a simple paradox, like humanism versus capitalism."

"That's what I've been trying to tell him," John butted in.

"Oh be quiet," Jevh commanded.

Assock went on, "In our early discussions, I was quite impressed with our Sapien's sense of individuality and his concern for human rights and dignity. Now, I thought, we have an unusual specimen, perhaps an exception from those Dark Ages. Then, in the next breath he objected to what he considered our extreme permissiveness. Our sexual freedom was most disturbing to him, even though that was what he wanted for himself. But he could not be honest about it. He had to have his own private little dome and his secret trysts with Vinya. He could not wait. It had to be instant gratification. And if he couldn't have what he wanted—"

John could not contain himself. "Your honor," he said, raising his voice to speak over Assock, "I protest. He's distorting everything."

"If you would please be quiet," Jevh said again. "You kept calling for Assock and when he finally comes you won't let him speak."

"I'm sorry, but he's doing the same damned thing as you—more half-truths and twisted god knows what."

"Be patient," Jevh said patiently.

"It's hard."

"Try." Jevh motioned for Assock to resume.

"Even Esop failed to recognize, or chose to overlook, the extent of his irrationality. He mistook the Sapien's fixation on Vinya as an innocent love affair, not as his last desperate flight from the isolation of his survival. Vinya became his *raison d'être*, not only for the fulfillment of his adultery and incest but as the eternal resurrection, the ultimate everlasting orgasmic indulgence. Without her, his identity would dissolve in the void of his despair, bereft of all loved ones.

"We had to question what would happen if she was taken from him. Would this unleash the rage of his species? Would this awaken in our own culture the remnants of irrationality we had fought so hard to destroy? Would his example be as a contagious disease to those in contact with him? How resistant was the Species Human to Homo Sapienism?

"As charming as he could be on the surface, we had to confront the issue, to remove our own blinders. The responsibility lay with me. I would have to conduct the experiment. I would have to assume various poses—friendly, patronizing, irritating, frustrating. I explored his emotional topography, but I had to be careful not to irritate him too much, not before the final confrontation, or he would reject me, short-circuiting the experiment." He turned towards John and said, "You understand, by *irritation* I mean psychological—nothing personal."

"You certainly succeeded," John replied irritably.

"Yes, thank you," Assock replied absently. "You see," he said to Jevh, "Vinya had three qualities which made her ideal for the role I had chosen for her. Beauty—quite compelling, don't you think?"

The mask nodded affirmatively.

"Intelligence and youth. Youth was particularly important because to recover from what I was exposing her to would require great resilience. She was the bait. I threw the lamb to the lion—but I had also fallen into the pit."

Again turning to John, Assock said, "You are quite right. I was not a disinterested spectator. I had my interest in Vinya but not the way you think, that is, not until that evening. I became so absorbed in the experiment that I was beginning to lose my own identity. I picked up most of your attitudes and I practiced them so well that when I tried to stop acting I discovered I was no longer acting, that it was me. I had come to be despised not only by you and by Vinya but by myself as well."

He paused, obviously disturbed by his recollection, acceding to Jevh who urged him to get on with it.

"I had to finish. I was losing control. It was too late. There was yet another scene and we played it out compulsively. I proved what I had feared—the Species Human is only one generation removed from Homo Sapiens." Assock sighed, "You could not be allowed to go free."

"So it is your conclusion," Jevh summarized, "that it was beyond the capacity of Homo Sapiens to avoid self-destruction and the destruction of everything surrounding them. And that this lone survivor is bound to infect others with his illogical and destructive impulses. Oh my, how dismal."

"Yes," Assock concluded, "only Humans can maintain a humane society."

"That is not very encouraging for our friend here, is it?" Jevh said.

"I'm afraid not," Assock concurred.

"Rubbish!" John exploded. "You speak of progress and rationality and logic and then play games with people's lives. You take a series of provoked incidents and then assume sweeping generalizations as though you have discovered incontrovertible laws of behavior. Couldn't I do the same with what I've seen here?"

"It is your privilege. That may be part of your defense," Jevh replied sweetly. He turned back to Assock, asking as a matter of protocol if there was anything further he wished to say in behalf of the defendant.

Before Assock could answer, John insisted that nothing had been said in his behalf, only against him. "Furthermore, you accuse me of immorality. What about him? What about what he did to Vinya?"

"Professor?" Jevh passed the question to Assock.

Assock faced John, his expression softening to match the softness of his voice. "My friend, if it were possible to relive the past in the knowledge of the present, much of this would not have happened and the world would not be as it is. If there was some way to convince you that what you correctly term my provocation was not intended to harm you, but to help you understand the character of your species, I would willingly absolve your guilt and set you free. Unfortunately, it is not within my power to do for you what only you can do for yourself. If it would help to say I am sorry, I would prostrate myself before you and beg your forgiveness. But that would change nothing. You cannot blame me for what I did to Vinya as though it was my doing."

"For god's sake, Assock, it wasn't mine," John appealed.

The reference to deity sent a shudder through Assock's frame as he recalled the moments before the Sapien's attack on him.

"I was no longer myself," he continued. "I was the actor who became the character he played. You…you were the author of the script and I the puppet fulfilling your fantasy."

John stared at Assock so intently that his eyes strained and his vision momentarily blurred. For an instant Assock's features resembled someone from the past. It was such a fleeting resemblance and it was gone as soon as it appeared, but in his mind lingered the image of his old friend Arthur Sokolsky.

Assock went on, "I wish I could say I enjoyed my role. I suppose I did, much as an actor who performs well, no matter how difficult or distasteful the part. What I regret most is that it made us antagonists when we are meant to like each other as we should ourselves. It may not be within you to like everything about yourself, but when you think of me, my friend, remember me as we."

With these words Assock bowed first to John and then to Jevh. Then he turned and shuffled out of the chamber without a backward glance.

As John watched him disappear a lump rose in his throat, blocking an unexpected surge of emotion, preventing him from crying out, *Assock, come back. Please, don't leave—not yet—we haven't finished.*

CHAPTER 17

The cell had become a refuge, not where he felt at home, though there was a secure aspect to it, but a place where he could stretch his legs, aching from the strain of standing long hours in the dock, and relax muscles taut with the tension of the trial. If only he could release his mind as well. But there was no valve to ease the pressure or switch to turn off thoughts that rolled and roiled in fits and starts before his eyes like an old-fashioned hand-driven flicker film.

He had left the chamber more confused than he imagined possible. Firmly convinced beyond doubt that the masked figure was Assock, the appearance of the professor completely shredded the last remnant of his defense. And in the moment of Assock's departure from the chamber, his antagonism towards him, indeed, his hatred, had fled his body like an exorcised demon.

Not so Jevh who obsessed him now as Assock had before. Every time he closed his eyes he felt the pressure of Jevh's mask against his pupils. There was even a lingering image when his eyes were wide open, yet he was no nearer to recognition. But if he carefully positioned his upper and lower lids so they barely touched and—squinting—stared straight ahead, the mask took on the character of a computer screen scrolling words like a transcript of the trial. He couldn't quite make out the words, but in his mind's memory the arguments spun around again, swathed in the emotions of the day.

He was still annoyed by the judge's preoccupation with his inconsistency. Even Assock felt Jevh overplayed that hand, perhaps an indirect admission that Humans were not themselves immune to inconsistency, which could hardly be a major crime, except in the madness of this trial. It was not wrong to see both sides of an issue and to choose one or another as befit the circumstance. Sure, he would like to be consistent, to be as certain as a religious zealot of scriptural truth. He would like to be a fool rigidly adhering to dogma like the fundamentalist rejecting evolution in the face of obvious contradiction. But he was not a fool. He was not a zealot. He was not a consistent person. If a willingness to listen, to learn, to weigh evidence, to admit fault and contradiction were not honorable qualities, then he would choose to be dishonored and yet retain an open mind.

He turned on his side, tucked the blanket around his shoulders and nestled his head against the pillow. Weariness transformed to numbness. His eyelids fluttered closed as he drifted into the comfort of that special exhaustion when one feels awake but is asleep with dreams as conscious as reality.

He was walking along a narrow path between fields of flowering millet. Gradually the land began to roll in small mounds, and the grassy ground gave way to pebbles and rocks. The path turned north in a steep incline. He was at the base of a high plateau, against a wall of rock rising nearly vertically. Nervous steps carried him upward along a dangerously narrow, hand-carved ledge zigzagging in switchbacks that seemed unending. The walk became a strenuous climb. His breath labored heavily. His legs dragged like lead weights. The trail skidded out beneath his feet twice before he glued his eyes to each precarious step.

Halfway up he thought of turning back, but the path behind had disappeared. The air thinned and his lungs cramped for oxygen. He forced himself on in counts of steps—ten steps up, pause, ten steps more. His mouth was parched and his lips encrusted with dried saliva. At each turn, he prayed it would be the last. The pressure of the climb was mounting like steam in his chest and he vented his frustration in a torrent of curses at the stupidity of starting out not knowing where he was going.

But he kept going—ten steps, pause, ten steps more. The determined rhythm carried him finally to the top.

He slumped to the ground and rested until his breathing steadied. Perspiration drenched his shirt, which clung to his back like a cold damp towel. A mound of rocks supporting a thin wood pole, from which fluttered bands of tattered gray cloth, crowned the ascent. He picked up a rock and tossed it on the pile, adding one more count to the countless travelers who had paused in gratitude for their safe journey.

The plateau presented a barren landscape of scattered scrub, rocks and boulders. Another path led up a slope towards a wall of layered stones surrounding flat-roofed adobe abodes that were clustered close together like an old pueblo village. He walked the path slowly, noting the silence and the stillness of the air, broken only by the occasional caw-caw of jet-black ravens and the fluttering of wings as they shifted their sentinel watch from roof to roof.

The village seemed empty. He climbed on top of the wall, cupped his hands around his mouth, and hollered *hellooo*. A raven cawed to the lonely echo of his voice. He called again. The sound of a muffled drum began to seep through the silence of the village. The beat continued steadily. As he followed to its source, the chant of a man's voice joined in, interspersed with the ringing of miniature bells and the mournful bleating of a primitive horn at measured intervals.

He paused before the doorway. Lowering his head to clear the wood-beam mantle, he stepped inside the darkness of the room and was surrounded by the low reverberations of the drum and the singsong voice. As his eyes accustomed to the darkness, he made out the figure of a man sitting cross-legged against the far wall before a low bench on which was set an array of small bells and icons. To his left was an altar lit dimly by candles on either side of a multicolored mask twice life-sized, with a painted expression that grinned and grimaced in the shifting light.

The moon-faced man was obscured in shadows but John could see his hair bore a topknot and his shoulders were draped by a dark red robe. Around his neck were colored strands of beads and a silver necklace shimmered in the dim, flickering light to his swaying motion. The man tapped the drum suspended from the ceiling with one hand, the other tingling bells, and his voice chanted on in entranced monotony, pausing every now and then to pick up the bone horn and sound its haunting tone above the beat of the drum.

As John started towards the figure, the beat slowed to the tempo of his steps and then stopped as he stopped before the bench. He knelt on the hard packed dirt floor, his eyes following the hand that beat the drum to the bench where it picked up the thick-rimmed glasses and placed them on the face of Assock.

"You were long in coming," Assock said.

"I came as quickly as I could."

"Will you stay?"

"I don't know where I am."

"This is the place."

"What is it called?"

"It has no name."

"Where are the others?"

"There are no others."

"What am I to do here?'

Assock's head turned towards the altar and his eyes fixed on the mask, which glowed between the candles. "You will take my place."

"Why?"

"You want peace and contentment."

"Yes."

"Here you will find it."

"Alone?"

"There is no other place, no other way, no other one."

"Won't you stay with me? There is so much I want to say to you."

"It is all said. Peace and contentment have no words but one." Assock's gaze turned towards the mask, which stared back blankly through the hollows of its empty sockets.

"Please, don't go," John pleaded, but Assock was gone. In his place, John sat cross-legged behind the bench and his hand began to strike the drum methodically to the beat of his pulse as his chest resonated in the hum of repeated *Ommmmm* and his eyes stared unblinking at the grinning mask—and the terror of eternity exploded in his brain.

John forced himself out of the paralysis of the dream into the pitch-black darkness of the cell. He fumbled for a match and lit the candle. Sitting uneasily on the edge of the bed, he ran his fingers through his hair, scratching at his scalp to shake himself fully awake. He pulled the blanket over his shoulders, shivering beneath the cold of his perspiration drenched shirt—and the clinging horror of the dream. He had climbed the mountain and found the village and been shown the way of peace and contentment—the beating of the drum to the rhythm of his heart, the bleating of a horn and the chanting mantra of a mind emptying into the grinning mask of death in the utopia of dismissed self. He knew that if he lay back on the bed and closed his eyes and began the chant of *Om mani padme hum...Om mani padme hum...Ommmmm....*

For the remainder of the night he battled with sleep. He paced the floor, slapped his face, jumped up and down, talked to himself out loud, doing anything and everything to stay awake. He tried imaginary conversations with Vinya and Esop and Lank and Zenar but he could not focus on their faces, not even Vinya's. They had slipped beyond his reach like sequences of a dream that linger just beyond remembrance. His thoughts kept returning to Assock. If Assock had stayed in the dream he might have also. He had pleaded with him to stay and talk, and then he was alone with the drum, the bells, the horn—and the mask.

He could not shake the vision of the mask even though his eyes, which begged to close, were propped open against the fear—the endless fear of endless sleep. He had the terrible thought that behind Jevh's mask was this mask, and behind that another and another and he would never discover what he was meant to know.

Morning filtered ever so slowly through the cell window in transparent veils of gray mist, gradually dissolving in the light and warmth of the sun. A persistent ringing filled his ears and a barely perceptible tremor rippled across the surface of his chest and abdomen and in the muscles of his legs. Reserves of adrenaline coursed through his arteries in victory over sleep with the same effect of skittish alertness, almost of exhilaration, brought on by amphetamines.

There was an irony to the renunciation of the dream's nihilism within the confinement of a prison. He was like a man convicted of a crime he did not commit to whom release meant return to a society offering not comfort and security but continued condemnation. How those poor, innocent souls who had fallen victim to the law could maintain hope and a sense of the importance of their lives was almost beyond reasonable explanation. There had to be something inherent in the soul, the instinct to survive and push on no matter what the cost, no matter how degrading the external conditions of life.

Was he any different than a *nigger* tried by a judge prejudiced against him not for what he did or was, but for the color of his skin? If only he could achieve the dignity of the black man who stood before the judge returning contempt with contempt, rejecting the preordained verdict of guilt even as he was forced to accept the sentence. In the least, he could be spared the endless words of explanation and apology for having to do what need not be done but for the perversity of an unyielding world.

John stepped into the dock and fixed his eyes on the mask of Jevh glaring down at him above the high judicial bench like a blank sheet of paper before a writer drained of words. The judge leaned forward, picked up the gavel and rapped it sharply. "This chamber is in session," he intoned. "John Altern, have you prepared your final defense?"

"No, your honor," John answered calmly, although his voice had the brittleness of an insomniac.

"No defense?" Jevh queried in surprise. "You must have a final defense."

"I have no defense," John repeated, "but I would like to make a statement."

"Call it what you will," Jevh shrugged.

"Your honor," John began, his voice firming up, "I have been tried without benefit of counsel and convicted without a jury by a judge without a face who has assumed my guilt."

"By your own admission," huffed Jevh. He rummaged through the papers on the bench, found the confession and waved it before John. "Signed and delivered."

John ignored the document. "If everyone is judged in black and white with no regard for circumstance, then no one is innocent. There is not a crime that has not been committed in thought, and it goes without saying that everyone, unless he is an absolute psychopath, has a conscience and must admit to himself, as you have made me admit, that he is guilty. If you judge everyone by his conscience, then we are all guilty."

"Is not that the case?" Jevh asked, perplexed by John's train of thought.

John's eyes lowered, his head barely nodding. "It is enough that one condemns oneself and has to bear the burden of one's own guilt. That is punishment enough. If people are to live at peace they must at least be allowed the privacy of their thoughts without having them dragged before the public like flags of filth. The things we do to each other, which we cannot conceal, are bad enough. For these things there are laws to protect society, and punishment when the laws are violated. I do not deny this. I do not challenge this. I submit to it. If I am guilty of violating your laws I will accept your punishment, but I have not been so charged.

"When you accuse me of violating the laws of my conscience, then I protest that is none of your business. It is something I must contend with and has nothing to do with you here or anyone anywhere except myself. These charges—this charge of adultery—I admit it. I did it, and I suffered for it. I knew it was wrong. But let me say also that I suffered when I did not, when I wanted to and could not, when my body desired what my conscience denied me. Not violating a law also has its punishments. That is why I say to you that I have been judged out of context."

"Is there a crime that cannot be rationalized by the criminal?" Jevh interposed.

"I must be judged by my actions, not my thoughts," John continued, ignoring Jevh's rhetorical comment. "Is there a law in the Seventh Millennium that says, 'Thou shalt not commit adultery'? Can it be adultery when your wife is dead?"

Jevh responded, "We are governed by mores. I think you call it common law, maybe even common sense."

"Okay—*mores*. Have I violated your mores?"

"You have violated your own," Jevh asserted sternly,

"That is exactly the point. I am guilty of violating my code, not yours, and my conscience is my condemnation. If I have not violated yours, I am innocent."

"You may continue," Jevh said non-committally.

"I am charged with incest—accused of perversion—not by Vinya who never doubted my love and refused to testify against me, but by Assock who seemed to be saying that he and I were the same as though...as though I was imagining it all."

"You do give the impression of a solipsist," Jevh observed.

"You're no better than Assock," John retorted.

"I appreciate the compliment."

"Assock was determined not to give me a chance, to destroy whatever hope I had of becoming a free citizen of Opalon."

"Conjecture, my boy. Quite incompetent."

"If you will let me pursue this!" John's annoyance was ill-concealed.

"There is no hurry," Jevh yawned.

"When Assock realized Vinya and I really loved each other, and that he had lost control of Vinya, he reacted like a jealous father, punishing his own child, and then blaming me as though I had abused my child."

"He claimed that to understand you he had to become you," Jevh said.

"That is so ridiculous. I can't even respond to it. I suppose you'll say next that I assaulted myself."

Jevh nodded. "It crossed my mind."

"I wish I could laugh," John said angrily, "but it's not funny."

"No, it isn't—not your adultery, your perversion, your assault or your inconsistency," the judged fairly shouted.

"I wish you would stop saying *your—your—your*—as though I am the only guilty one."

"You have confessed."

"Your assumption—"

"Assumption?" Jevh again waved the confession.

John pointed a finger at Jevh. "Yes, your assumption that my signature—on a piece of paper written by someone else that you have not allowed me to read—is a valid confession. I suggest it could as well have been your confession. You yourself said you can only be innocent if you are ignorant. Since you are not ignorant, you must be guilty."

"You are speaking in contempt," Jevh said slowly, glaring through the mask.

John thrust deeper. "No more so than you with your smug holier than thou pretense. You are as obsessed with guilt as I."

"Speak for yourself, sir."

"I will not be alone," John shouted in anguish, "I will not be the only one."

"You are the only Homo Sapien."

John's eyes searched the courtroom. The clerk was there taking notes, and there were guards and observers in the back of the room, but for all their presence, he was very much alone. He turned back to Jevh and affirmed with quiet dejection that he was the only Homo Sapien, and what it came down to is that Humans don't like Homo Sapiens. He added petulantly, "I'm not so sure I like *your* damned Species Human." He sighed, folded his arms across his chest and whispered wearily, "I have nothing more to say."

After a long pause Jevh imperiously rapped the bench with three slow strokes of the gavel and began his summary.

"The court has heard the defendant, John Altern. He asks to be exonerated on grounds of extenuating circumstances. He argues that people cannot be judged by their conscience or else all are guilty of all things. It is an interesting argument and has much merit. But it fails to consider that laws are the reflection of conscience. The distinction between conscience and common law is one this court is incapable of perceiving.

"The defendant argues that it is improper to be judged by his own laws rather than ours. This is undoubtedly a relic of his prehistoric origin wherein the accused was made to conform to the court, rather than the court to the accused. The court can sympathize with his confusion but it cannot accept it. We long since determined that no one shall be made to conform to pre-existing laws, and that each case shall be viewed on its own merits.

"Thus, one may be guilty of a crime of which another is innocent even though in both cases the outward facts are the same. It is not what has happened that is crucial so much as the individual's conception of what has happened. If a man judges himself guilty—it matters not how many courts proclaim him innocent—he is guilty.

"The defendant cleverly maintains that the Species Human has guilts, as well it may. But it is not Humans who have been accused here. It is not Humans who are being judged. The guilt of others cannot absolve one's own. By the defendant's own admission, he is guilty.

"The defendant claims he has been prejudged, but there was nothing in his argument that he has been prejudged wrongly. Both the court and the defendant are in agreement that he is guilty.

"What, then, is the problem? What is the defendant's challenge? It is essentially the competence of the court to sit in judgment of him and to provide the proper punishment for his crimes. Let us take each point in turn. Judicial competence is nothing more than the power of the state to impose its will. Deny competence and sovereignty is denied. The right to judge is sovereign. A state must have the power to force its citizens to conform. It must assume itself competent to rule in these matters. It can permit non-conformity only so long as the power and the stability of the state are not endangered. Non-conformity is therefore a privilege extended by the state to its citizens. It is not a *right*. It is tolerated only when it is harmless and does not threaten the *status quo*.

"The defendant recognizes the right of the state to rule. He has argued, however, that since his guilt derives from his conscience, it falls outside the purview of this court. Yet the court is the conscience of the state, and when he stepped into the dock he acknowledged the court's conscience as his own. If he had taken the position that the court had no jurisdiction because he was forcibly abducted to Opalon, and that this violation of his personal rights preceded any violation he may have committed here, the court would have had no choice but to dismiss the present charges and deport him back to the place of his origin. Since he has not rejected the court, he has by default accepted the prerogatives of the court to judge him on his own terms. So be it.

"There is no alternative but to find the defendant guilty of all charges—and it is so declared."

John leaned heavily against the railing of the dock, clenching it tightly. If only he had thought to challenge Jevh's jurisdiction.

He sighed to himself. What difference would it have made? Guilty or innocent, there was nothing left for him here.

Jevh continued, "John Altern, you present an unusual problem. Since it is the custom of the court to suit the punishment to the individual rather than the crime, you must understand our decision. I take no pleasure in punishment but I am bound to comply with your guilt.

"You were brought to Opalon with the expectation that you would have your freedom. I cannot fathom why you rejected it. Your world blew itself to oblivion and by some miracle you survived. But what was your first thought on reawakening? To go back! What was there so precious in a world hell-bent on suicide that a man blessed by escape would want to return? Should we dismiss him as merely insane? You insist you are not insane and the court agrees. What is it, then? Why should you be so guilty? Is it because you alone survived?"

John closed his eyes. It was a question he had asked himself over and over. It was not only that he survived, but that all his problems—the guilts and the *wants*—survived with him in a whirling suspension. There was no resolution outside of his past. He could not erase his sins like a sycophant in a confessional.

"You carried your indulgence into your new life. You would give up nothing for what you received. And when you were denied, you tried to destroy it all?"

"I did not. It was not like that."

"No, it was not quite like that. It was not all black and white. You have said so yourself. Well, all we have been trying to do is establish the nature of your guilt, that which you brought with you, that which must remain with you because it is etched upon your mortal being.

"You see, there is more to it than the crimes you committed. The real problem is *you*. You may think you have been prejudged or that you were not given adequate time to change, but you are so totally preoccupied with yourself it would take another millennium to disentangle you."

"What did you expect of me?"

"Perhaps too much, just as you may have expected too much of us. I suppose we are each at fault. We expected that you could free yourself of the past, that you would find your presence in this new environment liberating, that you would be interested in us sufficiently to at least modify your egocentricity. You lacked what we might call scientific curiosity."

"I wouldn't call what Assock did scientific curiosity," protested John.

"Must I continually remind you that this is not about Assock? It is not Assock who is being judged here. You are disappointed that we are not all perfect, that we still have human problems, and that it may take more than a cataclysmic catastrophe to transform a Homo Sapien into a calm, meditative, reasonable being.

"There is this much in your favor. You were able to see the vision. Without vision you would have been dismissed as an inconsequential nothing. Having seen the vision, do we now deny you the pleasure of retaining it? Shall we say to you now that you have learned your lesson, 'Come, John, join us, be one of us?' Saying it would not make it so. Perhaps if we had no choice, perhaps if we were each irrevocably stuck with the other, then we would have to make the best of it."

The mask slipped askance as Jevh spoke.

"What if I said to you that there are many aspects to a vision? This white mask, see how it reflects the sunlight. Is it now so white? Twist the kaleidoscope, the bits of broken colored glass are the same as the image changes. Watch the transformation. The eye is dazzled by the mirrored illusion.

"Twist your kaleidoscope, John. What do you see? Now a medieval dungeon with a black-robed, masked judge. Twist the dial, John. What do you see?"

John could not say how it happened or when but it seemed that all else had disappeared and he and Jevh were alone. Now there was neither thought nor desire to escape him, nor to deceive him, nor to withhold things he would rather keep to himself. Jevh had come to know him as himself. He wasn't even sure which of them was speaking.

"We must believe in something."

Was it he or Jevh?

"Bit by bit we have explored our motives, our feelings. We have destroyed all the little rationalizations and revealed our inconsistencies. We are left with a sense of futility, as though we can never really know anything and therefore nothing matters. Yet, there is something about us that rejects this logic, which is so useless if we are to go on living. We have come too far to slip back into the blathering of nihilism or the false security of mysticism.

"How can we find substance and meaning in all this banality? We've got to step outside ourselves, away from our own little involvements. We've got to look past the brush marks if we are to see the painting. We must believe in something if only the conscious experience of life.

"If everyone gave up because of disappointment, would we ever have emerged from barbarism? You say we have not, but I say we have."

"Ah—it is you who is speaking," John said.

"Who did you think it was?"

"For a moment…I thought…I thought maybe it was I."

"You don't know who I am yet?"

"I can't be sure."

"It is confusing."

"What will become of me?"

"You can't remain here."

"Where shall I go? You've left me nothing."

"You have yourself."

"It's not enough."

"You still have hope. Just a moment ago you said the positive has at least equaled the negative."

"I thought you…yes, perhaps it was me…I was saying that people always feel inadequate. But they don't all give up, not all of them. I keep asking myself why—why don't we just give up. Why should we give a damn? What keeps us from running out into the street screaming our horror at what we do to each other?

"All I can think is no matter what, we belong to each other. We have to care. Even if we went crazy and destroyed ourselves, still it was not absolute destruction. There were some left, just a few with hope and the dream of Opalon to sustain them through the terror of the long night...and the will to survive in towers and prisons and fight back against friends turned informers and faceless judges and their own guilt for having caused it all. Perhaps it will always be a mix of dream and nightmare—and ever the trial of conscience."

His mind was aswirl with echoes of Jevh's pronouncements. *The real problem is you—you are so totally preoccupied with yourself—it would take another millennium to disentangle you—you can't remain here—you can't remain here—you can't remain here..."*

The sentence was unmistakable. He was being consigned for an indeterminate term to his own life. He would have to contend with his fears, his guilts and his inconsistencies. No, they would not go away, he would never be completely free of them. He was, after all, a Homo Sapien. But he was not the same person uncovered by the Humans. There was an awareness, a sense of consciousness that had been missing in his increasingly dreary and mundane life before the Cataclysm. He felt, in a way, like a new person with the opportunity of a second chance to be...to be what? A decent human being?

If only he could go back. If only he had that second chance. Despite all the trauma, he felt so alive, as if he had been liberated by the trial and freed of the frozen past of indecision.

He couldn't change the world, but he could change *his* world. Given another chance, he would not spend the rest of his life living a lie. He would face up to his indecisiveness. His stomach twisted in knots as the pain he would inflict on Mary seared his heart. But she and he would survive, and so would Alice who was old enough to understand. And somehow he would do the right thing for Ina, though what that was he didn't know, except that it was all over between them. And he would get back to work, grateful that his profession enabled him to help and comfort and ease the pain of living—and of dying. If only he had that second chance.

Then his resolve wavered and it all seemed too much—the fear of his family breaking up, the mess with Ina, the endless round of sick and dying patients.

His mind was like a yo-yo on a string, bouncing up and down, swinging back and forth until it came to rest, its energy exhausted. He sensed the mantra of oblivion beckoning—humming its incessant *Ommmmmm*—exchanging all thought in his brain for mindless *peace and contentment*. His throat constricted and rejected the numbing sound as he grasped for consciousness.

His sentence was final and irrevocable. He could not remain in Opalon. But there was a part of Opalon that would forever remain with him. Like old friends whom he would never see again, they lived on in his memory: Esop and Lida, with their calm, assuring manner; Lank, for all his fumbling well-meaning caring; Zenar, whose bombast belied his gentleness; Assock, for whom his ambivalence was softening; and Vinya, dear sweet Vinya, who would always occupy a cherished place for him in Opalon. But what of Jevh? Would he forever remain in his mind—judge and jury—or could he come to terms with the man behind the mask?

Could he really come to terms with himself? Despite all he had been through, he still feared he was unable to contend with the unresolved issues of his life and that he would go on as before, recycling all his inadequacies and dissatisfactions, paralyzed by his ambivalence and indecisiveness.

Paralyzed? The voice came from afar. It could have been Jevh—or himself. *If you were paralyzed, would not you have remained to beat the drum and blow the horn and hum the mantra of oblivion? You are not paralyzed, John. Wake up.... Wake up, John.... The dream is over.*

His eyes fluttered open and slowly accustomed to the light of the room. The dark gray ceiling turned white and he realized he was no longer in the cell, no longer lying on a straw mattress. He was stretched out on...a hospital bed.

And then he remembered the blinding flash of light and the torrential downpour that swept his car over the embankment.

His body was so stiff, every joint and muscle and bone resistant, yet he managed to raise himself on elbow and slide over the side of the bed. Wobbly and woozy, he pushed himself upright and maintained his balance by stretching out to the cabinet nearby. On the cabinet was a mirror and in the mirror the image of a face appeared—masked by a white gauze bandage.... "Oh no," he gasped, "*he*—is me!"

Made in the USA
Charleston, SC
29 March 2015